SWEET THURSDAY

Sweet Thursday

A NOVEL BY

Ray Salisbury

ANDRE DEUTSCH

First published in Great Britain 1990
by André Deutsch Limited
105-106 Great Russell Street London WC1B 3LJ

British Library Cataloguing in Publication Data

Salisbury, Ray, *1942–*
  Sweet Thursday.
  I. Title
  823'.914 [F]

ISBN 0 233 98571 9

Printed in Great Britain by
WBC, Bristol and Maesteg

For Mark and Naoko

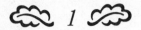

1

*M*y leg clicked as I straightened it and I ran my fingers over the pattern the sawdust in the chair seat had made on my knee. Then I knelt back again with my elbows on the window-sill. My breath hit the cold glass and spread and hung there and evaporated. The grey evening was thickening now, darkened by the drifting clouds of drizzle, and the bungalows opposite were sinking into it as if they were sliding out to sea.

I reached back and flicked the light on. The outside disappeared and the reflection of my bedroom flooded the glass. The white ceiling was going grey, especially round the light, where it looked as if the builders had run out of paint, and there was a white scar on the primrose distemper where I'd stuck a picture of Marilyn Monroe on the wall and ripped it down again when I'd heard Mum coming. I leant forward and rested my forehead on the window handle and two clouds of condensation formed where I was almost touching the glass. They looked like thunder clouds overhanging the reflection of my bed and I imagined a fork of lightning coming out of them and flashing down and setting fire to my new green school blazer and grey trousers that Mum had laid out for me for the morning and I said 'huh' to myself and steamed the glass up completely.

The paint on the window-sill was flaking. It came off in chunks when I got my fingernail under a cracked bit and lifted. Dad said it showed the bungalow was a proper utility job and it would probably come down round our ears before long, but we'd been here nearly seven years now and nothing like that had happened in the Close since Jimmy Phillips's bedroom ceiling had fallen in three times in the first month. I put a paint flake on one of the long bubbles of this morning's condensation and pushed gently. It floated. I bent down level with the sill to see how high the bubble stood above the tile. It was a long way. The water must be gluey. I pricked one bubble with a paint flake but it wasn't gluey. It broke and ran into another one and then I joined three or four together.

The mist had cleared from the glass and I pressed my finger against a blob where they must have trapped some air when they'd melted it to make my window. Maybe it was a bit that hadn't melted properly. Perhaps they'd been trying to make so much glass just after the war, to build lots of houses before the prices went up, that they hadn't let it boil long enough to get all the lumps out or perhaps they should have stirred it more and got it hotter, and . . . I pulled my dressing-gown around me tighter as the back door opened and I felt the draught from the kitchen that came through into the living room and across the passage and under my door onto the soles of my feet.

'Gi's the bucket, my Ine.' The back door creaked where Dad was leaning on it. 'And then I think I'll pop up 'ome.'

I closed my eyes and resettled my forehead on the glass.

'Just a minute, dear.' Mum tipped the last few bits of wood out of the bucket onto the fire and the handle clattered on the rim as she shook the sawdust out.

'Come on, Ina. Blimey! You don't have to polish it.' Dad would be craning round the kitchen door, with the water dripping off his mackintosh collar and cap peak, his arm reaching out for the bucket. 'I'm only going to fill it up again and it's coming down in chunks out 'ere.'

'There you are, my lamb.' Mum bumped the living-room door as she went out. 'And you shouldn't be out there wood-sawing if it's raining.'

'Thanks.' The handle squeaked as he took the bucket. 'It's only just started. The Nip all sorted out?'

I stood up and brushed my hair over to one side.

'Yes, I think so.'

'Good. P'raps he'd like to come up the road with me. Do him good. Take his mind off things for a while.'

I shook my head in the mirror and tried to make the lines on my forehead disappear and then I straightened my

Radio Luxemburg pop star calendar that I'd stuck under the clips on my mirror. Guy Mitchell looked fat although he sang thin and Johnny Ray was small although he sang big, and Lita Rosa wasn't as pretty as her name and Frankie Laine looked older than he sounded. And they all had creases in their foreheads so I let mine come back again and sat down on my bed with *Tom Brown's Schooldays* as my bedroom door opened.

'All ready, Simon?' Mum's red hair had a stand-up wave and she said it had gone thicker the moment it had been cut shortly after she'd left school. She'd used to hang her head back and make her hair hang down to her waist, she said, when they asked her to sing on special occasions at the Miners' Welfare Hall when she was little. But then she'd grown up and had her hair cut off and left school and home and got on the train at Newcastle, with her trunk, and come down south to work and met Dad and had me. 'Simon. You all ready?'

'What for, Mum?'

'Well, school of course.'

'Oh . . . yeah.'

'Got your pen and pencil set?'

I pointed to the dressing table.

'Well, it's no good there, Simon. Put it in your pocket.'

'But it'll make it bulge, Mum.'

'Not if you take it out of its box first it won't.'

'But you said, "Keep it neat and tidy in its box." '

She looked at the ceiling. 'When you take it out of your pocket. When you get home of an evening. Not all day, silly.'

'Oh.' I took the Conway-Stewart label out carefully and slid the pen and propelling pencil out.

They all said we'd have a different classroom for every lesson at the new school and that some of the corridors were a hundred yards long and the school bus was going to drop us at one place and pick us up from another and sometimes we'd have to stay late doing activities and get a service bus home and keep our tickets so that we could get the money back later.

'And have you got your school plimsolls ready separate?'

3

'Yeah.' I touched one with the toe of my slipper. 'But why have they got to be separate?'

'Because they're for wearing in school.'

'I know that, Mum.'

'Just inside school, mind. Not at playtimes, else you'll be through the toes in no time.'

'I know, Mum.'

'Well, what you on about then?'

'Nothing, Mum. Just wondered why you called them separate.'

'And what about your bus pass?'

'Here.' I pointed to my blazer top pocket.

'It'll fall out of there if you're not very careful.' She reached across me but I beat her to it. 'And be careful how you plonk yourself down on that bed.' She straightened the legs of my trousers. 'See how nicely I laid them out for you?' She put them back where they'd been before. 'You going up to Nan and Grandad's tonight?'

I sat back against my headboard. 'Don't think so, Mum.'

'Well, I think you should. Nan and Grandad'd love to—'

'Do I have to, Mum?'

'Nan and Grandad'd love to see you. And don't interrupt, my lad. It's very rude. And anyway, Uncle Edward and Aunty Sarah and Uncle Roger and Aunty Doreen and the children'll be there and it'd do you the world of good and help you take your mind off things for a while.'

I picked at a loose thread on my bedspread. 'Couldn't I take my mind off things by reading or listening to Luxy or something?'

'No you couldn't. You know how Nan and Grandad like to see the family all together occasionally.'

'Are you coming up, Mum?'

'Although you could read for a bit when you get home if you behave yourself.'

'Mum?'

'*If* you behave yourself, mind. And you'd better get a spurt on else they'll be gone by the time you get there.'

'Why aren't you coming, Mum?'

'And do get off that bed carefully, Simon. Go messing those nice clothes up.'

4

'Why, Mum?'

'Because I've got too blessed much to do getting you ready for school and it's given me a headache.'

'Oh.'

'So just you be a good boy and go up the road with Dad and don't forget to kiss Nan and ask Old Gran how she is.'

I waited for the door to close and then I said 'blimey O'Riley' loud enough for her to hear I'd said something but not loud enough to hear what I'd said.

Walking in the dark would have been like being blind if it hadn't been for the light from the living-room window. I'd been up to Nan and Grandad's with Dad so many times that I could have done it blindfold but Dad would have wanted to know what I was up to if I'd tied a handkerchief round my eyes so I shut them instead and followed him up the Close.

'What you walking behind me for, Nip?'

'Letting you keep the rain off me.'

'Oh.' Dad's mac scrunched as he hunched his shoulders. 'Well, don't keep treading on my heels then.'

Dad always walked to the top of the Close before he crossed: that's where he'd taught me to cross the road straight and not diagonally because there was less chance of a car hitting me that way. I don't think I'd ever seen a car coming down the Close after eight o'clock but he'd always said it was the principle that mattered and I felt my hand go to his as I stood next to him looking right, left and right again and then I followed him down Crouch Cross Lane.

The wind felt more solid when I had my eyes closed, as if I was being hit with towels and pillows. It wasn't that I could see it or dodge out of the way of it with them open, but somehow I felt less ready, when a gust hit me, with them shut and it was like when the boxing commentator said somebody was being rocked back on their heels.

'What the devil you stumbling about for, Simon? You all right?'

'Feel a bit faint, Dad. Hope I'm gonna be all right for school tomorrow.'

'You will be.' He was going on ahead of me.

My hand brushed against Jerry Henry's box hedge and then we were passing the new people's house who had lots of children and no curtains. I wanted to open my eyes and look in but if I broke my promise not to open them until we got to Nan's they might never open again.

'What's the new people's name, Dad?'

'I don't know. Bickers or Vickers or something. Why?'

'Nothing. Just wondered.'

I stepped over the cracks in the pavement where Baldy Cairns rode his motor-cycle and sidecar over it. Baldy wasn't bald at all. He had a shock of brown hair, that looked like a rolled-up porcupine when it was cut and folded out from the middle in two waves like a pair of kippers when it was long, and I couldn't think how Geoff Gibbs and Colin Gander had the nerve to call him Baldy when he was losing his temper kicking at the kick-start on his motorbike. Perhaps it was because Gander lived next door to them and his dad went up to the Men's Club with him most evenings.

Colin Gander's house was at the end of Crouch Cross Lane, by Ray Whittle's barn, and the light from his front room gave us space to stand and talk in on dark evenings when we weren't having a sit-down in the bus shelter or hanging about round the swings in the playing field. I could feel the light from Gander's on my eyelids and hear his mum shooing his little brothers and sisters into bed as if she was chasing out mice.

'Da-ad?'

'Yes, Simon.'

'Couldn't we manage a brother for me yet?'

Dad slowed in front of me and I stepped on his heels again. 'What's brought that on all of a sudden?'

'Well, goin' past Gander's. He's got lots ... and sisters.'

'Make things harder going, you know, Simon.'

'Well, they manage all right.'

'Strewth alive, Nip. I don't know. We'll have to see about that.'

'Yeah, well, I wish we could, else I'll be too old to play with 'im.'

'All right, Simon. Now be careful how we cross the road.'

We looked right, left and right again into the dark and then we crossed Crouch Cross Lane into the main street through the village. At one time this had been the only street but then they'd built the Council Estate after the war and cut out roads into the fields in one or two places for houses and now this street was the only street in the village without a name so that Nan's letters came addressed to '64' on one line, above the name of the village, and Chichester underneath and Vernons wrote and told Grandad that if he won a fortune on the pools they'd send notice of it to the post office in case it went astray.

We walked on through the smell of beer from the Men's Club and under the dripping laurel bushes, that separated the Arnolds' garden from Grandad's, and through his gate and up the long front garden path. The broken house-bricks and flints stuck up out of the path and the rock plants, like enormous pin cushions, flopped out underfoot and the lupins sagged over, where they were wet, and dragged cold across my face. I could tell when we were coming to the first corner because the path flattened out and I could smell the dry smell of the hibiscus bush under the kitchen window. And from there it was only a few more yards and two more corners to the back door. Dad tapped on the kitchen window, to let Grandad know we were coming so that he could warn Nan and she wouldn't have a shock, and then we walked in.

'Da-ad?'

'Yes, Nip.'

'Why don't we go in the front door?'

'Because Nan's got a draught-excluder curtain fixed up there and she keeps the door knob all nicely polished and she doesn't want all sticky finger-marks on it, *and* it's too much bloomin' performance to let people in the front door.'

'Well, they open it when they get the milk in.'

'Course they do. Because that's where Milky leaves it.'

'Well, why doesn't 'e put it round the back door?'

7

'What, and go trailing all round there when he can save 'imself a few steps? Have a heart, Simon.'

'Well, we 'ave to.'

'All right now, Simon. That's enough. Cheer up and speak up as if you're pleased to see them.'

Dad opened the back door and I followed him in. 'Aye-aye! It's only us.' He hung his coat up in the passage and I held my hand over the oil stove to see how hot it was.

They always lit the oil stove at half-past seven to warm the draught from the back door and they put a brick over the top to stop the smoke smudges from getting on the ceiling and, when Old Gran was staying with them, they put a round flint like a rugby ball on top of that to heat because she got cold feet in bed and one night her hot-water bottle had burst and she'd woken up thinking she was drowning and got such a shock that Nan sent Grandad straight down to Tangmere Corner, with his clothes on over his pyjamas, to call Dr Wilkins out, thinking she was having a heart attack.

'Gonna take your coat off, Nip?'

'It's not wet, Dad. I'll just keep it on for a bit.'

'No, you take it off. Then it'll look more as if you're staying.'

I unzipped my windcheater and held my arms back as he slid it off and hung it up.

'Go on then.'

I hated going first because it meant they all looked at me and said 'hello' before my eyes had got used to the light.

' 'ello, Simon. What a nice surprise. Got a booty for your old Nan?'

Nan was in her wicker chair in front of the cooker with her hair in curlers, and Old Gran was standing between the sofa and the kitchen table ironing the purificators. Grandad was sitting forward in his big armchair on the other side of the fire and his face was strained, as if he'd been eating radishes again and given himself indigestion, and Uncle Roger and Aunty Sarah and Aunty Doreen were squashed up on the sofa. Uncle Edward was standing with his back to the fire with my cousin Michael on one side and little Jonathan on the other. They both had their uniforms on for their private school.

I slid past Old Gran and let Nan kiss me on the cheek and then I came back to Old Gran and kissed her and asked her how she was and said 'hello' to my aunties and uncles and then I went and sat down on the arm of Grandad's chair.

'All ready for school then, young Simon?'

'Yes thank you, Grandad.'

'Boys're all fixed up for Oakfield then, Sarah?' Dad moved the chair by the door to the stairs forward so that it didn't scratch the wall when he sat down.

'Blessed job we had getting them kitted out though.' Aunty Sarah reached out and tucked Jonathan's shirt deeper into his trousers. 'And they grow so quickly at this age.'

'Don't I know it.' Aunty Doreen had unknotted her headscarf and now she took it off and shook her hair loose. 'Young Steve's absolutely shooting up.'

'But they do insist they're properly turned out.' Uncle Edward pulled his coat cuffs down more over his cuff links. 'They're very insistent on that.'

Michael and Jonathan were standing there like dummies in a shop window and I wondered if all posh schools had dark blue blazers with a black edge all round or if it was only this one or if this one didn't usually but they did now because somebody important had died.

'Looking forward to it?'

'School? No, not much, Grandad. And where's Stephen and Rachel?'

'Young Steve's got a bad cold, Simon.' Uncle Roger sounded as if he had one as well.

'And we couldn't risk him making it worse so we asked next door to pop in and look after them for an hour or so.' Aunty Doreen was having another baby. I could always tell because it made her face puff up and her eyes went brighter and she wore more make-up.

'That's not the attitude, you know, Nip.' Dad folded the peak of his cap into the crown and put it on the dresser. 'You'll get a jolly sight better facilities for sport there than ever we had at your age.'

9

'Ah, but not as good as 'e'd've 'ad at the High School.'
Nan dabbed at her mouth with her hanky.

'Well, he's not going to the High School, Fran.'

'I know that, Art. That's what I'm saying.' She smoothed
her frock down over her knees. 'Dear oh dear. Go biting my
head off the moment I open my mouth.' She looked above
Grandad's head at the photograph of my Uncle Steven in his
Air Force uniform. 'Remember, Art, 'ow they always said 'e
was the best all-round sportsman they'd ever 'ad and always
came towards the top in French and Latin an' all manner of
things.'

'Dunno as he was extra special at cricket.' Grandad
lay back.

'Would've been something pretty special by now, Art,
if 'e'd been spared.'

Grandad closed his eyes and seemed to go to sleep
and Dad folded his hands behind his head and Uncle
Edward moved forward as the fire crackled and sank and
flared and Michael and Jonathan moved forward as well
and Aunty Doreen sat up straighter so that Uncle Roger
could sit back.

'Such a pity you couldn't've followed on after 'im, my
duck.'

'Well, he might do yet.' Dad rolled his head around as
if he was exercising a stiff neck. 'They move the best ones
over when they're thirteen.'

'Just put this iron on the 'ot plate and pass me that one
up 'ere, Simon.' Old Gran's arm was so thin that I wondered
how she could lift a flat-iron. 'And these purificators'll need
renewing before long.'

'Mind you, there'll have to be a general all-round improve-
ment before that happens.'

I traced my thumbnail down the crease in my trousers.

'Going as thin as thin can be.' Old Gran held one
up to the light.

'And there's all his prize books you can 'ave as soon
as you're able to make good use of them, Simon.'

Old Gran folded the purificator into quarters and ironed
it flat.

'Do, for goodness' sake, take an interest, Simon, when

Nan's trying to help you.'

'I was, Dad.' I sat back on the arm of the chair and felt for the ring that fixed a silver pencil to a silver chain on the little lead penguin Uncle Steven had brought back from somewhere during the war.

'Darn near put the iron straight through them, they're so thin.'

'Blessed purificators!' Nan looked at the back of Old Gran's head as if she was drilling a hole into it. 'I was just sayin', m'duck, that you can 'ave all 'is prize books as soon as you can do justice to them.'

I could get my little finger through the ring on the silver chain if I twisted it.

'And what do you say, Simon?'

'What?'

'What do you say to Nan?'

'Oh.' I was struggling to get my finger out. 'Thank you, Nan.'

The fire settled deeper and Nan uncrossed her legs and recrossed them the other way.

'And what you keep harping on about those blinkin' purificators for, Mum, I don't know. They're perfectly all right.'

Old Gran ironed faster.

'It's not as if they get a lot of wear. Just to dab the cup after each person's 'ad it.'

'Course they're not supposed to go gulping at it you know, Edward.'

Uncle Edward looked up as if his name had been drawn in a raffle.

'Well, be that as it may . . .' Nan sniffed and touched her nose to her hanky. 'You wouldn't credit the blessed performance I 'ad with them when Pop first came 'ere and started using that jiggerin' awful wine from—'

'Claret!' Grandad was awake in a flash. 'It wasn't wine, it was a load of claret the bishop wished on him just after he took over the parish.'

'Well, whatever it was, it stained like billy-o and was the very devil to get out.'

'There you are then.' Old Gran put the squared-off pile

11

of purificators together and jammed the iron down on them. 'Darned near rubbed great 'oles in them.'

'Don't be so silly, Mum. That was thirty years ago.'

'Then it's high time they got some new ones.' Old Gran stood the iron up on its end to cool and sat down.

'Huh! You always must 'ave the last word, Mum. Blessed infuriating.'

Dad had started to whistle under his breath and Uncle Roger was tapping out the time on his knee. Aunty Doreen stretched the fingers on her left hand out straight and made her little finger peel off and come back and peel off again joined to the finger next to it and then three of them together leaving her index finger stiff to her thumb: she smiled at me when I tried to do it and then laid her other hand on Uncle Roger's hand and trapped it against his knee and Dad stopped whistling.

'That's something I was never very struck on.' Uncle Edward touched the bottom of his nose as if he'd got an itch.

'What, claret?' Dad asked. 'Cabby up at 'anover 'ad some at one time. I didn't fancy it much though.'

'Do you remember that time old Cabby doped Palmer's rooster?' Uncle Roger's hand escaped from Aunty Doreen.

Dad cringed.

'You must do, George. It was you who told me.'

Nan looked up at Dad and then to Uncle Roger and back again and Grandad opened one eye.

'Blessed thing kept crowing every perishin' morning.' Uncle Roger's face lit up. 'Kept waking Cabby up.'

'There never was much love lost between those two.' Old Gran wriggled back more into the sofa. 'Always at each other's throats.'

'Come on, George, you remember. Used to roost on Palmer's dung 'eap right 'ard up against the fence under Cabby's bedroom window. 'e soaked some raisins in rum one evening an' laid 'em out an' when the rooster picked 'em up 'e keeled over and Cabby wrung its—'

'Well, I 'ope he was pleased with himself then.' Nan was glaring and Dad had gone as white as a sheet. 'Really, Roger, and in front of the children.'

12

I tried not to be listening but I noticed Grandad's head had slid round so that he was shielded from Nan by the tea cosy and Dad went whiter still when Uncle Roger muttered, 'It didn't go to waste though.'

'Well, I think that's quite enough.' Nan did the top button up on her house-coat. 'Taking his spite out on an 'elpless bird.'

' 'elpless bird! 'annibal, they called it. He'd 'ave yer 'and off if you looked at 'im.'

Dad shook his head at Uncle Roger, under cover of stroking the bristles on his chin, and Uncle Roger settled back and Aunty Doreen made more space by drawing her arm out and putting it under his arm and I saw her whisper 'What happened to it?'

Uncle Roger shushed her and waited until they started talking again. Then he winked at me and whispered to Aunty, 'George brought it 'ome an' the old boy plucked it and spun 'er some yarn about being given it for grave-trimmin' an' she cooked it for Sunday dinner.'

They sat giggling together but I couldn't see anything funny about killing something when it was asleep.

The wind gusted under the eaves and a motorbike accelerated out on the Hanover Road and changed gear and disappeared towards Chichester. Grandad got up and Uncle Edward stood aside for him to put another log on the fire.

'And this blessed leg!' Nan touched her knee as if it was electrified. 'I really must get Ina to rub it for me with Wintergreen tomorrow.'

'Thought you were going down to Sarah's tomorrow.' Old Gran drew a loose thread out of her cardigan by frazzling it between her finger and thumb.

'Well ye-es. You do like me to come down of a Wednesday, don't you, Sarah?'

Aunty Sarah looked at her watch.

'Well then. Ina can't rub your knee if you're not 'ere, can she?'

'I know that, Mum. But p'raps she'd like to pop up during the morning for a cup of tea for ten minutes.'

Grandad's stomach rumbled and he twisted in his chair.

'What do you think, son?'

Dad refolded his cap and put it on his lap. 'I'll ask her, Mum.'

'Well, I can't see why you want to go traipsing off down there if your knee's playing up.' Old Gran touched her finger to the bottom of the flat-iron and gave it to me to put in the fender. 'Got any more darnin' needs doing?'

'No I 'aven't, Mum. Unless you 'ave a go at that lacy bit on my frilly nightie.'

A noise like a flushing toilet came from Grandad's chair.

'Do stop that, Art.'

'I can't stop it, my dear. I would if I could.'

'And anyway, Mum, Sarah likes me to get the fish in Chichester on the way down.'

'Lot of silly non—'

'Haven't seen much of you lately, Roger.' Dad stood up and straightened the creases in his trousers and sat down again.

'No-o.' Uncle Roger yawned. 'Been getting a lot of overtime lately.'

Nan was looking at Old Gran but Old Gran was pretending not to see her.

'Does me good to get out a bit. Dr Wilkins said so that last time I came over all queer.' Nan resettled herself in her chair so that she was facing more to the fire. 'No, we 'aven't, Roger. Do Doreen a power of good to 'ave a little break sometimes and come over and see us.' Her eyes followed Old Gran to the door. 'And where d'you think you're off to, Mum? I 'aven't put your brick in yet.'

'To get your nightie.' The door to the stairs closed behind her. 'Though what the point of a little flipperty-jib of a thing like that is beats me.'

The cuckoo clock clicked and struck nine, which meant it was ten to nine and Dad had ten minutes to get home for the Nine O'Clock News. He stood up and kissed Nan good-night and Uncle Edward said he thought it was about time they were thinking about it and they all got up then and said goodbye and how nice it had been to see each other again and I went up to say 'good-night' to Old Gran.

Old Gran was standing by Nan's dressing table looking

14

at the photograph of her and Great Grandad Grainger when Aunty Rene was in pigtails and Nan was still in her pram.

I stood beside her and put my arm around her. 'Good-night, Gran.'

'Good-night, young Simon.' She pressed my head down against her cheek. ' 'e wasn't much of a husband, so they say, but I still miss 'im.'

'Do you, Gran?'

'Yes I do. Always fiddling about with 'ome-made wine and full of a lot of silly nonsense 'e was. Used to infuriate me at times but 'e always managed to make me laugh.'

'Did he, Gran? Do you think I'll ever make Grandad laugh again?'

'Course you will. Especially if you make up for lost time at school. 'e thinks the world of you, you know, Simon.'

'Does he, Gran?'

'Course 'e does.'

'Come on, Simon.' The stairs door opened. 'You sit 'ere all perishin' evening and we can't get a peep out of you and then you disappear the moment it's time to go.'

'Just coming, Dad. I will try at this new school, Gran.'

'Good boy. God bless you, Simon.'

☙ 2 ☙

*M*um had me standing in front of the fireplace while she tried to remember anything we might have forgotten.

'And you'd better take a few sheets of toilet paper, in case this new school runs out, and a clean hanky.'

I tried to find something to do with my hands, apart from putting them in my pockets, while she dashed up to the toilet and back again and I lifted my arms up as she slid some rolled-up paper into one pocket and a hanky into the other.

'And your propelling pencil and pen in your top pocket.'

I flinched as she flicked a bit of invisible fluff off my lapel.

'And your dinner money in your purse in your inside pocket with the flap buttoned down. You will remember always to keep it done up, won't you?'

'What, Mum?'

She'd stopped and was looking at me with her hand still inside my jacket.

'Simon.'

'Yes, Mum.'

'You jolly well listen to me when I'm talking to you.' She pulled my blazer down at the front and then bent my arms at the elbow to see there was plenty of room in the sleeves. 'And I think you'd better carry your mac to balance your case.' She gave them to me. 'P'raps that'll help you keep your hands out of your pockets.'

'Blimey!'

'Never mind "Blimey". It's a slovenly habit.'

'Yes, Mum.'

'Right then. Off you go and I'll come out to the gate and see you off.'

'No. It's all right.' I threw my arm with my mac round her one way and my arm with my case round the other and hugged her and let her kiss me. 'I'm meeting the boys.'

She was still hugging me so I gave her another squeeze and said, 'I'll try really hard,' and ran.

Jimmy Phillips was a few months younger than me and he was a friend of mine although he didn't like football or cricket. His dad was a fireman and his mum was the only person who rode her bike over the Wobble Fields footpath without getting told off for it. She used to shout at jumble sales and she'd once caught me looking at her when she was saying that two shirts for sixpence each was sheer extortion and that she'd give them threepence for the pair of them. I stopped by our gate, pulled my socks up, straightened my tie, waved to Mum and went over the road. Mrs Phillips was banging her mat against the wall by their front door.

'Is Jimmy coming to school, Mrs Phillips?'

'Course he is.' She gave the mat a last whack that made me blink and blew the dust off her pinny.

'Well, is he coming now?'

'Jim-mee!' She reached behind her and pushed the front door open. 'You ready?'

'Yes, Mum.'

'Right. Off you go then.' She was watching me like a hawk. 'And don't you dare let Simon talk you into any mischief. And no dawdling on the way home after the bus's dropped you, either.'

'Yes, Mum.'

'And put your cap straight.'

She jammed Jimmy's cap over his head until his ears stuck out and I held his gate open for him to escape quicker.

'Your Mum in a mood again, Jim?'

'S'sh.' He waved to her and humped his satchel further up his back. 'She'll hear you, or lip-read.'

'Oh? She's pretty clever then, your mum?' I said it very loud and straight at her but she looked straight through me so I backed off and followed Jimmy up the Close.

Derek Brown was coming down the hill from his front door. He was small for his age and his mum had kept him in short trousers. They'd searched around for the smallest blazer they could find but even that was so long it came down over his trousers and he came towards us like a tent

17

on legs. We waited for him to catch us up and Jerry Henry met us by the hedge. His blazer was second-hand and it had lost its furry coating and was darker than ours and had a different badge.

'Shall we wait for Gander?'

'Can do, Simon.' Jerry tried to pull his sleeves down. 'Although I expect they'll've—'

'What? Oh strewth!'

Colin Gander was coming out of his house with Geoff Gibbs.

'If ya wanna know why I ain't wearin' one'a they snooty coats it's cos I dun bleedin' wan'oo.' Geoff was wearing his old school trousers and the brown jacket he usually wore to church. 'An' the firs' one 'oo says anything's gonna get this!' He waved his fist at us.

Colin scraped his toe on a hop-scotch line so that it smudged like an arrow feather.

'An' Col's only got one cos 'is cousin goes there'n's got one.'

'Hadn't we better be going?' I hitched my mac further up my arm. 'Bus'll be here soon.'

'Go on then, Lord Snooty. We ain't stoppin' ya.'

'All right, Gibbs. 'old yer 'air on. I didn't want this bloomin' uniform in the first place. I'd much rather be able to wear something scruffy.'

There was a ticking sound in the grass, of the moisture soaking in.

'Sod off, Wilson.' Geoff was clenching his fists. 'We don't want you with us, do we, boys?'

I went on ahead of them up past the old village school until I had to cross the road at the Wobble gates and then ran the rest of the way to Hanover Corner where we were to meet the school bus.

Dicky Mole and his sister Margaret were sitting on the wall of Mr Henty's bakery with Pat Smith and some of the children from the Greatwood Estate. It had always amazed me how Dicky Mole's nose only ran out of one nostril and I'd meant to ask him if there was anything wrong with the other one until he'd got hit in the face with a football one day at the village school and they'd both bled. Pat Smith had been 'confidently expected' to pass the eleven-plus and Kenny Lane's dad, who drove a caterpillar-tractor on the Estate, said her mum had put off buying her Lincs Girls' uniform until the last minute because they were sure there'd been some terrible mistake. Pat was slim and grown-up with her hair falling back in two long tresses, like a Greek goddess of something we weren't supposed to know anything about, and very pretty although her eyes were puffed-up and red this morning and she looked as if she had a cold. I felt more sorry for her than I did for myself because she'd been good enough to go to the High School but no matter how close she'd come to passing she'd still failed and that made her no better than me. I sat down on the wall between her and Dicky Mole, took a deep breath and folded my arms.

'Summer soon went, didn't it, Pat?'

'Did it? I really didn't notice.' She pulled her blazer out where I'd sat on it and brushed brick dust off it.

'Pity about the High School, but p'raps the Lincs won't be so bad.'

Pat sniffed. 'It'll be awful. And I'd rather not talk about it. In fact I'd rather not talk to you at all, Simon Wilson.'

I sat looking at her reflection in the side window of Mr Henty's bread van. If she'd been nice to me we could have gone on bike rides and walks and sat up against bales of straw and done our homework together and helped each other to get to the High School and I couldn't imagine how she could be so unhappy and not realise I was too. I tried to think of something horrible to say to her but it was too late now and I couldn't be bothered so I went and looked at the old-fashioned things for making bread in the bakery window until a van, with lots of children from Tangmere Camp singing 'Bless 'em All', drew up and Don and Stuart Norris and their sister Brenda and Mickey Leary and Paul Craven and the others spilled out. Skip Matthews was driving in his sergeant's uniform and he slammed the door after them and revved up and yelled that the coach would soon be coming and then he screamed round in a circle in the road and roared off back towards Tangmere.

Brenda Norris put her bag down next to my case and pulled her socks up.

'You're lucky getting a lift up here, Brenda. We had to walk.'

'We won't every day. Just when Sergeant Matthews is on NAAFI duty.'

'Oh.'

'Simon?'

'Yes.'

'You nervous about changing schools?'

'A bit. Aren't you?'

'No. We get used to it in the RAF. This will be my fifth, not counting the one in Singapore.'

'My dad was in Singapore in the war. He was a prisoner.'

'Was he . . . ?' Her voice was drowned in a great wave of booing as one of Breeze's coaches, with a sign saying SCHOOL BUS in the front window, drew up. 'Come on.' Brenda lifted my case up for me. 'Get in behind my brothers and me and then we'll get on first. You can sit next to me if you like.'

All the camp kids got on first and went straight to the back. Brenda looked back for me but I didn't want to push in front of Pat Smith. I stood back for her but she was staring the other way and Dicky Mole and his sister and some of the Greatwood children slipped past us. I was looking up through the window to see if anyone had sat next to Brenda and moving towards the steps when Pat did the same thing and my elbow bumped her in the chest. She blushed and sat down on the gangway side of a double seat and looked straight past me. Brenda had saved me a seat and I sank down next to her as the bus reversed up into the entrance to Brindle's Coal Yard.

'Well, here we go, Brenda.' My mouth was dry as if my tongue was coated with toothpaste.

'Yes.' She leant back and her elbow fitted into the crook of my arm. 'Won't be long now.'

The bus rumbled and bumped along the Westhampnett Road and Brenda chattered on about all the schools she'd been to until we got to the White Swan at Strettington Corner where we picked up a dozen or so children who'd

20

gone to the Church of England school there. They looked a
weedy bunch and three of them had buck teeth and glasses
and somebody said their dad was a merchant seaman who
only came home once a year. One of the others was small
and dark and looked as if he might be the Paddy Bishop
that Colin Gander had used to play with when he lived over
here and who got into so much mischief that Geoff Gibbs
got jealous and beat somebody up in a temper whenever
his name was mentioned: there'd never be any peace if the
three of them got together.

'Your brothers still play football down the camp of an
evenin', Brenda?'

'Yes.' She squiggled back against me more as she looked
up. 'Why?'

'Oh, just wondered. I might start coming down again
evenings.'

I lay back and watched the road rushing by until it
changed into the oily silver-green furrows of the Lavant
Course. It looked like the river described in Mum's book
The Fifth Form at Beck House that the boys tried to jump
over on a cross-country run and I felt sure the Lincs would
be more like that than the school in *Tom Brown's Schooldays*
and I wished I'd read that last night instead of *Tom Brown's
Schooldays* because I'd got up to the bit where some bullies
held Tom over an open fire and roasted him until his trousers scorched and I'd dreamt that Gibbs and Gander had
roasted me and the matron had peeled my trousers off in
front of a lot of girls and Pat Smith and Janet Rolls were
amongst them.

'Brenda?'

'Yes?' Brenda was like a plump little doll who'd come
to life.

'Will they have matrons an' things at this new school?'

'Yes. They usually have a matron. Why?'

'Oh, nothing.' I tucked my case more under my seat.
'Just wondered.'

We'd got well past Janet Rolls's house by now and
I hadn't seen her get on. I sat up and looked around.

'Who you looking for?'

'Dave Rolls. I didn't see 'im get on.'

21

'P'raps they've got seasons. They're not all coming on the school bus, you know.'

'Aren't they?'

'Are you still going steady with Janet?'

I tried to look like Dicky Jamieson when he was moaning to Mickey Leary about having three girl-friends at once and not knowing which one to take out, but it just reminded me that all the girls I liked didn't like me and the ones who did were the ones the boys said they wouldn't touch with a barge pole.

'Simon?'

'No, not really. She never was my steady girl-friend.'

'Who is then?' Brenda didn't seem to worry about having to wear a tweed coat, with a belt and buckle, and ankle socks and a brace on her teeth and she always looked straight at people when she spoke to them. 'Susan Farley?'

'Who's been telling you about Susan Farley? I haven't got one.'

'Oh good. You can come down to the camp social with me then, on a Saturday night.'

I looked at her chubbly knees and tried to imagine her with nylons on instead of ankle socks. 'Do you really want me to?'

'Wouldn't ask you if I didn't.' She'd turned and was staring out of the window and I wondered if I'd upset her.

I tried to think of interesting things to say about the Gaumont Cinema and Stevey Bacon's clothes shop, as we went down St Pancras, and about the police headquarters and the bus station, as we went over the level crossing, but she didn't take any notice of me. She didn't say goodbye either when we got off the bus by the canal basin, and made out she was talking to Pat Smith as we formed up behind a teacher at the entrance to the drive and then some other girls came and stood between us and I lost sight of her.

The canal basin lay deep and black and the gulls bobbed up and down on the chopping water. The wind blew my hair about and my arms were all goose-pimply where my blazer sleeves pulled up as I tried to put my mac on without putting my case down.

'Keep up, boy.' The master stood back from the line and hurried us up. 'What's your name?'

'Simon Wilson, sir.'

'Well, get a move on, Simon Wilson. We'll be there by the time you've struggled into that coat.'

I left the mac half on and half off and tried to catch up.

The school drive was wet black tarmac that looked as if it would come off on the soles of our shoes, smudged with dobs of mud and spilt cement powder. It was sunk below the level of the kerbstones so that they stood out like gravestones and I bent my head against the wind and watched my feet following the ankles in front of me.

There was a bungalow inside the school entrance that still had the slits in the brickwork where they'd fixed the scaffolding in place. The windows were smudged with white stuff, as if somebody had put Windolene on them and then gone off to do something else. The front garden was coated with turves, that were bald and dead where they lay on chunks of rubble and tufty and long where they touched the ground, and curls of wood shavings and paint flakes clung to the long grass until a gust of wind would blow some across the drive and into the chain-link fence that ran along the bottom of the police sports field. About twenty apprentice policemen, in short-sleeved singlets and long black shorts, were being shouted at by an officer in a high-peaked cap with a silver-topped stick under his arm.

'Shouldn't fancy that on a morning like this, would you, Jim?' Jerry Henry looked across me to Jimmy Phillips.

Jimmy smiled as if he'd just had a tooth out and I wished I could find a nice, quiet, warm hedge to lie down and die under.

The drive sloped down and the school rose up out of the weeds as we got closer. It had looked long and flat from a distance but now I could see it had four floors and was built of yellowy bricks, the colour of marzipan, with bright blue doors and windows. There was a big room at one end with thin windows running from the floor to the ceiling and peacock-blue curtains, and I could imagine Dad

23

saying they'd have done that to save on bricks but that it was a false economy and would cost them a fortune to heat in the long run. Behind that was a great square chimney with smoke curling out of it, that looked as if it had been copied from a factory or a hospital. I dragged my eyes away from it and over to the High School.

The High School was empty and there were no lights on. They must be starting back later than us. Their playing field ran right up to the edge of the Lincs tarmac playground and was separated by a narrow path. Our girls broke off from the drive and went down the path. Brenda was at the back with some of her friends from Tangmere. She turned, but it was only to catch her scarf and bring it inside her coat.

'Snooty bitch!'

'What d'you say, Simon?'

'Nothing, Jim. Just thinkin'.'

Brenda's head bobbed away until I lost sight of her behind what looked like a bike shed. The drive branched right now and we turned left and, for the first time, I could see the mass of boys in the playground. I'd never seen so many boys. The playground stretched the whole length of the school and was as wide as a football pitch and it was packed: some were standing in groups and others were chasing in and out throwing each others' caps in the air and ripping at jackets and jumping on backs, and all as if they didn't realise it was tarmac and not grass and that if they fell over on it they'd cut their knees to ribbons.

The teacher led us into the sea of green which parted to let us through and turned to face us.

'Right! I'm Mr Cherriman and this is as far as you go for now. You wait here until you're called for enrolment. Don't go in until you're told to unless you've got to go to the toilet and then only if it's absolutely necessary.' He looked at each of us to see that we were listening. 'All the floors are highly polished and normally you'll only be allowed in the main hall in plimsolls, but this morning's an exception. All right?'

We shuffled our feet and said 'yes, sir' and I was glad when he turned and left, because I couldn't bear the thought of any more instructions, but I wished he'd come back, as

24

soon as he'd gone through the blue double doors, because it seemed as if we'd lost the only person on earth who knew who we were.

We stood closer together and came into a circle, with our backs to the centre facing outwards, like a waggon-train being attacked by Indians. I backed into Geoff Gibbs. His nose was running and I gave him a hanky without asking him and he used it and gave it back without looking at me. We could see now that there were other groups like ours amongst the swarms of children charging around.

'They're in the same boat as us, Geoff.' I nudged him in the direction of half a dozen or so who looked as if they were waiting to be sold. 'Can you see any from Lavant?'

'Nar.' Geoff had picked a rough bit on his thumb and was biting at it. 'Gander's cousin was supposed to be meeting up with us. Wonder where the bloody 'ell 'e's got to.'

'Dunno. P'raps 'e can't find us.'

'Yeah, p'raps 'e can't.' Geoff pulled back as two boys chased round us. 'I ain' afraid but I expect Browner an' 'enery are.'

I searched the sea of faces but I couldn't find anyone I knew and I wanted to cry when I thought of how I could have walked up with Brenda's brothers and the other boys from the camp.

'Seen 'im, Nipper?'

'Who?'

'Gander's cousin.' Geoff Gibbs was looking where I'd been looking.

'Don't know what he looks like.'

'What you lookin' for then?'

'I wasn't. I was looking for—'

'Yeo-oo-oh!'

'Blimey, what was that?'

'Dunno.' Colin Gander was looking over towards the tennis courts. 'Oh, there it is.'

We all looked where he was pointing. A big boy was throwing a smaller boy at the high-wire fence so that he bounced off into the arms of another boy who hurled him back again.

'What're they doing that for?'

25

'Doin' what, Mush?' The voice came from so close behind it made me jump.

'Over there. Why're they chuckin' 'im at the wire?'

'I dunno.' The boy was about my age but smaller and there was a sharpness about him that made me shy away from him. 'See if 'e bounces, I s'pose.'

I winced as the boy sank into the wire again. 'Doesn't it hurt?'

'Gawd! 'ow should I know? You'd better ask 'im,' and he ran off again into the crowd.

The stream of children from the drive was never-ending and one or two fights broke out in the crush. The space in front of the main doors had filled up but there was a V-shape that had been left empty as if it was a big pit which nobody wanted to get too close to, yet they crowded forward until they made a solid wall around it. Everyone was looking in that direction and Jerry Henry said, 'Won't be long now,' when the handle on one of the doors turned and the door opened a fraction, stopped and then opened fully. Two masters came out and stood on either side of the doors, then another man came out and stood between them. Jerry Henry was shaking beside me. The man in the middle was wearing a tweed jacket and grey flannel trousers, and I knew, from his cold blue eyes, that he must be the head-master. He came down the steps and stood over two boys, who were fighting on the ground.

'I should think so too!' His voice sliced through the wind as the two boys looked up and slid back into the crowd.

'Devonshire, Ruell! Just lead them off into the main hall, would you? And Prefects—' One or two older boys stood to attention. 'Pick out any who misbehave and stand them outside my office.'

Jerry Henry was white and so was Jimmy Phillips. Only Colin Gander looked as if he wasn't frightened.

'You all right, Col?'

'What?' He sucked at his lower gum and touched his fingertip to it. 'Dunno really. I got a toothbrush bristle stuck in me tooth and it's given me this rotten toothache and it's bleed . . . ing . . .' His voice drained away and his

26

eyes glazed over and his pupils disappeared up into the top of his head and he fell all over me.

Mum said the best thing for shock was hot, strong tea and as I'd had a shock that's what I'd better have. It tasted sweeter and was blacker than usual but I couldn't feel it doing anything so perhaps I hadn't got shocked as much as Mum thought I had.

'And it's always a good idea to talk about these things, Simon.'

We'd had to stay at school until quarter to four and it had taken us half an hour to get home and another quarter of an hour to walk down from Hanover Corner and I'd thought how lucky we'd been at the village school, as I'd walked past it, that we'd been let out at quarter past three and been out to play by half past.

'Help to get things off your chest, you know, laddikins.'

If I half closed my eyes and made them flicker I could make Mum split into two. I tried to see which was the real one, as she came back together, when I opened them properly, then I split her into two again and wondered how she could seem to be in two places at once.

'Are you all right, Simon?'

'Think so. Why?' I could make her jump from side to side by closing one eye and then the other.

'Well, do stop making those awful faces and pay attention. You're giving me the creeps.'

I let my head drop forward and looked straight into the fire.

'Good.' Mum sat further forward and reached out and took my hand. 'Now drink your tea up and tell me all about it and then you'll feel much better.'

'Gander fainted, Mum.'

'Yes, I know that, Simon. But do try to be a bit more explicit. Mr Henty said he'd seen an ambulance outside the Ganders' when he was delivering next door and that Colin's curtains were drawn.'

'M'm. S'pect 'e was 'avin' a sleep.'

'But, dash it all, Simon, what happened?'

27

'I dunno, Mum. He jus' said 'e 'ad toothache an' that it was bleedin' an' then 'e fell over.'

'Nerves, I expect.' She stirred her tea but she didn't drink it. 'And how was your day?'

'All right.' A flame was licking up round a piece of wood.

'Only "all right", Simon? Didn't you make any nice friends?'

'Nope.'

'Don't you mean "no"?'

'No, Mum.'

'What?'

'No, I didn't make any nice friends.'

'Oh.'

'One or two were all right, but most of 'em were . . .' The flame edged into a knot. 'An old bloke called Hassell is our form-master and they say my form was the worst in the school at the old Lincs because there's a gang in it called the "Firm" who set fire to the bike sheds and shut the headmaster's cat in the staff-room all one weekend so that it had to be fumigated.'

'Dear oh dear.'

'Mr Hassell's the deputy headmaster. That's why 'e's got us.'

The knot started to bubble and brown pus oozed out of it.

'And a new fat boy from Hunston had to hand over the bar of Milk Motoring his mum'd given him for playtime to a boy called Ritson because he sat in one of the Firm's chairs by mistake.'

'But that's extortion!'

'And Mr Hassell calls them all by their christian names and he calls us by our surnames and it feels horrible to be called by your surname when you don't know anyone.'

'But you do, Simon.' Mum spread her hands. 'Why, there's Jerry Henry and Jimmy Phillips and—'

'We've all been put in different classes. They say we're all different ages and different ability streams or something.'

The knot suddenly caught fire and sizzled and Mum went and put the kettle on again.

'And we have a different classroom for each lesson and a locker to keep our plimsolls in.' I faced towards the door and shouted until she came back. 'And we're not allowed to wear our outdoor shoes inside the school but 'ow the 'ell can we help it if our plimsolls're upstairs and we've just come in and can't put them on without going up to get 'em?'

'Beats me, my darling.' Mum looked at the clock and out of the window and then put the curtains straight. 'I really don't know what to suggest.'

'And we've got to choose one out of gardening and woodwork and metalwork and I'd probably get frozen doing gardening and burned in metalwork so I'd better choose woodwork.'

'Looks like it.' Mum took the tea cosy off and felt the pot and put the cosy back on again.

'An' the roof of the gym's about forty foot 'igh an' we 'ave to climb up ropes to the very top an' touch the ceiling.'

Mum looked up at our ceiling as if she was expecting to see ropes screwed into it. 'Surely that's an exaggeration, Simon.'

'No it isn't, Mum, an' it means lettin' go with one 'and an' 'angin' on with the other.'

'Well, I really don't know.'

'An' ol' Cherriman makes us run round the gym with only our shorts on while 'e kicks footballs at us to make us go faster.'

'Now steady on, Simon . . .'

The more I told her the less she believed me and she said she couldn't possibly ask Dad to get me a transfer to another school because the Lincs was the only school I could go to, so far as she knew, and anyway it was only my first day and things might improve but that I'd better make a special effort and see if I couldn't get to the High School pretty quickly.

She left me staring at the smouldering black knot when Dad got home for tea and they spent ages whispering in the kitchen. I poked at the knot with the poker until a few sparks caught and a tiny blue flame curled up around it and then Dad came in and put his bike clips over the onion-shaped brass ornament on the mantelpiece.

'Busy letting the fire out, Nip?'

29

'M'm.' I gave him the poker.

'I expect there's enough left to catch, don't you?'

'Yeah, I expect so.'

He built the ashes up so that there was space in between and some charred bits caught and flared and I went and sat on the woodbox by the airing cupboard and stared into the flames, while Mum finished laying the tea, and wondered if it was really me that today had happened to.

There I was, in the middle of the crowd surging forward and being squashed through the doors and pushed up the corridor and into the main hall where we'd separated, like milk bottles on a machine to be labelled. First we split off from Colin, who they said was a bit nearer thirteen than twelve, and then from Kenny Lane and Derek Brown and Jerry Henry, because their birthdays were after 1st September, and then into streams according to what some masters had on their clip-boards. I was channelled into the twelves-before-1st-September with Gibbser and Jimmy Phillips and had to stand behind a little fat man with a red face who said his name was Mr Hassell and he called our names out alphabetically and sorted us into different lines . . .

I swivelled round on the woodbox and opened the palm of my hand to the fire and let the warmth lick in between the joints of my fingers: I'd read in a geography book once how all the animals crowded together in the pools when there was a forest fire and never attacked each other so that if a juicy little deer fawn had fallen over and caught its coat alight a lion or something would have grabbed it gently by the scruff of the neck and dipped it in the water and given it back to its mother. I made a V of my fingers and moved them up and down against the background of fire. Gibbser had been the first of us to go. He'd been put into 4R, with a crowd of boys we'd never seen before, and then they found Jimmy Phillips was in the wrong age band and he went as red as a beetroot when Mr Hassell asked him if they knew where he came from that the 23rd November came after 1st September and he'd been sent to 3R with Jerry Henry. That left me with a few others and we edged closer together. Mr Hassell called out 'Wilson S.G.' and 'Yes, sir' stuck in my throat and I missed my first grab at Old Gran's case and went where he pointed. 4B was a dozen or so boys lounging together as if they were waiting to be sent on errands and another dozen, dressed up like window dummies with cases and satchels that shone as if they'd been polished with cycle oil, who were shrinking together like sheep in a snowstorm. I took a deep breath and stood between them with my back to the stage facing outwards.

I fanned my fingers out, so that the fire-light showed through them, and screwed my eyes up against the picture of me trying to be helpful.

Mr Hassell was marking the register and there was a ping and a splintering squash as his pencil broke and the stub dug into the paper. I winced as I saw myself dive forward with my propelling pencil and my face flushed as the messenger boys grinned like cannibals and I made out 'arsehole-creeper' passing between them. I turned my hand over so that the tiny hairs glanced golden in the flames and wondered why I hadn't left it at that. Whatever had possessed me to go up to one of them, Farmer, afterwards and say I hoped they didn't think I was a creep for lending Hassell my pencil? The heat had built up on my cheek and it felt as if my skin was scaling. Farmer had looked at me as if I wasn't there but he and Ritson had bumped against me and called me something I'd never heard before as we went to our classroom.

'What's a prat, Dad?'

'I dunno, Nip.' Dad was on his hands and knees feeding the fire. 'With two t's it could be a name, I s'pose. Why?'

'Oh . . . nothing.'

'Don't mean "prattle", do you? That's a sort of childish way of talking.'

'Dunno. Doesn't matter.'

'M'm.' Dad went back to blowing the fire and I focused on a spark that had got hung up amongst the shreds of soot on the damper back-plate and was spreading.

'Ever heard of anti-glare lights, Dad?'

He knelt back on his folded knees. 'Don't think so, Nip. Why?'

'Well, there was this boy at school . . . they had all the lights on in the hall but they weren't very bright so

31

I asked him what the point was of having them on at all.'

'Oh yeah.'

'And he said I wasn't very bright either because they were the new anti-glare ones.'

'Oh arh.' He was waiting for a woodlouse to crawl out from a gap where the bark was peeling away on a log he was ready to put on the fire.

'Well, that wasn't very nice, was it?'

'No. S'pose not.' He knelt forward and pulled the damper over and the flames flattened. 'But you must try not to be so perishin' sensitive about every least little thing, you know, Simon.'

I closed my eyes and leant my head back so that my hair scraped between my scalp and the gritty brickwork of the fireplace and I took a deep breath and held it.

Mr Hassell had taken us to our classroom and shown us our lockers and where the cloakrooms were and explained about changing rooms when the bell went and then we'd gone out to play.

Standing by the corner wall to the toilets I'd remembered what they'd said about reading the timetable carefully and I'd kept taking it out of my pocket to see where I had to be next. I'd even showed it to a boy who was passing and pointed to the next square and asked him if that was where 4B were having Maths in the first period after playtime.

I leant back against the fireplace as I saw, again, the boys in 5B laughing at me as I stood in the doorway listening to their teacher telling me I was in the wrong class. He was writing numbers as well as letters on the blackboard and it looked so difficult that I could feel a dark hand beckoning me on for when I was older and went up to 5B to be tormented by sums with letters in them and I prayed that they'd lower the school-leaving age before that happened to me or that we'd emigrate to Australia and get shipwrecked on the way.

'Whatever's up with you, Simon?'

I'd sensed Mum come in and that she was standing there waiting for me to notice her.

I'd tried to find the right class but I kept coming back

32

to the wrong one and looking at my watch to see how late I was.

'Simon?'

'Nothing, Mum.'

It had got so late that I'd given up and gone down to the cloakrooms and sat amongst the coats waiting for playtime.

'And what're you up to in here, my lad?'

I could still feel the shock of the caretaker appearing from nowhere.

'Nothing, sir.' It had felt as if he'd caught me with my hand in somebody's pocket.

'Really can't think what's got into him, George.'

I could see her, through my eyelids, watching me as she poured the tea.

He'd taken my name and walked off in the direction of the headmaster's office but I couldn't see if he'd gone into it or the secretary's and then the bell had gone and I'd had to go out to play.

'What in the name of all that's wonderful is up with him?' Mum was holding Dad's tea out to him but he hadn't seen it. 'Sitting there sulking about heaven knows what.'

Maybe they'd call my name out tomorrow morning in assembly and I'd have to stand outside the office where everybody could see me as they went by.

'Simon!'

And if anybody had lost anything I'd get the blame and be branded a thief. I shivered and it came out as a whimper.

'Simon, darling.' Mum was over me and she was shaking me. 'What is it?'

'I missed a lesson, Mum.'

'Oh yeah.' Dad stood up and squeezed past us and sat down at the table. 'Weren't skiving, were you?'

'No I wasn't. I was soddin' well lost.'

'All right, all right, Simon.' Dad sat to attention and Mum looked as if she'd run into a wall. 'That's quite enough.'

'I didn't want to get left out there on my own and I couldn't go in late and have them all looking at me.'

'I said, that's enough, Simon.'

'And it's not my fault if I can't remember where I'm supposed to be . . . and I've never got any friends.'

'Come on. Calm down.'

'Leave me alone, Mum.'

'Steady on, Simon.'

'Never got anything to do and no one to play with and no brothers or sisters. Haven't even got a bloody cat.'

'Simon, ple-ase!'

'Don't touch me.' I shook myself free. 'Just leave me a-bloody-lone.' My elbow caught Dad in the stomach as I ran into my bedroom and slammed the door.

I'd expected them to follow me and for my bedroom door to crash open but it didn't and the curtains swayed gently where Mum had left the window open to the first notch.

'I don't know if he's over-sensitive, Ina—' Dad paused and I could hear him puffing on a cigarette as he lit it from a spill of paper. '. . . or just plain perishin' obstinate.'

'Beats me, dear.' It sounded as if Mum was opening a new pot of jam. 'But I do wish he could find something to occupy his mind.'

It wasn't raining too hard so they'd sent us outside at playtime. I'd passed the headmaster and the caretaker in the corridor and they'd ignored me but I didn't dare shelter in the cloakrooms again so I stood in the entrance to the toilets until the crush built up behind me so much that I got pushed out. Kenny Lane and Jerry Henry were sheltering against the wall by the dustbins and I ran over to them as they spotted Geoff Gibbs and Colin Gander just inside the bike sheds. We darted across to them but I caught my foot in the straps of a canvas bag lying by the wall.

'Come 'ere, Mush, an' I'll punch yer 'ead in!' It was the boy who'd been throwing another boy against the wire the first day and I put his bag straight without taking my eyes off him and slid into the bike sheds.

'What you done now, Nipper?' Geoff Gibbs was bending forward and holding his stomach, which meant he'd be dashing for the toilet soon.

'I tripped over that big bloke's bag.' I tried to shoulder in. 'An' move over so's I can get in, will ya.'

'Ain't 'ny more room.' Geoff nudged me away with his bottom.

'What about over there?'

'Nah!' Geoff groaned and bent lower. 'Somebody's been sick over there.'

'Oh . . . p'raps you want a good dose of Syrup of Figs, Geoff.'

'P'raps you wan' a good kick up the arse, Nipper.'

I hunched my shoulders against the misty drizzle and looked at the boy whose bag I'd kicked. He was sheltering against a wall talking to a small dark boy of about the same age who looked like a picture from a judo magazine. There were half a dozen or so other big boys with them but those two stood out.

'That's Pip Williamson.' Colin had come up behind me. 'And the other one's Tony Cato.'

'Oh yeah. How d'you know?'

'There's a bloke in my form from the Children's 'ome. 'e knows them. Williamson's an 'ard man an' Cato boxes for West Sussex.'

'Blimey, does 'e?'

'Yeah. So you'd better watch yer step, Nipper.' Geoff Gibbs stood up slowly as if he was seeing if the pain had gone. 'What you got next, Col?'

'Woodwork.' Colin did his jacket up as the bell went. 'What about you?'

' 'istory, I think.' Geoff Gibbs barged into me as he followed Colin. 'Watch it, Nipper. Don't you push me around.'

I tried to get into the middle as everyone crowded towards the doors but I kept getting edged to the sides and when I pulled my timetable and school map out, to see what my next lesson was, I dropped it and I had been swept halfway down the corridor before I managed to slip out to the side again and by the time I got back it had been trodden to shreds in the wet tarmac.

The corridor was empty and my plimsolls made a squishing sound on the vinyl floor. The vinyl was squashy and

35

thicker than lino and it was probably because they had stuff like this and anti-glare lights and marzipan-coloured bricks that they called it one of the most modern schools in the country. They couldn't call it that just because it was new because Dad said they were opening new schools all over the place nowadays . . . and modern couldn't be the same as good because everybody still wanted to go to the High School and nobody would have chosen the Lincs. Maybe it was the chemistry rooms that made it more modern than anything else, or the gymnas . . . !

Clip . . . clip! Footsteps on the concrete staircase.

I slipped back into the cloakroom amongst the shoe cages behind the coat racks wondering why it had to be me again, here again, and I put my hands together and prayed it wouldn't be the caretaker. It was the headmaster, and his chest seemed to fill the corridor as he peered through the round glass window in each of the classroom doors as he passed. I held my breath as his footsteps came closer. A hairy hand reached out and the macs in front of the shoe cages parted like a curtain.

'What in heaven's name've we got here?'

'I'm lost, sir.'

'Lost? You're skulking, boy. That's what you're doing.'

'Yes, sir. But, please sir, I don't know what lesson I'm supposed to be in.'

'May the saints preserve us.' He breathed out so hard the hairs up his nose quivered. 'What form are you in?'

'4B, sir.'

'Dear oh dear. Poor Mr Hassell. And what lesson should you be in?'

'Chemistry, sir.'

'Don't you mean Science?'

'What?'

'I beg your pardon!' His face was brown and wrinkled like the surface of cold gravy. 'I said it's science, not chemistry. If you'd been paying attention you'd have known. And where's your timetable?'

'I lost it, sir.'

'Get along with you.' His arm came out so fast it made

me jump. 'You're in there. Right opposite. And you'd better watch your step, my lad. I've got my eye on you.'

I edged past him and backed away across the corridor and into the classroom.

The boys looked up as I walked in and the master turned from the blackboard and then turned back again. I stood by the door waiting for him to say something. He was wearing a heavy blue suit with trousers that looked as if they'd been pressed and then had hot air blown up them, and crumpled pockets, and I wondered if he rolled it up at night instead of folding it on a hanger. His face was reddish, as if he'd been running and then washed it with a hot flannel and then had black pepper shaken over it.

'Any more behind you?'

'Pardon, sir?'

'The door, lad.'

'Oh.' I tried to close it but the handle wouldn't turn.

'Just pull it. They click closed.'

I pulled and it clicked and I went and sat down on the far side of the row, about halfway up the class, next to a boy with pimples and a grey pullover and grey trousers.

The teacher, Mr James, had written his name up on the blackboard. He turned and rubbed chalk dust off his fingers and slipped his thumbs under the waistband of his trousers and hitched them up.

'Right now! We'll start off by going over the last bits of last year's work for the benefit of those who were in 3B because they weren't paying much attention, were they, Farmer?' – Fag Farmer finished whispering and Chunky Halstow slewed round slowly to face the front – 'And it'll be a good introduction for the new boys. So you'll need a test tube between two of you and a sugar lump and a half-beakerful of sulphuric and don't make a mad dash for it.'

Nobody moved.

'Right. Off you go.'

Farmer yawned and Ritson and the others just in front of them turned round and it looked as if they were having a rugby scrum over the table until Aston and Hill leant back and got up and went to the cupboard behind Mr James and then some of the new boys got up and followed them.

'I'll get ours if you like.' The boy next to me slid off his stool. 'You check to see our Bunsen's working.'

I stared at the empty table and ran the flat of my hand over it to make sure I wasn't missing anything and felt underneath to see if there were any drawers that might have something in that might be our Bunsen. I couldn't find anything so I looked around the classroom for clues.

The classroom was square and high and the walls were painted white down to a row of metal sinks and draining boards on one side and grey cupboards on the other. The wall at the front had three blackboards made out of shiny black canvas stuff on rollers that looked too slippery to write on with chalk. There were no desks, just two rows of long, high wooden tables with space for four boys each to sit on high round-topped stools. There was a long hole in the top of each stool and I squiggled back on mine to make myself more comfortable, and gazed out of the window.

The grass on the playing-field was about three inches high; too long to play cricket and too thin for football. It didn't look as if it would ever be any use because the rough red soil that showed through was spattered with flints. There was a low hedge around the field and a gap leading to another field which had a high wire fence along the edge cutting it off from the by-pass where cars and lorries were flashing by. There were no tall trees so we could have looked right down to the sea if it hadn't been so overcast, and the willow trees across the by-pass ballooned in the wind as if they were going to take off and join the rain clouds that hung above the gravel pits.

'Does it work?'

'What?'

'The Bunsen.' The boy was back and he put a plastic pot with a plastic lid and five sugar lumps down on the table and offered me one.

'I dunno. What is it?'

'This.' He tapped a thing like a table lamp, screwed to the bench top, with a glass tube he had in his other hand. 'You're supposed to light it.'

38

'Oh.' I looked to see what the others were doing. 'I haven't got any matches.'

'You don't need matches. 'ere, you want that sugar lump?' I shook my head so he ate it. 'You use a taper and get a light off Jammer.'

'Oh . . . my name's Simon.'

'Yeah, I know. I'm Clements.'

'You done science before?'

'Course I 'ave.' He was searching through a drawer that pulled out from under the centre of the bench. 'Haven't you?'

'No. Is it difficult?'

Clements shrugged. 'I dunno. He tells us what to do and we do it.'

'Do you. What for?'

'I told you, because he tells us to. If you put a drop of this vinegary stuff in that tube and heat it up and then put a lump of sugar in it it steams and goes all frothy and bubbles up.'

'Then do you drink it? Sounds like Dr Jekyll and Mr Hyde.'

'Who?' Clements had spots and he was picking one. 'No, course you don't drink it. You slosh it down the sink and wash the test tube out an' then he tells us about acid an' stuff. 'ang on and I'll get a taper.'

Clements came back with what looked like a piece of string coated in sealing-wax, that Mr James had lit for him, and he showed me how to work the burner and made the flame go from a long, curved yellow shape, like a daffodil, to a hissing roar like a blow-lamp, and we cooked our sugar until it bubbled and foamed and stank and then we tipped it down the sink and he told me some more about 3B.

'They all think Pete Farmer's the worst cos he's the biggest and used to get into a lot of fights at the Central Boys.'

I looked back at Farmer without turning my head.

'. . . but Doug Ritson's the one to look out for.'

Ritson looked up and I closed my eyes as if I was falling asleep and opened them looking in a different direction.

'He lives with 'is old Gran over on the Weald Estate

39

an' he can get anything he wants off her; stardust shirts an' green gabardine trousers an' he gets five bob a week pocket money an' goes around with the yobs from the sixth form in the evening.'

'What doing?' I stole another glance at Doug Ritson. His tie was so thin it looked like a piece of string.

'Pictures an' out roun' the Rendezvous, I expect.' Clements nudged me to look back to the front and he rested his forehead on his fingers so that he could talk from behind his hand. 'An' the rest of 'em's Gipsey Hill and Yates an' Allsorts Bassett and Aston an' Elsworth an' 'im with the black 'air an' maggotty features is Lenny Long. He's not in with them really but 'e's got a sister called Singin' Jenny so they voted 'im form captain so 'e can't split on 'em.'

'Why not?' I couldn't help looking back at Long.

'I told you.' Clements dipped his pen in the ink-well and drew a swastika on the back of his book. 'Because they voted 'im form captain.'

'Oh. You mean about what they get up . . . out round the cafes an' things?'

'Yeah.' Clements grinned. 'You could say.'

I hadn't got a clue what he was talking about but I didn't think he knew that. 'And what about the others?'

'What others?'

'Well . . .' I looked around the class. 'All these others. I thought 4B was the worst class in the school?'

'Oh they were.' Clements pulled another sugar lump out of his pocket. 'But Povey's got sent down to 4R this year an' Hayward got sent away for settin' fire to an ol' barn in the 'olidays an' Tupper an' Denyer an' that lot're all right an' the rest're new.'

'Do you reckon we'll get in much trouble?'

'Dunno.' Clements scratched at a little outcrop of pimples at the corner of his mouth. ' 'spec so. 'ere, we'd better get cleaned up. Bell'll be going in a minute.'

The laboratory was big and cold and smelt of tin and water and paint but the geography room was small and warm and we helped Mr Heater put maps on the walls and pictures of special places, like the Grand Canyon and the Taj Mahal. And the English room smelt of lavender floor polish and had soft cork tiles that were nice to walk on and we had to do a story about the best day in our lives. I started one about my last day at the village school but I didn't finish it because I just sat there thinking how long ago it seemed already until the bell went for us to go home.

I passed myself in the mirror in the toilet as I was putting my mac on. My cheek was smudged and there was chalk dust in my hair and on my blazer and my socks had fallen down. A boy looked in and bumped up against me. He pulled his tie straight and tasted some water off his fingertips and flicked them dry on the towel and rushed off again without noticing me, so I wiped my nose on some toilet paper and ran out through the playground as if I'd been here forever because if I didn't know them they couldn't know me so they probably wouldn't notice me if I did just what they did, and now that my first week was over I couldn't think why I'd been so worried about it.

I soon got to know where the classrooms were and to having the masters call the register before every lesson and, as I passed the village school every day, it seemed less and less as if it was the only school I could ever have gone to and I soon found I was walking past it without even noticing it was there.

The boys in my class thought I was clever to keep finding different excuses for being late for lessons.

'That's one of the beauties of a school like this.' Clements was soaking toilet paper in a basin and rolling it up into tight balls and stuffing it up the taps. 'You can waste about five minutes between each lesson and even more than that if one or two of you can manage to be a bit later.'

'Yeah.' I was combing my hair with water and folding a wave up in front with the palm of my hand.

'And maybe a whole lesson if you can persuade 'em somebody asked you to do something.'

'Such as what?'

Clements turned a hot tap on, gently at first and then more as the water started to spurt up out through the handle. 'Perfect!' He turned the tap off and wiped his hands. 'Oh I dunno . . . getting something for somebody or runnin' a message down the gardens or gettin' glue out of the woodwork shops if something needs stickin'. Anything like that. You jus' 'ave to say you forgot who told you to do it so they can't check up on you.'

'M'm.' I shook my comb out and put it in my pocket. 'You goin' on first or second sitting?'

'First, I think,' and Clements slung his arm over my shoulder and we marched out to the canteen together.

Nearly all my class had school dinners and most of them said they were rotten, but I liked them, especially some pudding-stuff called Meat Loaf, and I always had a second helping, once we'd slung Fatty Nicholson from Sidlesham off our table for picking his nose and showing it to us.

At the end of the third week they said we could go out and play games in the bottom field by the by-pass and the following week Mr Levers, the headmaster, announced in assembly that we were going to have house football trials in the games periods so that the house-masters could pick their sides for the inter-house matches.

'Pointless you botherin', Nipper.' Doug Ritson had come up behind me and buckled my knees as I was writing my name down on the trials lists on the notice-board. 'Saxons never were any good.'

I straightened up the 'l' in Wilson where he'd jogged me and wrote '4B' after it. 'What house you in then?'

'Romans. You seen who we got?'

I ran my finger down the purple-headed paper. 'Dunno any of 'em.'

'You bleedin' will do after you've played us.'

'You can never tell with . . . football.' I groaned inside as I heard Dad's voice and knew Ritson had noticed it. 'We'll bleedin' murder you.'

'Yeah . . . well . . .' Ritson's eyes had narrowed and he veered off from me as we crossed the playground. 'We'll see who'll murder who.'

I slowed down deliberately and worked my way over to the footpath from the girls' school so that he went on ahead of me. I'd seen Henry and Phillips still in the cloakrooms as

I'd come out, so I wouldn't be last on the school bus, and I'd learned it was best to just have a few words with Ritson at a time because he always started hitting out if you spent more than about five minutes with him.

'Who's been murdered?'

A hand on my shoulder stopped me dead.

'You haven't hurt anybody, have you, Simon?' The head of a rag-doll was sticking out of Brenda's satchel.

'N'ho.' I tried to laugh as I said it. 'Rit's a friend of mine really, an' 'e reckons Romans'll beat us at football.'

'Well, my brothers think you'd be a jolly good player if you practised more.'

'Do they?' My shoulders went back and I pulled my stomach in.

'And you can come down and play with them if you like cos my dad said Skip Matthews is going to give them a few tips.'

'Cor yeah! When's that gonna start?'

'They might be playing tonight.'

'Cor, goodo!'

Brenda hadn't got any gloves and I could see her hand was getting cold where she was holding her case.

'Shall I carry that for you, Bren?'

Her little cheeks reddened. 'Yes please, Simon.'

I took a deep breath. 'Here, give it us then and you can put your hand in your pocket.'

Farmer and Ritson were sitting on the canal wall. Farmer nudged Ritson to look at me and I looked away. I opened the sliding door on the bus and stood aside for Brenda in full view of them and closed it behind me without turning round as a long wolf whistle cut through the wind. I sat down next to her just in front of Gibbs and Gander without going red and I didn't try to cover my hand when she held it going round the roundabout by the White Swan.

I met Mum coming out of Nan's gate as I was going home. She'd trodden in some mud and was wiping it off the heel of her shoe in the grass.

'Hello, Simon. You earlier or am I late?'

' 'bout the same, Mum.'

'How'd school go today?'

'All right.'

'You're getting on better now, aren't you?'

'M'm, s'pose so.'

'That's the ticket.' She stood up straighter and pulled her coat down where it had worked up under her belt. 'I expect it was just a question of getting used to it.'

'M'm, 'spec so, Mum.'

'Simon, where're you . . . ?'

I stopped and looked back. 'I'm in a hurry, Mum. I'm going down the camp.'

'But couldn't you just wait and walk down the road with—'

'I can't, Mum. I'll be late. I'll be back about seven or whenever it starts getting dark.'

I felt a gripping feeling in my stomach as I turned away from her but she didn't call after me and the distance fell in behind me as I turned the corner by Gander's house and ran up Crouch Cross Lane and down the Close.

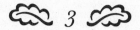

I'd cycled down through the village past the post office and the farm and across the main road and into the old married quarters out of habit. The shelves in the NAAFI had been getting more and more empty since the end of rationing and now it looked as if it was closing down. I drew an arrow in the dust on the window-sill and rubbed it out and rode off down to Mickey Leary's house where we'd used to play cricket. The bald patch where we'd had our wicket was knee-deep in grass and the earth air-raid shelter had been flattened and I sat there, with my elbows on my handlebars, wondering if they'd have bulldozed it if we hadn't gone off somewhere else to play. They'd put a smart new chain-link fence across the hole in the hedge we'd used to go through to get to the new married quarters, and I had to double back along it to get out onto the road past the guardroom. I stopped again, with my pedal against the kerb and balanced with my feet on the crossbar, and looked at where the old Spitfire had stood at the official entrance to the camp. There was nothing left of it except an oil stain on its concrete plinth. They'd taken the fluorescent light out of the guardroom as well, and all the furniture, and the paint was flaking off the doors. There had always been two Special Police with red armbands in there and sometimes they'd had motor-cyclists' boots and spats on and I'd always felt I was committing a crime just walking past them and that, even if the Germans had got across the Channel during the war, they'd never have got any further than the SPs in Tangmere Guardroom. But now it looked as if an infection was eating into it and had destroyed our Spitfire and was doing the same to the NAAFI and the place where we'd played cricket and that if anyone attacked us now there'd be nothing to stop them except Skip Matthews in his paint-stained track-suit waving a bike pump from behind a smart new chain-link fence.

I yawned and looked at my watch. It was still only ten to five.

I leant forward into my pedals and forced my way up the hill to the officers' married quarters but there was nobody about up there and the curtains were all drawn and it didn't look as if any children lived there so I went straight round in the turning circle and back down the hill and turned right into the sports field and leant against the pavilion wall waiting for the five o'clock hooter.

The hooter sounded from behind me somewhere over towards the runway. I'd always been home for tea before when it went off and it sounded foreign going off so close. I rolled my front wheel towards a worm-cast and then back again and stared down at the tyre print. I'd never thought before, why it was there and why it went off at all. They had hooters in the collieries up north, Mum said, to let them know when a shift finished but people didn't have to rely on them so much now because they were much better off nowadays and most of them could afford watches. I took my front wheel over the flattened worm-cast from a different direction and gave it a cross-pattern. Half a dozen or so people went by on bikes and then a few in cars. They all had air force uniforms on under their macs but I noticed one was a WAAF because she had a skirt on and a bike without a bar, but there was nothing to tell me what they'd been doing to need to have a hooter to tell them it was time to finish and I turned my bike round and came at the flattened-out worm-cast from the side and turned the lines I'd turned into diamonds into squares divided into diamonds.

Come to think of it ... what could there be for any of them to do now that the war had been over for so long that they didn't even need a guardroom?

I looked at my watch. It was still only ten-past five and Brenda had said they probably wouldn't start until about half past. A low whine started up down on the runway and built up to the scream of a jet. We often saw them flying but never taking off or landing and Mickey Leary and the Norris boys said they did a lot of training down at the camp now so perhaps they had a jet or two there they kept especially for the men to practise on. I sat up and stretched my leg down so that I could touch the ground and balance and still sit on the saddle. The jet whine softened and died. If the Norris boys had been here they'd probably have said they were burning off old fuel or testing something, but they weren't and I couldn't see how hundreds of airmen could be kept busy on a couple of jets because they'd be left standing around waiting for a turn; and if it never flew perhaps I could find out where it was and go and see it. It was still only quarter-past five so I sped off down Tangmere Lane again and turned right towards the runway.

The runway was behind a high hedge of spiky evergreen that grew close right down to the ground and I couldn't see through it even when I got down on my hands and knees. There was a heavy metal gateway, covered in wire, with a lightning flash and a 14 FT. MAXIMUM sign on it, but even that had been boarded up so I couldn't see through the cracks and I was halfway along the New Road, that came out by Shopwhyke where there was a lay-by with some trees in it, before I could get a proper look. All I could see, from between the trees, was rough fields with the runway in the distance disappearing amongst the weeds. I stepped back and looked up into the trees. There were no branches low down but they were growing close enough together for me to get my back against one and walk my feet up another like an upside-down caterpillar.

The runways were just like scruffy roads and the nearest one must have been half a mile away. There were some hangars or sheds in the distance with some things that could have been planes dotted about but I couldn't see anything that made it worthwhile having a blessed great hedge around and I climbed down again and rubbed the green, from the bark of the tree, off my back.

There was still nobody out playing football when I got back so I squiggled my front wheel in the soft grass, until it churned up some mud and rolled a few balls and threw them at the pavilion windows until I saw Brenda Norris coming down the road with Christine Lanagan.

47

'Hello, Simon.' Christine Lanagan looked like Montezuma's daughter in a film we'd once seen about the Spaniards against the Aztecs.

' 'lo, Christine . . . Brenda.'

Brenda didn't answer and Christine was clinging to her and whispering into her ear.

'Bren?'

'Yes, Simon.' She looked like one of the chubby infants in a nativity play and I found myself drawn back to the way Christine's creamy-brown skin seemed almost white against the glossy black-wire shine of her hair and to how much deeper brown her eyes were and how she'd stopped grinning and was looking at me with her lips apart and her pink tongue-tip just showing now as if she'd realised she'd lost something and wanted it back. '. . . Simon?'

'What? Oh yeah. I thought you said there'd be football tonight?'

'Well, I thought they said there would be.' Brenda was treading the heel of one shoe onto the toe of the other. 'But p'raps there isn't.'

'Are they still indoors then?'

'No.' Brenda swung round to Christine. 'They went out. We don't know where they've gone. We're going down to Susan Farley's to listen to records. You could walk down with us if you like.'

'What for? T'listen to records?'

'Leave him, Brenda.' Christine's hand was over her mouth again.

'I don't know.' Brenda shrugged Christine off. 'Just thought you might've wanted to walk down with us.'

'All right, then.' I turned my bike round and lifted it down the kerb. 'But I did want to play football really.'

'Well you can't, can you, if there's no one to play with.' Christine Lanagan tossed her head and took Brenda's arm and they went on ahead of me without speaking until we came to the guardroom and they broke off up into the old married quarters and I kept on down the road.

The road ran past the front of the cinema and through some lime trees with a high wire fence on the right where I'd never been before. Through the trees I could see a parade ground with buildings clustered around it on three sides and a young airman was sitting on a front step, with a cigarette hanging out of his mouth, whitening a pair of plimsolls.

'So that's why they call them the married quarters.'

'Pardon?'

I'd stopped and drawn up near the wire but I hadn't seen a man in an officer's uniform who'd stood up from behind a laurel bush.

'Married quarters, sir. I'd always wondered why they called them—' I pointed with my thumb back behind me. 'Why they were called the married quarters an' where the ones who weren't married lived. S'pose it's in there.'

He had a moustache like Professor Jimmy Edwards and polished black gloves.

'You don't live here then?'

'Oh no, sir. I just come down here to play.'

'Oh, you do, do you?' His chest went out and his stick came up under his arm and I stood more to attention with the bar of my bike between my legs. 'And I suppose it's all right for you to be playing about on government property?'

'No, sir.' I daren't blink.

'No. I should think not.'

'But I've been coming down here for years. To play with—'

'Straight out down there and on to the civilian road, please.'

'But—'

'*If* you please!' He took a half step towards the wire and I turned and rode away.

Mum was breaking a block of salt up with the bread knife and a thin cloud of white dust hung over the bread-board.

'Of course I'm sorry you were disappointed, Simon.' Sometimes she slid up and down the salt block so that it flaked off into a roasting tin but today she was cutting it into chunks and chopping them up as if they were onions. 'But I didn't at all like your attitude when you came home from school this evening.' The knife chop-chopped up and down. 'And you needn't think you can start coming home for your meals just when you feel like it.' She turned the

49

knife flat and crushed the salt to powder. 'You can count yourself mighty lucky Dad had to stop off at the Weston brothers on the way home else you wouldn't've got any tea at all.'

'Yeah, blessed performance that was, you know, Ina.'

'Pardon, dear?' Mum was grinding the salt now with the rolling-pin.

'This blessed football signing-on caper.'

'Oh.' She tipped the salt onto a sheet of newspaper and took it up in its fold and shot it into the earthenware jar that stood on two scrubbed bricks at the side of the cooker.

'First of all I didn't think they were in.' Dad was taking cards and letters and forms out of his pockets and arranging them on the table between the knives and jam and bread and butter. 'And then I spotted Len's bike behind the woodshed so I went round the back to make them hear.' He put the postcards in one heap, the forms in another and the two letters together. 'You listening to me, Ina?'

'Yes, dear.' Mum had been out to tip the old tea leaves under the cabbages.

'I thought it was fishy when they reckoned they couldn't find a pen and then, when I said they could use mine, they said they hadn't got the signing-on fee.'

'Would you believe it!'

'And when I said they could pay that later it turned out that Len may have to work some Saturday afternoons and young Peter's thinking of signing on for Lavant.'

'Oh surely not, dear.' Mum stopped as she was bringing the tea in and then she set it down gently. 'Surely not.'

'Yep.' Dad knocked the three cards into a neat pile and put them on top of the letters between the paste and the bread and butter. 'But fortunately old Ron came 'ome while I was still there and talked some sense into the pair of them.'

'So they've signed on then?'

'Yes, Ina. All three of 'em, and Ron an' Len'll probably come to the meeting.'

'What meeting, Dad?'

'The AGM tonight.'

'Oh. Why isn't Pete coming?'

Dad spread a slice of bread and butter and jam and licked a spot of jam off his finger. 'He's only a nipper, Simon. Good young prospect though, you know, Ina, when he learns not to run with the ball.'

' 'e scored a smashin' goal against Hunston last year though, Dad. Ran through 'alf their team on 'is own.'

'I know, Simon, and I stood out there on the left wing completely unmarked all the rest of the game while 'e tried to do it again.' Dad straightened his forms up square with his letters. 'No, much better to leave the question of selection committees and things to those with a bit more experience.'

'Boys were old enough to die for their country when they were fourteen in the First World War.'

They both looked at me and then at each other.

'What's that got to do with it?'

'Dunno, Dad.'

'What'd you say it for then?'

'Dunno, Dad. It's jus' somethin' I 'eard Grandad say once.'

They started each season with a selection committee meeting in the village hall and Dad typed the agenda up on an old typewriter he'd found outside the Men's Club one evening on his way home from Nan and Grandad's. He'd taken it down to P.C. Farr to report it but nobody claimed it for six months so they gave it to him.

'I've always resisted having the AGM in the Men's Club, ya know, Ina.'

'Shan't be a minute, dear.' There was a splash and a gurgle as the washing-up water went down the sink.

'Haven't been inside a pub since 1934, ya know, Nip.' Dad was laying out his clean hanky and the minutes from the last meeting and then he put a pencil out next to them. 'But p'raps having it in the snooker room won't be so bad and we can get your hair cut at the same time.'

'Oh, Mum, do I have—'

'Yes you do, my lad.' Mum was still wiping her hands as she came in. 'Now get your coat on and don't make a fuss.'

Albert Dainty and his son, Gerald, were playing snooker when we arrived and they just grunted at Dad when he said, ' 'ow do,' as if we had no right to be there.

'Right then, Simon.' Dad put his mac over the back of an old pew and dusted the seat off with his hand. 'You sit yourself down there until Mr Davis gets here to cut your hair while I go and get a table and chair.'

'What for, Dad?'

'The chairman. You always have a chairman at meetings and he needs somewhere to sit and put his papers and if I don't get them I don't suppose anyone else will.'

I sat listening to the click of the balls and tried to guess which pocket they'd fall into but I never got it right and I wondered why they left all the lovely red ones in the pockets and picked out the green and the blue when they went in. I tried to follow the score as well but they seemed to be putting up whatever they liked and it didn't make sense and then my eye caught the way Gerald's pants came out above his trousers, where his shirt had pulled out when he bent forward, until he saw me and pulled his pullover down over them.

The snooker room was an oval dome of white-washed corrugated-iron sheets. There were two old church pews running the length of the table against each wall and a space at the far end with a rusty army stove with a chimney going up through the roof. They'd made a coal bunker for the coke in one corner out of sandbags left over from when the Men's Club had been in danger of flooding one winter and there were two armchairs in the other corner that had been there ever since the night a courting couple had set a rick alight near Westhampnett during the war and they'd had to evacuate the village in case the Germans saw it and thought it was Tangmere and bombed it.

The door grated open and Mr Dainty paused over his cue. He glanced back as Dad struggled in with one of the fold-up card tables they used at beetle drives and a kitchen chair. Mr Dainty followed Dad all the way up to the space by the fire, where he stood the table up and tested it was level, and then all the way back to the door. Then he settled himself over his cue and mishit the white as the door grated open.

'Bugger!'

'Four away, Dibbler.' Taffy Davis pushed the door back with his foot. 'Ah, good, somebody's been kind enough to put me a chair out. You first, Nipper?'

He put a brown-ale crate on Dad's chair, sat me on it, wrapped a towel round me from his black bag, and snipped away until it felt as if I hadn't any hair left.

Geoff Gibbs and Colin Gander came in soon after that and made a dash for the far end of the pew, nearest Taffy, and started to argue about who was going next and the Brindle brothers and Ted and Billy Lovesey wandered in with their pints and I passed some RAF chaps from Tangmere outside as I was leaving.

It was nearly eight o'clock when I got home and Mum thought that, now that I was home, I might as well stay in so I got out all last week's newspapers and cut out any pictures I could find of Arsenal footballers to make a scrapbook. Mum made me some glue, out of flour and water, but it came through the paper when I stuck them in and the pictures didn't mean anything without the writing and when I put the writing in as well it just looked like pages out of a newspaper so I screwed them all up and threw them on the fire.

'What the p'liceman's up with you, may I ask?'

'Nothin', Mum.'

'Then why'd you screw that all up in such a nasty, ill-tempered way?'

'I didn't.'

'I was just thinking what a good boy you were, sitting there nicely making that book.'

'It was stupid and it looked 'orrible.'

'Well, I thought it was coming on very well.'

'It was all soggy and rotten.'

'Good heavens above, Simon. The look on your face! Whatever is the matter?'

'I dunno.' My fingernails bit into the palms of my hands. 'I was supposed to be playing football tonight but the boys didn't turn up and then I met—' I caught myself hesitating. '. . . met some other people who'd got somewhere else to go.'

'And who were these other people, pray?'

'Just a couple from school, Mum.'

'But *who* were they?'

'Just a couple of girls from school.'

'Girls? I see.'

'It was only Brenda Norris and her friend. It was her brothers I was going to play with. They're in Saxons with me at school.'

'Very convenient.' She folded her arms.

'And she said they'd be out to play tonight.'

'I see.' Mum appeared to be looking for cobwebs on the ceiling.

'Wasn't my fault they didn't turn up.'

'And it's not my fault if you let girls go inveigling you into things when I've warned you against them. If I've told you once I've told you a thousand times. And then you come home in a flaming temper when things don't pan out.'

'I'm not in a flamin' temper. It's just that the camp's the only place I've got any friends and now I've been stopped going down there.'

Mum's eyes left the ceiling and her nose came down. 'Oh, and why's that?'

'Because I went down where they do their square-bashin' and a man told me to clear off.'

'And what mischief had you been getting into down there, may I ask?'

'None, Mum.'

'What were you down there for then?'

'Nothin', Mum. I just was there. Brenda and her friend went one way and I went the other.'

'Oh, I see.' Mum fitted the top on her needlework box more securely and tucked a loose piece of elastic under the lid. 'You hadn't been up to anything then?'

'No, Mum.'

'Or giving him a lot of lip?'

'No, Mum. Course not.'

'Well then, I really can't see why . . .' The elastic was unravelling itself again and she pulled it out and rolled it up and stuck a pin through it. 'Perhaps they're not so keen on having older children down there nowadays.' She stood up and smoothed her skirt down and I poked holes with the poker through the charred pages that lay in black cones over the flames. 'And it's such a shame that you burned up all that nice work.'

'It was all gluey, Mum.'

'Silly old funnikins.' Her hands smelt of onions as she smoothed her palm against my cheek. 'That would've dried out.'

'Would it, Mum?'

'Course it would.' She looked at the clock. 'And now I suppose I'd better put the kettle on. Dad'll be home in a minute.' She went to the door to the kitchen but stopped halfway through it. 'And Simon . . . ?'

I looked up.

'I shouldn't go down that camp any more if I were you. P'raps Dad'll play football with you sometimes.'

I leant into the fire, with the poker poised over the black envelope of burnt paper. Little Joe Haverty's legs had curled up and his face had disappeared when the flames caught him and I wanted to reach out and pour some magic liquid over him to bring him back to life on the paper again but Mum called me to go and have my wash and I stuck the poker through it like a sword and scurried the bits about until they glowed and disappeared into the red-hot embers.

Mum had been pacing in and out of the kitchen for ages to tut at the clock and I'd gone to bed before I heard the gate click and Dad's steel heels clipped past my bedroom window.

'That you at last, George?'

'Yeah. Didn't even 'ave time to go up 'ome.'

'Sit down then, dear.'

'And if tonight's anything to go by you can keep football AGMs as far as I'm concerned.'

'You would like a cup of tea, I take it!'

'Argue, argue, argue!'

'Only I'll have to make some more because this'll be stewed to billy-o.'

There was a rubbery click as the top came off Dad's tobacco tin and his fingernail tapped the loose shreds to one corner. A cigarette paper crinkled and there was a short pause, while he licked it, and then his lighter flicked and a putt-putt, putt-putt puffing as he got it going.

'Pot-'untin'. That's all some of 'em're interested in. And would you believe what the silly twirps've done?'

'Search me, dear.' Mum was pouring the tea from a great height so that it sploshed into the cups.

'Voted Bladder Payton onto the selection committee.'

I sat forward in bed and screwed my eyes up like Mum did when she had a splitting headache.

'Oh, my goodness!'

'Wouldn't credit it, would you? But I saw it coming.'

'Did you, dear?'

'First of all Ray Brown turned up with half a dozen RAF chaps.' Dad puffed at his cigarette and I could imagine him with his head back catching the sparks. 'I do so wish they wouldn't turn up in their uniforms. Course this provoked the local 'erbs and they came straight out with a motion that we shouldn't have any Tangmere players at all.'

'But could they do that?'

'Not a question of whether they could or not, Ina. They did. And we'd be mighty pushed to field a team without the odd one or two. And Andrew didn't help.'

'Didn't he, dear?'

I screwed my nose up. I'd never forgiven Andrew Kenton-Benyon and his wife for being the first to live in the second of the pair of bungalows they'd built on the bit of ground next to us where we'd used to play cricket and now he had a car and always wore a suit and spoke with a posh voice and the only time I'd heard him stop talking was when Nunkey Knowles hadn't turned up for an evening match and he'd had to go in goal and the South Bersted centre forward had smashed him against the goal post and winded him.

'Is he chairman again this year, then?'

'I've no quarrel with him as chairman, but to go and suggest we have a maximum of five RAF in any one game just encourages them to ask for more and our blokes to dig their 'eels in.'

'Yes, well I should just drink that tea up, if I were you, while it's nice and hot.'

'And, really, I'd rather the Lovesey boys'd stay away from these meetings if they can't learn to control themselves.'

I sat further forward.

'Well . . .' The door from the living room closed and I had to roll forward out of bed and kneel with my ear against the bottom of my bedroom door to hear. 'I knew from the start that it was a mistake to have the meeting anywhere near the bar, and how the devil they think they're ever going to be able to play football if they keep swilling beer, I'll never know.'

'Another cup, dear?'

'The Lovesey boys and young Les Painter an' one or two others set to right from the start. "We don't want any Tangmere at all . . . village boys only" and a whole song an' dance about what they were and weren't going to do and that's when Bladder Payton put in an appearance.'

'More sugar, dear?'

'M'm, please.' The tea was stirred. 'Started off some cock'n bull story about democratic rights and putting it to the vote that it ought to be left to the selection committee. Course the 'erbs voted 'im on straight away and when I suggested it'd be best left to people with playing experience he said if watching Pompey every other week for the last twenty years wasn't qualification enough he didn't know what was.'

'Goodness me.'

'So now, I suppose, we'll 'ave 'im there on the touchline every week hurling abuse at us in the name of democracy.'

'Looks like it.'

I stifled a laugh.

'But surely there'll be others on the committee?'

'Oh yes.' Dad was draining a drop off the bottom of his cup on the saucer. 'Me as captain an' Nigel O'Neal as vice-captain. But they're pretty thick together so if the 'erbs don't get what they want I'll 'ave to carry the can.'

'So you're blessed captain again then?'

'Yes. And Secretary and Treasurer.'

'Oh, George.'

There was a scuffling sound as the rolled-up draught

excluder was pulled across the bottom of the living-room door and their voices became muffled so I bent back slowly and crept into bed without letting the springs creak.

I followed Dad up Grandad's front garden path with my hands in my pockets. I couldn't think what I disliked most: going up there during the dark evenings when I could have been home in front of the fire listening to the wireless or coming up during the light evenings when I could have been out playing. I kicked a stone at Dad's heel and looked away when it hit him.

'Tryin' to wear your shoes out, Simon?'

'Wasn't my fault. Path's all uneven.'

'Well, get your hands out of your pockets and straighten yourself up and try to look a bit more amiable, for Pete's sake.'

Dad tapped the kitchen window as we went by and Grandad had the back door open for us.

'Hello, son. Simon.'

'Dad.'

'Grandad.'

We went in together and I closed the kitchen door behind me. Grandad sat down in his armchair by the fire, Dad kissed Nan, who was sideways on to the fire with her back to the cooker, and carried on round the table to the chair by the door to the stairs and I sat down carefully on the sofa so that I didn't disturb Old Gran. Nan finished a row on the sock she was knitting and looked up.

'And 'ow're you, Simon, me duck?'

'Qua-ack!' formed in my throat but I set my teeth against it and nodded and pretended to cough instead.

'Football all sorted out again then, son?' Grandad had lain back and closed his eyes and it sounded as if he was talking in his sleep.

'S'pose so, after a fashion.' Dad sat forward and pulled the creases up in his trousers and sat back again. 'Be trying to get some of 'em out for a run a time or two before the season starts.'

'Oh ah.'

'Ray Brown reckoned it wasn't fair the RAF blokes should have to train and not be sure of a game when our blokes don't do any and get guaranteed one.'

'I preferred it when it was a proper village team.' Nan had dropped a stitch and she picked it up and nudged Old Gran who'd started to snore.

'It's beside the point really, as I told them. They'd have to train for the camp team.' Dad was tracing the line of the grain in the kitchen table through a hole in the oil cloth. 'But, jigger-all, it's part of their air force duty anyway.'

'That's just what I was thinking.' Nan looked up over her knitting.

'Still, I s'pose a bit of training won't come amiss so long as nobody comes a purler in the dark.'

'Never needed it in Mespot.' Grandad was sucking a sweet. I hadn't noticed it before but now I'd seen him change cheeks. 'Least mention of mess duties and looking after the 'orses and they were off to apply to train for the regiment team like lightning.'

'M'm, well. Can't do any 'arm, surely?'

Grandad straightened on his elbow and sat up. 'But I'm blowed if I like the sound of it.' He turned and wagged his finger at me. 'A house divided against itself, Simon, cannot stand. Did you know that?'

'Yes, Grandad.'

'Says that in the bible.'

'I know, Grandad.'

Nan cleared her throat and rubbed her bad knee and stuck her needles into her ball of wool. 'Well, we never used to 'ave to put up with all this silly palaver and I don't see why we should 'ave to now.'

'And I expect it'll be left to me to mark the pitch out and put the nets up and make sure the balls're pumped up and every blessed thing else.'

Nan tutted and turned the milk on.

'For two pins I'd pack it all up and go back to Portlees.'

Nan stiffened as she turned back from the cooker. 'Oh, don't say that, George. That's the one thing I look forward to of a weekend, and we're so proud you've been made captain again, aren't we Art . . . Art?'

59

'Wha—' Grandad roused himself. 'Oh ah!' and he opened one eye at Dad.

'And you'd better put a spurt on, young Simon, and start playin'. Be nice to see a Wilson on each wing again.' Her chin was wibbling now and she was staring at Uncle Steven's photograph and Dad was staring at me as if he was edging me sideways until I got up and put my arm around her neck and hugged her until I could feel her feeling for her knitting and then I sat down again until it was time to go.

They'd fixed training night for Tuesday because they said that would give them long enough to Saturday to get over it and that two sessions should be plenty to tone them up before the first match. Dad spent from half-past six to half-past seven on the sofa in his underpants wrapping his toes in lambswool and rubbing the backs of his legs with the white liniment Mr Lovesey used to put on horses and strengthening his cartilages by lifting two flat-irons, tied together with a handkerchief, up by his toes. It seemed odd to me that he was taking more precautions for training than he did for a real match but he said that running on the road was a different kettle of fish from a nice soft playing field and he knew from experience in the army what a mess hard roads could make of your feet if you weren't jolly careful and that this training lark was Brown's idea in the first place so there was bound to be a flaw in it even if it wasn't a deliberate attempt to cripple half the team so that he could find a place for his hot-stuff Irish left-winger.

Dad got home just after nine and he sat down on the sofa and unwrapped all the things he'd wrapped up before he went out and ran his fingers over his feet looking for blisters while Mum went out and made the tea.

'N-no. It went quite well, Ina, and I'd've been back earlier but I thought I'd better pop up 'ome to report.'

'Well, I was beginning to wonder what'd happened to you.'

'We had a blessed performance getting the Lovesey boys and young Les Painter past the Winterton though. I shan't go that way again.' Dad leant back on the sofa and bent

60

his knee and ran the palm of his hand down the sole of his foot. 'They insisted on stopping off there for a Jimmy Riddle and then they sent young Les out with some cock'n bull story about the landlord not letting them use the facilities without having a drink so they'd decided to stop for a pint and a game of darts to be sociable.'

'Would you credit it!' Mum put Dad's tea down and stirred it.

'Thanks. Bit closer, my geeze.' Dad dropped his leg and bent his other one up and Mum pushed his tea up to level with his elbow and I marked the place in my book with my thumbnail and left it open.

'They were in there for ages so Nigel O'Neal and the Weston brothers and the rest of us decided to do some physical jerks in the bus lay-by opposite to keep warm. Jigger me if the 156 single-decker from Singleton didn't sweep in as we were doing press-ups and darn near flatten us.'

'Huph!' I held my breath and forced against it.

'I beg your pardon, Simon?'

'Thought I was gonna sneeze, Mum.'

'That could've been nasty, dear.'

'Jolly nearly was.' Dad gave the sole of his foot a final rub and reached for his tea. 'Came swingin' in there at a hell'ov'a lick. We had a few words to say to the driver, I can tell you.'

'I'll bet you did, dear.'

'Still, there's one thing, Ina. All the commotion got 'em out of the pub, and pretty sheepish they looked about it too, and we jogged two telegraph poles and sprinted one all the way back down the Lavant Straight and home and I left it with them that we'd put the goal posts up on Sunday morning and mark out and have a bit more training afterwards.'

'That's good, dear.' Mum wiped her nose and put her hanky back up the sleeve of her cardigan. 'Well, hurry up and finish that cup of tea and then Simon can get washed and off to bed.'

It was the kind of cold on Sunday morning that felt like

61

walking in the shade on a warm day. I hung about at home until I was nearly late and then I ran all the way to church so that I could be genuinely panting and not look as if I was trying to get out of being candle-boy. I sat at the back and stared at the statue of St Blaise until I could make out the cracks in his face under the paint and I wondered if he was made of the same stuff as they used to mend broken arms or if he was concrete with that wire-meshing stuff inside that they used for the bus-station forecourt on our way to school. Whatever it was, we'd soon know because he seemed to be cracking up. They said Pop was cracking up too. His cheek-bones stuck out like little thigh bones and his eyes were like two crabs waiting for something to pounce on from under a rock. I got on my marks as he said the blessing and was out in Church Lane before the organ finished. Mum had her back to me, hanging out the washing, when I got home so I didn't have to hang around and speak to her and I changed into my football kit and ran up the field on the thin grass strip between the road and the pavement so that I didn't wear my new studs down.

The Lovesey boys were standing by the alms-house wall with Les Painter and the Weston brothers and Ron Keely from Greatwood and there was somebody else coming across the fields from the cottages on the Westerton Road. Dad was laying out the uprights and the cross-bars were leaning against the Hall roof.

'Come on, you blokes.' Dad was straining against the bend in the middle of the cross-bar. 'You surely don't expect me to do it all myself?'

'S'pose we'd better give 'im an 'and.' The Lovesey boys elbowed themselves off the wall. 'Keep 'im quiet.'

I pretended not to hear them and went over to Ron Keely. 'Reckon we'll 'ave enough for two sides?'

'Dunno. How many we got?'

'Eleven.' I counted them against the sun. 'Includin' me.'

'Well, we're not includin' you.' Ron Keely leant over the wicker basket on the handlebars of his mum's bike. 'Your brother comin' up, Painter?'

'Dunno. Don't s'pose so.' Les Painter side-scraped some dog muck off his shoe.

'An' what about the Brindles an' Alan Haines?'

'Ian was on taxi duty last night an' I dunno about the others, but I spect 'awkeye 'aines'll turn up later.'

'Come on, you blokes.' Dad had got the cross-bar down but it was too long for him to carry on his own.

'Blimey, 'ark at 'im.' Les Painter kicked the back of his heel against the wall. 'Come on then.'

I sat on the football under the overhang of ivy on the wall that separated the football field from the alms-house gardens and watched them put the goal posts up. Dad said they should slide the uprights into the wooden boxes let into the ground first and screw the cross-bars on later, but the others thought it would be better to screw the cross-bars on first and lift the lot up together.

'But you'll never get it up with the bar swingin' about all over the place.'

'Course we will.' Harold Lovesey was looking from the holes to the cross-bar and his brothers and Les Painter and Ron Keely stood holding the whole thing while they decided what to do with it. 'Two at each end an' two in the middle to 'old 'er steady an' she'll go up as easy as pie. Better'n tryin' to 'old 'er'n screw 'er at the same time.'

'Then suit yourselves.' Dad tightened the wing nuts on the cross-bar as they lay it in place and left them holding it while he went back to his jacket for his jar of Vaseline to stop the nuts going rusty. 'But you'd better keep it straight else the bar'll bend and crack.'

They raised the posts steadily and slotted them over the holes. Then they stood it up straight and stood back. The posts slid in like jelly coming out of a mould, and a mixture of mud and water spurted out of one and up the back of Les Painter's leg.

'There. You see. That wouldn't't've 'appened if we'd—'

'Oh, don't worry about it, George. It's only Painter. 'e's always puttin' 'is foot in it.'

'Yeah. Leave it. It'll dry off.' Wilf Lovesey sprinted off to the middle of the goal. 'C'mon, Billy. Centre!' and he threw himself at the ball and missed it and yelled out something about Nat Lofthouse and Dad started to tell them what Tracey Black would have done with a centre like that before the war but they'd gone to put the other goal up.

Dad tried to get them to do proper training, to loosen up, and he started off with a run round the field but when he looked back he found he was on his own and they said they just wanted a kick-about and then they argued about who was going in goal until Les Painter said he would, because he didn't like football much anyway, so long as somebody went behind goal so that he didn't have to keep running after the ball. I'd been centering from the right wing and getting it up onto their heads most times so I didn't see how they could stick me behind goal but they did and it wasn't so bad because Ron Keely couldn't keep his shots down and put nearly all of them over the bar until they nick-named him 'balloon boots'. They played for about an hour, centering and heading and shooting on the volley, and then they started tackling each other and scrabbling in the dust in the goal mouth and pulling each others' shirts while Dad stood out on the left wing with his arms folded saying that this wasn't what he called practice and that they might as well pack up now and start marking the pitch out. They quietened down then and played properly and I noticed that the boy from across the fields was a very good player. He could trap the ball with his instep, like a Hungarian, and score goals off the post and the underside of the bar. Jerry Henry turned up just after that and he came behind goal with me and we nick-named the boy Jimmy Jampot because he scored jammy goals and then he hit one against the bar and it went in off the back of Les Painter's head and we laughed and Les said he'd have to have a sit-down and the others sat down with him and then, when Dad had gone for the whitewash, they put their trousers on and went up to the Anglesey and Jerry Henry went with them because they said they might buy him a packet of crisps.

I played passing with the new boy, whose real name was Frank Parfit, and we moved away from the goal when Dad came back with his bucket of whitewash.

'They pushed off then?' He scraped some blobs off the side of the bucket with a stick.

'Yes, Dad.'

64

'Typical!' He carried on stirring. 'I put some weedkiller in this, Mush.'

'Did you, Dad?'

'That ought to sort the lines out. Shouldn't wash out with the rain either.'

'M'm.'

'You listenin' to me, Simon?'

'Yes, Dad.'

'Well, come 'ere then.' He touched his toe against the marking machine. 'And uck some of this out that's gummed up round the wheel.'

'Gaw' blimey. Must I?'

'You don't mind giving me a bit of a hand, do you?'

'Well, I was playing, Dad.'

' 'ere yar.' Frank tapped the ball over so that it rested against the back of my heel. 'I'll give you 'and.'

'Oh . . . thank you very much.' Dad went to shake hands but he had the bucket in one hand and a ball of string in the other. 'Thank you very much.'

I knelt down on the grass with Frank Parfit and broke the piece of stick in half and we poked the dried bits of whitewash out from around the wheels and Dad stirred them into his bucket and then Frank and I stretched the string out and Dad ran over it with the marker after he'd measured them with his surveyor's tape from the office and we'd finished by the time the 66 bus went down at one o'clock.

'I'm very grateful to you, Frank.' Dad wiped the perspiration off his top lip and licked a cigarette. ' 'ere, put this in your pocket.'

There was a flash of silver and Frank said 'thank you' and then we passed the ball to each other over to the ploughed field.

'You live over there?' There were two cottages across the field, with gardens that ran along the Westerton Road.

'Yeah. Next door to the Keelys.'

'That where Keely lives?'

'Yeah. 'e's a sort'a cousin 'a mine.'

'You live next door to your cousin. You lucky blighter!'

'Why?'

'Well . . . you'll always have someone to play with.'

'We don't *play* together. We never have.'

'No, what I mean is . . .' My face was burning. 'Who do you knock aroun' with?'

'Oh.' He'd started shaving. There were little nicks on his Adam's apple. 'Nobody really.' He looked at his watch and put it to his ear and shook it. 'Look. I gotta go for dinner. You can come over some time if you like.'

'Cor thanks, Frank. I will. Goodbye.'

I sat on the ball watching him stip-stepping through the newly turned furrows and once he turned and waved but then he disappeared under his mum's line of washing.

Frank Parfit's house was all high, narrow rooms, as if it had been built properly and then lain on its side. I went there most evenings and his mum let me listen to the wireless, unless the accumulator was running low, while he was doing his homework, and then we'd play WOT or darts on the back of his pantry door until his dad came home for his dinner.

Frank's dad had tattoos down his arms and he was so tall that he had to duck down when he came through the kitchen door. He wore his pullover tucked inside his blue overalls tied up with a wide leather belt round his stomach so that he looked like an iron-rimmed barrel. Frank told me he'd been nick-named Pugey when he was a boy but he didn't know why. It sounded to me like the old-fashioned name for a boxer and I imagined he'd have looked like a picture I'd once seen of Bob Fitzsimmons in *John Bull* if he'd had his shirt off and boxing gloves on, and I was always polite to him and listened quietly while he told Mrs Parfit what he'd found during the day sorting through the stuff at the refuse disposal headquarters. Mrs Parfit was very thin and wore her hair in a bun. She spent most of her time standing in the corner of the kitchen over the brown glazed sink or watching that things didn't boil over on the mottled blue enamel stove that stood on four bowed legs beside it, and I guessed she was grey because she spent all her time in that dark corner and never saw the light of day except for when she hung her washing out or caught the bus to Westerton on a Wednesday afternoon to see her mum and dad. Frank had an older sister, called Elsie, who was married to a car dealer from Fratton called Sidney who looked like a ferret. I'd seen them once when they came to visit and Frank had to go in and say hello to them. He said they didn't like Sidney much and that his mum could see right through him and I believed him because she saw every move we made even when she had her back to us.

Frank beat me at everything. He went out quicker than me at 'Round the Board' and finished all his reds and coloureds before I'd got my reds when we played a game of darts he'd made up called snooker and his mum made him fix a piece of hardboard behind the dartboard where I kept sticking them in the door. And he seemed to know what WOT cards I had by magic until he told me, one Saturday morning when we were playing in the dell out towards the Redvins, that he could see them reflected in the face of the clock that stood behind me on top of the wireless.

I hadn't liked this dell much before I'd met Frank. It was just one deep hole with trees around the top and nothing much in the bottom, but Frank rigged a rope up to a branch of a tree, growing out of the side, so that we could swing out over the dell and back again and he showed me how to strip out old tractor batteries and use the cartridges inside as ammunition for when we built barricades of tin cans and had wars. He had a rusted-up starting pistol, as well, that we used for when we were being attacked or heard a suspicious sound, and when *they* were coming we would crawl back from wherever we'd been and get inside our camp, by our swinging-tree, and shoot at them with our pistol and throw our flaking batteries as hand grenades through the trees opposite, so that they exploded in showers of dry dust, and then swing out on our rope to make sure they were all dead and the coast was clear for us to come out.

We were sitting on a rotten log one day after a battle, smoking a Gold Flake Frank had got from school, when I noticed his feet.

'Can you pass straight with feet like that, Frank?'

'Yeah, why?' He drew one leg up, dragging his heel on

67

the trunk so that it left a scuffed-up mark on the flaking white wood.

'Well, I know you can score goals, flukey ones, but your feet're all bumped up and the ball could bounce anywhere.'

He lifted his other leg up and put his feet together.

'Don't they 'urt when you do your boots up?'

'Nope.' Frank ran his finger over his high instep. 'Only when I wear slip-ons and they're new.'

'Oh.' I lay back against a stump where a branch had been sawn off. 'Reckon they'll be back today?'

'Nope.' He stubbed the cigarette out on the trunk. 'Don't s'pose they'll be back at all now.'

'We'd nearly run out of batteries anyway. Who'd you reckon they were?'

'Dunno really.' There was a bump on the bridge of his nose as well and his wiry blond hair came out in a tubed wave at the front like a V and I wondered if that was because he wanted to look like Tony Curtis or if he was going bald. 'Camp kids, weren't they?'

'Were they? I thought maybe they were the Russians.'

Frank stood up and dusted the loose wood-chips off his trousers and yawned and stretched. 'Comin' back to my place?'

'Can do. What for?'

'See if there's any mice in the rick at the end of my garden.'

'All right.'

I followed Frank across the road and along the side path between his dad's vegetable patch and the hedge and out through the gate into the field. The rick rose above us like a house overgrown with grass that had matted and died.

'You just need to prod about at the straw with sticks and get 'em when they run out.'

'We goin' up on it then?'

'Yeah, course we are.'

'But we might get our legs chopped off.' The rick looked as if it had been slashed down one side by a giant Japanese sword.

'How?'

I put my hands in my pockets and trod some stems

down so that the stubble cracked. 'Me mum told me they cut the ricks with a big knife an' they sometimes forget to take it out an' if you fell on it it'd 'ave ya leg off.'

'Oh yeah.' Frank reached up and pulled a branch down and let it fly back. 'Well, there's nothing else to do so I'm going in. Bye.'

I watched him go back down the path and then he ducked under his mum's washing line and disappeared and I walked back across the ploughed field and along the edge of the school playing-field and through the hedge to the lane.

The boys were playing sword-fighting on the bank where the lane joined Crouch Cross Lane but they stopped when they saw me coming and drew in around Geoff Gibbs.

'What'cha, boys?' I stuffed my hands in my pockets. 'What'cha doin'?'

'None of your business.' Geoff Gibbs slung his arm over Jimmy Phillips's shoulder. 'Jimmy Jampot gone in?'

'I dunno. I 'aven't been up there.'

'Liar.' Geoff nudged Colin Gander. 'See, Mush. 'e's got mud all over 'is shoes from over the field. You needn't think you're gettin' in with us again. Go on. Shove off.'

'Suit yourself. It's up to you.' I turned away.

'If we weren't good enough for you when you 'ad ol' Jimmy Jampot to muck about with we ain' good enough for ya now.'

I was drawing away from them now and they had to shout to make me hear.

'. . . or you can sod off down the camp again as yer ol' man's so frien'ly with them over football.'

They were still pointing and calling after me as I turned the corner into the Close and Mum wanted to know what I'd been up to all morning that had left me not wanting my dinner.

4

*T*he first stop the school bus made on the way to Chichester was a village on the other side of the aerodrome called Oving. Some of the boys from Oving had been at the old Lincs for a term and two of them had been in 3B. Alan Jasper was the bigger of the two and Eddy Hender was his cousin. Alan was tall and broad with a shock of blond hair and pink skin that made him look like an advert for toothpaste: he was always smiling and he hated Geoff Gibbs. Eddy played right-half for our form team and, although he was much quieter, he was even stronger than Alan and he was good friends with Doug Ritson. I watched for them out of the window as we drew up and they sat with me at the front.

'Got your footer stuff, Nipper?' Alan leant over from the seat in front.

'Yeah, but I'm not lookin' forward to it.'

'Why not?'

'They've put me left-half and I play right-wing.'

'You right-footed then?' Eddy Hender never spoke to anyone much and I looked round to see if Gibbser was watching.

'Yeah. I can't kick with my left.'

'Well, you could swap with me. Rit's playin' inside-left and I could team up with 'im.'

'Cor, I'd like that. Who we playin' first?'

'4R. They're 'opeless.'

'Who's 'opeless, Jasper?'

'You are, Gibbs. We've got you in the first form game.'

'Well, that's nothin' ta worry about. You've got Wilson playin' so you can't be much cop.'

'And they've got me, Gibbs.' Eddy Hender looked along the gangway and Geoff Gibbs sat back. 'Do you stand for that sort of thing, Wilson?'

70

'What?'

'Him comin' funny with you. If you're gonna be in with us you 'aven't gotta stand for that.'

'I'll get 'im one'a these days, I expect.'

The road flashed by and the rain scarred the windows and pock-marked the puddles. The tarmac was wet and shiny and it felt as if I'd gone to sleep a long time ago and woken up in the wrong place. We were coming up to Strettington Corner. Janet Rolls and her brother had been taken off the service bus because we had so many spare seats and we slowed down and they stood back and we stopped and they got on. Janet Rolls looked like Odette from the French Resistance, with her pale sharp features hidden deep inside her hood, and her mac tied tight around her waist. She was getting slimmer and taller. I looked the other way and she ignored me and sat down near Geoff Gibbs.

'Bitch!' I hitched my knee further up the back of the seat in front. 'I'll get 'im. One'a these days.'

The traffic lights turned to red at Shopwhyke and the bus throbbed in neutral and then went on past the gravel pits and the bus station, where the boys from Chichester went for a sit-down and to watch a big girl called Sabrina from Mundham, after school, and I got off with Alan and Eddy and walked up the school drive with them. The others were behind us and Janet Rolls was talking to Brenda Norris. Geoff Gibbs was just behind them but I couldn't see if they were taking any notice of him and I wanted to hang around and let them catch me up so that I could try to get Brenda talking to see if she remembered asking me to the camp social but Janet would have heard, and so would Gibbser, so I followed on after Alan and Eddy and we went straight into assembly.

Mr Levers was standing in the centre of the stage with his arms folded and his legs apart and the masters were fanned out on either side of him in order of seniority. Dan Hassell was on one side and there was someone new on the other.

'That's Hoggy Hogan.' Ritson leant my way and was scratching the side of his lip. ' 'e's been away on some course.'

71

'Oh.'

'They reckon he's gonna be the next deputy head when Dan retires.'

'Oh yeah?'

'Watch out for 'im. 'e's a right bastard.'

'Okay. Thanks.'

Hoggy's eyes were everywhere as Levers said the prayers. His greasy grey hair curled like iron filings from the metal-work shop above his thin grey moustache and, standing there in his blacky-blue suit with his blotchy red face and hooked nose, he looked like a frost-bitten vulture and a chill went through me as I caught him looking at me.

'And now listen to me.' Levers took his glasses off while we were still mumbling 'arm-en'. 'We have a pig in the school!' The veins stood out on his neck and he had turned bright red. 'There is a *pig* in the ground-floor toilet.'

'Best place for 'im.' Halstow had his head down and I tried not to hear him but then Fag Farmer went 'oink' and Ritson sniggered.

'A dirty, filthy pig.' Levers was shouting now and banging the lectern so that the bible jumped.

'Should feel at home.' Chunky Halstow took a deep breath and blew his nose like a train whistle in a tunnel.

'And when I catch this . . . this, this *ani-mal* who's had the effrontery . . . who's had the brass-necked cheek—'

' 'e's off now!' Chunky Halstow was staring at the floor and rubbing his hands together. 'Listen to 'im.'

'. . . to go scrawling all over the lavatory walls.'

'Oo-oh!' Chunky was spluttering behind his hand.

'When I catch 'im he'll regret the day he was born. Now dismiss.' He turned and whispered something to Hoggy Hogan and then he banged his lectern again and said, 'And I want to see Cato and Williamson outside my office.'

We shuffled out form by form and into the foyer. Pip Williamson was standing there already with his arms folded. He had black jeans on with big turn-ups and a red and beige Fair Isle sweater and, with his crew-cut, looked like a sparring partner waiting for a gym to open. As we went by, Tony Cato joined him. Tony Cato was wearing a chunky black sweater, speckled with grey, and black trousers and spongy-soled black suede shoes. His skin was oily brown and his hair was black and looked as if it had been sleeked down with engine oil and I imagined him swapping a little plastic packet of something hidden in the sole of his shoe for a carrier bag full of money in a film about the Orient.

We fanned out as we went further down the corridor and I followed Ritson and Farmer and Halstow and peeled off after them past the labs. The toilets stank of new paint and disinfectant.

'Where is it then?' Fag Farmer had looked in all the toilets and Chunky had checked the urinals and above the wash-hand basins.

'Must'a washed it off. Can't even see any scratch marks.' Chunky took a gulp of water from the drinking fountain and sprayed a fly crawling up the wall. 'What we got this mornin'?'

I pulled my timetable out of my pocket. ' 'istory an' Music.'

'Oh no!' Doug Ritson looked up from combing his hair in the mirror. 'An' Hoggy's back.' He held his comb under the tap for a minute and shook it out and put it in his top pocket and then walked out with Farmer and the others followed and I followed them.

History was one of my favourite lessons. Mr Pointing was short and thin and so brown he looked as if he'd been made out of cherry wood. He wore gold-rimmed glasses and he'd been telling us about Oliver Cromwell for the past fortnight which made me wonder what had happened between him and Harold and 1066, which we'd done at the village school, apart from Henry the Eighth having six wives and knocking our church down, and whether he'd ever read *The Children of the New*—

'. . . Roundheads, Wilson?'

It was suddenly quiet. 'What, sir?'

'I said, why do you think they were called Roundheads?'

'Oh.' I leant back and rested my arms on my desk. 'Because they wore those round steel helmets that made them look different from the Cavaliers who wore those big floppy hats and sashes and flowing feathers and—'

'Yes. Thank you very much. Very picturesque.' I caught sight of Fag Farmer and Chunky Halstow staring at me from

73

the front row. 'And where did you get all that from, may I ask?'

'Book, sir.'

'Oh yes. Which one?'

'*Children'a the New Forest*, sir.'

'M'm well, that's admirable but I'd appreciate it if you'd pay a little more attention to what I'm trying to teach you.' He closed his book and took his glasses off and Fag and Chunky turned back to the front and I relaxed and the bell went and we stood up and I followed them along the passage and down the stairs.

I was walking off the balls of my feet. Doug Ritson had spoken to me in assembly and I'd managed to answer a question right without looking like a creep. They thought I'd been cheeking Pointing by 'taking the piss out of his flamin' Cavaliers'. I smirked and let them go on thinking so but it left me wondering what would happen if I said something wrong and wishing I'd been learning to fight and get gangs on to people when I'd been young so that I wouldn't have to worry about people like Gibbs and Gander and I caught them up and put my hands in my pockets and let my shoulders slouch forward.

'What we do in Music, Fag?'

Fag Farmer counted the cigarettes in his packet of ten. 'Recorders.' He folded the silver paper over and slipped them back into his top pocket.

'Records? That's not too bad.' I didn't like the look of Hoggy Hogan but if all we had to do was sit there and listen to records . . . Maybe we'd even have some like they played on Radio Luxemburg.

I sat down halfway up the middle row next to Gipsey Hill, and in front of the rest of the Firm, and put my elbows on the desk so that Doug Ritson could see I was looking out of the window, but I could still see Hoggy's reflection in the glass. He looked worse close up. He had his blue-striped shirt sleeves rolled up and his arms were red-freckled and hairy, like a slaughterman.

'M'n'you, boy!' His arm was up like a finger-post. 'M'you. In the middle.'

I turned round.

74

'M'yes. You. What d'ya mean by it? Staring out of the window when I'm about to start a lesson. Get up to the front here.'

I eased my chair back with the backs of my knees.

'M'get a move on.'

I flew up the aisle and sank down under his pointing finger.

'Seems some of you think you come here to play about. M'you don't.' He was like a chill draught above me. 'Now get m'your instruments.'

The class dissolved and came together in a queue to the sink. We shuffled along and I shivered at the sight of an iron-grey bucket full of mauve disinfectant with a frothy scum, like mouthwash, and the ends of some pipes sticking out like snakes in a swamp. I wanted to put my hand up and say that I'd sit quietly and listen to symphonies and things without making a fuss so long as I didn't have to put one of those things in my mouth, but when I nudged Farmer and said I'd thought he'd said we'd got records he covered his mouth with his hand and breathed back 'be careful' and stared at the bucket and I knew there was no escape.

We had to take one of these long whistle-things and run the cold tap over it and then take it back to our place. I sat at my desk covering over the holes and pressing and making white rings on my fingertips and watching them fill up with blood again and Spider Webb passed among us, like a ghost, giving out the song books and Hoggy folded his rubber lips round a recorder he'd taken from his desk and then he peeled them off it and licked them and resettled over the mouthpiece.

'Page nine,' he said, out of the corner of his mouth. 'Good King Wenceslas. You'll see the fingering instructions on page two.'

I held the recorder in one hand and tried to find page two with the other but the book had got wet at some time and the glossy pages were stuck together so I had to go straight to page nine.

'After one.' Hoggy's hand went up like the starter in a race. 'One . . . and G and . . . G and . . . G . . . A.' He dropped and raised his hand as he called out each note and a hideous screech came out and I suddenly understood what

Pop had meant when he'd preached about souls in torment after we'd died and gone to hell.

The noise ground on, but so slowly that I couldn't recognise the tune. So I blew each note for the same length of time as everyone else and whenever I heard my recorder above the others I just pretended to blow and I could feel my eyes disappearing up under my forehead as I watched Hoggy to see if he was watching me. Good King Wenceslas went on for ages and Hoggy stalked down to the back to find out who was playing something sharp when it should have been flat and then he said we could turn over to page four and try something a little faster.

'On Ilkley Moor' had been one of my favourites at the village school but it wasn't any better and I felt as if I was getting a headache. We played it several times and then lined up to stir the mouthpiece in the scummy disinfectant and then drop it in. We crept out and I tried not to hurry but my legs wouldn't stop and I ran until I got to the bike sheds.

The High School boys were out to play but I couldn't see Frank and I had to stand in closer to the wall as Pip Williamson and Tony Cato went by playing a game of slamming Scabby Whitehouse against each other and telling him they were teaching him to be a stunt man. Dicky Denver and Les Whitfield were with them watching and I watched as well until they were all past me and then I crept into the library and asked Mr Titmarsh if I could come in and read. He helped me find *The Children of the New Forest* and I sat over it wondering how Edward and Humphrey Beverley and Pablo the gipsy boy could be the same here amongst so much darkness and cold with monsters like Hoggy and the yelling and screaming from the playground, as they'd been when I'd sat on Mum's knee, never dreaming that places like the Lincs existed.

It got dark straight after tea now and Dad said he'd soon have to be getting a new battery for his front light.

'Beats me why the front one never lasts as long as the

back'n. You haven't been 'alf-inchin' it to play "Moonlight, Starlight" with the nippers, 'ave you, Simon?'

'No, Dad.' I was sitting picking the sorbo-rubber out from under the sole of my slipper. 'They never want to play with me anyway.'

'You have to get out there and make friends, Simon.' Dad reached for the paste but changed his mind and went for the jam. 'Setting up this terrier's a massive job, you know, Ina.'

'Is it, dear?' Mum had made some cream by beating some sugary stuff into top-of-the-milk and she was spreading some of it on a scone. 'Like some of this, dear?'

'No thanks. Fattening.' Dad took a bite and licked his finger. 'Yes, it'll take years to record every council property. But I've been given carte blanche to set it up exactly as I want.'

'That's good, dear.' Mum chewed on her scone slowly. 'I thought I'd beat this cream for quite long enough but I think it could have done with a bit more.'

'M'm.'

The light was draining away outside and Mrs Phillips opposite put her light on and drew her curtains.

'Could I go and play with Laurence next door, Mum?'

'And the thousands of little strips we'll have to use, Ina, cos they all have to go singly into big sheets with grooves in so that they can be added to.'

'Mum?'

'And they all have to be typed you know, Ina.'

'Can I, Mum?'

'Oh, for heaven's sake, Simon. What?'

'I said, could I go and play with Laurence?'

'All right. No need to put it in that disrespectful tone of voice.' She moved her chair forward and sat up straighter. 'Surely he's a bit young for you, Simon. And anyway it'll be his bedtime soon.'

'Well, what can I do then?'

'Why don't you get off up and see Frank Parfit?'

' 'e don't like me any more.'

'S'st, blimey!' Dad shook his head.

'I shouldn't think he does if you talk in that slovenly way.'

'It's not that, Mum.'

'You should try to make yourself a bit more amiable, Simon.'

I picked some more rubber out from under the sole of my slipper but I said 'bollocks' under my breath.

'I don't know why you can't settle down with a nice book, Simon. Or do some drawing or something. You could even have a go at cleaning your own shoes, my lad.'

'Yes, go on, Nip.' Dad squeezed dead ash out of his cigarette end. 'Then you can help me do some wood-sawing.'

'Do I have to?'

'Yes, go on, Simon. And I'll clean your shoes for you else you'll only get polish all over your shirt sleeves and then it'll be the very devil to get out.'

Dad went and changed his trousers and I put my windcheater on. It was dark outside now with strips of deep pink in the sky across the back field by the dell and Dad said it wasn't quite dark enough to make it worthwhile lighting the hurricane lamp. I stood at the end of the sawing-horse and took each bit as he cut it and started to stack them against the shed wall under the window.

'I shouldn't bother with that, Nip, if I were you.' The saw swayed gently on its blade in the log as he stood back and flexed his shoulders. 'You could get 'old'a the other end of the saw if you like though.'

The saw teeth bit into the wood and made a ripping sound. The moon was out and I'd got accustomed to the light and when we pressed harder the sawdust came out thick and fluffy like snow and it smelt sweet and fresh and wet and burning and I felt my body warming as if the bar of an electric fire was on inside me.

'Just pull, Nip. Don't push.' Dad's face was flushed under his cap and the saw-blade was slipping forward and back and ripping and slicing through a knot that gave off a sharper smell. 'And don't jerk it. Teeth can't cut if ya jump 'em off't wood.'

'Did you ever live in Yorkshire, Dad?'

'Don't think so, Nip. Why d'you ask?'

We did a last lifting cut and the piece dropped off and we slid the log along.

'The way you said, "off't wood". That's how they spoke in *Wuthering Heights*.'

'You sure that wasn't just your mother, Nip?'

'No. She doesn't talk like that. That's how it's written.'

'Oh, I see.' He shifted the log along again and marked a groove out for us to cut into and then resettled it comfortably. 'Your grandad came from up round Ripon way originally.'

'I know, Dad.'

'How d'you know?'

'He told me.'

'Oh.'

'Ripon's mentioned in stories about the Civil War. It was a Cavalier stronghold.'

Dad took his cap off and wiped his wrist across his forehead. 'Was it? I didn't know that. Phew! Think that'll do us for one evening. You comin' up 'ome?'

I straightened my arm where my elbow had stiffened. 'Yeah. Might as well.'

'Good. We'll get straight off then.' Dad took the saw and left it by the shed door and tapped on the window to Mum and called to her that we were off.

'Where's young Simon, George?' Mum was looking from the lighted window into the dark and she couldn't see anything.

'He's coming with me.' Dad made it sound like a big joke and he put his arm over my shoulder and we joggled against each other as we went down the path and through the gate.

I felt taller when I'd been wood-sawing, as if I was made of rubber and been warmed and stretched. Our shadows arched away on the pavement ahead of us in the moonlight and I could almost match Dad's stride. He talked about indexes and files and searches and I made out I understood, especially as we went past Mr Stroud who was covering a new plant with straw against the frost.

'Course, going to County Hall was the best move I ever made, ya know, Nip.'

I nodded like a grown-up.

'If it 'adn't been for my accumulated army pay I don't know how we'd've got by.' We were walking into the moon

79

shadow from Henry's house. 'And that'd just about disappeared time I made the move.' Our two shadows slid out along the pavement as we came out into the light between Henry's and Baldy Cairns's. 'And I'm delighted with the work and getting three Saturday mornings in four off, although I enjoyed the work at Rapson's, ya know, Nip.'

'Seen ya, 'enery!' We were coming into the shadow again from Gander's house.

'An' you, Browner.' That came from down Church Lane.

'. . . don't think of it as work, ya know, Simon.'

'An' I've touched the post.'

The spring had gone out of me and I suddenly felt cold.

'It's more like a hobby than a job.'

They must have walked past my gate to call for Jimmy Phillips because he wasn't allowed out unless somebody called for him.

'Ya know, Simon.'

'You're up next, Jim and Jerry's with you.' Gibbser never called us by our first names. They must have got friendly.

'. . . Nip?'

'What, Dad?'

'What's up with you, Simon?' His arm barred me as we stopped to cross the road. 'You were right as ninepence a minute ago but now you've gone all morose again. Blimey, you're a difficult 'erbert to get on with.' He went on faster and held Grandad's gate open for me so that I had to walk ahead of him up the garden path.

Nan was standing over the cooker where she'd just saved the milk from boiling over and Grandad was mixing their cocoa. She gave him the pan to pour the milk out because her bad elbow was playing her up.

'My, what a big boy you're getting, Simon.'

'Yes, Nan.'

'You'll 'ave to bend down for me to kiss you, me duck.'

I bent down.

Grandad poured a little milk into each cup and then he stirred each one and rinsed the milk around in the pan and poured and stirred and rinsed and poured and stirred again and I strained my ears to catch some sound of the boys.

'You still enjoying your new school, Simon?'

'M'm.' There was a sound like running feet down towards the road but it was so far away that it might have been something else.

'And are you getting on all right with the masters?'

'M'm.'

'St't.' Dad put his cap down.

If they were going up past Nan's they'd be heading for the village hall to look through the windows, if there was a meeting on, or even up to the Common to see if they could find anyone poaching.

'I expect you'll be playing cricket regularly for the school next season, won't you, Simon?'

They'd be creeping low down in the bushes and sliding forwards under the holly and dodging in and out of the moonlit patches and getting those crinkly shivers up their backs when you don't know quite what you are going to stumble into in the woods or who may suddenly appear so that you have to lay flat until they go away.

'Won't you, me duck?'

'For goodness' sake answer Nan, Simon.'

'Eh, what's that?' Old Gran started up and stared at Dad before she was really awake. 'That Doug Houghton back yet?'

'S'sh, Mum.' Nan leant forward. 'He went missing years ago.' She strained to stand up but flopped back into her chair. 'Just pass Mum 'er cocoa, Art, would you?'

'Sit there dreaming when Nan's taking an interest in you, Simon. What the devil d'you think you're playing at?'

'You say young Doug's not coming back?' Old Gran was trying to fold her hair net forward but she'd got her wedding ring caught in it. 'Where'd 'e go then?'

'They left, Mum. The whole family. Years ago.' Nan sucked at her cocoa. 'Soon after the war.'

'But 'e's got my pension book!'

'He hasn't got anything of the sort, Mum.'

' 'e 'as I tell you.'

Grandad leant forward and plonked his cup down. 'Here we go again!'

'Strewth alive!' Dad slapped his cap down on the dresser

and went over to Old Gran. 'All that was in the war, Gran. Ten, nearly twelve years ago.'

'Eh?' Old Gran bent her head back and up so that Dad was speaking into her left ear. 'Speak up, George. I can't 'ear a thing if you whisper.'

Nan was sniffling into her cocoa. She had milk drips on the corner of her mouth and she reached out for me and drew me to her and clung me up closer to her.

Old Gran's face lengthened and her eyes went cloudy as she watched Dad's mouth. It looked to me as if she was still waking up but I heard Nan whispering to herself that she was losing her grip and that she couldn't stand it much longer.

A cobweb was waving gently on the ceiling in the draught from the passage door and I tried not to look at it in case Nan noticed it as well. Old Gran bent forward in her chair but she couldn't reach the table with her cup so Dad took it for her and she sat back again.

'Really only wanted to 'ear 'ow you were getting on, Simon.'

'Yes, Nan. All right, thank you.'

'Just interested, me duck. Because you really were very special to us, wasn't 'e, Art?'

'Aye.'

'. . . never knew what new catastrophe was going to hit us from one day to the next, and there was all that rationing and we were cooped up 'ere and couldn't get out and about anywhere.'

'Didn't stop you, Fran.' Old Gran was gripping the arms of her chair.

'What do you mean by that, Mum?'

'Well, you were up and down to Petersfield several times a year to see Rene and gallivanting off over to Eastergate.'

'Well, I like that!' Nan rubbed her bad knee. 'Nothing much wrong with your memory when it suits you, Mum. Life had to go on, you know.'

'Could I go and find the boys, Dad?'

'Eh?'

'Oh, my duck!'

'Go on. Let 'im go.' Grandad rolled sideways in his chair

and resettled. 'Go on, young maester. Bit of fresh air'll do 'im good.'

I got up and ran before Dad could change his mind and closed the door behind me and took a long, deep breath. The laurel bushes by the back door were caves of black against the hazy light of the moon and I fancied I could hear the boys away over the Wobble Fields towards the Redvins. They'd be playing hide and seek chasing by the park gates and throwing conkers at each other or talking to Sally Elliot and the Mole Sisters. I crept out past the coal shed to the back garden. Mum would be at home ironing or mending socks by the fire and if I went back she might pack up and read to me if I asked her, but I was too big now to sit on her knee and she got tired sooner reading now and it made her throat sore and her mouth dry and, anyway, I could read myself. The coal-shed door was so bent and rotten that I could have pulled it apart. I leant against it gently and looked up at the stars. There might be some boys out down at the camp or I could go and see if Frank Parfit was coming out, but he'd probably say he wasn't which would mean he didn't want me to come in. I ducked down and climbed through Grandad's hedge into Brindle's Field and started towards the Redvins but then I changed my mind and headed for home and then I changed my mind again and climbed back through the hedge and went up towards the school.

The moon reflected off the black windows of the school and there was a heavy drip, drip, drip from the cloakroom wall where the overflow pipe was leaking. I slipped in through the side gate and followed the sound until I found it. I stretched out my hand. The drips hit my palm and the sound softened to a putt, putt, putt. Each drip hit my palm in exactly the same place. At first I hardly felt it but the weight and cold accumulated and I found that I could eliminate the weight and the cold and the noise completely by drawing my hand away under each drop like a boxer riding a punch. I closed my hand slowly into a fist and turned it over. Now it reflected in the window like the backbone of some animal and, above it, my face looked down like some body floating dead in a pool. The drip fell and exploded off my knuckles and the glass splintered from the centre and flung out long, shivering cracks and a warm, sticky flow traced down the channel between my fingers and collected around my fingertips, in the palm of my clenched fist, and dripped off into the gutter. I let the drip splash onto my knuckles and twisted them this way and that. A loose shred of skin flapped back and up, back and up, like a window swinging in the wind, until it was numb and the water ran clear and it no longer seemed part of me.

I leant my head against the cold glass and let the silence fill me and then I got an old paper bag from the waste-paper bin on the school gate, and wrapped it around my knuckles and went up past the village hall and over the Wobble Fields and along the Hanover Road and down the lane and home up the back field. I stuffed the bag behind the forsythia bush on the shed wall and went in through the kitchen.

'That you, dear?' Mum was in the living room and the chair creaked as she stood up.

'No, Mum. It's me.'

'Oh . . . hello, Simon. Dad not with you?'

I took my coat off and squeezed past her and sat down with it on my lap covering my cut hand. 'I came away early and went for a walk. Isn't he home yet?'

'No, he jolly well isn't. I hope everything's all right. Was everything all right when you left?'

'M'm. S'pose so.'

'Oh ye-es?' Mum used her deep voice that she used when she was reading a gloomy bit out of Charles Dickens. 'Come on. Out with it.'

'Well, there was a bit of a row.'

'What about?'

'Dunno. Nothing really.'

'It must've been about something. Sensible people don't row about nothing.'

'It was Old Gran. She couldn't remember who Doug Houghton was.'

'Oh dear.' Mum glanced around as if she was expecting to find somebody lurking in the airing-cupboard. 'He went about the same time as . . .'

'Yes, I know, Mum, but lots of people got— didn't come

84

back. And we ought to be thinkin' a bit more about them 'oo are 'ere.'

'That's not really the point, Simon. And don't use that slovenly way of speaking . . . whatever is the matter?'

'Dunno, Mum.'

'Well, why are you crying then?'

There were a couple of tear stains on my windcheater and I put my arm across to hide them. 'It's just that . . . Chor!'

She grabbed my arm and hauled me up and plonked herself down on my chair and pulled me back onto her lap and I balanced there like a cuckoo in a hedge-sparrow's nest, crying like a baby.

'It's just that I've never got anything to do or anyone to play with and everything I do is wrong and I want a baby brother and—'

'All right, all right.' She patted my back and I started to cough. 'That'll do for a while. Love-a-duck, that's enough for a start. Dear oh dear, Simon. We'd no idea things were as bad as all this.'

'Hadn't you, Mum?'

'No, of course not, laddikins.' She eased me off her lap and stood up and sat me down. 'Course we hadn't. I think we'd better have a hot, strong cup of tea and then we'll get you off to bed for a nice refreshing sleep and then we'll see what Dad's got to say when he gets home. All right?'

'All right, Mum.'

'Right!' She stood looking at me for a moment as if I was new. 'Cup of tea.' She nodded as if she was agreeing with herself and disappeared into the kitchen.

I sat so close up to the fire that the backs of my hands burned and then I held one of Dad's spills over a flame so that it leapt up to touch it. The warmth from the fire crept over me and into me and I sat swaying in the waves of heat. I stayed like that long after she'd come in and noticed my cut hand and bathed it and put a plaster on it and told me not to play rough games at school any more else next time I fell it might be my face I cut and spoil my beauty. She folded my clothes up for me as I undressed in front of the fire and walked beside me down the passage to the bathroom, to clean my teeth, like she did Old Gran to make sure she didn't fall when she went to the post office for her pension.

I couldn't see the broken window, on my way to the bus in the morning, without looking round and if I'd done that somebody might have seen me and thought I'd done it, but on the way home I noticed it had been replaced because there was new putty, doused in red primer, with putty finger-marks all over it. I looked the other way and stared at the evergreens behind Mrs Evans's wall and imagined I was with somebody and saying something interesting about how I used to play in them when I was little but it felt odd trying to think what to say about doing something then that I wouldn't be allowed to do now, so I slung a stone at a blackbird sitting on the wall.

Part of the flint wall had crumbled where the ivy had grown over and it had been chipped back to where it was strong and had house bricks built into it. They stood out against the flints and mortar like a bloodstain on a bandage. Grandad said he'd had a running battle with Mrs Evans over that ivy ever since he'd worked for her because she liked to see it growing over the wall and he'd explained to me how it sucked the life out of the cement with little feeler, feeder things that grew into it and made it crumble, but then he'd laughed and said, 'It's taken the better part of twenty years to devour a bit that's been there nigh on two hundred so it might as well get cracking on Hubert Pendentary's bit of patching now and keep m'lady happy because, God willing, I'll have other fish to fry by the time it next becomes a problem.'

I couldn't imagine Grandad in twenty years' time. I'd never met anyone that old except Old Gran and she'd been the same ever since I'd known her. She was completely different from her photograph, when Nan and Aunty Ina were girls. Perhaps she'd had an accident that had made her go thin and shrivelled up, like Grandad's Beauty of Bath when they'd been hanging around too long. I ran my hand along the top of the Arnolds' box hedge under their apple tree and found a big red one. I rubbed it on my school blazer, bit a

86

worm out and spat it through the Smithys' gate and lobbed the core into Stroud's fish pond before I crossed the Close and closed our gate behind me.

I knew the house was empty before I got to the back door. Florence, next-door's dog, was lying on their front step with her muzzle on her paws and their cat beside her. She watched me with one eye as I went past and then closed it. A flock of starlings took off from our back lawn as I took the back-door key from under the mat and unlocked. A note on the kitchen table said Mum wouldn't be long and I slumped down on the sofa. The blue covering on the sofa was fraying. I picked at it, to straighten it up, and then folded the loose ends in and smoothed them down. When we'd first moved down to the bungalow from Nan and Grandad's I hadn't been able to touch the floor with my feet and sit on the sofa but now I could stretch out full-length with my head on one end and my feet on the other. I lay back and looked at the ceiling. There was a crack right across it. It had been there ever since we'd moved in and in all those years it hadn't got any bigger. I yawned and turned over onto my side. My reflection in the china-cabinet doors looked back at me between the table legs and Mum's ornaments on the glass shelves. She had a set of green cups and saucers and tea plates with a bigger plate for bread and butter with a fairy on it dancing on a mushroom. She looked like a baby. Maybe she was growing down instead of me growing up. There was another tea set, of thin china cups with flowers on and knobbly handles and some glasses and two little Japanese vases she'd been given by a lady she'd worked for in Northumberland soon after she'd left school and before she'd moved down from the North and met Dad up a tree when he'd been out for a walk with Den Payton in Hanover Park one Sunday afternoon. Mum got a lot of sick headaches. That was probably from when she was a little girl during the National Strike and the miners had been so poor that the children had to go wading waist-deep for sea coal, washed up the river Wansbeck. She must have got soaked to the skin bending down to pick it up and there had been no hot milk drink waiting for her when she got home because they couldn't afford it. If I'd been Mum's big brother I'd have got the coal for her.

A spot of light was shining off one of the fancy sherry glasses they used at Christmas. They kept the port and sherry on a cold slab in the pantry and Dad was always telling people he always had it in the house but that he never thought about drinking it from one Christmas to the other. The posh people in the plays on 'Saturday Night Theatre' usually had a drink when they got home from work. First a car would draw up on the gravel outside and an outside door would open and close and the swish of a coat being hung up and the settee creaked as a lady got up off it.

'Hello, d'w'arling.' I imagined it was Janet Rolls and I was smoothing my hair straight in one of those mirrors, in one of those chunky gold frames that always hang in the hallways of big houses, and then she was standing in the doorway to the drawing room in a dress made of some stuff that kept swinging after she'd stopped moving. 'Like a drink?'

I scratched below my nose as if I was thinking about it and something else at the same time. 'M'm, might as well.' I screwed my nose up in the mirror. That wasn't right. That sounded more like Dad telling Mum he'd like another cup of tea. I put my face back the way it was before. 'Yes please, Sonia. A small one.' Janet Rolls had lost weight and was about nineteen and I was about twenty-one and I'd just rescued her from Geoffrey Gibbs, who'd been holding her prisoner in a sewer, and I'd knocked him out and left him to the rats.

'Ice?' Janet was standing with a pair of silver tongs over a thing like a pineapple chopped in half that stood on the folding flap of a cocktail cabinet.

'Please.' I turned the key in the china cabinet and took out one of Mum's glasses by the stem. Funny how they always had a name like Sonia and kept their bottles in a cocktail cabinet instead of on the cold shelf in the pantry.

The smell of bacon and cheese and cold rice pudding wafted out of the pantry as I opened the door. There was always a glugging sound on the wireless when they poured it out but this came out in an oily-smooth flow. I kept on pouring to make it glug but it wouldn't and the glass was so full that I had to bend down to drink it and then I tried the other bottle. The label was the colour of autumn leaves and

I liked the sound of the name 'Tawny' because it reminded me of the owl in my children's books, but I didn't like the word 'port'. This bottle didn't glug either. I tried to pour it slowly and then I did it fast but it just came out in a brown stream like melted syrup. Port was a fat word. I sat up on the kitchen table and swung my legs and said it to myself, by building it up inside my lips and letting it burst out like a bubble in the bath. A roly-poly word. Mr Pickwick would have liked port. I ran my tongue down the side of the glass where a slow drip was trailing and filled it up again. Sitting there on Mum's lap, staring into the fire, I could see him with his legs splayed out in his swallow-tail coat and tight trousers and his white waistcoat and his stomach sticking out, like an electric light bulb, in front of a roaring fire, making an announcement to Mr Snodgrass and Mr Topman. I leant back against the kitchen wall and pictured Jimmy as Snodgrass by slimming him down and Jerry as Topman by leaving him as he was.

'Right, you chaps.' No, that sounded more like *Tom Brown's Schooldays*. I cleared my throat. 'I say, you blokes.' Blokes? No, fellows. 'H'I say, hrm. H'I say, you fellows. We r'h'eally h'aught to do something about . . .' About what? 'I say, you fellows. We really should do something about . . . Oh sod this!' I drank off the rest of the port and swished it through my teeth until it went watery and my gums burned and then I swallowed it and breathed in and nearly choked and wiped my eyes. 'Blimey O'Riley! Bledder swash thish glassup.'

I slid off the table and found I'd got pins and needles and my legs were rubbery and my ankles bent over. I aimed the rubber extension on the tap at the glass and missed and wiped my hands on the tea towel and then wiped the glass up and put it back and locked the china-cabinet door and then I went back into the kitchen and straightened the tea towel. They always got caught in the plays on 'Saturday Night Theatre' by leaving some clue behind, like a hair or a glove or something, and I went back to the china cabinet, like Raffles from a story in a magazine Pop had lent Grandad, and wiped my finger-prints off the key with my tie and then I opened it again and wiped the glass.

'S'no v'lies on me.' I winked at my reflection in the mirror and started to giggle because I was whispering and there was nobody here to take a blind bit of notice of what I did anyway.

I changed my clothes in my bedroom and folded them up and counted the money in my money box and then I stood twisting my head from side to side in time with a sparrow that was standing on the rainwater gutter and peering in at me upside-down. I twisted my head into the same position, so that I could see him the right way up, and then I started to spin and I spun into a bank of darkness.

'Simon!'

My eyes moved under my eyelids and sent a pain rippling across my forehead and my mouth was glued together.

'Simon, dear?'

'Headache, an' I feel sick.'

'Oh my poor darling. When did that come on?'

'When I got home.'

'Does it all feel black?'

'Yeah.'

'And does it feel as if your head wants to be sick as well as your tummy?'

'Ugh.'

'Oh my goodness. That's what I get. But I've never heard of it in a boy of thirteen before. It must be hereditary.'

I felt a burp coming but I daren't let it out in case there was something attached to it and my mouth felt as if I'd been sucking lemons. 'Drink'a water, Mum, please.'

'Do you think that's wise, Simon? I can't keep a thing down when I get like this. And there's no cure.'

'Jus' leave me then, Mum.'

I rolled over onto my face to see if the pillow would take the strain off my forehead.

'P'raps something you've eaten. What did you have for dinner?'

'Oh don't, Mum.'

'Ah yes, I know just how you feel.'

The sweet smell of port on my pillow nearly choked me.

'Sleep's the only thing, my boy. You just lay there and I'll close the curtains.'

'Thanks, Mum. And Mu-um?'

She drew the curtains without making a noise. 'Yes?'

'Don't wake me up for anything.'

'I won't, my darling.' She came back and tucked me in. 'Of course I won't . . . 'ere! What've you been eating?'

'Nothing, Mum.'

She sniffed up close to me. 'Smells like liquorice.'

'Does it, Mum?' I held my head away. 'Oh yeah. A boy at school gave me some. A lot, an' some aniseed balls.'

'And you ate them all?'

'M'm.'

'Cor, no wonder your tummy's in a state.' I could feel her over me. 'P'raps that explains it. You just have a good sleep now.'

My head felt like an egg cracking and there was a soup-simmering feeling in my stomach. I curled myself into a hard ball that reminded me of the new-born baby I'd once seen in a jar of salty water at the Chamber of Horrors at Sloe fair and . . . h'ploor! I rolled out of bed and flew down the passage to the bathroom and shoved my head down the toilet and prayed that Mum wouldn't hear me. I stayed there, clinging to the cold china pedestal, until I heard Dad come home for tea and then crawled back to bed.

I slept for hours in a close, dark pit, but then I felt myself start to rise up through it. I could feel my head was aching but it was as if I was a flounder on the sea bed and the rippling ache was a rough wind disturbing the surface of the water. My arms were aching and my legs were aching and even my fingers ached but they all melted away as I lay limp and followed the drifting movement of the deep.

Mum came in sometimes and once I felt her standing there, wiping her hands on a tea towel, and I fancied she was shaking her head and saying 'Wonder if I should get doctor in to have a look at him?' as if there was somebody there with her but I couldn't be bothered to find out and just let myself drift back deeper into sleep because that meant she wasn't going to get me up to go to school; but then, another time, she was standing outside my bedroom window telling

91

Aunty Win over the garden fence how 'blissfully peaceful he looks' so that it sounded as if I'd died but the very thought of having to move and get cold getting up to find out convinced me that I hadn't so I drifted off again.

It wasn't so much the jangling of brass rings on a metal rail as she drew the curtains or the shaft of sunlight that it flung across me, like the lid coming off a coffin, but more the two combined that woke me up and left me gasping and raw and grounded. I managed to doze off again and the next thing I heard was the music at the end of the Nine O'Clock News; then they were switching the lights off and their bed springs pinged and settled and as they settled I sat up against my headboard and opened my eyes. They talked softly together for a little while but I couldn't make out what they were saying and their voices gradually disappeared into the dark and I leant my head back and stared at the black ceiling until they'd been quiet for a long time and then I got up.

The bottles chinked against the cold tap as I refilled them and put the corks back in before putting them back in the pantry with the labels facing outwards and wandered into the living room and leant over the newspaper that was lying, open, on the sofa. Apparently yesterday had been the day after tomorrow and that must mean I'd missed Hoggy for Technical Drawing. I sat down on the sofa and leant back and closed my eyes; a whole week before we had to suffer him again. I sat there dozing and dreaming until I was frozen and then I went back to bed.

Mum came in soon after the milkman had put our two pints on the front step and I could feel her watching me as she drew the curtains.

'You feeling better, laddikins?'

'Dunno, Mum.' I stretched and rolled over. 'I'm not sure yet.'

'You've had an awful time of it, poor old feller. Did you realise you'd slept through two nights and a day?'

'Nope.' I felt my head. It was still in one piece. 'Why'd you think that was?'

'Search me, Simon.' Mum sat down on the bed. 'I wish

to goodness I could sleep like that when I've got these sick headaches.'

'Do you, Mum?'

'I'll say I do. And Dad's been ever so concerned about you.'

'Has he, Mum?'

'Course he has. Old funnikins!' She leant forward to ruffle my hair but stopped and sniffed as if she could smell burning. 'You sure you're all right?'

'Yeah. Course I am. But I'm starving.'

'Ah well, you just hold your horses.' She put her hand over my forehead. 'I don't think you'd better have much to eat until we're quite sure you're better. So you'll have to go easy at lunchtime.'

'What do you mean, "lunchtime"?'

'Well, at school of course. I shan't be there to make sure you don't make a pig of yourself, shall I?'

'Does that mean I've got to go to school?'

'Of course you've got to go to school.' She stood up and got my clothes out of the drawer and my blazer from the wardrobe. 'No point you staying home if you're better, is there?'

I lay curling my lip in the mirror until she brought my tea and I moaned as loud as I could that my head ached as I washed and dressed but they didn't take any notice and I forgot I was supposed to be ill when I stubbed my toe on the leg of the bed and swore and punched the roll of lino behind the bedroom door in temper.

Mum poured the milk on my Weetabix without asking me if that was enough and Dad read the newspaper without asking me how I was but I knew they were looking at me when they thought I wasn't watching.

'Dad?'

Dad measured a half-spoonful of marmalade onto his toast and refolded the newspaper to a new page. 'Yes, Simon.'

'Mum said she was going to speak to you.'

Dad spread marmalade from the centre and then down the sides. 'Did she?'

'Yes she did, Dad. When I got home from Nan's the other night.'

Mum looked at me as if I was giving false evidence.

' 'bout a brother or somethin'.' I looked straight at her.

'I wonder he's got the gall to mention such a thing at a time like this.'

I scraped up the last of my Weetabix and put the spoon down.

'Really, that language in the bedroom just now. Wherever does he get it from? And whatever kind of an example would he be to a baby brother, I'd like to know?'

Dad scratched a marmalady crumb off the corner of his mouth and shook his head.

'If he feels well enough for language like that it makes me wonder if he was as ill as he made out he was.'

'Well it hurt, Mum.'

'P'raps it did, but if half the other boys in the village had stubbed their toes they wouldn't have carried on like that.'

'No, but the other 'alf would.'

'Well then p'raps it's time you stopped mixing with the other boys.' Mum was flushed again.

'Steady on, Ina.' Dad reached over and eased her back into her chair. 'See, that's the whole point really.'

'What is, Dad?'

Dad resettled himself and straightened the tablecloth and lit a dog end. 'You're mixing with all sorts of boys now, Simon, and you're getting older.'

'Not so much older that he doesn't have to still behave himself though.'

'No-o.' Dad leant back and puffed until his cigarette was properly alight. 'But he is getting older and I think it's time he had something to take more of an interest in.'

'Cor, yeah.'

'Something that'd keep him out of mischief, that he could concentrate on and look forward to.'

'What, Dad?'

'Something that'll stop you brooding over every perishin' little thing.'

'Yeah, Dad. But what?'

'The Club.'

'The what?'

'The Boys' Club.' Dad stroked the ash off his cigarette into the ashtray and laid it down. 'See, Steven used to run a Boys' Club for Pop before the war and he was thinking of opening it again if he can find anyone to run it. And if I was to run it p'raps we could have a—'

'What, Dad?'

''old on an' I'll tell you. We could p'raps go up for a game of billiards occasionally.'

'Yippee!' I shot up and banged my knees on the underside of the table and rattled the cups.

'Steady on, for heaven's sake, Simon.' Mum stood the cups back straight. 'And you needn't think you're going to be stuck up there all evening every evening.'

'No.' Dad touched the end of his dog end into the ashtray and relit it. 'It'll just be for the occasional game.'

'And you've to get straight off to bed the very moment you come in afterwards.'

'Depends what the time is, Mum.'

'And absolutely no arguing.'

'But—'

'Else there'll be no billiards or any bloomin' thing else, my lad.'

I stirred what was left of my tea slowly and then rested the bowl of my spoon on the surface of my saucer and lifted it carefully so that it felt as if they were stuck together. Mum looked as if she was covered in nettle-rash. She was staring at Dad.

'More tea?'

'No, thanks.' Dad put his tobacco tin and cigarette papers in his pocket and stood up. 'I'd better be off. You ready, Simon?'

'Yes, Dad.'

I buttoned my coat up as he put his bike clips on and he held the back door open for me. He wheeled his bike through the gate and I closed it after him and the curtain in the living-room window fell back as I turned and followed him up the Close.

95

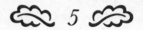

5

*W*inter seemed to have come on while I was ill. I was usually hot and sweaty by the time I got to Hanover Corner, carrying my case with my mac on against the warm drizzle, but now the clear, sharp cold cut through the warm fug of tea and toast, and dazzling splinters of hoar frost danced around me. The grass was dried out and powdered white and crunched underfoot and the puddles were like broken teeth where the milkman's van had smashed the ice and they'd re-frozen and my fingertips throbbed where I was gripping the handle of my case. The bare trees were swathed in frozen mist as if the night's breath had been caught and held and turned to silver and the sunlight splintered through it, orange and violet and red and green and it clinked and tinkled when a bird landed on it or flew away and when I half closed my eyes the colours flashed like Arctic lightning.

The patterns changed as I walked up the path and I stopped by a blackberry bush, laced with spiders' webs and spangled with dew and set in silver and I could imagine the spiders being spread out somewhere, fixed and frozen and white. The ploughed field stretched away to Common Woods in long, cable-twisted, frozen furrows and the Downs, beyond, were rolled out clean and white and sparkling and I imagined myself up there looking down to the sea and walking along the sloping ridges and running down them and up again and skating over frozen ponds and—

'You going to school?'

'Eh?'

'We're late, you know.' Jimmy Phillips turned as he passed me and I followed after him. 'Where you been the last few days?'

'I been sick.'

Jimmy Phillips wasn't as tubby as he'd used to be and

he was nearly as tall as me now but he still smelt of boiled eggs and milk.

'What you been doing evenings lately?'

'Nothing much.' He hitched his satchel up higher and moved over for me to walk next to him. 'Hide'n'seek chasin' if it's not raining.'

'Oh.' I ran my forefinger along my thumbnail. 'Spec I'd get fed up with that. I think I'd rather play billiards or snooker or something like that.'

Jimmy edged closer to me. 'You can't play that. They only let the men play that.'

'Oh, do they?'

'Yeah. Up the Men's Club.'

'Ah well, I wasn't thinking of up there.'

'Oh yeah.' Jimmy put his head on one side. 'We'd better get goin'.'

'Don't you want to know where, Jim?'

'Come on.' He was running. 'The bus'll be coming.'

'Oh, all right then.' I held my mac to stop it flapping and ran after him.

I sat looking out of the bus window at the fields trying to think of ways of telling him about playing billiards without showing off but Janet Rolls got on with her brother at Westhampnett School and they sat down near Geoff Gibbs and he boasted to them about how he'd climbed a fir tree in the corner of the churchyard to a squirrel's nest and pinched their nuts and I went bright red when I saw Brenda Norris had seen me trying to ignore them. And it was the same at school.

I stared at the blackboard in science when Mr James drew a cluster of molecules and tried not to see them as a centre-spread of reds and when Dan Hassell showed us how God had made the sun and the moon and the earth I found myself working out how many ways Gerald Dainty could have scored a cannon off them while we were waiting for a haircut at the Men's Club on a Tuesday evening, and I hung around the boys at dinner time trying to find a way of telling them but Geoff Gibbs kept on about how he couldn't understand why Janet Rolls liked him so much when he didn't much fancy her and I knew he was trying

97

to get at me when he nudged Colin Gander and said there were plenty of kids who were crackers over her so what was it she saw in him that was so special and I imagined the end of a snooker cue cracking the back of his skull where it joined his neck. I waited until they went to the toilet and then I slipped off round by the metal-work shops and watched Pip Williamson and Scabby Whitehouse playing fag cards until the bell went.

It was the same at playtime and all the way home and Janet smiled at Geoff and stuck her nose up at me and I ground my teeth and wondered what I could do to make her like me instead of him.

It was dark when we got to Hanover Corner and the boys went on ahead of me in a huddle as they crossed the road in the lights of the school bus. I stepped off the kerb to follow them as the bus pulled away and it jerked to a halt and the driver yelled at me and waved me back and started off again. By the time it had gone, and two more cars had gone past, they'd disappeared and I couldn't tell if they were walking along the road or up on the path behind the hedge and I was sure they were keeping quiet so that I wouldn't know where they were. I stood at the top of the road wondering which way to go until my hand got cold holding my case and then I went up on the path and walked until I got to the downhill bit and then I ran all the way home.

Mum had made some jam tarts and she was busy taking them out of the oven as I came in.

'Wiped your feet, Simon?'

'Yes, Mum.'

'Don't tell fibs.'

'I have, Mum.'

'Go back and do it.'

'Grrh!'

'And then wash your hands for tea.'

'Blimey! Give us a chance.'

'Cor!' She stood up from lifting the tarts out of the baking tray with a spatula. 'You're in a pretty good mood again.'

'I'm not in any sort of mood. I'm just ruddy fed up.'

'Well, you can just go and get fed down then and wash your hands while you're about it.'

'Blimey!'

'And don't "blimey" me. Dad'll be home in a minute and I expect he'll want you to go up to Pop's with him.'

'Oh, Mum, I don't wanna go. What for, Mum? What's 'e goin' up there for?'

'You just wait and see.' She scooped out more tarts and licked hot jam off her fingers. 'Be blessed Boys' Club morning, noon and night for evermore now, I suppose, and I'll never see anything of either of you.'

'Does that mean I'll be able to play billiards, Mum?'

'Don't ask me, Simon. I'm sure I don't know anything about it and— Blast it! C'mon, out of my way.' She pushed past me. 'Couldn't you see that kettle was boiling its head off? Now go and wash your hands and do as you're blessed well told.'

I went through to my bedroom and dropped my case on the bed. My Radio Luxemburg calendar had fallen off the mirror and the edge frayed up when I tried to push it back under the clip that held the glass and the first bit of firm edge was too low down so that it slewed round crooked. I tried it on the other side of the mirror but the clip was too tight and Mum's metal nail file bent when I tried to prise it open and left a rough bit where she had to hold it. I lay the calendar down and put the nail file back on her dressing table and then went and sat on my bed. The primrose wall was empty and it reflected sharply in the mirror and flat and watery in the windows. A fly was walking across the mirror and stopped. His legs were joined to his legs at his feet and he stood so still that I couldn't tell what was him and what was the reflection; then he flew off over my head and into the mirror at the same time. I got up and went to the dressing table and put my ebony box straight on its yellow cotton circle, that Gran had put a lacy edge round, and moved my brush and comb over onto the other side. There was a key in my box but the lock had never worked and I didn't really know where it had come from. Perhaps somebody had seen it and thought I'd like it for when I got older. If the lock had worked I could have got some valuables and locked them up. I opened the lid. I had two silvery tie pins and a goldy one which was a bar with a chain on it and a cricketer. I liked the gold bar and the chain but the cricketer made it look childish. He was held on by a bit of solder and I dropped him on the floor but he wouldn't break so I put him back. I had a couple of whale bones as well, that I'd had in shirts I'd grown out of, and three farthings I'd forgotten to spend before it was too late. I sat back on my bed and turned the farthings the same way up. The three wrens stood in a line. I remembered once I'd been out bird's-nesting with the boys up in Hanover Park when we'd found a wren's nest in the ivy on the wall. We'd gone to stick our fingers in the hole, to see if she had eggs, when old Jennie shot out and flew straight at Kenny Lane's head and then she dive-bombed the rest of us. Derek Brown had squeaked that she was going for his eyes and I'd taken a whack at her with my stick and missed and hit her nest by accident. I'd made out to the boys that I'd meant to do it, but I'd felt sick about it for days and the way she'd sat up on the wall and stood forward off her wispy legs and flapped her little wings at us and then, as we'd gone away, I'd looked back and seen her swoop down and hover at the entrance hole that she'd woven out of moss and spiders' webs, and seen all her babies' eggs smashed . . . I sniffed and wiped my nose with the back of my hand but the picture was still there and I closed my eyes and reached out to stroke her and try to make it better but she wasn't there and I imagined her going back, like Old Gran to Grandad Grainger's grave, and I let my head hang forward and my shoulders shook.

'Simon, will you please . . .' The door banged back against the roll of lino but Mum pressed it shut and crept up on me, half-bent, like an old Indian under a blanket. 'Whatever is the matter?'

I flung my head on her lap and she collapsed down onto my bed and I coughed and sobbed together.

'Dear oh dear! I only asked you to wash your hands, for heaven's sake.'

' 's not that, Mum.'

'Whatever is it then?'

'Dunno, Mum.'

'Well you must know. You don't sit around sobbing like this for nothing. Great thing like you.'

I buried my head deeper into her lap.

'Simon?'

'What, Mum?' I sounded like somebody calling up a mine-shaft.

'Oh do stop this. Tell me what's the matter.'

'Squeeze my head, Mum.' I reached up behind me. 'With your arms and elbows.'

She pressed down.

'Harder.'

She bent forward and added the weight of her chest to her forearms pressing down so that my head was buried into her lap and it was dark and a rushing sound filled my ears as if I was in a furnace.

'That enough?' She was panting.

'No. Harder.'

'Oh but, Simon, I'll hurt—'

'Harder.'

'But why?'

My ears were squashed against my head like prunes to the inside of a jar and a button off her frock jammed against my cheekbone.

'Simon, you're frightening me. For heaven's sake. Why?'

'I wanna get under your skin.'

'Eh?'

'Blimey! I-wanna-get-under-your-skin.'

'Oh my poor lamb.' She threw her arms up in the air and my head stuck to them and I could feel my face all red and blotchy and she hugged me against her. 'Do you still love your old Mumpser?'

'M'm.' I rested my chin on her shoulder and wiped my eyes with the back of my hand.

'And you're still Mum's baby boy, aren't you?'

'Strewth! Yes, Mum.'

'And you're feeling better?'

'M'm. S'pose so.'

'Good.' She held me away from her and then grabbed me back again. 'Come on then. Ups-a-daisy and come and

101

wash your hands and face for tea. And then—' She held her head still and sniffed and then she jumped. 'Oh my giddy aunt, my rock buns! They'll be burnt to a cinder.'

I smoothed my arms out and trod the pins and needles out of my legs and went to the bathroom and washed the tear stains off my face and straightened my ears and got the lashes out of my eyes and combed my hair and then went and sat in the living room.

Mum was bustling about in the kitchen. 'Bust it, that's hot.' A baking tray clattered on the kitchen table. 'Just look at that.'

The back door opened and the draught brought in the smell of burning. 'Burnt offering, my Ine?'

'I got interrupted, George. Burnt these rock buns to blazes.'

'Scrape off, won't it?'

'Of course it won't scrape off. They're not fit for the pig bin.'

'Stick a cherry on top of 'em.'

'I did put a cherry on, before I was . . . oo-oh.' The oven door slammed.

'Steady on, Ina. What interrupted operations, anyway?'

The kitchen door closed and their voices became muffled and then Dad came in.

'Hello, young Simon.' Dad sounded like Colin Gander's dad when his mum told him she'd found Colin in their chicken house with Shirley Lane and she thought it was about time he had a chat with him man to man. 'I'll be going up to see Pop this evening.'

'I know, Dad.'

'About opening up the Boys' Club again.'

'I know, Dad. You told me.' I narrowed one eye, like Humphrey Bogart squinting out from under the brim of his hat.

'So I'll probably have to pop in there and see every-thing's all right. That all the cues've got tips on and there's no damp about and brush the table and light the fire to see it doesn't smoke and one thing and another.'

'Yes, Dad.'

'And I know Pop'd like to see you. And it'd please him to see you're showing an interest.'

'Does that mean I can go, Dad?'

'Take it easy, Nip. You mustn't be so impatient about everything, you know.'

'Yes, Dad, but can I?'

'You can come up to Pop's with me. And then you can come over to the club while I have a look round.'

'Yeah, but can I come to the club when it's opened?'

'Don't get so perishin' excited about every little thing, Simon. I don't know yet what age it'll be for.'

'Blimey!' I slumped back in the chair and left my leg sticking out so that Mum would have to step over it to get past. 'What's the point of me coming over then?'

'Because . . .' Dad leant closer to me. 'Because we can 'ave a game while we're up there.'

'Hooray!'

'But for crying-out-loud be quiet about it.' He stepped back from me as Mum came in with the tea tray. 'And we've to drop in on Nan and Grandad on the way back so we won't have to be over there very long.'

'No, you make jolly sure you're not.' Mum sat down and she had a long face all through tea and I had to hang about afterwards while Dad helped her to wash up.

The boys were standing in the doorway of Ray Whittle's barn in the light from Colin Gander's front-room window. They looked away as we came up to them and I hoped we might be able to make out we hadn't seen each other but Dad sang out, ' 'ow do, you 'erbs' as we came level with them.

'Hello, Mr Wilson. Simon.' They stood forward and reams of cigarette smoke wafted out from between Geoffrey Gibbs's legs.

Dad nudged me.

'Geoff, Col . . . rest'a ya.'

Dad speeded up and I walked faster and tried not to look as if I was running after him.

'That wasn't much of a way to greet your friends, Simon.'

'They're not my friends.'

'I'm not surprised if you talk to them like that.'

'Well, I couldn't run through the whole lot, could I?'

'Thought you liked Jimmy Phillips and the young Henry boy.'

'They're all right, I s'pose, but they're always with Gibbser and Gander nowadays.'

'What's wrong with that then?'

'They don't want me with them.'

'Why not?'

'Dunno, Dad.'

'Well, try and be a bit more pleasant. Not so moody.'

'I ain't moody. It's just that I get bored and they never want to do anything.'

'Well, they seem happy enough. Do you good to mix with boys of your own age a bit more instead of relying on me to amuse you all the time.'

We'd crossed the road now and were going down Church Lane between the high wall at the bottom of Mrs Evans's garden and the rows of farm cottages, and then past the bigger houses fronting the road where rich people who'd retired lived. The furry light from the windows looked as if it had been strained through steam, and bowls of apples and pears that had been picked before the frost got at them stood on the window-sills ripening, and I wondered what their children did in the evenings because they never came out to play and they couldn't have any friends here because they all went to private schools somewhere: perhaps they weren't like us at all.

Dad stopped outside the last house, at the entrance to Pop's drive, and did my mac up and folded my shirt collar in. A boy of about ten lived in this house and he had a younger sister with red hair and green wellingtons. I'd seen them playing in the garden shed with a train set one day, when I came past from getting fir cones up at the church, and I'd watched him putting the rails together and spotted where the key to his clockwork engine had fallen when he dropped it. I'd opened the gate and picked it up and given it to him and he'd thanked me, very politely, but he hadn't asked me to play with him and his little sister had stared at

me until I felt out of place so I'd told them I had a better
train set than that and I'd gone home.

'Who lives there now, Dad?'

'Landers. 'er family were related to the Vines years ago
and lived in that big house along the Strettington Road for
a while and then she married. He was something in the army
in India until that lot came to an end. Now he's a big-nob
London solicitor or something. Now take your hands out of
your pockets and speak up when Pop speaks to you.'

'Think they'd let me play with their little boy?' There was
a dresser full of willow-pattern plates through the window.

'Blimey, I dunno, Nip. They're pretty well-to-do.'

'Oh.' I looked back as I followed him round the drive.
'What do you mean, "when 'e speaks to me"? What's 'e
gonna say?'

'Cor, strewth alive, Nip! You're a suspicious blighter.'
Dad pushed the bell button and stepped back. 'Just how
you're getting on at school and things like that.'

'M'o-oh . . . Dad?'

'M'm.'

'Why'd you step away from the door when you're jus'
gonna go in?'

'Huh?' Dad looked down on me from the second step.
'I dunno, Nip. Because Mrs Pope'd 'ave a fit if she opened
the door and found me standing over 'er all of a sudden, I
s'pose.'

'Why, Dad? She'd've known somebody must've rung the
bell, wouldn't she?'

'Well yes, I s'pose she would.'

'Well then?'

'Do stop it, Simon.' Dad rang the bell again. 'And take
your blessed 'ands out of your pockets and stand up straight.
C'mon now. 'ere she comes.'

Mrs Pope opened the door and stood full in the doorway.
She had her brown woolly jumper on and a tartan shawl,
tweed skirt and thick stockings and grey socks, rolled down
to the ankles, and men's brown brogues, and her face looked
as if it had been left on the cold slab all afternoon and she'd
picked it up and put it on on her way to the door.

'Evening, Mrs Pope. Is the vicar in?'

Mrs Pope stood back and pointed to the study and Dad took his cap off and rolled it up and held it like a packet of biscuits and I followed him in and stood with him outside the study door. Mrs Pope closed the front door and pulled the curtain across and tapped one knuckle on the middle panel of the study door and opened it as a plummy voice called, 'Come in.'

A chandelier, with bulbs like raindrops, gave off a yellow light that edged out dark patches around the fireplace surround and flaffing shadows of firelight reached out across the carpet as far as Pop's brown leather slippers. Pop was sitting at his desk with his forearms, from the elbows, reflected in the polished brown mahogany with heavy floral curtains behind him that reached to the floor. He was leaning forward into the arc of light from his table lamp with his bible and binoculars at his elbow, reading a copy of *Country Life* and I wondered if he gave them to Dr Wilkins for his surgery when he'd finished with them or if Dr Wilkins gave them to him.

'George, how lovely to see you!' Pop's face shone pink, as he reached forward to shake Dad's hand, as if he'd had a hot bath and shaved with a scalpel and his white hair fell forward like a skein of silk. 'And little Simon. Dear oh dear. Not so little now.'

'H'hrm.' Dad blushed and twisted his cap.

'Getting quite the little man, George, isn't he?'

I couldn't think why he was making such a song and dance because he saw me most Sundays at church, but then he was usually in such a flap getting his robes on and the bread and the wine out and wiping the rim of the cup with the purificator, that he never really noticed us unless we were missing.

'Dear oh dear, Simon.' Pop was shaking his head as if somebody's washing line was coming down in the mud. 'I remember your first service carrying the incense with Mr Bright, faithful as ever. A-ha, how time flies!'

I grinned and wished they'd get on with it.

'Well now, George. So you want to re-open the Boys' Club?'

'Well I—'

106

'Good . . . splendid. But there'll be one or two things'll need seeing to, I expect.'

'Yes, I expect—'

'The flue, for instance.'

'Ah . . .' Dad shifted to his other foot and I wondered why we didn't sit down.

'It hasn't been cleaned since before the war. And I don't remember when it was cleaned before that.'

There was a row of chairs along the wall by the fireplace facing an oval table under the window, and a lion's skin laid out with the head facing the door so that it snarled at your back as you went out. I'd sat and stroked him one day, when Old Gran brought me up with her to deliver the purificators, and tried to get my little finger up his nostril, and then I'd tied a piece of cotton round one of his fangs and stretched it across the inside of his mouth and wound it round the other one and pinged it and got down on my hands and knees and listened to see if the sound echoed up in his head. They must have cleaned his teeth before he was too dead and they'd laid him out, because his breath didn't smell of anything, except faintly of furniture polish, and I could see he had false eyes by the layer of dust in the rims and I'd have blown it off for him if I hadn't thought he might wake up and roar and bite my head off.

'So perhaps if you'd give the cloth a brush and iron it, George, and then I expect you'll need some money for new tips and chalk and one thing and another.'

'I'll see what I need and let you know.' Pop's hand had moved towards his desk drawer but Dad waved it away. 'I can get cue tips and chalk at Bowman's and table tennis balls. You 'aven't got the bats and nets and snooker balls 'ere, have you?'

Pop shook his head. 'No . . .' They were both looking at the same point on Pop's blotting pad and then Pop's wet eyes met Dad's. 'He always looked after that sort of thing. Better ask your father if he knows what happened to them.'

'Yes.' Dad was resting his hands on the desk. 'And then we'll pop back and see if the fire'll light and give the table a testing.'

Pop nodded. He looked as if he'd never moved from that spot since he'd heard that Uncle Steven had passed his scholarship and he'd told Grandad he'd meet all the expense of sending him to the High School and, later, how he'd have started back and stared at the pattern on the carpet when Grandad came over to say Steven'd been shot down and killed, and all the time during the war he'd have been wondering where the snooker balls were but not have wanted to ask because Steven was dead and my dad was a prisoner and there was nobody left to run the club and the Germans were bombing us and they'd probably blow it up anyway. Maybe, now, he remembered how much it had cost to go to the High School before the war and be thinking how ungrateful I was for not bothering to get there now it was free.

'Right then. We'll be off. C'mon, Nip.' Dad's arm was across my shoulder.

Pop pushed his chair back, as if he was going to stand up, but he sat back and gazed at the ceiling. 'I'm glad the club'll be opening again.' He had his hands together as if he was praying. 'Village still needs it. Different people, of course. Never met most of them. Very different.'

'M'm.' Dad shuffled his feet as if he'd got something on the sole of his shoe.

'Ah well.' Pop straightened in his chair as if he was collecting his thoughts from the different parts of the room. 'There it is. No going back, I suppose.'

'No. S'pose not.'

'Off you go then, George. Keep a note of what it costs and let me know, will you?'

'Yes, sir.' Dad stood more to attention. 'Good-night, sir.'

I didn't turn my back on the lion's head as we left but I gave Pop a small wave as the door closed and I peeped back in at him, through the lead diamonds in the windows, as Dad did his coat up on the front step. Pop looked the same as he always did but, sitting there behind the pool of lamp light, he really did look as if he'd never moved since that summer's day in 1941 and that it was just his shadow I'd seen walking about ever since.

'Eh?'

'What, Dad?'

'Oh.' He turned his collar up. 'Thought you said something.'

It was deep dark now and we felt our way down Pop's drive past where it bent to the right and the rhododendron bushes shielded us from his outside light. Our feet found the tarmac of Church Lane and we turned right through the church gate and up the flint path between the graves until we came under the dripping shadow of the church and veered left through the squelching leaves under the beech tree to the archway in the wall and out onto the path that swept around Mrs Evans's garden to the main street through the village.

Dad fiddled in his pocket as we came to the old stables, built into the wall, which they used as the Boys' Club and I tingled as if I was holding a cue already as Dad ran his fingers over the door in the dark looking for the key hole.

'Strewth alive!' He struck a match.

'What's up, Dad?'

'Dunno.' The match flared and reflected off the green gloss paint. 'Bloomin' lock's blocked up with something. Bit of stick, or paper. Blessed kids, I s'pose.'

'Why kids, Dad?' It was ages since I'd tried to open it with a broken lolly stick.

'Who else'd be daft enough to break something off inside?'

'What we gonna do then?'

'Blowed if I know, Nip.' The match burned low and he dropped it and shook his fingers. 'Gotta go up 'ome sometime anyway. See if we can locate those perishin' balls. P'raps see if Grandad's got a pair of pliers. Blow this for a game of soldiers.'

Nan got in a stew when we walked in because Dad forgot to tap on the window and she said she'd be flummoxed all evening now when he said we'd have to go straight back over to the Boys' Club and probably not have time to come up and see her again and then he went out to the shed with Grandad to look for the pliers.

'You can't imagine how I look forward to somebody coming up to see me of an evening, Simon.'

'Can't I, Nan?'

'It's often the only thing I 'ave to look forward to.' She was rubbing her bad knee. 'Up 'ere all on my own all day.'

The back door opened and I stood up.

'You coming, Simon?'

'Yes, Dad.'

Nan had both arms round me. 'Nigh-night, my duck.'

' 'night, Nan.'

'I'd come out and see you off if I wasn't afraid the damp night air'd set my neuralgia off again.'

'Yes, Nan.'

Grandad held the door open for me as I bent to put my shoes on on the back door mat. 'So you're off playing billiards with Dad then, Simon?'

'Yes, Grandad.'

'Aye well, have a good game then.' He was holding his hurricane lamp down and I noticed he'd buttoned his flies up wrong as I stood up. 'P'raps see something of you tomorrow night, son?'

'Yeah, spec so, Dad. C'mon, Simon.'

A squall had passed over while we'd been at Nan's but a high wind followed us and caught drips off the trees and tossed them at us as we stepped high through the grassed-over mole hills to the club door. Dad felt for the round lock and fiddled in his pocket for Grandad's pliers.

'Ah, that's it.' The pliers grated on the lock. 'Just get a good, firm 'old. If this snaps off, Simon, we're sunk.'

'Is it coming, Dad?'

'Easy, easy. Not too . . . fast.'

'Dad?'

' 'old on, Simon. Can't you see I'm— Ah, got it!'

'Good. Well done, Dad.'

He slipped the pliers through the slit pocket in his plastic mac and into his jacket pocket and then lit a match inside his coat to look at the piece he'd pulled out. I turned my back more into the wind and licked the rain water off my top lip.

'Looks like a bit off one'a them bloomin' ice-lollies.'

'Oh yeah.'

110

'Wonder what the devil that was doin' in there?'

'Dunno, Dad. Can we go in now?'

'Just a moment, Simon. I want to keep this safe and have a closer look later.'

'What for, Dad? What good's that gonna do?'

'I want to know why it was there, Simon, and that's an end of it.' He felt in his other pocket. 'Remains to be seen if this blessed key'll fit as well.'

'Easy enough to find out.'

I felt him turn in the dark as the key scraped in the lock. 'Any more of this moaning and groaning and we'll go home right now.'

I stuck my hands deeper into my wet pockets.

'Moan, moan, moan.' The lock clicked and the hinges creaked. 'That's all you do.'

'Yes, Dad.'

'Yes Dad what?'

'Yes, I do, Dad. Now can we go in, please, cos I'm soaking.'

The door grated against the floorboards and a stale smell escaped and Dad's leather soles echoed on the bare boards.

'Hang on, Simon. Lights're 'ere somewhere.' A switch flicked and a single bulb lit up to our right. 'Wrong one. Oh, 'ere we are.' He slipped through a doorway in a partition and flicked again and another single bulb came on in a larger room and I followed him.

It was enormous, about half the size of the village hall, with two old church pews down one wall. In the centre stood a full-sized billiard table on legs that looked as if they'd been taken from the fat lady in the circus and stained and polished. It was covered by a loose grey cloth and when Dad flicked another switch a long light, like an upturned pig trough painted green, came on above the table. The walls had been white but they had patches of green and grey and black on them and they felt wet-cold and I shivered as I followed Dad up to the other end where he stopped in front of a round coke stove, like we'd had in the infants' class, and opened the door in the top and poked inside it with a long bent poker.

I held my hand over it. 'Is it hot, Dad?'

111

'Shouldn't think so, Nip.' He lifted the ash trap at the front. 'Hasn't been used since the last time they opened it for the club and that must've been before the war.'

Dad was standing over the stove so I sat down on a pew and picked around at the side of my thumb and tried to think what Uncle Steven would have looked like bending over that same stove and tipping in coke and seeing that the boys didn't muck about and it struck me that if I went over to the heap of coke in the corner I might be the first one to touch the handle of the shovel since he'd used it and I might even find something he'd dropped. But I didn't think I should move about until Dad did and sitting there with my eyes closed trying to hear the echoes of the last words that had been spoken here all those years ago, was like waiting for the spell to wear off a king who'd been cursed.

'Ah well . . .'

'What, Dad?'

'Oh . . .' He turned and half smiled and rubbed the underside of his fingers against his chin. 'I dunno. Better see if this fire'll go, I s'pose.'

'Can I light it, Dad?'

'Better let me do it, Nip. It's a devil of a job to get going from what I remember.'

'Did you use to come over here then, Dad?'

He was taking his mac off and feeling in the pockets. 'I used to give him a hand sometimes but I wasn't very keen.' He pulled out a bundle of rolled-up newspaper and spread it on the billiard table. 'Lord knows if this table'll be any good now. It's as damp as old socks.' Next he took a handful of kindling wood from his other pocket. 'And I doubt this'll be enough to get that coke going. It'll be soaked. Still, p'raps we can use some of the old . . .'

I followed where he was looking but he wasn't looking anywhere. 'Some of what, Dad?'

He jerked as if I'd woken him up and passed his hands across his eyes. 'Oh, some of the old embers, Simon.' He drew in a deep breath. 'I'm not enjoying this much, you know.'

I couldn't think what he wanted me to say so if I said anything it would probably be wrong. I wanted to take the

112

cloth off and hit one of the balls with a cue like the men did at the Men's Club and see it hit another one and go down a hole and put my points up on the sliding scoreboard and take a puff of my cigarette and moan about work tomorrow while my opponent tried to get out of the fix I'd put him in; but it felt as if I was walking over somebody's grave so I went and straightened the stray bits of coke back into their pile with the top of my shoe.

'Gi's that little shovel over, Nip.'

I looked to where he was pointing and picked it up and gave it to him handle first. The handle had been shiny smooth but there were rust spots on it now that left a brown-red stain on my palm.

'Just get this lot out and put it in the ash bucket there and pick out the big bits.' Dad crumpled the newspaper and laid the sticks on top and fitted chunks of burned coke on top of them.

'Right then. Let's see what we can make of it.' He lit a match, cupped his hand as the draught from the window caught it, and lit the paper. The flames crackled up through the sticks and Dad closed both the little doors and rubbed his fingers clean. 'Well, that's that.' He slivered the round lid at the top so that it fitted better but a curl of smoke still crept out. 'Smoking a bit but p'raps that'll cure itself.' He turned away from the stove as if it would do as he told it if he didn't watch it. 'Shall we have a look at this 'ere table then?'

'Yes please, Dad.' I grabbed the corner of the cloth and started to pull.

'Not like that, Nip.' Dad darted forward and I let it fall. 'You drag that down on the floor and it'll get covered in grit and then it'll get all over the table when you go to cover it up again. You have to fold it up nice and square and put it on the seat there.'

I stood back.

'Well, get on the other corner then. We'll walk it down to one end and back again and across and that should do it.'

The cloth felt as if a slug had crawled all over it. I folded it towards Dad and he lifted it off and laid it on one of the pews.

113

'What's up with the table, Dad?'

'Blimey, Nip. It's worse than I thought.' He ran his finger along one of the cushions. 'Bald as a badger.'

'But is it all right?' The only sign of the fluffy green stuff they called the nap was under the cushions and that was coated in black dust and the rest was like a stretched-out grey skin.

'Not much pile left but at least it's flat.' Dad smoothed his hand across it and wiped gritty fragments off his palm. 'And it looks as if it could do with a brush.'

'But can we play, Dad?'

'Oh we can play all right. But it'll need a brush first.'

His footsteps echoed to the end of the table to the scoreboard, with its numbers on rollers and brass markers, and he unhooked what looked like a giant's clothes brush off the end.

'This is damp too.' He ran his finger over it as if he was testing a razor's edge and then shook it like a paint brush. 'But it'll 'ave to do for now. P'raps take it home and dry it out.'

He brushed at the table a section at a time and built up a ridge of dirt and grit like a beaver's bulwark across a river and then he scurried about under the cushions with the ridged edge of the brush.

'What're you doin' that for, Dad?'

'Gotta get it all out, Nip.'

'But it's not doin' any harm under there.'

'It's all got to come out, Simon. Can't do a job by halves.'

'Bloomin' waste 'a time.'

'It's not a waste of time. It'd all come spilling forward as it dried out and we'd be forever brushing it up.'

'Well, do it then, then, instead 'a now.'

Dad took his cap off and shook the drips off it and then leant forwards again under the long light and over the table. 'Go and see if that fire's still going.'

I trudged back to the stove and put my hand over the top and lowered it until I was touching the lid. It was cold and the lid was damp. I lifted it and sniffed. It smelt of sludge and soot.

'It's out, Dad.'

'What, completely?'

'Completely.'

'Blast it!'

There was a rack of cues on the wall by the stove and I ran my hand along them and they rattled like loose railings.

'You tryin' to mess those cues up?'

'No, Dad.'

'Well, leave 'em alone then.'

The rack was made with a length of wood at the top with holes that the cue points went through and another length at the bottom with round grooves cut in it that the ends stood in. I ran my hand along them again, at the top.

'D'you 'ear me, Simon?'

'Yes, Dad. Da-ad?'

'What?'

'Did I ever have a harp when I was little?'

'Don't ask me, Nip. How should I know?'

'Just wondered.' I played my fingers along them again.

'Will you leave—'

'Sorry, Dad.' I clapped my hands down by my sides. 'How're you getting on?'

'Just about finished.' He'd brushed all the rubbish against one pocket and was looking from the pile to the pocket and back again.

'What you waiting for then?'

'What?'

'Shove it down.' I pointed to the pocket. 'And then let's have a game.'

'Don't be in such a deuce of a hurry, Nip. If I shove that lot down there it'll get 'ung up in the 'oles and stick to the balls when they go down and then get back on the table and we'll be back where we started.'

'We won't, Dad.'

'Course we will.'

'We won't.'

'Why not?'

''Cos we can shake most of the dust out an' then wipe the balls as we get 'em out.'

'That'd make a hell'ov'a mess on the floor.'

'We could sweep it up.'

'Well . . .'

'Or even—' I pulled my school timetable out of my pocket and flattened it on the table. 'Make a cup for it to go in.' I rolled it into a loose tube, pinched it at the end and then twisted it and flattened the end down so that the longer end flared out like a tulip, and stuffed it in the pocket. 'See, Dad. You can shoot the dust in and then lift it out.'

'Think that'd work?'

'Don't see why not. 'ere, see.' I grabbed the brush and started to scrape the dust into the pocket.

'Hold it, Mush.' Dad took the brush back. 'Do it carefully like this.'

He brush-brush-brushed, in little rasping strokes, and the pile edged to the lip of the pocket and held there and he went back and brushed up the last fragments.

'Right. Hold the pocket steady, Nip.'

'It is steady.'

'Hold it. It won't be when I shoot it in.'

'Blimey!' I held the pocket in the palm of my hands as Dad edged the pile of damp dust forward and it gradually fell in like blobs of cold gravy with the odd fleck of white-wash off the ceiling that looked like flecks of grease. 'That's it, Dad.'

'Just finish this bit off.' He brushed some more at the lip of the pocket and stood back. 'There you are. How's that, Nip?'

'Great, Dad. Now can we play?'

'Just hold your horses, Simon. What do we 'ave to do now?'

'I dunno . . . oh, yes.' I lifted the packet of dust out and dropped it into the stove and grabbed a cue and turned on the table. 'Oh bugger—'

'I beg your par—'

'We've forgotten the rotten balls.'

'The "rotten balls", as you call them, are under the pew there and if I hear—' I dived down under the pew '. . . get the biggest thrashing of your— And be careful!' He tried to pull me back by my shoulder. 'You'll get gummed up to the eyeballs scrabbling about under there. 'old on. Not so fast.'

The box was stuck and I pulled at it because there was nothing to lose but Dad pushed me aside and lifted it out.

'That old box 'asn't been moved for donkeys' years. It might be rotten and fall apart.' He flicked the clips at the sides and lifted the lid.

'O-oh!' I was drawn over them like one of Ali Baba's forty thieves.

The reds were in a V of mahogany and the coloured balls clustered around them in a bed of cottonwool, each with a twinkling star of gold where the light caught them and separated them from the cloudier red of the red billiard ball and the ivory cream of the whites.

'They're like diamonds, Dad. Like precious stones.'

'Yeah, they're expensive, all right. I shouldn't like to 'ave to lash out for a set of snooker balls nowadays.'

'Well, I promise not to 'it 'em 'ard, Dad.'

'Oh, you couldn't damage them by hitting them, Simon. But you mustn't drop them and you have to be careful how you cue up not to rip the cloth.'

'Yes, Dad.'

'See here.' He lifted one of the billiard balls. 'That chip? That's where— You listening to me, Simon?'

'Yes, Dad.'

'That chip's where young Alfie Gardner shot it straight off the table one night tryin' to make it jump.'

'Oh, yeah.'

'Whatever's the matter, Simon?'

'Nothin', Dad. But can't we get a move on?'

'I don't want you trying any fancy stuff like that.'

'I won't, Dad.' I grabbed a couple of reds and a yellow.

'What you doing?'

'Setting them up. Well, getting them out for you.'

'Not them, Simon.' He took the reds and the yellow from me and put them back. 'Snooker's a bit complicated. You'd better start off with billiards. There's more skill in billiards, unless you play snooker properly, which most people don't.' He went to the rack for a cue and I dived for the dull balls in the box and put them on the table and tried to knock them with my cue.

117

'Simon!' Dad grabbed my arm. 'What d'ya think you're playing at?'

'Jus' gonna hit it, Dad.'

'Blimey, you can't without a tip.' He stuck the end of the cue under my nose. 'See that?'

'Yes, Dad.' There was a brass bit at the end with a screw thread inside it.

'You have to put a tip in there. You go uckin' about without a tip and you'd jolly soon be through that cloth.' He rested the cue on his hand and reached it forward over the table and drew the last few inches backwards and forwards between his finger and thumb like a tortoise's head over a lettuce leaf. 'See, Mush, you'd rip the cloth as easy as pie without a tip.'

'Yes, Dad.'

'Or chip the ball.'

'Yes, Dad.'

'So never use it without a tip.'

'Cor blimey, ye-es. Now 'ave you got one?'

He straightened. 'Yes, I have. Left over from when—'

'Well, put the bloomin' thing in then.'

'All right. All right.' He undid his plastic mac and took it off and folded it up and laid his cap down on top of it.

I stood with my cue at my side and gripped it and let my hand slide up and down it.

Dad unbuttoned his jacket and felt in his pocket.

I changed my cue into my other hand and leant against it.

Dad took something out of his pocket and eyed it up and held it to the end of his cue.

I closed my eyes and started to count.

'You ready then?' He'd screwed a leather end into his cue.

'Yes, Dad. But what about the ball?'

'You have to learn to cue-up first.' He was leaning forwards and the tortoise was flicking its tongue again and he screwed his head round to make sure I was watching. 'And you 'ave to 'old it at the end 'ere, see?' He waved the ebony end of the cue. 'And you have to stand close to it, see. So that it brushes your side. See, Nip? Now you do it.'

I lined it up, did a couple of practice shots with the cue tip to the ball and then followed through. There was a clean thud. The impact went solid through the cue into my fingers and the ball sped off like an arrow and bounced off one cushion onto another and I knew I'd done it right.

'Well done.' Dad caught the red as it bounced back. 'The best way to teach you 's by having a game.'

'Goodo!'

'But we won't keep the score else you'll be concentrating on that instead of what I'm saying to you.' He put the red ball on a spot at the end of the table and shuffled the whites behind his back and then held his crossed hands out. 'Which one?'

'Dunno. What's the difference?'

'One's got a spot on it. Spot starts.'

'Oh.' I tapped one of his knuckles.

He turned his hands over and splayed his fingers. 'I'm spot. See that spot?'

'Yes, Dad.'

'Spot starts.' He put his ball down in a half-circle at the scoreboard end and leant forwards and poked at it a couple of times and then stood up again.

'Wha's up, Dad?'

'Need some chalk.'

'Thought we weren't gonna keep the score.'

'No . . .' He was rummaging in his jacket pockets. 'For the cue tip. You have to rough it up a bit else it gets 'ard and shiny and skids off the ball and you could wind up ripping the cloth.'

'Yeah, come on then.'

'What?'

'Well, take your shot and then I can 'ave a go.'

Dad rubbed the end of the cue with a square of blue stuff and blew a puff of blue dust off it. 'Some of the blokes reckon to do this after every shot but I think that's overdoing it a bit.' He settled himself over his cue again. 'You start off from anywhere in what's called the D,' and he prod-prodded and then hit it gently.

Dad's white trundled up the table and smacked the red against the end cushion and they both rolled back towards us and I waited, watching, until they stopped.

119

'Do I start from where you did, Dad?'

'M'm.'

I put my ball down and took aim.

'Stop!'

'What?' I was stretching forwards and I could have rested my forehead on the table.

'You can't go straight back behind the D.'

'How'm I s'posed to 'it it then?'

'That's the idea of the first shot, you see. Try to make the other player miss.'

I looked down the table and then back again. 'That's a bit unkind, isn't it?'

'Don't think so, Nip.' He folded his arms across his chest. 'That's just the way they play it. Go on. Hit it up the table and back. It doesn't matter much which one you hit.'

I prod-prodded like he'd done and aimed at the blank cushion. The ball jumped as it rebounded and shot back and hit the cushion at my end and bounced off the red and onto his white.

'Strewth alive!'

'What, Dad?'

'You got a cannon as well as hitting it.'

'That's good, isn't it?'

'Yeah. You get two points for a cannon. That's when you make your ball hit the red and the other white. And you get another go.'

He told me all about pot-red and in-off red and in-off white and how it was ungentlemanly to play to pot your opponent's ball, as well as being a bit short-sighted because you couldn't get any more cannons, and we started to keep the score when he thought I'd got the hang of it.

'What do I do now, Dad?' I'd whacked it as hard as I could and they'd all gone down.

'Blimey! Pot-red's three, and a cannon before that's five, and I believe it was red you went in off so that's eight and you potted my white, you blighter, that's ten.' He looked around the empty table. 'I dunno, Nip. Swallow your cue and go 'ome I should think.'

'Cor. Was that good then, Dad?'

120

'Well, yes.' He got the red and my white ball out of the pockets and set them up again. 'Flukey though. You'd never go for a shot like that intentionally.'

'Why not, Dad?'

'Cos it wasn't really possible. You could never anticipate that's how they'd run.'

'I did, Dad.'

'No you didn't, Simon.' He chalked the end of my cue. 'Get on with it. It's your shot again from the D.'

We played billiards until we were too cold to hold the cue and then we covered the table and turned the lights off and went back to Nan's, but we came straight away again when we saw it was half-past nine and Nan had finished her milk drink and Grandad was washing up. Mum went from one job to the other when we got home, splashing things she was washing up and wiping them with stiff fingers and pushing past us in the doorway from the kitchen to the living room to get the tea pot because she expected we'd want a cup of tea now that we'd finally decided to come home, and I found myself in bed before the cold of the club had worn off, with the musty damp of the table still on my hands and the blue chalk on my fingers, and I closed my eyes and watched the three balls flowing up and down the table and slipping into the pockets and then they kept on spinning without stopping and I felt myself spinning away with them.

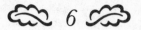

6

*N*an and Mum had always said how time flew as you got older but I'd always thought that was just something old people said until Mum told me one day that Laurence, next door, had started school when we'd gone back after Christmas. The boys at school all said you were really grown up when you became a teenager and that people had to stop bossing you about then and I started combing my hair back in my bedroom in the evenings and standing staring into the mirror and imagining how I was going to grow up without getting like the grown-ups, but I found myself thinking about all the games I'd never played when I was young and I rushed off out to play them all because I hadn't got much time left. Cowboys and Indians was my favourite for a week or two and I never forgave Mrs Keen, next door, for buying me a book for my birthday when I'd asked Mum to tell her I wanted a Winchester repeater cap rifle if she asked what I wanted. Aunty Win had started letting Laurence out to play now that he was older and Mr and Mrs Stroud's little boy, Billy, who was friendly with Laurence, used to play as well, but they weren't allowed out of the Close. I moaned to Mum about that but I was glad, really, because it meant I could stay and play with them instead of having to chase around after the boys. We played football in the road most of the time when we weren't playing Cowboys in my back garden. We were in the back garden one day, and Jimmy and Jerry were with us, when I saw Brenda Norris and Christine Lanagan coming up the back field past Vine's farm. I didn't want the boys to see me talking to them, or them to see me playing Cowboys, so I ran back down the garden and told the boys to go and hide out the front somewhere and I'd give them a hundred and fifty before I started looking and then I raced back and combed my hair in the reflection from the shed window and wandered up the garden as if I was looking for something.

'Hello, Simon.'

'Oh hello, Brenda. Christine. I didn't see you coming.'

'Didn't you?' Brenda stood up on tiptoe to see over the hedge. 'Is this where you live?'

'Yes.' I looked back down the garden and wished Dad's underpants would stop swinging about on the line. 'We've been here since my dad got back from the war. I don't usually come up 'ere but I was looking for my ball.' I bent down and poked about in the hedge and was too embarrassed to stand up again when I heard, 'Go on. Ask him,' and 'No, you,' from the other side.

'Si-mon?'

'What?'

'You still there?'

'Yes.'

'Would you like us to come and help you?'

'No.' I scrabbled about in the dry leaves. 'You'd get all stung in 'ere an' there's all spiders an' beet— Ouch!' I held still and picked a hawthorn needle out of my finger.

'Is it bleeding?' Brenda Norris had her head stuck down through where the branches forked and she was looking right down on me.

'No.'

'Simon?'

'What?'

'There's a social down the camp on Saturday night.'

'Is there?'

'They have dancing with Mantovani and Petula Clark and Frank Sinatra records.'

'Yuck!'

'Frank Sinatra! O-ooh!' Christine looked as if she'd lost her balance, but then she flashed a look at me as if I'd stood on her foot. 'Three Coins in the Fountain . . . O-ooh! What's up with him?'

'I like Guy Mitchell and Johnny Ray.'

Brenda glanced at Christine. 'Well, my brother's got "Such a Night".'

'Oh 'as 'e? What's that?'

123

Christine giggled. 'Johnny Ray's latest.'

'Oh, yeah, course it is.' I ignored Christine, and the way the light sparkled off her hair and her black eyes glinted from the cushioned surround of her creamed-coffee skin. 'An' I like Dicky Valentine.'

'I adore Dicky Valentine.' Christine's lips puckered up like a daffodil. 'Will you come, Simon?' She stretched over and took my hand and stroked my palm.

'Yeah. Yeah. I'll come.' It was like having hold of the wire with the electric pulse, that kept the cows in. 'I should be able to make that.' I tried to make my voice sound deep but it was just clogged up. 'What time?'

'Shall we meet you there or will you call for us?'

'Well I—'

'Oh, do call for us. We don't like walking into the social on our own, do we, Bren?'

'But I'll 'ave me bike with me.'

'Well you can push it, can't you?' Christine had been hugging up to Brenda and looking all lost but now she spun round.

'Well I s'pose so.' I stood with one foot on top of the other and prayed I wouldn't say anything stupid.

Christine nudged Brenda and Brenda looked back at me. 'And would you ask Peter Bennett from Moulscombe if he'd like to come?'

'M'yeah . . . I dunno though.'

Christine's eyes narrowed. 'Why not?'

'Well, I dunno really. I don't s'pose he's got a white shirt.'

'What's that got to do with it?'

'You're supposed to wear a white shirt, aren't you?'

Christine shrugged at Brenda. 'Doesn't matter, does it?'

'Most of them do, but it doesn't really matter.' Brenda seemed a very sensible girl. 'We'll see you about half-past six on Saturday then, Simon?'

'Right. Yes. I'll be there.'

'Bye then.' Brenda smiled and gave me a little wave and then they turned and stroked the tops of the long stems of grass as they walked away.

I made out I was going back down the garden but I ducked down as I went under the clothes prop and crept back up and watched them from the gap in the hedge by the chicken house. Brenda was shorter than Christine, and rounder, and her sky-blue bobble hat sat on her head like a cosy on a tea pot. Christine was tall and I sensed her moving under her dress and fawn overcoat. Her hair was glossy black and, as I closed my eyes and saw her face again, I felt the creamy warmth of her skin and a fizzing feeling went through the pit of my stomach and I searched the edge of the field for a last sight of her but they'd gone.

I turned and kicked the mud off my boots as I went down the path. It was nearly half-past six and it looked as if it was going to rain and there'd be nobody coming out to— The boys! I shot down the path and round the house and out to the front gate.

Jerry Henry was talking to Jimmy Phillips over his fence. I stood at my gate for a minute but they didn't look at me so I went over.

'What'cha doin'?'

'Goin' 'ome.' Jerry Henry didn't turn round.

'Why?'

'Cos we're cold an' fed up, aren't we, Jim?'

'Yeah.'

'Where're the littluns?'

'Gone in. They were cold an' fed up as well.'

'Where d'you hide then, Jim? I couldn't find you.'

'You didn't look.'

'I bloody did.'

'No you didn't. We went down the cess pit.'

'Wha-at!'

'In the cess pit. It was perishin'.'

'You dope. They're not allowed down there.'

'We know that now, Simon. And stop shoving.'

'What'cha mean, you "know it now"?'

'Laurence's mum.' Jerry felt the side of his head. 'She gave me a thick ear. But it was your fault, Simon.'

'Yeah.'

'It wasn't. And you can shut up, Fatty Phillips.'

'Good-night, Jerry.'

'Was his mum annoyed with me?'

'Yeah, good-night, Jim. See you tomorrow.'

'I'm talking to you, 'enry.'

'Better ask 'er.'

'I'm bloody askin' you, Phillips.' The gate clasp caught as I barged it open and Jimmy bolted and I skidded to a halt as his front door opened and his mum came out onto the step.

'What you doing, Simon?'

'Playin', Mrs Phillips.'

'Well, you'd better play somewhere else. Jimmy's coming in.' She stood aside. 'And who else is that out there?'

'Jerry, Mrs Phillips.'

'Oh, is it?' She stood out over me from her front step. 'Off you go home now, Jerry. It looks like rain and Mummy'll be wondering what's become of you.' She stayed standing over me until Jerry had disappeared and then she closed the door.

The toilet light was on when I got back so I took my boots off by the back door and went straight to my bedroom. I pulled the curtains and lay down on my bed. The ceiling was a fretwork of cracks. I'd read a book once, about Africa. The people had herds of cattle and they moved to another place when they'd eaten all the grass and then they moved on again. They must have run out eventually, although they could have gone back again, when the grass had grown, in a massive circle. I pressed my ear against my bedroom wall to see if I could hear Aunty Win talking about me. It was all quiet. Maybe she'd smacked Laurence's bottom and put him to bed. Maybe by the time Saturday came Jimmy and Jerry would have forgotten about today. Maybe if I went up for Frank Parfit he'd ask me to come in and ask me where I'd been and what I'd been doing for so long. But what about if the boys at Tangmere asked me what I was doing at their social or if Peter Bennett told me to push off when I asked him to come to the social. I stared back at the cracks in my ceiling. It was broken up into blocks like a map of the states of America. They all seemed to come back to one crack in the middle. I got up and found my book about African tribesmen, but it didn't say what happened to them when they ran out of places to go to.

*

Doug Ritson said that plain white shirts looked like girls' blouses. He said the proper spivs wore white stardust shirts and that I should get a silk tie with a nude on it to wear with it. I'd seen Geoff Gibbs with a tie like that once, that had belonged to his uncle, but I didn't think Skip Matthews would have liked it and Mum would be upset if I got one. I helped Mum wash up on Friday evening after tea and I didn't have the wireless on too loud and I cleaned my teeth without being told to and I finally got around to asking her when she was saying good-night to me.

'Mu-um?'

'Yes, Simon?'

'Could I have a new shirt?'

'A new shirt, laddikins? But you've got several.'

'A white stardust one, for best.'

'A what?'

'A stardust shirt, Mum.'

'Whatever for?'

'I'm going— I've been invited to a children's social. Down the camp on Saturday night.'

'But that's tomorrow, Simon.'

'Yes, Mum.'

'And what in heaven's name are they?'

'Nice white shirts, Mum.'

'But what's the stardust bit?' She put the light on and looked at me more closely.

'Sparkly bits, Mum.'

'Sounds flashy to me.'

'Oh no, Mum.' I sat up in bed and tried to look horrified. 'They're really nice. You'll like it.'

'Oh, will I? And will I like the price?'

'Seven and six, Mum. In Bishop's.'

'Bishop's! That's an expensive shop, Simon. We always go to Stevey Bacon's. And it'll mean a special trip to Chichester.'

'Well, I'll put my pocket money towards it.'

'What pocket money?'

'Well, if I had pocket money. The other boys have pocket money and I could've saved it up.'

'What, to go off buying a lot of sweets and ruining your teeth?'

127

'Or to have bought a shirt and pleased myself.'

'And we buy all your things for you. You can't tell me you go short, Simon. Why, there isn't another boy in the vill—'

'I know, Mum.'

'Who else in the village has got a football and all the nice cricket stuff you've got?'

'I know they 'aven't, Mum.'

She stood biting her lip. 'And what is this social anyway?'

'Down the camp, Mum.'

'I know that, Simon. But who runs it and what'll be going on there and what time'll you be back and things like that.'

'Does that mean I can go, Mum?'

'Weren't you listening to a word I was saying?'

'Yes, I was, Mum. But does it?'

'Answer me.'

'Does it?'

'Simon!'

I clenched my fists under the bedclothes and my nails bit into my palms. Mum's face was set and she was staring and I fixed my eyes on the eiderdown until I saw her blink and re-focus on me and I lay down and closed my eyes.

'Well?'

'Well what?'

'I beg your pardon?'

'Granted.' Frank Parfit always said that.

'Simon!'

I jumped up. 'What?'

'Don't speak to me like that.' She tucked at the side of my bed. 'And look what a mess you've made of your beddie-byes.'

I said 'beddie-byes' under my breath and sat up stiff as she tucked me in.

'Now, who's running this club?'

'It's a social.'

'Social, then.'

'Skip Matthews and some of the camp kids' parents, I s'pose.'

'And what'll you do there?' She sat down on my bed.

'Dancing and games, I expect.'

'Dancing, with girls?'

'Yes.'

'What kind of dancing?'

'Blimey! Waltzes and quickstep and the flamin' polka, I expect.'

'And will they put the lights out?'

'Strewth alive, 'ow should I know if they'll put the lights out?'

'And I thought you didn't like dancing at school?'

'I don't.'

'Well, what you want to spend your weekends doing it for then?'

'All right then, I won't ruddy go,' and I flung myself back and banged my head on the headboard.

'That was clever.' Mum rubbed the back of my head but I pulled away. 'And don't make such a performance. I only want to know what you're going getting up to.'

'Mn-n.'

'And what about this flashy shirt you're after?'

'It's not flashy, it's smart.'

'Well . . . whatever it is.'

'It's an ordinary white shirt but silky with like silver diamonds in it.'

'Will it wash?'

'Course it'll wash. Doug Ritson at school's got one and it's always clean.'

'M'm, but I wonder how it'll stand up to washing though?'

'All right, I expect. And I'll only wear it for going out in.'

'And what time d'you expect to get home from this social or whatever it's called?'

'When it finishes, I expect. It won't be late.'

'How d'you know it won't be late?'

'Well, it's for people of my age so it'll finish at the right time, won't it?'

Mum was silent for a moment and I wondered if she was running out of excuses and going to be angry. 'But you've got to cycle back after that, don't forget. And cross that main road.'

'I've done that hundreds of times, Mum. Please let me go.'

129

She moved slowly to the door. 'I don't know, Simon. I'll have to see what your daddy says about it. But I do wish you'd give us more notice of these blessed new schemes you get involved in.'

I lay back and stared at the ceiling and tried to imagine how I'd feel in my new stardust shirt but all I could see was Mum handing over a clean, sharp ten-shilling note and just getting two and sixpence change to put in her purse; and I'd have to wear grey trousers with it and my black shoes that were for church and squeaked, and that made me angry and then I felt sad because I kept getting angry with her and she didn't know why and I knew it hurt her and I wished she wouldn't get hurt so that I could lose my temper without having to worry about it; and I turned over and stuck my face in the pillow and tried to remember when I hadn't had anything to worry about but I had to go right back to before I started school and that was so long ago that it felt as if it was somebody else and then I started to cry and I lay there saying 'bugger, bugger, bugger' until I went to sleep.

We got off the bus at St Pancras and Mum made me hold her hand as we crossed the road. I knew, as soon as we'd got off the bus, that she'd head straight for Stevey Bacon – Boys' and Gentlemen's Outfitters, but I didn't argue because it was only twenty-five past nine and I didn't want to go past the Gaumont with her holding my hand before the cinema opened, at half past, in case the boys from school were there and saw us. I managed to let go to open the door for her but the way she smiled and said 'Thank you, Simon' made me feel horrible because she didn't know why I'd done it.

Stevey Bacon's shop looked as if it had been burgled. Half the shelves were empty and there was dust on the toes of a row of wellingtons that stood in front of the drawers opposite the counter. There was nobody in the shop so Mum went and looked at some horrible check lumberjack shirts and I stood stroking a cat that was asleep on the customers' chair by the cash register. A woman's face peered in around the curtain of the place where Mr Bacon took people to try things on. She stared at us as if we had no right to be there and then

130

she disappeared and a hoarse whisper sounded, from halfway up some stairs, that he'd better come down because he'd got a customer.

'Morning, ah . . . Mrs Wilson, isn't it?' Stevey Bacon was thinner and looked as if he'd just got up. 'Haven't seen you for a while.'

'Morning, Mr Bacon.' Mum dragged herself away from the horrible shirts. 'There was Simon's new school trousers about this time last year.'

'Goodness me, was it a year ago? And they grow so fast at his age, don't they? S'pose he's grown out of them by now.'

'No. We're all right for school trousers just at the present thank you, Mr Bacon. We got them a bit big, if you remember, and we've let them down now and there's still plenty of room round the tummy.'

'Oh.' Stevey Bacon slid his drawer of trousers back.

I'd sat down with the cat but I wondered if I ought to stand up.

'No, what we're after today is—' Mum drew closer to him '. . . a stardust shirt.'

'A star dust-shirt, Mrs Wilson?'

Mum looked as if she'd always thought it was a hoax and not a thing that sensible people would take seriously and that if there was any explaining to be done I'd better do it. 'Yes, Mr Bacon. That's what he wants, if there is such a thing.'

'Well, I . . .' Stevey Bacon stood scratching the side of his head. 'I've got some very nice shirts with big fashionable collars I've reduced.'

I got in closer to Mum and whispered 'No' as Stevey Bacon's back was to us but she stood up straighter away from me.

'Little bit creased but that'd iron out.'

'But they're not stardust, Mum.'

'No. But they're very serviceable.' Mr Bacon looked me in the eye and I was glad we had the counter between us.

'They really do look jolly nice little shirts, Simon. They'd wear and wear and—'

'Oh but, Mum.'

131

'Dear oh dear. What *are* these new-fangled stardust things?'

Stevey Bacon sighed and looked down at his tray of dusty white shirts with the pointed collars that would cover the knot in any tie. 'I suppose it's the latest craze amongst the youngsters. No sooner do you get a supply in than they move on to something else.' His eyes moved to the piles of horrible lumberjack shirts. 'A year ago it was cowboy shirts and they'd pay the earth for anything check.'

'Are they exp—'

'Now I can't shift 'em for love nor money.'

'Are they expensive, Mr Bacon?'

'They're a give away now for what I paid for them.'

'Oh *no*, Mum.'

'S'sh, Simon.'

'And beautiful quality.' Stevey Bacon scuttled round from behind his counter and grabbed a handful of tartan shirts that made me itch just to look at them.

'No . . . the other ones.' He stood there with yards of tartan dripping off his arms. 'I was wondering if *they* were expensive.'

'Oh.' Stevey Bacon shook his head over his heap and folded a yellow and green and red and purple one into its creases and put it back on its shelf. 'I haven't had any call for them so far so I haven't got any in stock.'

'Will you be getting any?'

'I need it *tonight*, Mum.'

'*Tonight*.' Stevey Bacon went white. 'It'd take me a fortnight to get one even if I knew what I was ordering and I ordered it today.'

'Dear oh dear, a fortnight. Whatever are we to do?'

'Go down to Bishop's, Mum.'

'*Will* you be quiet, Simon.'

'It doesn't look as if I can help you, Mrs Wilson.'

I opened the door for Mum.

'I really am sorry to have put you to all this bother, Mr Bacon.'

'Oh, can't be helped.' He didn't say 'Good morning' but turned back and started folding and stacking again and I'd have felt sorry for him if I hadn't been desperate to get away.

Mum was well ahead of me down the street and I had to run to catch up with her.

'Well, I hope you're satisfied, my lad.'

'What, Mum?'

'Wasting Mr Bacon's time and embarrassing me like that.'

'Wasn't my fault he hadn't got what we wanted.'

'What *you* want, you mean. It looks to me as if you may have to do without.'

'But we can try Bishop's, can't we?'

'Looks as if we'll have to. You were determined to go there in the first place, weren't you?'

'Not really.' I stepped off the pavement to let an old lady go past. 'Only if that's the only place you can get 'em.'

Mum didn't answer me and she stared straight ahead as we went past the entrance to the Gaumont. The cinema steps were mottled with muddy footprints and sweet papers and the foyer looked like a clearing that a herd of elephants had gone through. We crossed opposite the Granada where all the softies went to Saturday morning pictures, and Mum rummaged in her handbag as we got level with the Pallants.

'What we stopping for, Mum?'

'Just seeing if I've got Nan's old pill bottles.'

'What? We gotta go off down the doctor's?'

'Just to pick up her prescription.'

'Well, couldn't I go and have a look in the shops?'

'I'd rather you didn't, Simon.' Mum looked at her watch and then checked it against the clock on the market cross. 'See, it's nearly quarter to ten now and if we hurry down there and then get this blessed shirt-thing of yours we can get back for the half-past ten 57.'

'Yeah, but if we took our time we could catch the quarter-to 66 and save walking up from Tangmere Corner.'

'Yes, but I don't want to be hanging about that long.'

'Thought you said we were short of time?'

'Yes, I know, but . . . oh, do stop being so argumentative, Simon. For pity's sake. C'mon now.'

The Pallants were narrow with little pavements and enormous rounded kerbstones. The houses were built so that the upper storeys came out like jaws, and almost touched in some places across the street, and the doors had scrubbed steps leading up to them and there were brass plates on the walls of the solicitors' offices. Some of them had the windows blacked out and their names written across them in brass-coloured paint.

The entrance to the South Pallant was like coming out of a tunnel. The houses fell back on the right side of the road and the pavement arched up a grassy bank with a row of beech trees growing out of it. We crossed over and Mum turned the big black knob in the middle of the heavy black door and we went up three steps and closed the door behind us.

The doctor's surgery was like stepping back in time. There was a broken floorboard, just behind the front door, that had bent every time I'd trodden on it, but it never broke, and the lino around it was cracked but it never seemed to get any worse, and the gas fire, in the green-glazed tile hearth, whispered up the white columns of cellular firebricks, both summer and winter, and the strained light, through the net curtains, played a freckled pattern on the mountain of green metal boxes on the table where the doctors kept their record cards. There was usually a lady there to meet us when we arrived, to ask us our name and thumb through the cards and pull out a packet and put it on one side: then she'd give us a coloured disc with a number on it and lead us into the waiting room, where we'd ask the other patients what their numbers were and wait until our coloured light came on above the door, and it was our number next, and then we'd go back into the little waiting room, and sit by the fire, until it was our turn to take our packet of notes and be led into one of the dark little surgeries and sit down across the desk from one of the doctors, all snug under a desk lamp like a drowsing moth, and explain what seemed to be the matter: but the dumpy lady was missing today and we just stood there waiting and trying not to look at the cards in the drawer that stood open.

'Perhaps they're closed for some reason, Simon.'

'Can't be, Mum. The door was open.'

'M'm, so it was.' Mum stood back so that she wasn't standing on the receptionist's scuffed patch.

The door from the big waiting-room opened and I stood more to attention. A lady in the receptionist's overall came in. She was short and slim and her overall fitted tight around her waist, so that she looked like an egg-timer. Her hair was short-cropped and black and glinting and her features were sharp, like an Italian film-star we'd seen in a trailer to an X-film once, and I'd never imagined that a receptionist could look like this.

'Name?' She sounded Italian and her black eyes flashed.

I stared at her, as Mum explained we'd called for Nan's sleeping capsules, and tried to imagine what it would be like to take her to the Gaumont where the big boys took their girl-friends.

'They'll be in the cupboard outside. Shall I take the empties?'

'They're here somewhere.' Mum groped in her handbag. 'I had them a minute ago.'

The receptionist had a silky orange blouse on under her overall and a thin line of dark blue tartan was showing at the bottom and I wished we'd caught her without her overall on.

'Thank you so much.' Mum gave her Nan's empty pill bottle. 'Good morning.'

'Good morning, madam.' She held the door open for us and I followed Mum slowly, drawn up to my full height, so that I looked like Jeff Chandler in *Flame and the Arrow*, but I sagged back when she said, 'Bye, sonny,' and closed the door before I was out properly.

'Steady on, Simon.'

'What, Mum?'

'Well, barging into me like that. Darn near had me over. Whatever are you thinking about?' Mum was stretching to see into the flat, black cabinet that was fitted into the surgery entrance. 'I'm blowed if I can see this blessed prescription.' She was holding up bottles and tubes and reading the names and putting them down. 'Ah, here we are.'

'Isn't that dangerous, Mum?'

'What?'

'Well, leaving them out 'ere. They might get pinched.'

'Who'd want to pinch them? They've got people's names and addresses on.'

'I know but—'

'Oh do come on, Simon. You shouldn't be thinking about pinching things at your age. Now come on and let's see about this blessed shirt.'

Bishop's stood halfway down East Street amongst the banks and opposite Marks and Spencer's. It had three windows on to the street and the canvas awning, that kept the rain off the customers and the sun off the suits, came out on criss-cross metal arms instead of folding struts. It had been the first shop in Chichester to have an electric fire stuck up over the front door and Dad said that was to encourage people to go in on a cold day and to make them not want to come out again. Everyone said it had always been an expensive shop, even before the war, but that it was still worse now they'd put in a new manager who'd run a similar shop in Portsmouth because he'd fitted it out with loads of chrome and mirrors and flash carpets and that anybody who went there'd get stung for a start to pay for them having the electric lights burning all day.

We'd been into Marks and Spencer's to see if they had any stardust shirts and Mum had gone very tight-lipped when the assistant said they were a special kind of fashion shirt and that Bishop's was the only place in Chichester that stocked that sort of thing and now she was standing on the pavement opposite it and I could feel her wondering how she could get out of going in.

Their window had been done up like a scene from a play. There were two men in dark suits and trilbies, with their jackets held open by strands of invisible cotton, to show off the shiny blood-red linings, standing together over a bicycle with autumn leaves stuck in the spokes and one was lighting the other's cigarette and the window and mirrors were angled so that it looked as if there were four of them and two bicycles. The next window was laid out with sloping pale blue stuff with pairs of trousers pegged out as if they were alive and leaping over pullovers that had been

136

folded up like people bending forward playing leapfrog in the sky.

'S'sh!'

'What, Mum?'

'Did you see that?'

'What, Mum?'

'Over there. Just going into that shop.'

I waited for a David Greig's delivery van to move on in the traffic and stared in through the plate-glass window. 'Cor, that's—'

'Who is it?'

'What, Mum?'

'What were you going to say?'

'Nothing, Mum. Just that suit. It's only nine pounds, nineteen and elevenpence.'

'That's nearly ten pounds.'

'I know it is.'

'And that's not what you were going to say anyway.'

'What wasn't, Mum?' I tried to look puzzled and turned my back on Bishop's in case Charlie Milo looked round and came over and spoke to me. I hadn't seen Charlie since he'd finished laying the drains up at the village school and I'd been looking out for him ever since I'd been coming into Chichester because he'd promised he'd teach me to box.

'I'm sorry, Simon.' Mum put her shopping-bag down on the pavement and stood over it. 'I'm not going in there.'

'Why not, Mum?'

'Oh, Simon. Didn't you see him? What an awful sight. And he went into that precious shop of yours.'

'Did 'e, Mu—'

'S'sh, don't look.'

'No, Mum.'

'He might see you.' She was whispering. 'He had those flashy thick-soled shoes on and awful lurid yellow socks. But it was his mac . . . ! I suppose you'd call it a mac . . . with the most enormous built-up shoulder pads you've ever seen, and his hair! Well, that defies description, all greased and quiffed-up at the back . . . Never in my wildest dream did I think you'd ever be wanting to go into shops like that. And he looked foreign to me, Simon.'

'Maltese.'

'What?'

I bit my lip. 'P'raps 'e's Maltese, Mum.'

'Well, these spivvy types put the wind up me, Simon. You never know what they might get up to.'

'P'raps wait until 'e's gone, Mum.' If she ever found out this was the Charlie I'd gone to see *Zulu* with I'd never hear the last of it.

'Wonder if he'll be long?'

'Shouldn't think so, Mum.' Charlie had said he was getting a new coat for half a crown a week, and he'd made me a roll-up and explained to me what the 'never-never' was.

'How d'you know he won't be long, Simon?' He might be in there ages.'

'Well, if he is, we'll 'ave to leave it, Mum.'

'Leave it!' She tore her eyes off Charlie's D.A. 'But you'd set your heart on it, Simon, and we came into Chichester especially to get it.'

'I know, Mum.'

'But . . .' She looked back at the window and then at her watch. 'Won't you be desperately disappointed?'

'S'pect so, Mum.'

'Oh my poor darling.'

I edged back.

'Perhaps we'd better just get on with it, then.'

'What now, Mum?' Bishop's was reflected in Marks and Spencer's window.

'Well, of course now. For heaven's sake, the bus'll be going presently. And why're you looking at me like that? Is my hair all over the place or are you getting that squint back again?'

'Dunno, Mum.'

A door opened over the road.

With his thin black moustache and nicotine-stain colouring he looked like a Chicago gangster. He hunched his shoulders in the doorway, stuck his hands in his pockets and set off down East Street towards Timothy White's.

'C'mon then, Mum.'

'What?'

'We'd better get goin' else it'll be too late.'

138

'But I thought—'

'Come on.' I'd started to cross the road and a butcher's delivery boy cut in behind me.

'Be careful, Simon.' Mum grabbed my hand and I led her through the traffic that was being held up by the policeman by the Cross. 'Why're you in such an all-fired hurry all of a sudden?' She put her hand on Bishop's window-sill and caught her breath. 'And what do you mean by going dashing off like that? You nearly had that boy off his bike.'

'I didn't.'

'And I say you did.'

' 'e was pullin' into Greig's.'

'Ah'h'oh!' Mum held her hand up. 'And that reminds me. I must pop in there and get some of their sausages.'

'Blimey! Why didn't we get them when we were over there?'

'Because you kept on about this blasted shirt, that's why.' Mum adjusted her headscarf. 'Now come on in and make it snappy else I shan't come in with you at all.'

The door brushed the carpet and closed slowly behind us and blotted out the sound of the traffic. There were lots of glass counters, edged with chrome, but you couldn't tell which was the customers' side except for the one with a cash register. Lines of chrome hangers on wheels were littered about and there was a whole forest of dummies dressed up in blazers and sports flannels and pullovers and trousers and suits and one of them came over to us.

'Does madam require any assistance?' He sounded as if he'd been lacquered and polished. A double-band of shirt cuff showed out from under each jacket sleeve and he had gold cuff-links to match the brass ends on the tape-measure round his neck. 'May I be of help?'

'It's not me, it's Simon.' Mum stepped back but I was behind her.

'Ah yes. The young gentleman.' He was smiling as if I was some sort of joke. 'And what can we do for you, young sir?'

'Wanna stardust shirt.' I scuffed my feet on the carpet and my face burned with embarrassment.

'Oh r'heally.' He stood off one leg and folded his arms across his chest.

139

'Yeah.' I tried to hunch my shoulders forward like Charlie'd done, but he hadn't had his mum with him with a shopping basket. 'A white one.'

'A white one?' He stepped back and wiped a sud off his lapel. 'And what neck size is he, madam?'

'I think it's—'

'We don't know, Mum.' I glowered at the man. 'You'll 'ave to measure me.'

'Oh, very well.' He marched back to his counter and stood there looking back at us over his shoulder.

'Go on, Simon.' Mum pushed me and smiled at the assistant.

'If you'd just be so kind as to stand here, sir.' He pointed to the side of his glass and silver counter. 'And perhaps I could take madam's shopping?'

'I'll just hold on to it, thank you.' Mum changed her basket to her other hand.

'I'm sure I don't mind.' He twitched his shoulders and stooped behind his counter and came up with a thing like one of Pop's dog collars.

'What's that for?'

'For measuring sir's—' he dropped it over my head and pulled it '. . . neck. Oh, I am sorry. Is that too tight?'

'Y'h'hes.'

'I'm so sorry.' He loosened it. 'Is that better?'

I ran my finger round under the measure where it had pinched. 'Yes.'

'Good. That's size 13½, madam.'

'Will that allow for growth?' Mum changed hands again.

'Oh, I should think so.' He looked me up and down and I thought I saw his lip curl. 'He's got plenty of neck for his age already.'

'Oh well, that's one blessing.'

'Yes, isn't it?'

I ground my teeth.

'Would he like large or small sequins?'

'Sequins!' Mum sounded as if she was talking through a small hole in the top of her head.

'It was a stardust shirt I wanted, Mum.'

'Huh, we'd better see what we've got then,' and he went

140

out through a green curtain where there should have been a door.

'What, in heaven's name, is a sequin shirt, Simon?'

'I dunno, Mum.'

'You haven't been telling fibs and got me here under false pretences, have you?'

'No, Mum. Course not.'

She backed back against a square pillar with a mirror on each side. 'Well, I don't much like this place, Simon.'

'Neither do I, Mum.'

'Shall we scoot while the coast's clear?'

'S'sh, 'ere 'e comes.'

The curtains parted and the assistant flounced in balancing three wooden trays in both hands. He pulled the curtain back behind him with the polished toe of his shoe. 'Here we are now.' He looked as if he'd brought up a sour taste. 'Three styles of sequin, small and medium diamonds.'

'See, Mum. Stars.'

'Ah yes.'

'I was about to ask . . . which one you'd prefer.'

'Dunno.' I felt Mum cringe beside me. 'Le's 'ave a look.'

'You can see them.' He turned the boxes round for me. 'You don't have to touch.' His fingers were drumming on the edge of the drawer and I drew my hand back.

'Is this the sort of thing you're after, Simon?'

'M'm. Think so, Mum.' They looked shiny but they didn't sparkle the way Doug Ritson's did. 'P'raps if I could see one stretched out?'

'Or even try it on?'

'Of course, if you really feel that's necessary, but if you went by the collar size you'd know it was ri— Not here!'

My fingers froze on the back of my pullover and I looked at him out of the hood of its neck.

'You don't undress *here*! You try it on in one of the fitting rooms. Dear oh dear!' He scuttled round, thrust a shirt at me and pointed to some curtained cubicles at the far end of the shop and I crept into one wishing I'd thought about it early enough to let Stevey Bacon order it for me.

The curtain slid so easily, on silver rings along a silver pole, that I stood back from it in case I opened it by

141

mistake. Then I took my pullover and shirt off and put them on a chair but they slipped off and, as I went to pick them up, my bottom bumped up against the wall and shot me forward so that I barged into the chair and sent it clattering up against another pole that held the curtain in place. The sound gradually died down and the curtain swung into long green folds. I flattened the shirt out and held it against me. It felt like glass against my warm skin and when I shook it it shimmered like icicles and the puffy sleeves ballooned out. I undid the buttons across the front and slid it over my head. The chill, as it settled across my shoulders, took my breath away, and then my arms were stuck and I was standing there with my head down and my arms jammed up to the wrists in the buttoned-up sleeves.

'Everything all right?'

'Can't get me arms . . .' I struggled but my fingers wouldn't move.

'Hold still or you'll rip the buttons off.'

I could only see him from the middle down.

'Pull your arms back so that I can undo the buttons.'

He smelt of talc and sugar.

I flexed one shoulder and pulled back as he held the sleeve and I felt the cuff loosen and my head slipped through, and he did the same with the other one and I stood up.

'Rip those buttons off and the material'd fray.'

'I'm sorry.'

He was stroking the sleeves back into their original creases. 'And you'd've had to pay for it.'

'I said I'm sorry.'

'All right then. Now try it again, properly.'

It felt as if slugs were crawling all over me as he hovered around and buttoned the shirt up to within one from the top and then priffed the sleeves out. 'Now, tuck it in and have a proper look.' He closed the curtain and I jammed the shirt in round the top of my trousers, without undoing the belt, and walked out casually as if buying a new shirt and looking at myself in the mirror in full view of the street was the sort of thing I did every day.

I couldn't help smiling. It looked better than I'd thought it would but it still looked all wrong from the neck up and from the waist down and then I realised that was the rest of me.

'Well?' The assistant was looking in from the side of the mirror.

'Well what?'

'Do do something with your hair, and tuck it in properly here. You've got it bundled up like an old sack.'

I tensed as he unclipped my snake-belt and released the top button on my trousers and slid my shirt down over my thighs.

'Now do yourself up and put your hair straight.'

I did my belt and top button up without looking at him and tried to comb my hair back.

'Not like that. Dear, dear! Let it fall forward. That's the way it wants to go. Here, look.'

I froze again while he stood over me and parted my hair in the reflection of the mirror and sent a wave across my forehead.

'There you are. Get Mum to put some brilliantine on it and some creases in your trousers and you'll look quite presentable. D'you like it?'

'Yeah. It's smashin'.'

'M'well.' The movement behind us made me start.

'What, Mum?'

'Well, don't you think it's a bit ... well, a bit theatrical?'

'What'cha mean, Mum? It's only cos it looks different.'

'It certainly does. It's a bobby-dazzler. Is it real?'

'Course it's real, Mum. It's just what I wanted.'

'What's it for?'

I screwed my face up so that Mum wouldn't answer him but she didn't take any notice.

'He wants it to go off down to Tangmere to a social or some such thing with dancing and ...'

'Nice.'

'Well, yes. I s'pose so, if you like that sort of thing.' Mum did the top button up on her coat. 'Well, come along, Simon. If you're satisfied let's get it wrapped up and be off home and get the dinner going.'

'Does that mean I can have it, Mum?'

143

'Yes, yes. For goodness' sake . . . Now get it off and let's go.'

The assistant put my shirt in its box and wrapped it up and tied it with shiny string and when we got outside Mum said it was probably all that fancy stuff that made it cost nine shillings and elevenpence and that we could have got two perfectly good shirts for that at Stevey Bacon's and that I needn't think I was coming that old game too often. I didn't answer because I'd seen some of those black jumpers with grey flecks in them and white tapes down the sleeves that Pip Williamson and Tony Cato wore and if I had one people might think I was friends with them; but if they thought that they might tell Mum whose company I was getting into and she'd stop me wearing it anyway. By the time we got home I wanted one so much that I didn't really want my new shirt and I kicked the gate as I went in because I'd been looking forward to having it so much that I wanted to keep on wanting it now I'd got it.

I hung it over the back of my chair in my bedroom, so that the folds fell out, and spent most of the afternoon wondering whether people would notice and think it was flashy and laugh at me or whether, if I wore a pullover over it, nobody'd see it, until it was nearly four o'clock and then I remembered Peter Bennett and had to dash out on my bike.

Mum was ironing when I got home and I came in quietly so she couldn't have heard me.

'. . . dashing off out just on tea time without a word about where he was going.' She was ironing my trousers under a wet towel and she jammed down so that the iron fizzed. 'And then he'll be demanding his tea the moment he gets in, no doubt.'

'I went up to see Peter Bennett.'

'And who's Peter Bennett, may I ask?'

'Boy at school.'

'And what did you want him for, pray?'

'See if 'e was goin' tonight.'

'And is he?'

144

'No.'

'No, I should think not. Perhaps his parents've got more sense.'

' 'e was out.'

'How d'you know he's not going then?'

'Cos I didn't ask 'im.'

'I see.' Mum carved a deep furrow through the damp towel and the ironing-board legs bent. 'So you'll be going all on your own and leaving me here sick with worry if you're late home.'

'I won't be late home, Mum.'

'*If* . . . you're late, and I dread to think what they'll be getting up to down there.'

'We'll only dance and play records and that, Mum.'

'Well, if that's all there is to do why's it so all-fired important for you to go down there?' The legs of the ironing-board bowed as she smoothed the towels and ironed over them. 'And you needn't think this craze for new clothes is going to become a habit.'

'It won't, Mum.'

'Or that you'll be off out late every night.'

'I know I won't, Mum.'

'Oh.' She leant on the iron and looked round at me. 'Why not?'

'Cos you won't flamin' let me. What's for tea?'

'I don't know.' Mum dropped her head and ironed as if she was trying to polish the underside of the iron. 'And don't you dare use that sort of language to me, if you please. I'm only taking an interest in you for your own good—'

'Yeah.'

'You wouldn't like it if we were like some parents and left you completely to your own devices, would you?'

I pressed my fingers on the glass of the china cabinet and watched the print evaporate.

'If we let you roam around at will all night and never took a blind bit of notice what you were up to?'

My mouth shaped out 'wouldn't mind' into the reflection in the glass.

'Well *would* you?'

'No, Mum.'

145

'No. Course you wouldn't.'

I breathed in deeply and watched my chest expand and let it out so that it flopped. 'When is tea, Mum?'

'As soon as I've finished this.' She folded the top towel off and peeled my trousers off the bottom one and held them up by the turn-ups. 'Lovely smart creases. Wish they'd stay like that.'

'They would do if you got me some green gabardine ones.'

'What d'you know about green gabardine trousers?'

'Dicky Jamieson down the camp's got some.'

'Oh.' She held my trousers under her chin and pinched them between her fingers and thumbs and folded them in half. 'And what's so special about him?'

'He's about sixteen and always looks smart.'

'Sure you don't mean spivvy?'

'No, Mum. Smart.'

'And why *green* gabardine?'

'Well, that's what all the boys wear and they'd go nicely with my new stardust shirt.'

'Well, I think your new stardust shirt'll go very well with these nicely pressed trousers. Grey and white is ever so smart.'

'M'm, s'pose so. 'ere, 've you ironed it?'

' *'ere!*' Mum lay my trousers over the arm of the sofa and wiped a wisp of red hair away from her eye with her little finger. ' 'ere! Is that any way to speak to your mother?' She looked at me until I looked sorry. 'Yes, of course I have. It's on your bed.'

'You didn't scorch it, did you?'

'No I didn't scorch it. And what about that little word?'

'What little word?'

'Thank . . .'

'Oh yeah. Thanks, Mum.' I suddenly noticed how blotchy her face was and that she'd been indoors all afternoon on her own, while I was out in the sunshine and Dad was at football, and how the skin under her eyes was wrinkling and she had to put rouge on to make her cheeks red and that I'd been teasing her and she was my mum and she was getting old and that one day she'd— I looked around as if I'd woken up alone. There was a picture of her on the sideboard when she

146

was young in a pleated mauve dress and white shoes with a brown pattern, standing with her hand on a posh polished table with a bowl of white lilac. She'd never have a bowl of all-white flowers in the house nowadays because she said it was bad luck but she wouldn't be able to get away from all white when she was in heaven. You couldn't ever get young again once you'd got old.

'What you staring at, Simon?'

'Just thinking, Mum.'

'Well, p'raps you'd better start thinking about having a wash and getting changed before tea.' She'd wound the flex of the iron round its handle and was folding up the ironing-board. 'And wash properly, mind.'

'Oh, Mum, do I have to?'

'Yes you do. And use some of that pretty violet soap that Nan gave us for Christmas.'

I curled my lip in the reflection from the china cabinet and watched myself as I moved towards the door and 'Be careful, Simon. Oh do look where you're going,' followed me as I bumped against the door and up the passage.

Mum's violet soap was lavender scented. I'd loved the smell of lavender ever since Grandad had used to bring it home and dry it and I'd gone out into the shed with him and he'd let me crush it and put it into bags for Nan, so I washed three times with it and rubbed it under my armpits until it all went sticky and I had to wash it again with clear water to clean it up and it was when I was looking in the medicine cabinet mirror to see if I'd got all the soap off that I noticed that I had hair growing under my armpits and when I looked closer in the other places, where the boys said it would grow, I found it coming up like grass seed and then Mum called me to know 'what the p'liceman' I was playing about at in that bathroom with the door locked and then I went into my bedroom to change.

My stardust shirt was so clean and shiny and my face so rosy from washing that it didn't look like me in the mirror and the glassy cold touch of it on my shoulderblades took my breath away as I combed my hair. My hair was just wet enough from the steam in the bathroom for it to hold in place when I combed it back and I kept looking from the mirror to my Radio Luxemburg calendar to see if I was looking any more like Dicky Valentine. I pulled my stomach in and stuck my chest out but my shirt was so loose that I couldn't see any difference so I just let it go and turned sideways on to see how much my nose stuck out and I wished I was old enough to start shaving. I put a tie on but it made my collar pucker up so I took it off again and undid the top button. This left too much white down my chest but when I undid another one the shirt opened up so that I could see right down to my navel, when I bent forwards, and if the boys saw that they might grab me in front of Christine Lanagan and stick chewing-gum in it, or the packet of salt out of a bag of crisps, so I did it up again and then tried my shirt sleeves buttoned and then rolled up and then Mum called me for tea.

'Cor, look at old spivvy-cum-spivvy!' Dad was stirring his tea with one hand and running a finger of the other down the column of football scores Mum had taken down for him from 'Sports Report'. 'Luton managed a draw away to Arsenal then. Just goes to show you can't go on form.'

'Do you really think so, dear?' Mum was arranging the jam spoon in the jam so that it wasn't jammed all up to the handle.

'What's that, my Ine?'

'Does it look flashy? I had my doubts but it's really rather pretty.' She reached in round the waistband of my trousers. 'If he'd only tuck himself in properly and stand up straight and not slouch forward and—'

'Get out of it, Mum.' I wriggled free. 'It's s'posed to be loose.'

'And turned his collar down so that it lay nice and flat.'

'Hold still, Simon, when Mum's trying to sort you out.'

'Well, does it, dear?'

'Well, I dunno.' Dad stroked his chin where he hadn't shaved. 'Bit bright, I s'pose. Hadn't realised he was growing up so much. Bit more sugar, please.' He held his cup out. 'Is 'e off out?'

'Dear oh dear. You know he's off out down that blessed camp tonight.' She tipped sugar in slowly until he looked at her. 'Else what do you think took me scampering off into

Chichester for on a Saturday morning? And then spending all afternoon getting his clothes ready.'

'Yeah, pity. You missed a good game this afternoon. If we could just play like that for a week or two—'

'And now he's dashing off without even bothering to finish his cup of—'

' 'ere, 's this right, Ina?' He sat over to one side on the shiny surface of the chair to unstick his leg where his football shorts had rucked up. 'Did Dundee lose at 'ome to Partick Thistle?'

'I don't know. If that's what I wrote down they did.'

I slid my chair back but Mum noticed me so I stopped.

'Oh well then, that's another fortune we 'aven't won again this week.' He folded the newspaper and put it under the cushion of the sofa. 'Washed your hands, boy?'

'Yes, Dad.'

'Washed his hands! He's been itching to get away for the past ten minutes. And wash? I should say he's washed. Wonder he's got any blessed skin left.'

I spread a slice of butter and paste.

'All these blessed extra preparations. I don't know what he thinks he's going to be getting up to down that camp tonight.'

I folded my slice over and cut it in half and chewed.

'And what he thinks he's going to be doing from half-past six to nearly ten o'clock I don't—'

'Start at half-past six, Simon?'

'Yes, Dad.'

'Better be off, then. It's almost that now.'

'Yes, Dad.' I pushed my chair back and stood up.

'And I s'pose you'll be back about ten?'

'Yes, Dad.' I bolted and, as I was getting my bike out, I heard Mum telling Dad that I'd been angling for ten o'clock ever since I'd started on about this blasted social, and now it looked as if I'd get my own way again.

My trousers felt like layers of cardboard and my shirt brushed glassy cold against my chest as I wheeled my bike out through the front gate standing up straight so that people

149

didn't think I was slouching to show off. I could imagine Mrs Phillips turning back from her living-room window to Mr Phillips and saying 'Just look at young Simon Wilson all spivved up with his hair greased back and such a deceitful look on his face. He's surely not off down that camp tonight chasing after that Jamaican girl' and Mr Phillips putting his newspaper down and getting up and looking at me and noticing that I'd started to pedal with my heels so that I didn't flatten the creases in my trousers.

Mr Stroud stood up slowly in his shirt sleeves in his front garden to ease his back from raising potatoes but he turned on his fork and followed me as I went past and I waited for him to speak to me first so that I could know how to answer but he went back to his potatoes muttering 'cheeky young devil' and I realised I'd been staring at him but it was too late to say anything now because I was out into Crouch Cross Lane.

One of Jerry Henry's sisters was talking to Lucy Brown outside Derek's house and I looked away from them by pretending to look round to see if anything was coming up behind me, but they nudged each other and I thought I saw Mr Brown's round face at the window calling them in. Further down, Pauline Tennant was sitting on her front grass with her dress pulled down over her knees with Margaret Gander and I said 'hello' to them, so that they didn't think I was snooty, but gruffly so that they didn't think I was sissy. Margaret put her head up close to Pauline's ear and whispered and then Pauline flung her head back and laughed. It was a put-on laugh and anyone watching would have known they were laughing at me so I stuck two fingers up at them.

'You vicious little beast, Simon Wilson.' Pauline's dad was yelling out of the fly window.

I bent my head over the handlebars and didn't look back. I wondered why he'd called me vicious instead of filthy-minded; that's what they usually called us when we did that, but I couldn't see what there was about a V sign that was either vicious or filthy-minded; perhaps the boys down the camp would know.

I stopped at the bottom of Crouch Cross Lane to let

old Mrs Wilkins, from the alms houses, across with a heavy bag from the shop. She looked straight at me and I thought she'd recognised me so I said hello to her and she stopped and turned as if she was treading round the outside of a threepenny bit, and squinted at me.

' 'oo's that?' She shaded her eyes. 'Can't see you.'

'It's me, Mrs Wilkins. Simon Wilson.'

'Simon!' She completed the full circle and tottered towards me. 'My, how you're growing up.'

'Yes, Mrs Wilkins.' I glanced behind me to see if Colin Gander was coming out of his house.

'And all togged up so smart. You're not off out, are you?'

'Yes, Mrs Wilkins. Going down the camp to a dance. And I'm late.'

'Going dancing are you, my love? Well, I'm blowed. S'pose you get that from your Nan.'

'Yeah, spec so.'

'She was a one for dancing, you know.'

'Yeah, I know.' I trod down on my pedal and leant forward against my handlebars.

'Beautiful dresses she used to wear. Course she always was a wonderful needlewoman. Got that from her mother, you know, Simon.'

A centipede was crawling under my front tyre.

'And how is old Mrs Grainger?'

'All right. She's up me aunty's at the moment.' I spun my pedal round and reset my foot against it.

'And Grandad?'

'He's all right, thank you.' I sat forward again. 'I s'pose I'd better be go—'

'Shouldn't wonder if 'e won't be going off up the Common wooding again one'a these fine days.'

'Dunno, Mrs Wilkins.'

'Lovely wood you used to bring us, Simon.'

'Yeah.' Colin's gate latch clicked and I heard him putting the chain on it and telling his little brother to clear off.

'Could just do with a nice load of logs now to set us up for the winter.'

'Yeah, well I'll tell 'im when I see 'im, Mrs Wilkins.' I pulled my sleeve across my chest to look at my watch.

151

'And old Aunty'd love to see you both again some time. She'll be a hundred and one on 17th November, God willing.'

'Cor, well I'm blowed.' I tried to sound amazed as I pictured old Mrs Ewing's wispy hair and sagging wrinkles and the snake-hiss voice, like a pair of squeezed-out bellows, as she said what a lovely little chap I was, and the warm paper feel of her hand as she pressed a sixpence into my palm and the clinging oil-lamp smell of their parlour, with drop-scones warming by the fire, all made me long to close my eyes and sink into her armchair by the fire and snuggle down into her cushions and it made me wonder if I really wanted to go to a social with Brenda Norris after all, but the 66 bus went by so I set myself off and yelled back to her that I'd try to pop up and see her some time, but I wished I hadn't gone off so suddenly when I looked back and saw her standing there as if she'd been stranded at a bus stop.

I put my head down and pedalled as fast as I could but I had to swerve up onto the verge by the bus shelter as Bimbo Lovesey's dad reversed his car out of his drive. He waited for me to go by and I could imagine him making a note of who it was who'd come roaring down through the village far too fast and nearly bumped into him.

Geoff Gibbs's gran was sitting on their wall talking to Mrs Poulter. I eased up and said hello to them but then I ducked my head down so that they couldn't see who it was. They stopped talking as I went by and they were still watching me as I held my breath and turned out of sight past the bend in the road past the entrance to Vine's farm and by the time I'd got past the stink I was nearly at Tangmere Corner and could breathe again.

I crossed the road and rode in and out of the white-bar barriers across the footpath to the camp by standing on the pedals. I got off when I saw an airman coming and got on again when he'd passed me. The lime trees along the estate road smelt of evenings playing cricket and the concrete road hummed against my bike tyres. I went out of my way to go past the swings and the maypole and the witch's hat but they were just hanging limp and grass was growing up through the tarmac and the smooth bits, under the swings, were stippled with rain-dried powdered mud, and then on past where we'd used to play cricket by Mickey Leary's house, but the grass was ankle-deep and they'd boarded up the entrance to the air-raid shelter with corrugated-iron sheets. I stopped off at the cinema but there was nobody about outside and no music from inside, and I didn't want to go in on my own, so I cycled on down past where the Spitfire used to stand, at the main entrance by the guardroom, and over the road and past the sports field towards the airmen's new married quarters.

They'd put new kerbstones in along the road, behind the sports pavilion. They stood out white and smooth against the black tarmac and the wind had blown the hawthorn leaves in drifts against them and I rode through them to make them crunch and to see how close I could get to the kerbstone with my pedal without touching it. I caught a wet cigarette packet full on with my front wheel and it splat open, like a blown-up crisp packet between a bricklayer's palms, and I stood on my pedals to get up more speed to crash through a dead hawthorn branch lying in the leaves. I hit it where it bent and waited for the crack but it sprang sideways and my front wheel slid along it. The back wheel reared up and I went half over the handlebars and collapsed in the leaves with the bike on top of me. The sky was like a cracked blue plate against the branches of the bush and the straggling puffs of white cloud, turning to grey to black in the middle, looked like the belly of a mackerel before Nan cooked it and I wondered if I could get up without getting my shirt dirty. I'd somehow got my left leg trapped through the angle where my pedals were fixed to the frame and my trouser bottom was resting on the chain. I lay still. My back wheel spun slower and stopped. A hawthorn spike was sticking out of the tyre. Perhaps it hadn't gone right in. I gripped it and pulled. There was a hiss and my tyre sank back against the wheel rim. I let my head fall back against my saddle and closed my eyes. Perhaps if I lay still and thought about riding up to the branch and swerved to miss it and counted to fifty and prayed with my eyes closed it would be all right when I opened them again. I put my hands together and wished I hadn't got a puncture and that I could see ahead to what was going to happen before it happened so that I wouldn't do it if it was going to get me into trouble and then I opened one eye to see if I still had a flat tyre. I had so I jumped up and down and kicked my front wheel and sent it slewing round in the leaves and then I bent down to see if I'd broken any spokes and when I saw I hadn't I stood it up roughly so that the front tyre bounced and the back one clattered and it humped every few steps as if it was running over a succession of fingers and I wheeled it up as far as Brenda Norris's house and left it standing against the kerb outside.

One hinge on the front gate was broken and it had been tied up with baling twine. I tried to shut the gate behind me but it wouldn't close so I put it back the way it had been. The front door looked as if it was made of three-ply under the flaking paint and somebody had chalked a target on the wall and there were lots of dents in the brickwork and one or two air-gun slugs were stuck in the cement. I brushed the palms of my hands down my trousers and knocked. A dog barked inside and I stepped back as it started scratching at the bottom of the door and then a heavy curtain was pulled back and the door opened and a leg and a dog's head stuck out together.

'Get back out of the way, Jess.' The man was looking the wrong way. 'Who is it?' His leg was hooked around the dog's neck hauling it back. 'Who're you?'

'Simon, sir. Simon Wilson.'

'Oh yeah.' The man was a bit younger than Dad and he had an airman's blue shirt on, without a tie, and braces. 'You after young Don and Stuart?'

'Well I . . .' Brenda had asked me to call for her but I didn't know if she'd told her dad, and if she hadn't . . .

'Well, come on, lad. Else the dog'll eat through my leg.'

I held my breath and stiffened my fingers. 'Is Brenda coming out?'

He turned away from me and shouted, 'Will you get back, Jess,' and then he leant back into the darkness as if he'd got a burglar round the middle and opened the door a bit wider with his ankle. 'Yes, you'd better come in.'

Jess's nose was sniffing out between his legs and I didn't

know whether to smile at what a playful dog she was or try not to notice he was having trouble with her.

'You off up the social?'

'Yes.' I could feel my shirt pulling out from inside my trousers and I couldn't think what to do with my hands. 'She asked me to call for her.'

'Oh did she ... will you get down, Jess.' He reached back behind him and then stood up with a collie's head between his legs and the black hair bursting out from between his fingers. Its eyes were bulging and its pink tongue was frothing like a river between two banks of teeth. 'You'd better go on in, then maybe she'll settle down.'

I looked back at my bike. If the Norris boys were in they might wonder what I was up to with Brenda and if they weren't I'd have to stand there and talk to her mum and dad and it might be like one of those old books where the man had to go and stand in front of the girl's parents and ask for her hand in marriage and I'd always thought that if that ever happened to me they'd know straight away what I was thinking and give me a clip side the ear.

'It's just through there.' He pointed past me and then he hauled Jess back on her hind legs and I squeezed through with my back against the door post and backed away up the passage and into the living room and he closed the door behind us. 'Sit down, lad. She'll quieten when you're sitting down.'

I tried to look at him and take notice of what he was saying but I was thinking about what that frothing tongue and scrabbling claws would do to my trousers and shirt if she came for me. I dropped into the first chair I came to. Jess stopped hauling at Mr Norris when I sat down and she stopped whining and just panted as he let her go. She came and sniffed up around the tops of my legs and I was glad Brenda wasn't there to see it, and I stroked the rough oily hair around her neck and then she went and lay in a basket under the living-room table with her chin resting on the side and the whites of her eyes watching me. It was then I noticed Brenda's mum. She was sitting in an armchair opposite me by the fire and her skirt and cardigan and brown hair so matched the material on the armchair and the cushions and

155

curtains behind her that I wouldn't have noticed her at all if she hadn't reached down to her needlework basket for her scissors to cut the thread off her darning.

'Just give young Bren a call, John. She's been up there an age already.' She smiled at me over her glasses and smoothed the sock out where she'd been darning it. 'She won't be a minute, Simon. And then I must go up and get ready as well. I'll be along later to help with the tea.' She took her glasses off and folded them into her case and put them into her needlework basket. 'Only use them for sewing you know, Simon.'

'Do you, Mrs Norris?' I sank back into the cushions and let my finger run along the braided bit on the chair arm. It didn't seem as if she'd heard the dog yelping or noticed the damage it might have done to the door with its claws and the way she just sat there re-winding her loose ball of darning wool and humming to herself and arranging her bits of patching material and folding her cloth tape-measure I couldn't imagine the social starting without her or buses leaving her behind or her dashing out into the kitchen because her milk was boiling over and the way she just carried on with what she was doing when she'd never seen me before made me think she wasn't worried about me running off with her spoons or knocking anything over.

'You been to the social before, Simon?'

'No, Mrs Norris.'

She leant back into her chair. The pattern was like falling leaves.

'But I've been in the cinema before.'

'Have you?'

'M'm, to see Randy Turpin boxing once. My grandad didn't come though.'

'Didn't he, dear?'

'No.' The sun through the living-room window caught the longest leaf of her Mother-in-Law's Tongue pot plant and threw its shadow into the fireplace and my eye rested on a spot where the light sparkled on the round bald head of a little brass buddha and, as I watched, the points of light got longer and less distinct.

'Doesn't he like boxing then, Simon?'

'Not much, I don't think. I don't really know. I thought he did.'

'Ah but you do, don't you?' She laughed as she said it and sat forward in her chair. 'So do my boys, and their cousin David.'

I blinked and the buddha stopped sparkling. 'I know. He gave me a black eye once, at the old school.'

'Oh dear.' She stood up and went to the table and felt the tea pot. 'And what did your mother think of that? Cup of tea?'

'I dunno ... m'm, yes please ... I don't think she knew really.'

'But how could she miss—' Her hand hovered over the cups with the milk jug. 'Sugar?'

'Just one please.' I sat back and closed my eyes. 'It's funny really. She must'a done. But I don't remember her ever saying anything about it.'

She stood stirring my tea. 'Ah well,' and then she laughed. 'I expect you come home with so many bumps and bruises she wouldn't've seen it as anything out of the ordinary.' She touched the end of the spoon on the rim of the cup so that it drained dry and didn't leave a mark on the saucer and gave it to me. 'Never mind. I'll just see what's keeping Bren— Here. Hold on a minute.' She was staring down at my feet. 'What's that?'

'What?'

'On the bottom of your trousers.'

'Grease.' I turned the inside of my ankle towards her. 'Off my bike chain. I came off by the pavilion and got a puncture.'

'Dear oh dear. Here, don't touch it.' Her hand rested on my elbow and she went down on one knee. 'It's only on the surface. That'll come off in a jiffy with a drop of turps.'

'Will it?'

'Certainly. And then you'll be the smartest looking lad at the social tonight.'

'Will I really, Mrs Norris?'

'Course you will.' She gave me a sudden squeeze that took my breath away. 'Be done in a trice and I'll get our

John to have a look at your puncture as well. Can't have you walking all the way home pushing your bike, can we?'

'No, I s'pose we can't.' I tried to say thank you as well but my voice was all choked up and I felt daft and then Brenda came down and got me to do the little hook up on the back of her dress while her mum finished off my trousers and then we went out together while her mum hung on to Jess and said she hoped we'd have a lovely time.

I kept Brenda on the inside of the pavement so that if a lorry came swishing round the corner it would hit me and not her – at least that's what Grandad had told me when he was teaching me to be polite – and held my hands behind my back, like Prince Philip did when he and the Queen were looking at special things, in case people saw us and thought we were going steady. She had low cut slip-on brown shoes, with goldy buckles, and long white socks that came to just under her knees and a sort of tartan check skirt of blue and dark blue and bluey-grey and a white blouse that tucked in under the top of her skirt and was covered at the join by a belt, like a gold ring, that had ridden up at the back and showed where she was tucked in. She was plump and warm and made me think of a bantam hen and I could imagine her darning, all cosy in her mum's chair by the fire, and pouring out the tea and making me feel all sleepy just to watch her, but then we stopped at Christine Lanagan's house as she was coming out of the front door. She stopped and put her nylons straight and her snaky long fingers searching for the seam sent shivers down my back and I stood off the balls of my feet with my stomach pulled in and away from Brenda as if I'd only met her by accident and was going to the social on my own.

'I like your shirt, Simon.' Christine Lanagan's pink fingertips touched my sleeve in the crook of my arm and I swallowed over a lump as her fingernail traced a pattern down my forearm. 'Cool and silky. Where'd you get it?'

'S'hat— ugh-h'm— Saturday. Yes, I got it today.'

'I said where'd you get it, not when.'

I was burning from the neck upwards.

158

'It's lovely.' She slid her gold bangle up her arm until it was tight and then down again. 'Did you see Peter?'

'I tried to.'

'You mean you haven't?' Her hand stopped, clasping her bangle. 'You promised.'

'Yeah, I know but—'

'Why didn't you see him?'

'He was out.'

'Oh.' She folded a wisp of hair back behind her ear. 'But you did try for me, didn't you?'

'Yes.' I moved closer to Brenda and tried to believe she was prettier than Christine. 'But he was out. Like I told you.'

'Oh well . . .' She shook her hair back from her shoulders and picked a strand off her pink cardigan. 'Never mind. Perhaps . . .' She giggled and whispered something to Brenda and Brenda laughed and pushed her away and then they went off up the road arm-in-arm and I followed wondering if I was with either of them.

The glass-panelled doors swung shut behind me and I stood on the thick bristle doormat and looked around to see if there was anyone there to let me in. The WAY IN to the cinema was marked, over the top of some red swing doors, in big yellow letters like they had on the sides of the air-force lorries and I was going to follow Christine and Brenda through them but they peeled off to the left and shot off down a passage, which turned out to be to the Ladies when I tried to follow them, so I went back and combed my hair in the reflection from the empty ticket office. I bent my knees forward, to make out I was too tall to see into it properly like I'd seen Big Bim doing in a shop window, and tried to look as if I didn't care who saw me combing my hair. By angling my head to the left I avoided the reflection from outside and could see who was coming. Mickey Leary walked up to the swing doors and stopped and hitched his trousers up and pulled his pullover down and paused with his hand on the handle as Dicky Jamieson appeared. I blew my comb and put it back in my pocket and

159

stood there as if I'd just been going to go in but thought I might as well wait for them.

Mickey Leary had started wearing light-coloured trousers and chunky pullovers, he called sweaters, and thick-soled shoes and, with his black crew-cut glistening with Brylcreem and his eyebrows growing over so that they joined in the middle, he was beginning to look like one of those people the Americans called teenagers from a film about something on the west side of somewhere that the girls were always going on about on the school bus nowadays. He pushed the swing doors open and walked in.

'What'cha, gormless! Anyone about yet?'

'Dunno. Jus' got 'ere meself.'

Mickey stood aside to let Dicky Jamieson in.

'Seen the others?'

'Nope.'

They were both looking at my shirt.

'Coupl'a the girls're in the bog.'

Dicky Jamieson was re-tying his Windsor knot in the reflection from the kiosk.

'I saw 'em as I came in.'

He grinned. 'Where'd ya get that shirt then, Simon?'

'In Bishop's. This mornin'. D'you like it?'

Dicky palmed his wave forward. ''s all right, I s'pose.'

'What's up?' There wasn't anyone at the High School we didn't like who'd got one. 'What's wrong with it?'

Dicky looked at Mickey Leary and they both shrugged. ''s all right, if you like that sort of thing.'

'All the boys at school wear 'em.'

'M'we-ell . . .' Mickey straightened one of his pullover sleeves. 'For school, p'raps.'

I looked down at my shirt and then at his fluffy fawn jumper and Dicky's green herring-bone jacket and green gabardine trousers. 'Don't you like it?'

'Ain' up to me.' Mickey made for the WAY IN. 'You gotta wear it.'

'Well, Christine likes it.'

'Christine would.' They went through the red swing doors together and I followed them and caught the doors as they swung back on me.

It felt like a sin to be turning my back on all that sunshine and I could imagine what Dad would have said about them having all the windows blacked out and the lights on in broad daylight. There were seats on either side of the swing doors and they were stepped so steeply that they looked as if they were stacked on top of each other. There was a low wall, painted cherry red between them and the dance floor and the dance floor ran the length of the building and was as wide as a cricket pitch. It was made of shiny bits of wood and had been polished up like glass and they must have had an awful job not scratching it when they put the boxing ring up there. Beyond that was a stage, with a little staircase going up to it on each side, with heavy red velvet curtains right across from the floor to the ceiling, that were crumpled as if they'd been washed and hung up without being ironed. I put my hands on the top of the low wall and leant back on my fingers. The wall ran down to the end of the seating, marked by a red fire-bucket full of sand, to a gap with a sign over it saying FIRE EXIT. The far wall had two doors in it marked LADIES and GENTLEMEN. Brenda and Christine must have got in there through a back way. Mickey Leary's mum was laying some sandwiches and cakes out on a trestle table against the wall and I watched her so that I could see when the girls came out without anybody seeing me watching for them.

More people were arriving all the time but only a few came in past me through the main door. They seemed to be coming in through the walls; Paul Craven and Fatty Morris emerged from the curtain up on the stage and then Fatty's brother, Charlie, and the Norris boys came down from the high seating beyond the wall above the main entrance and Maurice Geer and Johnny Evenden and Peter Hay appeared from nowhere down by where they were getting the food ready and then a movement caught my eye down towards the girls' toilets. There was a flutter of colour and then the entrance went empty; then another movement as they pushed Brenda out first and the rest of them followed hanging on to each others' arms and collapsing into each other giggling. I stepped back as they went by because they made me think of the geese up

161

Common Lane when I was little and went wooding with Grandad that had hissed at me. I made out I was looking over their heads until they'd gone past and then I went and sat down behind the low wall. The seats were narrow and hard and covered with cloth that felt like bristly suede and kept tilting backwards. The red-curtained stage looked like a castle, set in the middle of the lake of polished wood, and the strip-lights, hanging from the roof on chains, glistened off it and made the browner bits stand out like ripples and then it was water that was moving and if I stood up on the wall I could dive into—

Crash! The swing door slammed back against the wall and Skip Matthews said 'blast it' under his breath and then, 'Gi's 'and, somebody.'

I was on my feet before I'd thought about it and down on the dance floor. My heels clicked on the polished surface and I walked on the balls of my feet in case I scratched it and came face to face with him struggling through the doors with an enormous mahogany radiogram with a plug on a lead wrapped round his ankles.

'Who's that?' His chin was resting on the top of the radiogram and his black beret was crooked. 'Oh, it's you, young Wilson. Untangle this plug for me, will you, and follow me over to the stage else you won't get any scat-singin' or jitterbuggering or whatever it is that you get up to nowadays.'

'I like Johnny Ray, Mr Matthews.' I threaded the plug lead through his legs and lifted it carefully so that it didn't get snagged up around the folding rule in a long slit pocket in the leg of his overalls.

'Oh, do you? Well, I hope you get it. But you'll have to let me fix this up first and then I'd like to get off the premises before you make a start because if it's anything like the caterwauling purgatory our Denis puts us through at home I'd rather be spared it.'

I tried to tell him that Denis liked the Ink Spots and that he wasn't that struck on Johnny Ray but the way he looked as if the camp goalkeeper had let one in through his legs in a cup match made me laugh every time I tried to speak and then he started to laugh as well and before I realised it we'd got across the floor and he'd struggled up the steps to the stage and was asking Mrs Leary where she wanted it and where he could stick the plug.

'He's a humorous little character,' he said to Mrs Leary as she stood wiping shreds of potted meat off her pinny and watching him make sure there was a full supply of needles and that the lid stood up on its own. 'Never 'eard 'im speak before. Must be growing up.'

I made out I hadn't heard and gave the plug a final whack to make sure it was right in and then went back and stood behind him.

'Is that lead long enough, Skip?'

Skip Matthews looked up from peering at the gramophone head where he was screwing in a new needle. 'Ah, there you are. And there's a new box of needles if you use up all those in the box.' He pinched a few between his finger and thumb and let them clatter back into their Bakelite dish set in the brown gauze top. 'What's up with that lead?'

'It's stretched.' I pinged the lead with the toe of my shoe where it reached across the floor from the gramophone to the socket. 'Somebody'll trip over it.'

'Not if they look where they're going, they won't.' He got up off his knees and wiped his hands down his overalls. 'Still you can't bank on it, I s'pose.'

'Can't we have a record on yet, Simon?' Christine Lanagan's head was about level with the top of the stage but Brenda had to peer up from under it.

'Yeah. We're nearly ready.' My feet felt so big compared to their faces that I felt like John Newton looking down on the slaves in the hold of his ship. 'What ones you got?'

'Dicky Valentine and Ann Shelton and my friend's bringing "Shoes that Set my Feet a'Dancing" by Petula Clark.'

'She used to live in Chichester, you know, Christine.'

'Oh did she?' Christine Lanagan was straining back and up to see me. 'Do you know her, then?'

'Oh no.' Some of the other girls had come up now. 'I just heard she did.'

'Oh.'

'Are you putting the records on, Simon?'

'Well, I . . .' Johnny Evenden's sister had never spoken

163

to me before and I was surprised she knew my name.

'Dicky Jamieson usually does that.' Rita Benson had buck teeth. 'And we're not allowed up there.'

'Yeah, why's he allowed up there?' The crowd had got bigger and they were all looking at me.

'I was helping Mr Matthews get the gramophone up.'

' 's not fair if he's allowed up there and we're not.' Rita Benson had always had a runny nose and she'd never stopped moaning when we'd been at the village school. I'd wanted to wring her neck just from looking at her but we'd never been allowed to get angry with her because she had to wear leg-irons. 'And he doesn't even come from Tangmere.'

'But I came down with Bren—'

'Right then.' Skip Matthews stood up from twiddling the tone and sound knobs. 'You know how to use this thing?'

'No, but they say Dicky Jamieson does.'

'M'm. He ought to. The time him and young Denis spend in our front room with it. Where is 'e?'

'Over there.' I pointed to the door. 'Well, he was just now.'

'Just nip out and get 'im then, Simon.' Skip Matthews rested his hand on my shoulder and patted me off down the steps while he bent forwards over the edge of the stage and took records from the girls.

I couldn't see Dicky anywhere, so I went down to the end furthest from the door where Paul Craven and David Harris were having a game of seeing who could hang longest from the wall bars. They'd both gone purple and wouldn't answer when I asked them if they'd seen Dicky. Johnny Harris and Maurice Geer were talking to Johnny Evenden up in the high seats, but they were both looking at his sister, Avril, and they said they didn't know where he was and the girls by the entrance drew in closer as I came up to them and the whisper went up 'Here comes Simon Wilson' like an air-raid warning, so I didn't even bother to ask them. Mickey Leary's mum hadn't seen him either but I had to wait with her while I ate one of her cheesy biscuit things, with a slice of tomato and a blob of bloater paste on top, before I could get away and then I went to the Gents.

It struck cold as I went in and it got colder still nearer

164

the open window. Curls of white paint were flaking off the metal frames and it didn't look as if the windows'd close over the row of iron bars. I stood over the channel for a while but I couldn't go so I did myself up and was walking out when I thought I heard a whisper from one of the cubicles and then I noticed smoke coming out from above one of the doors.

'You in there, Dicky?'

The whispering stopped.

'It's me, Nipper.'

The bolt slid back and the door opened. 'Come in quick.'

I squeezed in beside Dicky Jamieson and Mickey Leary and they closed the door behind me. 'What you doing?'

'Having a fag. Wanna drag?'

I took a puff and passed it on to Mickey. 'What is it?'

'Abdullah.'

'Oh . . . 'ere, Dicky, they're waiting for you.'

'Oh, are they?'

'Yeah. To put the records on.'

Mickey Leary laughed. 'That's messed you up, Dicky.'

'Why's that? I'd do it, Dicky. Would they let me?'

'Do it if you like, Nipper.'

'See, he wants to dance with my sister.' Mickey lifted the toilet seat and spat through his teeth.

'Well he can, can't he?' I could imagine Dicky putting the records on and then dancing down the stairs and flinging his arms round Mickey's big sister Ann, who looked lovely even though she had a big nose and always kept her overcoat on, as the music started in one of those old films from before the war that Dad said were just a lot of silly make-believe.

'Yeah, but that means Larry Eccles'll get in behind 'im as soon as his back's turned. Is he out there?'

'Yes.' I manoeuvred a matchstick so that it lay in the cement channel between the tiles. 'And he was talking to her.'

'M'm.' Dicky put his hand on the bolt and then took it off again.

'But if she likes you she won't go with him and if she doesn't you're better off without . . .'

They were both looking at me and I could hear Mum in the echoes.

'Oh yeah?' They were looking at me as if I'd trodden in something. 'And what makes you such an authority on the subject.'

'Well, jus' stands to reason, don' it?' I edged closer to the door. 'Come on. Let's get goin'.'

They pulled the chain on the cigarette end and I slid the bolt back and stepped out. 'It's all clear.' I dashed out but then I had to wait while they combed their hair.

'What you in such a hurry for anyway, Nipper?' Mickey took a kick at some little kid's ball and two of them U-turned like Jack Russells after a stick.

'He's after Don Norris's sister.'

'I'm not.' I was in between them and people could see we were chatting. 'Has Christine Lanagan got a boy-friend?'

'A-ha!' Mickey nudged me so that I knocked into Dicky and he nudged me back. ' 'adn't when we came in but she might 'ave by now. Better ask her,' and they both stepped back as I was going forward. 'Now's your chance.'

Christine was standing in front of me as if she was playing statues. I shoved my hands into my trouser pockets and then pulled them out again and clamped them to my sides.

'Ask me what, Simon?'

'M'well, I . . . ah . . . nothing.'

'Yes you were, Nipper. You wanted to know—'

'If you'd care to dance, Christine.'

Her lips parted as she caught Mickey Leary grinning. 'But they're not playing anything.'

'Oh, well . . .' I could have kicked Mickey Leary. 'Well, Dicky's just going to . . .' I turned to Dicky Jamieson and mouthed 'go on' at him.

'Come on, Mick.' With the light behind him and his bushy eyebrows and suntan, Dicky looked like an off-duty airman home from abroad. 'We're not wanted here. Let's see if they've got "Such a Night".'

'No, not that.' I coughed and lowered my voice. 'Put on . . . blimey, I dunno. Put on "Charmaine" or something we can waltz to.'

The girls stood back and stopped talking as Dicky Jamieson climbed up onto the stage. He picked a record up, turned

166

it over, then put it down and slipped another one out of its sleeve and looked at first one side and then the other. At last he put it on the turntable and closed the lid and I took Christine's hand and held it forward, like the pointed bit on a sailing ship waiting for the start of a race, as the crackling sounds of waves breaking came out of the amplifier and the needle hit the groove. I closed my eyes and waited to float off to the growing swell of Mantovani but I froze, and the hair stiffened on the back of my neck, as a long accordion note shattered the silence and then, after a pause like somebody coming out of shock, the stuttering stiff-legged chunter of the 'Black and White Polka' and Christine was laughing and spinning with me and my legs were getting all knotted up as round and round we went doing long spinning swings down the length of the hall and a tight turn at the end, like a skater swerving away from a barrier, and then along the wall and turning again, so that my heel clipped the fire bucket, and up again with my hair flopping up and down and getting in my eyes and hers flying back like a black angel in the wind and her dress swirling out so that sometimes it wrapped around me and it felt as if I was wearing it with her. The music stopped with a sudden wheeze, like somebody sitting down with bronchitis, and we came to a stop more or less together and bowed to each other like they'd taught us to at school.

Now the dance had finished I supposed I'd have to say thank you to Christine and leave in case she thought I was pestering her. I wanted to dance with her again because I didn't like the polka much and yet if I hung around she might be annoyed and if I didn't I—

'You're very light on your feet.'

'What?'

'You're very light on your feet, for a boy. Most of the boys clump about like elephants.'

'Am I really?' I flicked my hair back out of my eyes. 'I don't usually like the polka. I prefer waltzing, if I have to do anything.

'Don't you like dancing then?'

'Oh, yes. Here I do but not at school.'

The needle of the next record scratched and hit the

167

groove and there was silence before the whispering, swirling sound of 'Charmaine' filled the hall and Christine leant into me and I leant into her and it seemed as if the lights had gone out because I was pressed right up against her cheek and I knew I was doing it right because I could see out through her hair at Dicky Jamieson who was doing the same thing with Mickey Leary's sister. He opened one eye and winked at me but I made out I hadn't seen him because Mum had once said that dancing cheek to cheek was a serious thing that adults did and nothing to laugh or poke fun at so I concentrated on my feet so that I didn't tread on her toes.

I tried to shuffle into the centre of the floor so that people couldn't see I couldn't dance and I was just getting my arm nicely round her waist so that my fingertips could rest on her ribs when the music stopped and the palm of my left hand felt as if a plaster had been ripped off where she let go so fast.

'Thank you,' she said, as if I was a bus conductor, and she dashed off to the main entrance.

I tried not to look too disappointed. I wished she'd told me if she didn't like people hugging her like that because she'd never understand there was nothing special about a girl's ribs and that I hadn't meant to go any higher and it was her fault anyway for pushing herself so close to me when she must have known how nice it felt, and then I heard her yelling, 'I'm over here, Peter,' and she was running with her arms outstretched and Peter Bennett was holding her where I'd been holding her while her warmth was still on me so I stuck my hands in my pockets and tried to look as if I didn't care.

I drifted off up the side staircase and sat down in the back row and looked down from the dark to the floodlit floor. Peter had horrible, greasy hair that stood up at the front in a hollow wave like the inside of a black shell, and spots, and his trousers were too short and showed his ankle bones, and he was even wearing brown sandals. I stared at my dimmed reflection in the surface of the brass ashtray and tried to work out what was wrong with me.

They were putting on any sort of record now and standing around in groups eating sandwiches and sausage rolls and

168

drinking tea or sucking Kia-Ora orange for sixpence out of cartons with a hole in the top for the straw. Peter pinched the end off the paper covering on his straw and peeled it back a bit and blew so that it flew off like a dart and stuck in Christine's hair and she laughed and poked him in the tummy and then she snuggled up against him and perhaps I should have carried on talking, when she did that to me, like he was to Larry Eccles and not even noticed she was there. There was a rough edge on my thumbnail and I picked at it. Larry Eccles was holding hands with Ann Leary but she was looking past him at Dicky Jamieson, who was making out he was talking to Mickey. I sat forward and bit at the side of my thumb: it smelt of Dicky's Abdullah. Johnny Ray's record of 'Cry' had just finished and Dicky was walking up behind Larry Eccles. Ann drew in closer to Larry and she must have said something to him because he looked round. He had rosy cheeks and looked like Laurence next door had when he'd had wind. He smiled at Dicky and showed him a record in a brown paper sleeve. I couldn't hear what he said but it looked as if he was asking Dicky to put it on for him. Then he turned round. Dicky looked from Larry's hand holding Ann's and then to the back of Larry's head and then his arm came over like a bowler in slow motion. There was a snapping crack and Larry's neck went stiff. Chips of black plastic fell out past his ears and off his shoulders and onto the floor. Dicky slid his hand off Larry's head, as if he was scraping grease off his palm, so that the brown sleeve looked like an Australian hat and he gave it to Larry and walked out.

'Oh dear!'

'What?' I turned round.

'Do you think that hurt?'

'Dunno. Why'd he do it?'

Brenda Norris sat down next to me and put a plate of sandwiches and sausage rolls on my lap and took one that looked like sardine. 'He's jealous, I s'pose. He's been going steady with Ann for ages.'

'But he shouldn't've hit him with that record, should he? They're expensive.'

'Oh yes.' Brenda bit into her sandwich and pushed a

piece of sardine into the corner of her mouth with her little finger. 'But I expect it was Larry's anyway.'

'Does that make it all right then?'

'Well, not really. But he's only got one ... of Guy Mitchell singing "She Wears Red Feathers" and we don't like that one much now. Would you like a sandwich?'

'M'm. Yes please.' I took one and opened it up. It was tomato and some seeds fell onto my lap. 'But it might've been a good one on the back.'

'Doubt it. They aren't usually.'

'Oh.' I ate my sandwich and waited until she looked away and then wiped the tomato seeds off. The boys from the camp were always talking about new records and saying things like 'the one on the back'a' some record or other and I thought it might be the right thing to say but I guessed she knew I didn't really know what they were like because they'd never let me hold one in case I dropped it. 'Do you think he'll get into trouble?'

Brenda munched and shook her head and swallowed. 'Don't suppose so. Anyway it's rotten to tease' – I could feel her looking at me – 'I expect Christine's glad Peter came after all, don't you?'

'Yeah.' I looked around as if I didn't know where they were. 'I expect she is.'

'Would you like some orange?'

'Cor yeah.' My throat felt as if it was lime-scaled like the inside of the kettle. 'But I didn't bring any money.'

'Didn't you?' Brenda licked the tip of her finger and dabbed up pastry chips off the plate. 'I did. I'll get one and we can share it.'

I sat back trying to look unconcerned, as if we were grown up and she was just getting my dinner, but my hands felt awkward folded across my lap and I felt silly when I lounged back and crossed my legs and spread one arm along the backs of the seats. I couldn't look at the others in case they saw me and wanted to know what I was staring at so I looked at Brenda. She went in and out of the groups of people carrying our plate and she gave Paul Craven a little kick when he pinched at her in fun and they all looked as if they were just one big family. I could see Mickey Leary's

170

mum mouth the words 'thank you, dear' as Brenda handed our plate back and the way she smiled as she gave her the Kia-Ora and showed her where her bow had gone crooked in her hair made my skin crinkle with a cold embarrassment.

Brenda was bent forward, like the pictures of Hillary and Sherpa Tensing climbing Everest, as she plodded up the stairs with our drink. She giggled as she bit the end off the straw and blew it at me but that reminded me of Christine so I folded the wrapper up and put it in the ashtray. The plastic hole in the top of the carton cracked as she pushed the straw in and then her lips folded around it and the lines on her neck moved as she swallowed.

'Three coins in the fountain . . .' somebody'd put a Frank Sinatra record on – must be one of the big girls '. . . each one seeking happiness.'

'Would you like some, Simon?' She bent down over me and then sat down.

'M'm, yes please.' I took the carton but she held on to it as she gave it to me and the record went on, 'Three coins in the fountain. Which one will the fountain bless?' and I couldn't make out if I was supposed to be saying an especially big 'thank you' for the drink or if there was something important I should have noticed in the song.

I put the straw to my mouth and went to suck but she was watching me and I wondered if she'd think I was dirty if I didn't wipe it first or if she'd be annoyed if I did, as if I thought she had germs, so I pointed over in the direction of the wall bars and said 'who's that?' so that she looked away and I fumbled with the straw and then put it in my mouth so that she'd know I'd done something but she wouldn't know what.

Brenda had pushed forwards past me but now she relaxed back. 'Who, Simon?'

'Eh?' I looked around as if I was trying to see something. 'Oh, I thought I saw somebody I knew.' I smiled at her as if it wasn't important and sucked at the drink. It was ice cold and had bits in it and Brenda must have still got the taste on her lips because she licked them and raked her bottom one with her teeth.

'Make it mine, make it mine.' I could feel Frank Sinatra

building up to a big finish and he stopped and took a deep breath and then let go 'Ma-ake it mi-h'ine' and Brenda came closer. I watched her out of the corner of my eye and carried on sucking but I could feel my eyes coming together and focusing on the straw until they crossed as her head came in and up from my chest level and then I almost fell out of my seat as I ran out of orange and made that sucking noise on the straw in the bottom of the carton, like the bathwater going down the plughole, that made Mum smack my fingers and turn round to see who'd heard when I did it in the pictures, and when I realised what she was doing I'd got the straw stuck to my lips.

'M'mew b'on't m'weally m'like 'er, m'blew you?' Brenda sounded as if she was talking through a pillow. I tried to listen to what she was saying but the picture of me sitting crushed back against the wall, with an orange carton squashed against my chest so that the straw was almost sticking up my nose, and a shred of sardine sandwich trapped between us made me grin and—

'Simon!' She jerked back and her little face was strained. 'Are you laughing at me?'

'No, Brenda. Honest.'

'You were.'

'I wasn't. I was suffocating.'

'You're not making out I was ... well, that I was ...?' She let out a howl that froze the hair on the back of my neck. 'I hate you, Simon Wilson. You're horrible,' and she jumped up and ran.

My head spun as if somebody'd let a banger off in my ear and 'I hate you' hung in the air like smoke from a green bonfire. I cringed back in my seat as Brenda flounced down the stairs and shook her head as people turned to see what was the matter and I held my breath as she went past her brother Don, but she didn't speak to him and he took no notice of her. She went straight into the Ladies and Mrs Leary followed her and I waited a moment until they put another record on and started dancing and then I slipped down the stairs and went out the side exit by the Gents.

It was cold outside now and dark and the road beside the cinema was flooded with flame-coloured light from the orange street lamps. I expected to hear a posse following me but the only noise was from the music and that snuffed out as the automatic spring on the door pulled it closed. I shivered and shoved my hands in my pockets and started to walk towards the guardroom.

The leaves lay deep and dead at the side of the road. It was only a couple of hours since I'd ridden down here. Then I had one girl-friend and the chance of two but now I hadn't got either of them. I scuffed through the leaves and kicked at a fir cone. Before today I'd have been pleased to have had Brenda for a girl-friend but I hadn't been satisfied. Brenda was always nice to me and she knew lots of people and her brothers would have been friendly if I'd been going steady with her but I'd gone chasing after Christine. I could hear Dad saying 'You're never satisfied with anything, Simon,' but that wasn't the reason Brenda'd gone off in a huff. I looked both ways and then crossed the road to the sports field. Why had she gone off in a huff? It wasn't my fault she'd tried to kiss me before I'd finished my drink and she couldn't possibly know I liked Christine more than her because I hadn't said so and, anyway, she'd got me some food after that and a drink. I was still trying to work it out when I got to her gate and I stopped with my hand on the gate post. My bike was nowhere to be seen.

I walked on up the road for a little way hoping I'd gone to the wrong house but I hadn't so I walked back again. The kitchen light was on and so was the one in the living room but I couldn't see who was in there because the curtains were drawn. I stepped inside the gate. My bike wasn't under the hedge or leaning up against the wall. I stared around the garden hoping it would suddenly appear, but there was nothing in the garden that I could have mistaken it for. There was a path down the side of their house, with a privet hedge alongside, and it was dark where the street light was cut off by the corner of the brickwork. I tiptoed over to it. If my bike was there I could take it and make out I hadn't wanted to disturb anybody.

I had to blink my eyes to get them accustomed to the dark and, when I could see, I found only a heap of coal and a rabbit hutch. I felt with my hands all the way down

173

to the back door but there was no sign of my bike and on the way back I got my foot caught in the rungs of a ladder and tripped forward into a spider's web. I was still wiping it off my face when I heard footsteps on the pavement and the sound of somebody sniffling.

'Oh do come on, Bren.'

'I can't, Mum.'

Their heels slowed on the pavement and I heard their coats brush the hedge as they came through the gate.

'You silly girl. Whatever made you do it?'

'I don't know, Mum.'

There was the crinkling sound of two plastic macs being rubbed together and the grate and click of a key in the lock and the door closed behind them.

I leant back and let my head rest on a rung of the ladder. I didn't know what had happened but whatever it was it was something to do with me and Brenda had told her mum about it. I peeled a shred of spider's web off the side of my nose. Pity, because her mum was nice and she might think that making Brenda cry was a poor way to say 'thank you' for mending my bike. Perhaps her dad hadn't finished it and I'd have to wait there making out I was grateful while her mum was in the other room trying to make Brenda feel better. Maybe it would be better to leave it and tell Dad it had been stolen, but if I did that I'd never be able to take it home again: although I could pretend it had turned up somewhere dumped in the bushes or—

' 'ello' – I froze back against the wall – 'what we got 'ere?'

'Me, Mr Norris.' I moistened my lips. 'I couldn't find my bike.'

'M'm.' I could see him wondering if I was telling the truth. 'Course you couldn't.' He bent and opened the flap on the front of his coal scuttle and started to shovel coal. 'Because it's upside-down in my kitchen.'

'Oh.'

'Mother said you had a puncture.'

'Yes, I have.'

He closed the flap and stood up. 'Well, let's hope that now you haven't.'

174

'Yes, I hope so . . . not.'

He brushed the coal dust off his knees and bent against the weight of the scuttle. 'Come on. Let's see if it'll pump up and have a cup of tea.'

My bike felt better than it had ever felt before. I held the brake handles underneath the handlebars, so that I could sit right back on the saddle and get my head down as if it was a racing bike, and shot up Tangmere Hill as if I was going down it and when I got onto the main road I sat upright and just idled along fast enough to avoid falling off. Mr Norris had made a cup of tea and he'd let me give the tyre a final pump and I was still doing it when Don and Stuart came home and he'd even said he'd seen my dad playing football once and that he'd thought he was very good. Mrs Norris had come down from upstairs and given me a biscuit and then she'd called Brenda to come and have her cocoa and to mind and put her dressing-gown on. I'd drunk my tea and eaten my biscuit as Brenda sat at the kitchen table blowing the froth on her cocoa to the edge of her cup in her teddy-bear pyjamas and a fluffy blue dressing-gown and pink slippers with a thing like Mum's powder puff on each toe. I'd caught her looking at me once, through the steam, and I'd smiled, because her mum had been watching us, and she'd smiled back and then her mum had had a coughing fit and told her dad that she needed her back rubbing with something and that would leave a chair free at the table and that I might as well sit down as stand up, and she'd taken Mr Norris into the living room although he'd said there was plenty of time for that and I'd thought he meant her back but she laughed and coughed again so I wasn't sure. Brenda said she always had cocoa before she went to bed because it was important that she had lots of sleep so that she didn't get bags under her eyes for when she got older and then she'd held the front door open for me while I'd wheeled my bike out and she'd smelt all pink, of Pears soap and talcum powder, as she'd leant across the cross-bar to kiss my cheek with her eyes closed. I'd even been careful to remember to close their gate as I came out and I hadn't sworn when I clouted myself on the ankle with the pedal as I tried to turn and wave and get on at the same time; but as I turned into the village I remembered that I hadn't said thank you to Mr Norris . . . or perhaps I had, earlier on, and just hadn't remembered. Somehow I didn't think they'd mind.

Mum met me at the back door as the last strains of the signature tune of 'Saturday Night Theatre' were draining away.

'You're looking mighty smug, Simon. What've you been up to?'

'Nothing, Mum.'

'Well you're jolly well late enough. Wherever have you been?'

'Down the Norris's.'

Her eyes narrowed as she switched the kettle on. 'I thought you were going to some blessed social.'

'Oh yes, I did. But I went to the Norris's after.'

'Whatever for?' She was standing over the empty tea pot with the spoon from the caddy poised above it.

'I took— I had to pick my bike up.'

'Whatever—'

'I got a puncture and her dad mended it for me.'

'*Her* dad?'

'Mr Norris.'

'Oh, I see.' Mum sank back like a pricked balloon. 'And now you'd like a cup of tea, I suppose?' She'd put two scoops in and was ready with a third.

'No thanks, Mum.'

'Why not?'

'I had one down the—'

'Huh.' She slammed the tea-pot lid down and jammed the tea cosy on top of it and left her hands pressing down on it as if she thought it was going to jump off again.

I put my arm around her shoulder and pressed her head against my neck. 'What's up, Mum?'

She was straining away from me and then she pulled away. 'Nothing.' She was suddenly brisk as if it was Monday morning and I was late for school. 'Nothing at all. Off you go now and get washed and ready for bed and then come

176

out for your cup of tea, if you're not too big to be about in your jimmy-jams.'

'Oh, Mu-um.'

'No. Off you go. Quick.' She made out she was giving me a playful pat on the bottom but her eyes weren't laughing and when I got back I sat and drank my tea and watched her not looking at me and wondered what I'd done wrong and then I went to bed and tried to think how I could make it up to her but all I could think about was pink teddy-bears and fluffy slippers and I went to sleep with the smell of Pears soap in my pillow.

7

I'd been sitting on the school bus with Brenda for months and it was like having a sister and a mum all rolled into one. She never made a fuss if I couldn't think of anything to say and sometimes I didn't speak to her at all, if I was staring out over the fields or watching the streaks of rain trembling across the window, but I only had to say 'What did you do last night?' and it was like turning on a tap and she chattered on until we stopped at the end of the school drive and got out and even then she kept on going until I said 'Bye, then. See you tonight' and she'd smile and march off with her friends.

'I like cooking.' She'd made an apple tart at school today and she was sitting there with it on her lap in a Tea-Time Assorted biscuit tin. 'And I help Mum dressmaking sometimes and we go round the shops on a Saturday morning.'

'Oh yeah.'

'And I still like playing with dolls.'

'Oh do you?'

'I don't see why I shouldn't if I want to.'

'No, course not.' I sat down lower so that the boys couldn't hear. 'It's none of their business.'

'That's what I told my brothers.' She looked back at Don and Stuart and snuggled down next to me and told me a lot of other things she told them that sounded as if it was really her mother talking and I listened to the babble of her voice without having to hear what she was saying.

I touched my finger against the window and moved it up and down tracing the outline of the horizon. Mum had told me once that she'd had a china doll, when she was a girl, that she'd worshipped but another girl had got jealous of it one day and smashed it to smithereens: poor old Mum had lost her temper then and bitten into the girl's arm until she screamed but Mum had hung on until the headmaster and his wife came out and forced her mouth open and she'd said nothing could ever replace that doll for her. I hadn't realised I'd remembered her telling me that and that made me wonder if I'd dreamt it, and after that I didn't sit much next to Brenda because she made me remember things that made me sad and the boys started saying I was getting softer than ever so I started sitting over with my legs down the gangway and talking to Alan Jasper and Eddy Hender.

Alan was a good cricketer and the cricket season had started about the time it started raining. I didn't like playing cricket at the Lincs because we could only play at lunchtimes and in the games periods whereas we'd played every playtime at the village school but we hadn't had pads and nets and batting gloves there and it took ages to cart the cricket bag over to the nets from the store in the gym so I supposed that was the reason we could only play at lunchtimes. At first I'd stood back and watched Alan and the boys in the Firm playing, because they were big and strong and always pushing people about and I'd assumed they'd be able to bowl fast and slog the ball about, but most of them only wanted to play for a few minutes and then they got bored and went and played wrestling in the long grass by the sand pit. Spider Webb was over six foot tall and had lived in Rhodesia. He could bowl fast but he looked like the sails of a windmill as he came lollholloping up to the wicket, and he often bowled short outside the off stump so that even I could hit them and once I hit Ritson up the backside and after that they had their play fights behind the hedge. I tried to show them how to hold the bat like they did in Tom Graveney's book about batting in the library but they couldn't seem to get the hang of it and they all jumped out of the way if we bowled on their leg stump. Alan was the best of the lot and he bowled fast and had a good length but somehow they all bounced properly so they were fairly easy to hit and he never took a wicket. They all said I was the luckiest bowler alive because mine either skidded along the ground or hit a bump and swerved all over the place and if they did hit one it usually went for a catch and one day I hit Pip Williamson on the ankle.

179

'Bloody 'ell, Nipper!' Pip dropped the bat and hopped over to me and I ducked. 'You could've told me you were a fast bowler.'

'Sorry, Pip.'

'Lotta fuckin' good bein' sorry, i'n' it?' He knelt and pulled his jeans up and his sock down. 'Look at the size'a that bleedin' bruise.'

'Shall I get you a cold cloth from the gardening class?'

'You can stuff yer cold cloth up yer— Cor blimey!' He hauled himself up by grabbing hold of Scabby Whitehouse and hobbled off between him and Tony Cato and they disappeared amongst the raspberry canes for a smoke.

'Try to keep 'em off the leg, Simon.' Mr Heater had been watching from the roller. 'Especially when the boys aren't wearing pads.'

'You should always wear pads, shouldn't you, sir?' Eaton was a first year with pebble-dash glasses.

'Yes, Eaton.'

' 'specially when Wilson's bowling, eh, sir?'

'Go on, push off, Eaton.' Geoff Gibbs was trying to bowl at Eddy Hender's legs.

'You're one of the best bowlers in the school, Wilson.' Eaton had stuck two fingers up at Geoff's back.

'Clear off, Eaton, you're puttin' me off.' Geoff shielded his eyes as his ball sailed over the fence and onto the by-pass and bounced between a Ford Consul and a dustcart. 'And you can go and get that, Hender.'

'Off you go, Gibbs. Get it yourself. If you bowl rubbish you can expect to be carted . . . and, Simon?'

'Yes, sir.'

'If you bowl to leg pitch 'em on middle and leg stump because you're moving them both ways.'

'Am I, sir?'

'Yes. You're coming on very well and we may want you for the game against East Dean.'

Ritson and Farmer and the rest of the Firm started talking to me more when they heard I'd been picked for the school.

'It's usually only the pets in the sixth form 'oo get time off to play cricket.' Ritson had started shaving and using

180

after-shave. 'An' they never pick anyone from the scruffs' classes, do they, Fag?'

'Nah.' Paul Farmer looked as if he was asleep. 'Chance ta show the creeps.'

'Yeah, then p'raps we'll get a chance.' Ritson trod on a piece of chalk and scratched it out on the tarmac. 'C'mon, Fag. Le's see if there's any apples worth 'avin' down the farm.'

I went to follow them but I noticed Tupper and Denyer watching me.

'What's up with you lot?'

'Nothin'.'

'Yes there is.'

Tupper edged his toe towards Denyer and looked at him and then they both looked at me. 'S'pose now you're in with the Firm you'll be pushin' the rest of us around?'

'Don't s'pose so.' – Clements and Webb had joined them. 'They probably only want me cos I'm in the school team but I don't s'pose I'll do much good.'

'M'm.'

'An' I expect I'll soon get dropped an' then they'll sling me out again.'

'Yeah, well, that's all right then.'

They wandered off in the direction of the science lab and I started off after Ritson and Farmer, but they weren't in the lane to the farm and I didn't want to get caught scrumping apples so I went down to the cricket nets to see if I could improve my batting.

Mum and Dad made me start going to bed early when they heard I was going to play for the school and Mum showed me how to whiten my cricket boots and she and Nan looked to see if my trousers still fitted and they found the white plastic belt off one of Nan's dresses and they got her friend, Mrs Kaley from Eastergate, to knit arms onto the sweater she'd made me last year and they bought me a new pair of socks and I practised putting my cricket boots on in the back garden and Dad showed me how to tie them up. It rained without stopping up to the day of the match

181

and Gibbser and the rest of them laughed at me as I walked up to Hanover Corner for the school bus that morning, with my kit in Old Gran's little case, and they said they didn't know about cricket boots but that if I'd had any sense I'd have worn my wellingtons, but they weren't laughing at half-past three when I went out of school early to get on the coach.

I couldn't believe it. Mr Hainsworth was the same Dougie Hainsworth that the camp kids had talked about before we'd started at the Lincs. He was always in charge of the football and cricket first team and he'd once played for Charlton Athletic and yet he called me by my first name when he told me to take hold of the other end of the cricket bag and he even said 'thank you' when we put it down in the gangway of Breeze's 23-seater; and I hardly dared breathe when the school captain, Bob Heller, and Gordon College, the vice-captain, got on and sat down behind me; and there was Philip Witney, who they said could bowl googlies, and Mick Miller, who was studying for something called O levels, and several others who were all in the sixth form and wore full school uniform and spent their time doing special studies and mock exams and were always getting their names read out in assembly for doing something special.

The bus rolled out over the tarmac and then steadied as the driver lined it up onto the narrow road that linked the playground to the drive through the fields of chickweed that were going to clear and seed one day and turn into lawns and cricket pitches, and turned right, out of the school drive, past the bus station and on up through the town.

I'd never been to West Dean from this direction before and I wondered if the driver knew the right way when he doubled back around Adelaide Road, by the St Richard's Hospital to go up through the posh houses in Summersdale because it would have been better to have gone the way Dad told the coach driver to go when we played football there: but he must have known what he was doing because he stopped just before the Royal West Sussex Hospital and jumped down from his driver's cab and left the engine running and dashed across the road to post a letter.

'Remember they've got a short boundary on the leg

182

side from the end you usually open from, Bob.' Dougie Hainsworth had filled his pipe but he hadn't lit it. 'So you'll need a deepish fine leg and a backward square.'

Bob Heller's rosy cheeks rounded and I noticed how white his face was where it wasn't red. 'Bowl on the off then.'

'H'm.' Dougie Hainsworth adjusted the pencils in the top pocket of his Harris tweed jacket and covered them over with his fancy handkerchief. 'You'll have to, but that Pasterman pulls everything to leg anyway, doesn't he, Witney?'

Philip Witney's head dropped.

'We don't bowl half-volleys into Pasterman's leg stump, do we, Witney?'

'No, sir.'

'No, sir. We don't. Especially if we want to hang onto the ball long enough to finish the game.' Mr Hainsworth looked severely at the back of Philip's seat and then he turned back to Heller and College. 'And you'll be keeping wicket of course, Gordon.'

Gordon College pursed his lips and I couldn't tell if Mr Hainsworth was asking him or telling him; the main thing was that I didn't have to go there so I might get a bowl.

The rain had stopped about lunch-time and the wind had got up and it was blowing the mock-orange blossom off the trees as we came into East Dean and the car in front left two print patterns of squashed petals on the road. I'd expected us to turn off under the railway bridge where they played football but we slowed down in the middle of the village and turned right down a side road with a little shop at the corner. The road dropped suddenly and the Downs loomed up in front of us as if we were going to drive under them and then we slowed down. There was a stream running along the road with a hedge the other side that grew out and over and into the water in places. The coach stopped by a gap in the hedge. The meadow had been mown in the middle and two boys were sticking in the stumps. I'd expected that playing in a proper match would mean changing in a proper wooden changing-room with steps going up to it and an old man in an overcoat and trilby marking out the creases with a pot of whitewash and a distemper-brush and a sight screen at

183

each end and deck-chairs for people to sit in and watch, but all I could see was the two boys slinging the stumps about like spears and an old shed that looked as if it had been taken off an allotment and the grass was too long for football let alone cricket. I couldn't see how I was going to see if the ball had gone for four because there were no flags to mark the boundary and there was an oak tree growing in one corner of the pitch.

'Is this it, sir?'

'M'm.' Dougie Hainsworth pressed the tobacco into his unlit pipe and sucked on it and then put it, stem first, into his breast pocket. 'Yes, here we are. Out you get.'

I stood up to get off but the others all went first and I got further behind because I couldn't close the sliding door on the bus with one hand so, in the end, I had to put my case down on the soggy verge and use both hands. They'd disappeared by the time I'd got it closed and there didn't seem to be any way into the field except across a little bridge made of railway sleepers so I crossed that and saw them stip-stepping onto dry bits along the side of the hedge about a hundred yards further up and heading for the shed. The door opened and a man with long wisps of hair combed right over his head and a navy roll-topped pullover came out.

'Doug!'

'Cecil!'

They met and shook hands.

'Is it playable?' Dougie Hainsworth lifted one foot and looked at the wet hole his shoe had made.

'Ah, that's just where it lays under this hedge.' Mr Cecil stroked a clump of grass with the toe of his wellington boot. 'It's firmer further out and the wicket's in quite good shape. But we've had to settle for one of the outer tracks, I'm afraid, because the village've got a fixture here on Saturday.'

'I see.' Dougie Hainsworth was nodding as Mr Cecil was speaking and the rest of the team had formed up behind him like a flight of migrating geese. 'I suppose you've got pretty much the same team?'

'Ye-es, pretty much the same.' Mr Cecil looked up at the shed. 'You . . . ? Any gains or losses to speak of?'

184

Dougie Hainsworth took his pipe out of his mouth. 'N-no.' He shook his match box and slid it open. 'One or two of the older ones've left and we've drafted in replacements.'

'Endersby?'

Dougie Hainsworth scraped his match and cupped his hands around his pipe. 'Working. Left and got a decent job with Plumber and Reading.'

'Not playing then?'

'. . . and doing very nicely, I'm told.'

'Good. Good, Doug. I'm pleased to hear it.' Mr Cecil put his arm along Dougie Hainsworth's shoulder as if he was showing him the way. 'Wonderful opening bat. Glorious range of shots. We'll miss seeing him in the school matches.'

'M'm. But I suppose we can still look forward to fireworks from Master Pasterman?'

'Oh yes, bless you, Doug.' Mr Cecil's wellingtons squelched as he clapped Mr Hainsworth on the back. 'He's in great form. Wonderful eye. He'll hit anything. Mind you—' He pulled Mr Hainsworth aside and closer as if he was going to tell him something that they weren't supposed to talk about. 'His younger brother looks an even better prospect.'

'You don't say.' Mr Hainsworth blew a puff of smoke into the air and shot short spurts into it. 'Just a first former yet, I suppose?'

'M'm. Still very young of course.'

'Be asking a bit much to pitch him in at this level.'

'It is asking a lot, but . . .'

'But what?' Dougie Hainsworth stuck his pipe in his mouth as if he was plugging a leak.

'Well, I'm so short of—'

'He's playing then?'

'Yes.'

Dougie Hainsworth flexed his shoulders and resettled his jacket. 'Good!' He clasped the bowl of his pipe in the palm of his hand. 'But lead on.' He forced a smile that looked as if he'd just been asked to take the Chairman of the Chichester Ladies' Guild on a tour of the school. 'Because I don't suppose the light'll hold long this evening.'

185

They said we could get more light in the changing room by leaving the door open but that that would take up more space and one of their players said he thought old Gaffer Jenkins had an oil lamp about somewhere and they found it hanging on a nail on the wall behind a wheelbarrow. It would have been cosy with the oil lamp making shadows amongst the rafters if I hadn't been preoccupied with getting my trousers off, standing up, without losing my case or treading on somebody or putting my foot down on the earth floor and getting all dirty so that it would come off on my new white socks. It got so tight at one point that I had to wait to put my other leg in until Mick Miller stood up straight so that I could bend down to find my other trouser leg; and then my toe got caught up and I hopped about like an upended carrot where I'd stuck my foot in my pocket. I had to wait until the West Dean team had gone out to practise before I could put my boots on and then I found that the eyelet on Nan's belt had broken and I either had to have it too tight, so that my trousers puckered up at the front like a pigeon's crop, or too loose so that they slipped out from under it and showed the waistband of my pants, so I had to wait until they'd all gone out and do it up tightly with the belt and then fold the spare bit over at the top and cover it with my sweater. In the end it looked quite good except for making my trousers a bit short, but I'd noticed Bob Heller's trousers were a bit short as well so perhaps that didn't matter.

Our team were all in white and were out looking at the wicket. I went out to join them and skirted round West Dean who were practising in front of the hut. Two boys were batting and the others were bowling at them with compound cricket balls, a hairless tennis ball and a golf ball that stuck in the mud like a bullet. Some of them had white shirts on and one or two had whitish trousers that weren't cricket trousers and they wore an assortment of boots and plimsolls but none of them had cricket boots and they swung the bat as if they were playing in the road and stopped the ball with their feet and didn't bring their arms over properly when they bowled and they looked so like a group of boys who were just having

a game of cricket that they couldn't possibly be any good at
playing in a proper match and I couldn't think how even
Pasterman, whoever he was, could be any good if he played
for a team that couldn't be bothered to get the proper outfit;
but as I watched I noticed they made the ball whizz in the
air as they bowled and when they hit it it went knee-high
for a long time before it came down and they were tossing
the balls about to each other as if they were throwing-in to
the wicket keeper and the spray from the grass was flying off
the balls as they threw them and it made my fingers sting to
watch them and I backed away out to the pitch to see if I
could see what the others were looking at. I'd seen the men
in the village team go out to inspect the wicket before they
played sometimes and once I'd been playing near them and
listened to what they'd been saying but, when I'd gone and
looked at the bit of grass they'd been talking about, I hadn't
seen anything about it to show it would 'take spin' or 'kick
up a bit' and I wondered if it was something to do with the
way they cut the grass or some sort of special weedkiller or
fertiliser that they used but I seemed to be the only one who
didn't know so I thought it was better not to ask.

'There's precious little life in this.' Dougie Hainsworth
was pressing the short-cut wicket with his thumb.

'And there's a rough bit over here.' Bob Heller was
pointing with his toe at a patch of plantains and I could
imagine the ball bouncing towards the wicket or away from
it, depending on which side it hit, or skidding straight
through on the ground if it hit in the middle, where the
heart was below the level of the grass and the leaves were
deep green and hard and slippery.

'Ye-es.' Dougie Hainsworth touched his toe under the
head of a daisy the mower had missed. 'It's a bit wide of
the off stump but if Witney can get them to move in a bit
it could be useful.'

Philip Witney gauged the distance from the centre of the
plantain to the stumps and then he looked over towards the
hedge on the leg side. 'What about Pasterman?'

'What about Pasterman?'

'Well, he hits them over there, sir.'

'Not if you vary your pace.' Dougie Hainsworth waggled

187

his pipe at Witney. 'Pace and length. Keep him guessing.'

'Well, it didn't make much difference last time, sir.'

I sidled in closer because Witney didn't sound as if he wanted to bowl and the way Mr Hainsworth explained it it was going to be easy to take wickets and they wouldn't have a chance.

'I could turn 'em in from there, sir.'

Dougie Hainsworth re-lit his pipe. 'We'll start off with our usual seam attack and go for some early wickets and change to spin when Pasterman comes in because I've an idea this evening will be the scene of Witney's revenge.'

Bob Heller won the toss and Mr Hainsworth told him to bat first.

'Good luck, lads.' Mr Hainsworth was buttoning up his umpire's coat. 'Now you keep your end up and just stay there, Witney, while Gordon goes for the runs.' He patted College on the shoulder as if he'd already got his fifty. 'And remember . . . once we're out there I'm absolutely impartial.'

Dougie Hainsworth marched out puffing on his pipe and holding his hand out occasionally to show it had stopped raining but our openers trudged after him as if they were being expelled.

The West Dean opening bowler was a boy called Sainty who was over six foot tall and worked weekends with his uncle felling trees. His first ball felled the wicket-keeper and his second nearly speared him with College's middle stump. We were three wickets for no runs at the end of the first over and a leg-break bowler called Hutson reckoned we'd be home in time for 'Dick Barton' at quarter-past six. Bob Heller and Witney made a bit of a stand, with the ball flying off their arms and legs, until Heller slipped ducking a bouncer and sat on his stumps. Mick Miller hit Sainty's brother for a four through the slips but then Sainty sent his bat spinning out of his hands and the wicket-keeper caught him off the handle.

'Better get padded up, Wilson.' Miller kicked mud off his boots against the shed step.

'When'm I in then?'

'Last.'

'Oh.'

My fingers were numb and I couldn't do the buckles up on my pads and the plastic box they gave me took my breath away when I slid it inside my pants and there were holes in the batting gloves that left the fingers flapping about like soggy sausages.

'You any good, Wilson?'

'Dunno.'

'Well, we'll soon see. Grant's out.'

My feet sank into the muddy grass up to my ankles and my pad straps flapped and I felt sick.

John Grant stopped as I passed him. 'If you can see 'em, hit 'em.'

'Right.'

'An' if you don't, duck.'

'Okay.'

'The bloke the other end's not much, if you can survive that long.'

'Thanks.'

I stood my bat up and asked for middle and leg and scratched a mark in the mud as if it was my last will and testament and looked up. Sainty was standing away in the distance tossing the ball from hand to hand as if it was a grenade. I stepped back and looked around the field. The boy at square-leg was picking his nose and there was a rook asleep in the oak tree.

'Pla-ay!' Mr Cecil hunched up over the stumps and Sainty trod the ground.

My arms froze and I leant into my bat. Sainty took a step back and his shoulders swelled. He took a half-leap in the air and thundered down on me. There was a swirl of arms and legs and a black dot appeared out of nowhere and whizzed past my ear.

'Over!'

The West Dean players changed over and they looked at me as they went by as if I'd narrowly missed an accident. I leant back off my bat and cold sweat ran down my back and it felt as if I'd wet myself. I prayed when they appealed for leg-before-wicket against the mud-spattered Witney and

189

gave thanks when Dougie gave him out and I got back to the shed as fast as my flapping pads would let me.

They clapped Witney in for lasting all the innings.

'And you should have held back for him, son.' Mr Hainsworth had taken me on one side. 'And clapped him in with the others.' He was fiddling with the six pebbles in his umpire's pocket. 'But that's just inexperience.'

'Yes, sir.' I was too cold to be upset.

'And now lads . . .' Mr Hainsworth gathered our team around him and College looked up from putting on his wicket-keeping pads. 'I know forty-eight's not much of a score but it should take some getting if you bowl tight.'

I shivered and clamped my jaw to stop my teeth chattering.

'And I suggest we take a chance, Bob.'

Bob Heller took his hands out of his pockets.

'You bowl the first over and we'll have Witney open at the other end with spin.'

Witney looked as if he had a migraine.

'That ought to fox 'em.'

'Beats me!'

'Pardon, Hutson?'

'Nothing, sir.'

Dougy Hainsworth re-buttoned his umpire's coat and re-lit his pipe. 'Right. Get your field set up and stay on your toes.'

They put me at fine leg in a patch of slurry that was seeping through the hedge from the silage pit in the next field and I felt it filling my boots as a weasel-faced boy took centre.

'Go on, Tich. Then we can all go 'ome,' came from the shed as Heller came up to bowl and a great cheer went up as Pasterman leg-glanced it and it sprayed my face with muddy water as it shot past me for four.

The Pasterman brothers got our runs after six overs with Teddy hitting the second ball of Witney's third over for six into the oak tree and Tich finished with another one off the fourth that cleared the hedge and bounced off the top of our bus and plopped into a rain-water butt at the side of the Hare and Thistle on the other side of the road.

Mr Hainsworth and Mr Cecil shook hands and we trailed off.

The settling sound of the misty drizzle on the tin roof seemed to dampen the light from the oil lamp and we whispered, if we spoke at all, even if it was only to tell somebody to watch where they were sticking their great feet. Mr Cecil shushed a boy who said half of them could have stayed at home and Mr Hainsworth said we might as well stand on our cricket trousers to change our socks because they couldn't get much dirtier and not to worry too much because we'd have proper changing facilities when we had the return match at the Lincs, but Mr Cecil reminded him that we didn't know when that would be because we hadn't got a pitch fit to play on yet.

I took my wet cricket socks off and wrung them out and then wrung my dry socks out and put them on. My dry socks felt as wet as my wet socks, but colder, and they clung to my trousers when I tried to get my leg through so that I overbalanced into Miller who bumped into somebody else who trod on Dougie Hainsworth's toe and smeared mud all over the brown brogues that he said he'd spent all afternoon preserving from the elements in galoshes. When I'd finally got my trousers on I found I'd lost a shoe and when that came to light my fingers were too numb to tie my laces and the others had gone and I had to run after them through the mud with my shoes half on and my coat over my arm because I'd hung it under a leak in the shed and it was soaked all down the back.

Mum couldn't believe how I'd managed to get my clothes in such a state if I hadn't bowled and had only faced one ball and Dad wondered why they'd put me in the team in the first place if they weren't going to let me do anything. I lay in the bath wondering if I'd lost my chance of playing for the school for ever or if, in years to come, people would look in the scorebook and wonder how many runs I might have got if I hadn't gone in last and run out of partners.

That first summer at the Lincs was the wettest in living memory, everyone said, and was probably due to the atom bomb tests they'd been carrying out in a place in the Pacific called Christmas Island. It was too wet for cricket and too wet for our gardening lessons and too wet even to go out to play at playtimes and I was beginning to think there was no other smell in the world except warm wet mackintoshes, as I sat in the cloakrooms wondering if Christmas Island was at all like the Coral Island in the book or even Treasure Island and if it was I hoped they wouldn't blow them all up but leave a few for me to get lost on when I got older, when I heard a whisper that some of the soft kids went into the library to read at playtimes. I went past it a few times to get something from my locker and then I had a look at it from the back stairs and then one day I went in.

There were rows and rows of shelves of books from the floor to the ceiling that came out between the windows and in the gloomy bit at the end of each row they'd put a bambooey-looking table with a jungly green plant that made me think of Croc and his men being pursued by headhunters through the undergrowth in *Amazon Adventure*. In the middle of the room they'd put squares of tables sideways on so that they looked like diamonds. They were made of a special yellowy wood that had a flared-out grain like a tea stain that had dried and they'd been varnished up so smooth that you could draw on them with ink and then wipe it off again.

The windows were misted up and they reflected the electric light back into the room. Most of the brainy kids from 4 and 5A were here and one, called Simpson, who always carried a briefcase that was too full to close and looked as if he had a cushion stuffed up his back, nudged a boy called Smythe next to him and nodded at me and Smythe took his glasses off and turned his book over.

'What you doing in here, Wilson?'

'Lookin' f'ra book.'

'Have you had permission to come in here?'

'Much as you 'ave.' There they sat with their rosy-pink faces and dark-green pullovers with creases in the sleeves like best blooms at a flower show drumming their white fingers, with perfectly rounded half-moons, on the desktops.

'It's our form room.'

'So what?' I scuffed the heel of my right shoe over the

scuffed toe of my left one where I'd been kneeling down on the tarmac to play fag cards, before it had started to rain harder, and I could feel where my trousers had gone tighter at the back where Pete Farmer had put some chewing-gum down for me to sit in when we changed from Scripture to Geography. 'It's all the same school, ain't it?'

'But it's our classroom. We've been given it.' They were clustering together like rabbits in a cage.

'And some of us are trying to study.' This was a boy called Liversidge from 5-Academic. 'Some of us are taking O levels.'

'So might I.'

'O-ho!' Smythe and Simpson bent their heads and sniggered behind their hands.

'I might do, one day.'

'One day!' Liversidge sniffed and went back to his book.

I clenched my fists and hoped we played them at cricket in the inter-form matches some time and then I got a book out about boxing and went and leant against the radiator under the window until the dried chewing-gum on my trousers softened and then I leant against their nice clean wall until the bell went so that when I moved a chunk stuck to it and came away from me in a long thinning trail that finally broke and curled up in the heat from the radiator, but I regretted it later when I found I was stuck to the seat in History.

Mum held my trousers up to the light and said they were ruined. She said it again and added 'well and truly' when she saw I wasn't listening and then she wanted to know what stupid nonsense I was on about when I said if it was as bad as all that she could cut a bit out and patch it. If she'd asked me quietly how it happened I think I'd have burst into tears or if she'd boxed my ears I'd have laid my head on her lap and howled but seeing her holding them up as if the future of the world depended on them made me want to throw a brass ornament through the china-cabinet door and then walk out, like some men in a factory had done in the *Daily Express*, when the boss had closed their canteen, and which a spokesman for the National Union of Boilermakers had said was 'totally justified in view of management's unreasonable attitude' over something I couldn't really understand, so I slammed the back door behind me and went up and smoked a dog end behind the chicken house.

It had stopped raining at last but the summer had gone mildewed and black and the blackberries were bloated and rotten and covered in cobwebs. There was a chilling wind coming over the back field that made me feel as if I was wrapped in wet bandages and I clenched my arms around myself and pulled them tight, like a picture I'd once seen of a man in a strait-jacket in an asylum, until the blood throbbed through my arms but my fingertips were still freezing and I was still trying to get warm when I heard Mum picking her way up the back path between the cabbages.

'What you up to here on your ownsome then, laddikins?'

'Nothin' much.'

'Wouldn't you be better off indoors in the warm?' She was shivering and the wind was blowing her hair about.

'Be better if you were.'

She smiled the way she did when somebody bumped her in Woolworth's and she made out it was her fault when it wasn't. 'Be nice if we could have an evening in together for a change.'

'Yeah.' I imagined the fire roaring away up the chimney and my eyes getting heavier, listening to her reading *The Gorilla Hunters* or *Coral Island* until I could almost taste the fleshy sweetness of some stuff called breadfruit and feel the salty grit of the coarse coral sand between my toes.

'Simon!'

'Nar. I'd be bored.'

'We-ell, maybe we could have a shot at making a Christmas list then?'

'Bit early, in' it?'

'Or even read?' She said it as if she was expecting me to shout at her and it sent a flush through me that made my cold fingertips tingle. 'Simon? I haven't had a good read for ages.'

There was *Robinson Crusoe* and *The Swiss Family Robinson* and *Treasure Island* and *Ivanhoe* and *Captain Cook's Adventures*

194

and *Black Bartlemy's Treasure* and I wondered why they never wrote books about desert islands nowadays.

'Would you like to, Simon?'

'Nar.' I could imagine what the boys would have had to say about pirates and desert islands and buried treasure. 'I'm too old for that sort of thing now. Anyway, you didn't want to when I was little.'

'*Simon.*' She sounded winded. 'How could you?'

'What?' I could feel myself smiling. It was an odd feeling.

'That was a cruel thing to say.'

'Was it?' It felt as if I was falling over myself down a hill.

'Yes, you know it was. Why, I spent hours and hours reading to you.'

'Did you begrudge it then?'

'Simon!' Her voice dropped to a whisper and broke and I couldn't think why I was talking to her like this, but somehow it didn't really matter because I'd only wanted to hear what 'begrudge' sounded like and I couldn't remember where I'd heard it . . . maybe *Barnaby Rudge.*

'How can you say that, and in such a callous way?'

Callous . . . ? That was a 'begrudge' kind of word. Perhaps I'd picked it up from her in the first place.

'Why'd you used to say you were fed up then?'

'I never said I was fed up.'

'Yes you—'

'Tired, maybe. I may've said I was tired.' Her face had gone blank, as if she was looking back into pictures of the past. 'But I never, ever, said I was fed up. Why, I—' She reached out around me and I tensed. 'I loved reading to my little boy.'

My arms hung like dead weights and I had to haul them up to hold on to the chicken-house roof so that I didn't over-balance as she hugged me round the middle and, looking out over the back field towards the dell, it made me realise how much she must have loved me when I was small and I suddenly wanted to run back down the garden to see if I could still get inside the airing cupboard.

'Do you remember how we used to—'

'Yes, Mum.'

'Well, wouldn't you like to . . . ? Oh, I see.' She pulled

away from me. 'I suppose you think yourself too blessed high and mighty for that sort of thing now.'

'Well I—'

'Surely you could manage a Christmas list. You used to enjoy doing that.'

'Yes, I know, Mum but—'

'Stt-t.' She made that noise, with her tongue off the roof of her mouth, when she dashed at the cooker when the milk was boiling over. 'Well, it beats me to know what I can find for you to do.' She wiped mist off her eyebrows. 'But do, for goodness' sake, let's go in and talk. And pity help you if you dare moon about the place and upset Dad.'

I stood where I was for a moment but she'd gone so I followed her down the path and under the prop and around the shed and into the kitchen. The door scraped shut against the draught excluder, and the vibration sent the condensation running down the inside of the windows.

'Cuppa tea, Simon?' She was already pouring water into the kettle.

'M'm, please.'

I stood with my back to the fire and looked around the room. The curtains were still drawn back so I closed them. I pushed Mum's chair right under the table as I came back, by pressing against it, and tried to sit on the woodbox, but the corner of the mantelpiece was in the way of my shoulder. The door to the airing cupboard would only half open before it came up against the brown armchair and I was too long to get in and too wide to turn round and I couldn't go in backwards because my head banged on the shelves. And even when I sat down in the brown armchair there was no space to sit to one side and curl my legs up and I knew I'd never be able to sit in it comfortably again.

'Here we are then, laddikins.' Mum was looking down at the brown armchair as if she was trying to work out how we could both fit into it. 'Don't move.' She put my cup and saucer down on the corner of the table and moved a dining chair out and sat down. 'You're fine there, and I really prefer a high-backed chair nowadays.'

'Do you, Mum?' I reached out for my cup.

She sipped her tea. 'Oh, this is nice,' she said but her eyes had darted to the hands on the clock.

A swish of rain fell across the side window and I could imagine the boys crouching back into the bus shelter and keeping Kenny Lane and Derek Brown in front of them to keep the draught out.

'Haven't had you all to myself for ages.' She touched the tip of her tongue along her lips to moisten her lipstick and then touched the rim of her cup to her lips again. 'What would you like to do tonight?'

'Dunno.' I finished my tea and gave her my cup and saucer. 'Mu-um? Did you play much with your brother and sisters when you were a little girl?'

'Cor, search me, Simon.' She rested her saucer on her lap. 'I s'pose I did. But your Aunty Bertha was a bit funny and Betsy had a gammy leg and was always slipping off out somewhere and the others came along later when my dad got married again.'

'What happened to your real mum then, Mum?'

'Oh.' Mum put her cup back on the table. 'Surely I've told you. She died when I was a tiny baby.' Her fingers went to her wedding ring. 'Don't know why really.'

'Oh.' I could imagine the cobbled streets with the rows of miners' cottages, each with a scrubbed front step, as she'd described them to me, and the grey sky with the misty rain drifting in from the moors with the slag heaps in the distance and a horse and cart pulling up, all draped in black, for the coffin, and my other grandad coming out in his black suit and his high wing collar and black hat and never showing what Mum had called a trace of emotion because men didn't do that sort of thing.

'Course, I used to play with dolls and things sometimes. Did I ever tell you about that doll I had that Bessie Braithwaite smashed against—'

'Yes, Mum.'

'Oh, did I? M'm. But there was lots to do in those days, you know, Simon. What with the cleaning and washing and getting the coal in and one thing and another. But what brought all this on?'

'Dunno. Just that I can't ever find anyone to play with.'

Mum sniffed and brushed her hair back. 'Well, can't I play with you for heaven's sake?'

'Not boxing, you can't.'

'Boxing! Whatever do you want to go boxing for?'

'Well, it's good and it keeps you fit.'

'Oh, Simon. I really don't know about that.'

'Oh go on, Mum.' I sat forward because I could see her looking around the room as if there was just a chance she would box with me and she was working out if there'd be enough space between the china cabinet and the table.

'Crumbs, I don't know, Simon. I'd just about go off hooks if I banged my funny thumb.'

'I'd be ever so careful, Mum.'

'And I wouldn't want you hitting me in my tummy, you know.'

'No, course not, Mum. But what we gonna use for boxing gloves?'

'Blest if I know. There's my furry ones.'

I dashed into her bedroom and got her leather gloves with the brown fur backs and rubbed them against my face. 'They're good, Mum. They won't hurt at all. Now what can you use?'

Mum pursed her lips. 'Those sheepskin mitts of Dad's. The ones he had for motor-cycling?'

'They've got a few holes in, Mum.' I couldn't remember if she knew I'd been using them for goalkeeping.

'Where are they then? In the shed?'

'Think so, Mum.'

'Better go and get them then.'

The shed was dark and cold and I found them by touch amongst the sacks of potatoes by the cricket stumps that we used for goal posts and she had the clothes brush ready when I got back. She frowned when she spotted the mud all over the palms but she sponged it off with a damp floor cloth and brushed the backs and shook the loose dust into the sink and then I grabbed them and started shadow-boxing in the reflection from the china cabinet. The gloves had big quiffs coming out at the wrists like swordfighters wore and I fancied I'd have looked like the Prisoner of Zenda if he'd had a sword fight with the

Count of Monte Cristo or something like that on the pictures.

'You be careful what you're up to near that china cabinet, my boy.' Mum was pushing the table back up against the sideboard to leave space in front of the fire and then she turned and put her hands up like a mouse nibbling cheese. 'Come on then. Let's make a start and then I must get Dad's tea.'

Mum led with her left as if she was dabbing on rouge and I ducked around it and then she gave me one in the tummy with her other hand. She dropped her guard to say sorry as I gave her an uppercut and then we had to stop while she turned the toast under the grill.

It had always embarrassed me when people commentated and once, when a boy called Mousy Trapper had done it, as I was coming up to bowl when we were playing cricket in the school field one evening, I'd got so self-conscious that I'd slung the ball at him instead of bowling it and Big Bim had sent me home with a thick ear, but now, in front of the fire with just Mum, I was Randolph Turpin and she was Luc Van Dam and I was knocking her out in thirty-six seconds of the first round at The Hague and then I was doing training for the championship of the world while she got Dad's tea and then she was Sugar Ray Robinson when Randy won the title off him and I was bobbing and weaving under his guard and snaking out that rapier left and crossing with that lethal right that sunk in up to the wrist, and Mum's eye bulged and she said, 'Steady on, Simon. Not so hard.'

'. . . and Turpin's got him on the ropes and he's pounding away left and right, left and right to the body.' I paused and wondered how Eamon Andrews managed to keep going without drawing breath on the wireless. 'Left and right, left and—'

'Steady up, Simon.'

'But now Robinson counters. A good one-two that forces Turpin back but Turpin's back again ducking under and—'

Crack! A jarring sensation went through me like splintered Bakelite.

'Aa-agh!' Mum's arms flopped down on my back and there was a moment when the world stopped turning.

199

I crept out carefully from under her. Her arms dropped and swung and one of Dad's mitts fell off her. Her face was set and puffy and her bottom lip was blown up like a football. It was split on the inside and the blood was collecting along her teeth.

'I'm sorry, Mum.' I felt my lower lids fill up and a couple of splashes landed on the back of her furry gloves. All the things I'd thought and said and done came back to me; the times she'd played with me when I was bored and read to me when she was tired and even up to a minute ago when I'd been trying to hit her hard in the tummy because I liked the feel of it and now she was reaching for the newspaper to drip on. 'Oh, Mum. I didn't do it on purpose. Honestly I didn't.'

She shook her head slightly and two more great splodges hit the newspaper and stained it like red candle grease. 'B's'all b'right. B'r'ust b'ro and b'rinse it.'

I followed her into the kitchen and stood behind her as she put her head up under the tap and ran cold water into her mouth.

'Will it be all right, Mum?'

She nodded, and I wiped the water out of her eye with the dish cloth, and then she let it run until she said her gums were numb and that she was going to have a lie-down.

I sat by the fire with the light out listening to the wind up under the eaves. The flames flickered and a loose tile clattered on next door's roof and I prayed that it hadn't really happened. I prayed until the clock struck half-past five and then I crept into Mum's bedroom and lay down beside her.

'How is it now, Mum?'

'Oh, 'it h'etter, h'imon.'

'Oh. Good. I am sorry, Mum. It was an accident. I'd never want to hurt you.'

'I know, h'imon.' She slid her arm under my head and cradled me against her cheek and we lay there until the clock struck six and she said she was feeling better and that the fire would need making up.

It was after six o'clock when Dad got home from work

now because he had to work until twenty-five-past five to make the hours up so that he didn't have to work one Saturday morning in four. Mum said that twenty-five-past five was a mighty awkward time to work to but I'd said it was as easy to stop work then as at any other time and Dad said it was all pretty much the same to him because it was just as much of a nuisance getting round Chichester Cross whatever time he knocked off and he couldn't think what had possessed them to stick the Market Cross slap in the middle of the town where they might have guessed the traffic would converge and once, when we were all together for Sunday tea, Grandad had said they wouldn't have realised what chaos would be caused because there hadn't been so much traffic then, but then Old Gran had woken up and told him it had been just the same in her day and if he thought it was a nightmare now he ought to have tried crossing East Street in the old days with a heavy basket of shopping in one hand and Rene and Young Fran in her pram in the other while your bonnet was being nipped off your head by some blessed great milkman's horse that had been standing there like a donkey for ages. I'd thought it was obvious they'd put the Market Cross in the middle of the town because it had a clock on each side facing down each of the four main streets because if they'd put it anywhere else people wouldn't have been able to see the time, but I hadn't said so because by the time I'd worked all that out, and decided that grown-ups didn't know what they were talking about, Dad had turned the wireless on for 'Songs of Praise' and I'd had to be quiet. And he was home again now. The shed door closed and the back door opened and 'strewth-alive!' came from the kitchen as the back door closed slowly.

'What the devil you been up to then, Simon?'

'Playing boxing with Mum, Dad. I hurt her by accident.'

'I can see you did.' Dad took his tea from Mum and held it while she put his sugar in. 'Do you think that was a good idea, Ina?'

Mum sat down and passed her hand over her forehead and then she passed him the bread and butter. 'Not really, perhaps. He's getting mighty strong now.' She dabbed at her lip with her hanky and looked at it. 'But, heavens above,

201

what am I supposed to do? He's always moping about with nothing to do and—'

'Where's all your mates then, Simon?'

'I don't—'

'Oh, for crying out loud, George. They won't be out to play in weather like this.'

'Well, couldn't he amuse himself with something or other?'

'I don't know.' Mum passed him the fish-paste but he shook his head and took the jam. 'He doesn't seem to be interested in anything at all nowadays.'

'Blimey, Nip, when I was your age I was off—'

'No you weren't, Dad.'

He stopped, with his hand above his plate, and stared across at Mum. 'No I wasn't, what?'

'Out bird's-nesting with Den Payton. Not at this time of year you weren't.'

Dad ran his knife round the inside rim of the jam jar. 'How'd you know that's what I was going to say?'

'Wasn't it?'

'Well, p'raps it was. But it's a bit rude to anticipate what people are going to say, isn't it?'

'Why?' I stirred my tea slowly.

'Well, because it is. Blimey, Nip, it makes us sound as if . . .' Dad shook his head and spread raspberry jam on his bread. 'We're not as predictable as all that, are we? What the devil's up with 'im all of a sudden, Ina?'

Mum sighed. 'It's beyond me.'

'Well, what about the boys down the camp?' Dad folded his bread over and took a bite. 'You always used to be off down there of an evening.' He chewed slower and sniffed out of one nostril as if he'd caught a whiff of something odd and then he opened his half-slice flat. 'This our usual butter, Ina?'

'No. Not exactly.' Mum put the top on the jam jar. 'They'd run out of St Ivel down at the shop so I got some of this new Australian. It's all right, isn't it?'

'M'm, s'pose so.' Dad refolded his bread and jam and took another bite. 'Different though.'

'They don't seem to do much nowadays, Dad.'

'Who's that, Nip?'

'The boys down the camp. There doesn't seem to be much to do down there now.'

'M'm.'

Mum poured more tea.

'Dad?'

'M'm.'

'What about that club you were gonna start?'

Dad moved the crumbs on his plate to the centre with his finger.

'When you gonna start it?'

'Blimey, I dunno, Nip. When the darker evenings come, I s'pose.'

'Well, they're 'ere already.'

'*Here* already, Simon.'

'They're h'here now, Dad.'

Dad took his second cup of tea and spread more jam.

'Dad?'

'What, Simon? Cor blimey, I know they are, but giv'us a chance.'

'Yes, for goodness' sake, don't go on so, Simon. And did you wash your hands before you sat down to tea?'

I put my hands on my knees under the table and stared at Dad until he looked at me and then he grinned as if I'd just guessed what he was thinking. 'Soon, Nip. In fact Pop's been on about it to the Old Boy again recently so I'd better be seeing about it.'

'What, is Grandad going to help, Dad?'

'No, Simon. Pop just mentioned it to him.'

'Oh.'

Mum cut through her bread and her knife ground on the plate. 'So I s'pose that'll be another couple of evenings a week I won't see either of you?'

'A couple!' I sat forward so fast I sent my spoon clattering off my saucer.

'No, Nip. Just once a week.' Dad was looking at Mum. 'And it won't be every week.' He swallowed the rest of his tea. 'We'll just see how it goes for a start and I'll get Pop to see what kind of a reaction we can expect from the nippers.'

*

Word soon got round that my dad was going to start a church boys' club, but he told me it would be up to the boys to make sure it was a success.

'An' they needn't think I'm gonna waste me time every evenin' sittin' aroun' drinkin' tea an' tyin' knots in fings.' Geoff Gibbs was standing outside the bus shelter spitting at Kenny Lane's feet to make him dance like a cowboy. 'Less'n it's a knot in Nipper's neck if 'e comes funny.'

'Well, we'll go if we can play snooker, won't we, Jerry?'

'M'm.' Jerry was watching where Gibbser was spitting.

'You'll be able to play, Jim, but you won't be able to monopolise it.'

Gibbser looked up and sucked around his teeth and spat out 'bollocks'.

'An' I'll only go if Laner does.' Derek Brown was sitting up in the window opening of the shelter.

'An' I ain' goin' if Gibbs does, so fuckin' pack it up, Gibbs.'

'Shut up yer whinin', Lane.' Geoff hoiked and spat and wiped his mouth like the old man in the Hopalong Cassidy films did when he hit a fly on the wall with tobacco juice. 'I was aimin' ta miss.'

I scratched two lines down in the dust with my toe, and two across. 'Well, you'll 'ave to behave yerselves up there else 'e'll—'

'Yar har! 'ark at Lord Snooty.' Geoff Gibbs scuffed through my noughts and crosses. 'Sod off, ya snooty bastard. We don't want him with us, do we, boys?'

Mum and Dad spent all the following evening getting everything ready. Dad had to sort through all the things he'd bought at Bowman's and he'd laid out a dozen snooker tips on the living-room table and two new table-tennis bats and half a dozen good balls and half a dozen ropey ones for us to get the hang of it with; he drew a line under his column of figures and wrote under it and then sat back.

'Two pounds, seven and ninepence, Ina. That lot.'

'You'd hardly credit it.' Mum was mending the table-tennis net with a piece she'd cut out of a vegetable sack the milkman had used for carrots. 'It certainly doesn't go far nowadays.'

I sat taking an interest in Dad making lists of other things he needed to buy and how much threepence a head would bring in over a year, not counting the summer months, and how much electricity we could expect to burn, assuming the club was open from seven to nine once a week, until he went to the toilet and then I grabbed my coat and disappeared out the back way. I crept low down behind the hedge until I was well clear and then I ran the rest of the way to the lane and down Crouch Cross Road. The boys were standing in the doorway of Ray Whittle's barn and Derek Brown was crying.

'What'cha.' I slowed down as I got closer to them. 'What's up with Browner?'

'Gibbser threw 'is ball in the pond.' Kenny Lane had had a crew-cut.

'Oh.'

'That right you 'ave ta pay ta play snooker, Nipper?' It looked as if Gibbser's Gran had given him a crew-cut.

'Yeah. To pay for the lights.'

'See.' Gibbser looked as if he'd won a bet.

'Only a penny a game, though, and threepence to get in.'

'So if you 'ad three games'a snooker it'd cost ya a tanner?'

'Yeah.'

'Bloody 'ell!'

'That's not bad.' Colin Gander had been sitting up in the rafters but now he swung down. 'Tanner's not bad.'

'But if there's ten of us. That'll be five bob a night?'

'Yeah.'

'An' where'll that go?' Geoff Gibbs stood forward like an attacking rat. 'Into your old man's pocket?'

'No. It'll pay for electricity an' coal an' table-tennis bats an' things.'

'Yeah-h?' Geoff Gibbs was sneering now. 'You'll 'ave ta prove that to us, won' 'e, boys?'

'I soddin' won't, Gibbs.' My knuckles hardened into fists. 'Got it?'

'Calm down.' Colin was looking towards his front-room window. 'If my mum 'ears us she'll be out an' moan.'

'An' if there's any arguin' 'e won' open the club at all.'

'Well, 'e can please 'im-bleedin'-self, Nipper.' Geoff Gibbs kicked straw at Kenny Lane. 'I'm goin' up be'ind the church fer a shit.'

Club night was on Thursday because there wasn't much on the wireless on Thursdays. It started at seven but Dad and I would go up at half-past six to light the fire and we'd have a game of snooker together while it burned up before the boys arrived. I liked this time better than the real club but when the boys found out we got up there early they shook their fists at me through the window, when Dad wasn't looking, and pointed at the door and made out they thought it was stuck instead of locked and kept banging at it until Dad had to tell them it wasn't seven o'clock yet.

Dad had agreed the entrance fee and snooker charge with Pop but that table tennis would be free because the entrance fee would cover the cost of the coke and the snooker would pay for the electricity. Darts was free as well because we'd all got fed up playing darts during the holidays, and there was draughts and ludo and chess if we wanted a quiet game. The stove dried out after a week or two but it still smoked and Dad spent most of one evening with it out trying to push a flue brush on a long handle of twisted wire up and round the bend in the chimney. The boys played snooker with their gloves on to keep warm.

'What the devil they up to in there?' Dad was on his knees in front of the stove. 'Like a herd of elephants stampeding around.' He had a soot smudge above one eye and rust scales in his hair. 'Simon?'

'Dunno, Dad.'

'Well, go an' see and tell 'em to stop it.'

Geoff Gibbs had trodden on a ping-pong ball and they were playing football with it.

'You could get that kink out, Geoff, if you sucked it and softened it up.'

'If I 'ad a mouth like yours I would, Nipper.'

'They're not for kickin' about, ya know.'

'Sod off. We're only tryin' ta keep warm.'

206

I drew the door to. 'Me dad wants you to make a bit less noise.'

'Bollocks!' Geoff kicked the ball at the door and then went and stood close up to it. 'Why can't 'e light it instead of muckin' about wiv it. We'd rather be smoked-out an' warm than frozen to death, wouldn't we, boys?'

'Ssh, Geoff, 'e'll 'ear ya.'

'Dry up, Nipper, 'e's s'posed to.' He slipped into the snooker room and came out with the broom from under the table. 'C'mon, Col,' and they went out.

They shinned up Mrs Evans's wall and the roof creaked as they climbed across it.

'They're heading for the stove pipe,' Jerry said.

I was watching Dad through a knot-hole in the partition.

'An' now they're sticking the broom down the chimney.' Jerry was dancing about as if his pants were on fire.

'Something's moving, Nip.' Dad was ramming the flue-brush up and down like a piston. 'Gets so far and then it seems to come back.' He pulled the brush out and looked up the chimney from the bottom. 'As if it's sticking to the— Who-oo!'

There was a sudden scratching rush and when the dust settled he was covered with soot and we had to blow it off and dust him down with the billiard-table brush while he yelled up the chimney that whoever it was that was up there had better come down quick before they fell and broke their silly necks and what did they think Pop would say if he had to fork out to repair a blessed great hole in the ceiling?

Dad said, later, that he thought the starlings had probably started nesting in the chimney in 1940, soon after war had broken out properly and they'd stopped lighting the club fire, and if he knew anything about starlings they'd have come back every year so long as they weren't disturbed. Geoff Gibbs swaggered his shoulders and tapped the broom handle and huffed on the knuckles of his right hand and rubbed them on his left nipple when Dad said this, and he asked Dad if that meant he could come in free next week and he asked again when Dad set fire to the nests and piled coke on top so that it got so hot that we had to open the windows and they said he wasn't such

207

a bad bloke after all when he let them play snooker free all evening.

News got around that we'd got the fire sorted out and more people came each week. I met Frank Parfit up by the swings one evening and he started to come and he showed us how to play table tennis properly and we had tournaments amongst ourselves and soon Dad had to draw up a rota and pin it on the wall so that everyone could be guaranteed at least two games of snooker or billiards and three games of table tennis and I heard him telling Grandad that he'd been thinking about opening it two nights a week if he could find somebody to give him a hand now and again.

I tried to get the boys not to talk about the club at school but news of it got around and then David Harris and Don and Stuart Norris and the rest of them from the camp got annoyed when I said they couldn't come because Dad said Pop would want to keep it for the boys in the village and they told me that if that was the case I could piss off evenings and keep away from their socials on a Saturday night so I started going out with the boys in the evenings.

8

*T*he boys had always played hide and seek chasing in the churchyard and around the school but now they told me they'd made it more interesting by extending the boundaries down to the Tangmere Road and up to the edge of the Common, but not into it, and out to the Redvins towards Greatwood and they had the telegraph pole by Ray Whittle's place for home. They had two on guard at a time and you weren't allowed to hang around at home. I asked them if there was a boundary on my side of the village and they said that nobody ever went that way but they might do now I'd started playing so we set a boundary of the end of the lane where it came out onto the Hanover Road. Whoever was up had to give the others five minutes' start and I said I'd go first with Jimmy Phillips so that I could talk to him and get the hang of the new way of playing. We leant with our backs against the telegraph pole and shared a roll-up he'd pinched from his dad.

'What is this?' I peeled the cigarette paper off my lips and blew a shred of tobacco off my tongue.

'Dunno. Golden Virginia I expect.' He took a puff and breathed it in and blew it out.

'Do you take it in?'

'Yeah.'

'What, right down?'

'Yeah.' He looked at the end of the cigarette and tapped the ash off with the index finger of his other hand. 'You're s'posed to, aren't you?'

'Yeah, I s'pose so.'

'Ain' up to much though, this.'

'Ain' it?'

'No. Wish 'e'd smoke proper ones in a packet.'

I took it back from him and pinched the end off up to a dry bit. 'My mum smokes Minors.'

'Din' know your mum smoked.'

'Yeah, she does. Not much though. Minors . . . De Reske Minors.'

'Oh yeah.'

'They're all right, and me grandad smokes Turf an' Woodbines an' sometimes Weights n' Park Drive.'

'What they like?'

'Not much.' I sprayed a thin jet of smoke at the telegraph pole so that it sprayed back. 'Bacca comes outta Park Drive an' Turf're a bit ropey an' ya know what Woodbines're like' – Jimmy winced – 'but Weights're all right, I s'pose.'

' 'lease ya get fag cards in Turf.'

'Nar.' I dug my heel into the earth and spun on it. 'Not good'uns ya don't.'

'Don't you collect 'em then?'

'No, not really. They're all right for swaps, I s'pose. I collect 'ousehold 'ints.'

'Do you? They say Pip Williamson collects them.'

I tried to look surprised. 'What, that big bloke in 6B?'

'M'm. You don't know him do you, Simon?'

'Oh yeah. Not well, like. I 'it 'im on the ankle once playin' cricket.'

'Cor! Reckon 'e'd do me any swaps?'

'Spec so.' I took the cigarette end from him and took a drag and offered it back to him but he shook his head so I trod it out. 'Shall I ask 'im for ya?'

'Yes please, Simon.'

'Right then.' I followed the lights of a car up the road. 'S'pose we'd better start lookin' fer 'em. Do we 'ave ta shout "coming" or anything?'

'No.' Jimmy pulled his pullover sleeves down so that he could bury his hands in them. 'They'll be miles away by now anyway.'

'How d'we find 'em then?'

Jimmy shrugged. 'Dunno. Jus' look.'

'Right-o then. You go one way and I'll go the other and if you see anything make an'oise like a n'owl an' I'll come runnin'.'

I sent Jimmy off down Church Lane, so that he could go over the fields behind the vicarage and come out down the road below the shop, and I said I'd look around the school and then go up past the Boys' Club and through the churchyard and back again up Church Lane and meet him by the pole and he set off into the dark to-whit to-whooing into his cupped hands.

I tucked my trouser bottoms into my socks, so that they didn't flap against my ankles and give me away, and went along the Smiths' hedge and up the side path by the Men's Club towards Brindle's Yard. I stopped and listened, where the path crossed the one to Arnold's chicken run. All the chickens had gone to roost and they made a gurgling, murmuring sound as I passed. The moon was full and shining down through the branches of the greengage tree. It silhouetted an old nest I must have missed last spring or perhaps it was even older. I slipped through Grandad's back garden keeping to the shadows flung out from the hedges by the moon. The bricks by the back door felt smooth through my plimsolls and I opened the side shed door and slipped into the smell of apples and dust. Grandad's old gardening jacket was hanging on its nail behind the door but he hadn't got any cigarettes in the pockets. I took an apple off the top shelf and held it out in the moonlight to make sure it hadn't got any bad bits in it and bit into it with a crisp cracking sound as I turned the corner at the side of the house away from the back door. The flints in the walls of the old house reflected the moonlight where they'd been chipped and it took me back to when I was in Wadey's class and he'd told us how many millions of years it had taken them to form and before that to when they'd reminded me of the kind of sheep's eyes Grandad had told me the Arabs used to put in their stews in Mespot and how, if you were a guest, they used to give them to you as an honour and you had to eat them no matter how sick they made you feel and if you didn't they'd think you were insulting them and more than likely slit your gizzard.

They had the wireless on in the kitchen and I could hear it plainly with my ear up against the window pane. When the music stopped it was 'Down Your Way' with Wynford

Vaughan Thomas. Nan would be in there watching to see the milk didn't boil over and Grandad would be going to sleep reading a Sexton Blake until Dad came up to say good-night to them and then he'd eat his supper. Something moved on the path at the bottom of the garden and a blackbird startled out of the bushes. I shrank down against the wall and picked my way through the forsythia bushes and lay down on the cold, crumbly earth between the sprout plants and peered out. The gate latch clicked, then the hinges creaked and the latch clicked again and Dad's dark shape came up the path etched out against the moonlight. I put my head down and pretended he was a German guard and, when he'd walked by and tapped on the window, slithered forward on my tummy until I was under the concentration camp wire and then crawled on my hands and knees until I was out of range of the gun turret spotlights and made for the border where the Resistance—

'Seen anyone?'

I stopped dead.

Jimmy Phillips rose, like a spirit from a grave, out of the trench where Grandad had been rough-winter-digging to let the frost get at it, in the place where he'd had his main-crop potatoes.

'Strewth! You scared the life outta me.'

Jimmy dusted dirt off his knees. 'Seen anything of 'em?'

'No. Any got 'ome?'

'Don't think so.'

'Wonder where they are?'

'Dunno. Might've gone in Gander's to listen to "Dick Barton".'

'Do they do that then, when we're s'posed to be playing?'

'Did once, when Gibbser wanted a— S'sh!' Jimmy dropped and I dropped too.

'What was it?' I'd put my hand in something nasty.

'Up there, past the school. Thought I saw something.' He knelt forward and crawled up behind the gate post and I followed him wiping my hand on the grass. 'Something crossed the road from the church and went into the alms-houses' gardens.'

'Think it's them?'

212

'Might be. They might've split up.'

'Come on, then.' I took the lead and dodged across the Simms's front garden and through Nurse McLaine's hedge and across her lawn and through a hole in her fence into the garden in front of the infants' class. 'We'll creep up on them.'

Jimmy Phillips was puffing and panting and he flopped against the wall behind me. 'Gi's a chance ta catch me breath.' He stooped down to tie his shoelace and I cupped my hands to cape my eyes against the window so I could see into the infants' classroom.

' 'member when we started school, Jim?'

'Yeah, just.' Jimmy was leaning forward off the wall looking past me.

'An' them "Jus' So" stories?'

'M'm, sort of.'

'An' what about Wendy Brewer when you went to sleep?'

'When did I go to sleep?'

'That day in ol' Shelter's class. An' she was tryin' to play footsie with Roger Davies an' got you instead.'

'I don't remember that.'

'Don't you? I do.' I tried to give Jimmy a friendly nudge but he overbalanced and banged his knee on the wall and went very quiet.

We crept up the side of the alms-houses' wall and around by the entrance to the old school canteen and then back down the other side of the alms-houses by the village hall.

'No sign of 'em then.'

Jimmy Phillips flexed his knee. 'Well, I'm sure I saw something.'

'Don' matter.' I etched my toe along the outline of light on the path from the hall window. 'Reckon there's a meeting on?'

'Might be.' Jimmy Phillips had his hands in his pockets and he wasn't bothering to stalk any more.

'Shall we see 'oo's in there?'

Jimmy shrugged.

'Come on. Spy on 'em.'

My toes sank into the ashy soft soil round Miss Turner's roses as I climbed the alms-houses' wall and then we were wading waist-deep in dead nettles but we couldn't see in through the window because the ground sloped away to the edge of the hall where they'd put the rainwater gully and we couldn't pull ourselves up because the window-sill was rotten. The grass on the other side of the hall where the dustbins stood had been cut and it was flatter, but it was still too high and we stood under the window listening to the voices inside.

'Stand on top'a one'a the bins, Jim.'

'Can't.' Jimmy kicked a bin gently with his plimsoll. 'It's empty an' it ain't got a lid on. It'd fall over if I stood on the rim.'

'Need somethin' to put over the top of it.'

'Hang on.' Jimmy dashed back the way we'd come and came back almost immediately. 'This any good?'

'That's just right.' I took the Watney's sign that had hung over the hall entrance until its arm had rusted and it had fallen down in a gale. 'But won't somebody miss it?'

'Not if we put it back.'

'S'pose not.' I put the sign on the top of a bin under the window. 'Gis'n 'and up, then.'

'Cor, that's not fair, Simon.'

'What's not?'

'Well, I found it so I should have first go.'

'Yeah, but it was my idea.'

'So what?' Jimmy put his hand on the edge of the sign and started to pull it.

'You leave that where it is, Phillips.'

'If I can't get up first I'm putting it back.'

'You're bloody not.'

'I am.' He was heavier than me and I had to let go of the board because he'd almost trapped my fingers. 'Cor, it's the old gals' Women's Institute meeting an' ol' mother Mole's makin' a speech.'

'Well, get down then an' let me 'ave a look.'

'You should see 'er. She ain' arf soundin' off.'

'P'raps I could if you'd jus' get out the bleedin' way.'

'Flingin' 'er arms about she is and there's all those old dears—'

'Come on, Fatty, for cryin' out loud!' I grabbed him round the knees and tried to pull him.

Crack! 'Whoo-a.'

The centre of the sign collapsed in a shower of splinters and Jimmy's yell echoed up under the corrugated iron roof. A sound like scalded turkeys came out of the hall and I turned and fled and was up by the Wobble Fields before I drew breath.

I rested against the gate trying to look as if I couldn't hear the commotion down by the hall and saw the wedge of light on the pavement disappear as someone closed the hall front door and I breathed in that heavy smell of grease and dusty mud that always hangs around tractors and wondered if it was still possible to run away to sea if I got caught and expelled from school.

'All right, Nipper.'

I gripped the top of the gate.

'Don't piss about. We know you know you've found us.' It was Gibbser's voice and it was coming from the hedge to my right almost under my feet. 'You might as well say cos there's all prickles in 'ere and we're gettin' stung ta death.'

'Seen ya, Gibbser, an' you . . .'

'C'mon, Laner.'

'An' you, Lane.'

Geoff Gibbs's head appeared through a tangle of beech saplings and brambles and I held them apart for him but he pushed my hand away.

'Sod, you are, Nipper. You knew we couldn't move so you just kept us stuck there.'

'Couldn't get at you.' I stared down at the tangled hedge. 'You could've run.'

'We couldn't bleedin' move, could we, Lane?'

Kenny Lane shook his head from between Geoff's legs.

'Come on. Get up. What's bleedin' keepin' ya?' Geoff bent down and hauled Kenny out by his armpits. ' 'ave ya got Whittle an' Gander yet?'

'No, don't think so.'

Geoff wiped his nose on the back of his hand. 'Only they was with us at the start. If they split on us . . .'

'They didn't.' I turned and started back towards the

215

hall. If I stayed with them it might look as if I'd been with them all the time. 'It was luck. I didn't know you were there.'

'Then why'd you come straight to us?'

'I told you, luck.' We were getting close to the hall now. In a few more minutes we'd be past it and I'd be safe. 'I thought you might've been over the Wobble Fields or up the—'

'Right! Gotch'a.'

We stopped dead as two shapes leapt out of the gap in the beech hedge where Flick Fenner had once poured his old motor-bike's engine oil and killed it. 'Simon Wilson and Geoffrey Gibbs. We might've guessed, and leading poor little Kenny Lane astray . . .'

'What's up, Missis?' I'd never seen Geoff Gibbs looking innocent before and I tried to look the same way. 'Git orf, we ain't done nuffin'.'

'I think we've got the culprits now, Clara.' Mrs Mole looked like the Butcher's Wife in 'Happy Families' with her arms folded across her stomach and her legs apart. 'I'm sure their headmaster will know how to deal with them.'

'What's she on about?' Geoff looked as if he'd been caught in the girls' toilets and Kenny Lane was almost in tears. 'Silly ole ba—'

'I beg your pardon, Geoffrey Gibbs.'

'Well, we wanna know . . .' but Geoff was left talking to himself as they turned on their high heels and clicked up the steps and closed the door behind them.

The light from the moon made a criss-cross pattern on the patch through the bare branches of the lime trees they'd planted for the Jubilee and I made a pile out of the loose grit with my toe.

'What the bloody 'ell was she on about?'

'Dunno, Geoff.'

'Silly ol' bag, what's she accusin' us of?'

'Don' ask me.' I flattened the peak of my grit pyramid with my toe.

'An' she's gonna tell ol' Levers.' Kenny Lane's nose was running.

'Yeah, but what's she gonna tell 'im? We ain't done nuffin', 'ave we?'

216

'I told ya, I don't know.' I overbalanced and stood on my heap of grit and flattened it.

'Well, it ain't bloody fair.' Geoff Gibbs stood back from the hall door and clenched his fists. 'We got a right ta know what we bin accused of.'

'Yeah.'

'Cripes!' Geoff Gibbs turned on Kenny Lane and hauled him forward.

'What's up? I was only agreein' with ya.'

'Yeah, well p'raps you were.' Geoff Gibbs re-positioned himself in front of the door. 'But lurkin' about behind me like that . . . scared the flamin' life outta me.'

'Think we'd better be goin', Geoff?'

Geoff Gibbs's fists tightened again. 'Sod you, Nipper.' He bent forward towards the door again. 'I ain't goin' 'til I got this sorted out. We got our rights, ya know.'

'An' why should we get into trouble for something when we weren't even there?'

'Yeah. That's right.' Geoff hunched his shoulders up and then he cocked his head and looked at Kenny Lane. 'Weren't where?'

'I dunno.' Kenny Lane brushed his eyes with his sleeve. 'Wherever it was that it happened.'

'Oh . . . yeah,' and then, looking at me, 'That's right, i'n'it, Mush?'

I stuck my hands into my pockets. 'S'pose so.'

' 'an' we got a right to 'ave our say.'

'What we gonna do then?' I could imagine Dad's face when he got a letter from Levers in Chichester about me misbehaving in the village.

'We go in an' 'ave our say.'

'We can't do that.'

'We can, Nipper. Come on.'

'Well I ain't.'

'You are, Lane.' Geoff grabbed Kenny Lane. 'If we go you'll 'ave ta come. What'cha say, Nipper?'

'Might as well.' I moved towards the steps of the hall.

'Good.' Geoff opened the door for me. 'You do the talkin'. You're good at that,' and he pushed me in.

The bright light and the smell of eau-de-cologne and

nylons stopped us dead in our tracks. Mrs Keen, the cow-man's wife, was up on the stage making a speech but she went dumb and stood there with her mouth open looking at us from under her glasses. They all turned round and sat there gawping and one said 'well r-h-eally!' and I cleared my throat and waited for the sound to disappear amongst the rafters.

'Me'n' my friends've been accused of somethin' we didn't do an' we wanna know what it was.'

Mrs Mole had left the stage and was coming down the gangway between the chairs.

'. . . cos we wasn't there when it 'appened, whatever it was.'

I looked back at Gibbser as Mrs Mole marched up to me.

'An' we've got a right to 'ave our say.'

Mrs Mole and Mrs Pargetter took me by an arm each and walked me back towards the door.

'An' it's not right to accuse somebody without sayin' what it's about.'

They swept Geoff Gibbs and Kenny Lane back behind me and closed the door on us.

'D'ya think they believed us?'

Geoff Gibbs shook his head.

'Think we'll get into trouble?'

'Dunno. But I ain't gonna 'ang around'n find out.' He darted past me and kicked the door. 'Might as well be hung for a sheep as a lamb,' and he and Kenny Lane dashed across the road and up towards the church.

I watched them and then I ran too.

The bin Jimmy Phillips had been standing on was over-turned but there was no sign of the Watney's sign. Perhaps they'd found it and taken it in and were going to use it as evi—

'Nipper!'

I crouched back into the shadows and slewed round.

'Over 'ere. I'm stuck. Can't get this soddin' thing off.'

Jimmy eased himself half out of the bushes. The remains of the Watney's sign were stuck round his waist like a square ballet skirt.

'What 'appened?'

'You can see what 'appened. Get it off.'

'Yeah, but 'ow'd it 'appen?' I tried to press it down at the sides.

'Ouch! Leggo!'

'You wan' it off, don' ya?'

'Yeah.' His eyes bulged. 'But don't bloody pull it. Me ol' man's trapped.'

'You go straight through?' I ripped at some of the loose bits and they came off in layers.

'Looks like it, don' it?'

'Did they see you?'

'No. I hid behind the bins and they never looked there. But I bashed my bonts on the side'a the bin and I think I grazed my side.'

'We'll 'ave a look in a minute.' I tore at the five-ply and Jimmy cringed as I pulled it away from around his thighs. 'An' we'll 'ave ta find somewhere to dump these bits.'

'What they gonna say when they find the sign's gone?'

'Don' matter. It was probably the brewery's anyway.' I pulled at the outer frame until it snapped and Jimmy shook himself free. 'Can't say anything much if they can't find it.'

'An' where we gonna dump it?' He was undoing his flies carefully and then he let his trousers drop.

'Any permanent damage?'

'It's not funny, Simon.' He was leaning forward looking into the palm of his hand. 'If one'a those flamin' great splinters 'ad gone through . . .'

'Le's 'ave a look.'

'Git orf.'

'Well, get on with it then. It's still there, ain' it?'

'S'pose so.'

It took us nearly half an hour to clear all the bits away. We put some over Farmer Price's wall and some in the middle of Mr Norbitt's bonfire on the allotments and we scattered the chips and flakes over the Wobble Fields.

The boys had all gone in when we got back to the telegraph pole. The wind got up and it started to rain and Jimmy Phillips said he probably wouldn't come out to play in the evenings any more and I went and stood under the eaves of our front door and had a think about how lucky he was to have fallen in the dustbin and not get caught and what a fool I'd been to go in and make a fuss when they couldn't have proved anything anyway and then I heard Dad coming down the Close so I made out I'd just got home.

'You're 'ome late, Nip. Haven't been getting into any mischief, have you?'

'No.' I fell into step with him. 'But that didn't stop us getting accused though.'

'Oh, strewth alive, what's happened now?'

'Dunno, Dad.' I tried to say it like Geoff Gibbs had but it didn't sound the same. 'We'd been playin' hide an' seek chasin' and were coming down past the hall when some old girls grabbed us and said now they knew who'd done it.'

'Done what?' Dad unbuttoned his mac and shook his scarf free from where it was tickling his neck.

'I don't know, Dad. They didn't say.'

'Sounds mighty strange to me. Blowed if I know.'

'Think we'll be in trouble, Dad?'

'I don't know, Nip. Can't be if you haven't done anything, can you?'

'No. S'pose not.'

'Anyway—' He held the door open for me. 'It's getting late. You'd better get in and have that bath and get ready for bed.'

The rusted hinge of the Watney's sign stayed there for ages and nobody ever asked what had happened to the board or made a fuss about us interrupting the meeting and Levers didn't call us up to the front in assembly. I told Jimmy Phillips to be quiet when Gibbser was sounding off about being wrongly accused because, with a mouth like he had, if he got to know what had really happened it would only be a matter of time before the whole village knew and by the time we'd got our end-of-term reports we'd forgotten about it.

They had given us our end-of-term reports a week or

so early so that the parents could comment on them before we broke up for Christmas.

'This is not, Simon, all that we'd been hoping for.'

The brown envelope with 'The parents of Simon George Wilson' on it was lying next to Dad's cup of tea and he smoothed the single foolscap page out in front of him.

' "Shows promise at games" is all very well but you really will have to stop wasting your time and get down to some real work soon.'

'I don't waste my time, Dad.'

'Well, what else do you call chasing around the village every night?'

'And going off out to socials and things all the time.'

'That was only once, Mum.'

'. . . and hanging about after a lot of girls.'

'I spend most of me time playing football an' cricket.'

'That's as may be, young man, but your chances of being a professional footballer or cricketer are a bit thin.' Dad opened his tobacco tin and laid his piece of cabbage leaf out on the lid and shook the loose shreds to one corner. 'You'd have to be exceptional already to have any chance of that.'

'I could practise more, Dad.'

'Practise more, indeed!' Mum made a face. 'What you need is to stop chasing around and get down to something serious.'

'Like what?'

'Well, for heaven's sake, I don't know . . . You used to be as happy as a sandboy to settle down with a good book.'

'Get fed up with readin'.'

'And you'd amuse yourself for hours with a nice scrap-book.'

'That's kids' stuff.'

'Well, what *do* you want to do of an evening then?'

'Dunno. It's borin'. Every evenin' borin', borin', borin'.'

'Surely you've got your blessed club!'

'That's only one night a week.'

'Well, then, I suggest you just buckle down and at least concentrate in class.' She plonked her hands down on the table and I knew she'd run out of ideas.

'Just try, Nip.'

'I can't concentrate, Dad. The other boys keep mucking about.'

'Well, don't sit with them then.' Mum had started wearing glasses and I sat and stared at them until all I could see was my reflection in the lenses.

'I did try, the other day, in Technical Drawing.'

'You did, did you?' Dad was so small in the reflection that his mouth didn't move. 'And what happened?'

'Ol' 'oggy came in an' said, "M'I suppose it m'would be too much to expect you to ask permission before m'you change m'your position?"'

'Didn't you explain why you'd moved?'

'' 'e didn't even look at me when 'e said it, the sod.'

'*Simon.*'

'Jus' walked in an' put 'is case down an' was takin' 'is scarf off. I didn't even know it was me 'e was talkin' to.'

'But didn't you explain, Nip?'

'' 'ow could I with all the boys there?'

'You could have had a quiet word with him afterwards.'

'Tol' me to get back to me seat before 'e lost 'is temper completely. 'e don' care, Dad. 'e's jus' a miserable ol'—'

'Well, I think that's enough of that, Simon.' My reflection disappeared as Mum stood up and they cleared the tea things away together. 'And we'd appreciate it if you'd show a bit more respect for your teachers.'

I stayed at the table until Mum told me to move so that she could shake the cloth and then I settled down on the woodbox by the fire. I'd got a book out of Mum's bedroom about the feudal barons and I read for a while until the lines all ran together. I tried to concentrate by running the point of my protractor along the lines but then I started to pick at the corner of my thumb with it and then to measure out the point to see if it would penetrate Hoggy's jacket and pullover and shirt to his heart. My eyes flickered and closed in the heat from the fire and I wondered how I'd feel when we got back to school and I saw the scratch I'd put in my desk top to remind me that we'd got three weeks' Christmas holiday to look forward to when I'd put it there, and I wished I hadn't done it now because it'd be bad enough to have to go back at all.

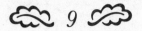

9

*M*um and Dad said they'd like to go to Holy Communion this Christmas morning and they expected I could be relied on to make sure we were all awake bright and early. I lay staring at the dark until it started to pinprick and I prayed that I'd be able to go to sleep quickly, and not wake up too early to open my presents or else it would be all over, again, before it had hardly started, when I felt myself falling and I woke up as I was about to hit the ground and realised I'd been asleep, but I couldn't tell for how long.

I scrabbled my hand about in the dark until I felt my stocking. It crackled as I grabbed it and I rolled over and out of bed and felt my way into Mum and Dad's room. Dad grunted as I turned their light on and rolled over when I snuggled down between them.

'Strewth alive, Simon. Watch where you're putting your cold feet.'

'Happy Christmas, Mum.' I kissed her cheek and she opened one eye.

'Oh dear . . .' She shut her eye and shook her head and opened them both. 'I was in the middle of a lovely dream . . .'

'Well, he's put paid to that.'

'Don't you want to see what I've got in my stocking, Dad?'

'Blimey!' He turned over again and squinted at the light. 'S'pose so, but I'd've preferred to 'ave a bit more shut-eye.'

'Yes, course we do.' Mum hauled herself up onto her elbows. She had a lime green nightie on that was the colour of the fairy on the plate in her best set in the china cabinet. 'Let's see what Father Christmas has brought you.' She nudged Dad in the ribs and he sat up as well.

'Go on then. Let battle commence.'

Mum had tied the top of the stocking with Christmas tape and I pulled it into a knot and she had to get the nail-file for Dad to undo it. She'd wrapped each parcel separately and I undid them carefully so that we could use the wrapping paper again. I pulled out a chocolate Father Christmas and a chocolate reindeer and a box of metal puzzles and some new coloured pencils and a box of dates.

I peeled the shiny paper off the Father Christmas and bit his ear and half his head off. 'Want some, Dad?'

He took it from me and held it in the palm of his hand. 'Look at this, Ina.'

'Look at what, dear?'

'This perishin' chocolate. It's hollow. You're paying through the nose for fresh air.'

'So it is.' She took it from him but she raised her eyebrows at me as if she wasn't really surprised at all. 'What a swizz.'

'I'll 'ave a date though.'

There were a couple of tangerines in the foot and a packet of fudge and a thing like an old cricket ball.

'What's that, Mum?' There was a sort of seam round the outside that I could have got a spin on.

'That's a pomegranate.'

'Is it? What do I do with it?'

'You eat it, Simon. That's what you do with it.'

'They're not up to much, Nip.' Dad was on his side now, resting his head on his elbow.

'Oh they are, George. I went right down to the bottom of South Street to get that.' Mum took it from me and pressed it. 'That's all crammed full of lovely fleshy seeds, Simon.'

'Tasteless.' Dad sucked at his date stone and put it on top of the box. 'We used to get them out East occasionally. Some of the blokes made a fuss about them but I was never very struck.'

'You'll get struck, my lad, if you put the mockers on that pomegranate.'

'Oh yeah.' Dad yawned and stretched and Mum winked at me. 'Better get the kettle on then, and the fire lighted.'

225

'Yes, and I must get a move on else we'll wind up late for church.'

'Do you have to go to church, Mum? It's Christmas.'

'That's exactly why we're going, Simon. Now up you get and get cracking.'

I felt my way out to the gate and opened it with my hand stuffed up my sleeve so that I didn't have to touch the cold latch. Nothing moved and the wet darkness weighed down on us as if we were dead and buried and waiting to go to wherever we were going to.

'You walk in front, Simon. That way you'll keep up.'

I edged forward sideways so that I could keep my hands in my pockets. 'Can't see a thing, Dad.'

'Let him come in between us, George.' Mum's furry glove was searching for my hand. 'Then we can all walk in the road together.'

We edged forward together.

'Not sure about this, Ina.' Dad was picking his way ahead like Grandad searching for a mole run with a long stick. 'What if we go blundering into a blasted car parked in the road 'ere?'

'Oh, I shouldn't think we will, dear. After all, Peter and Peggy're away and I don't for a moment suppose Mr Latterell'll've brought his lorry home for Christmas.'

'Why don't we go back then, Dad?'

'Because we've decided to go and we're going.'

'And you can start coming with us regularly as soon as you've been confirmed, my lad.' Mum was walking off the balls of her feet so that her heels didn't clatter. 'We really must see about getting him done before long, George.'

'Do I have to, Mum?' I could feel Dad turning so I turned as well down Crouch Cross Lane.

'You'll enjoy it, Simon.' Mum squeezed my hand. 'Why, it was the most wonderful experience of my life when the bishop put his hand on my head and . . .'

Dad was yawning but he covered it up by going 'te-tum, te-tum, te-tum' under his breath.

'It felt as if an almighty fire was covering me all over and I was all aglow.'

'Oh yeah?'

'And then you'll be able to come with us and take communion.'

'But I don't want—'

'Blimey O'Riley, Simon. Don't argue.' Dad's arm pulled me to a stop. 'And where the devil's the gate?' We'd mounted the pavement from the road at what felt like the bottom of Nan and Grandad's garden. 'Just for goodness' sake do as you're told.'

I was too cold and tired to argue so I hunched myself up tighter in my overcoat as the warm fringe of light showed out round the edges of Nan's curtains and I held my breath, from their front door right round the house and while they were unlocking the back door to let us in.

The smell of frying bacon and eggs and porridge poured out of the kitchen and a man on the wireless was saying 'Howdy, Pards. This is Big Bill Campbell welcoming you to the Gran' Ole Oprey' as Mum and Dad and Nan and Grandad whispered 'Happy Christmas' to each other so that they wouldn't wake Old Gran up.

'Aren't you coming in 'long'a us, my duck?' Nan had come out into the scullery. 'You don' 'ave to stay out 'ere on your ownsome, you know.'

'Jus' gettin' warm, Nan.'

'Any other Christmas 'e'd've been jumping about like a two-year-old, Mum.' Dad put his trilby back on and kissed Nan goodbye. 'We must be off now else Pop'll be starting without us.'

Mum kissed me and I braced myself as they opened the door and went out and then I followed Nan into the kitchen.

Grandad was pouring hot water into the tea pot. He rinsed it around and poured some more and winked at me.

'Happy Christmas, young Simon. How are you?'

'All right, Grandad.' I went to kiss him but I wasn't sure if I was too big for that sort of thing so I nuzzled up against him instead.

227

'Haven't you got one for me then, Simon?'

I kissed Nan and took my coat off.

'Sit you down then, young maester.' Grandad was still rinsing the tea pot around. 'Cuppa tea 'n then we'll 'ave'us break'us.'

I stood with my backside over the fire and bent backwards and forwards so that the heat covered me evenly.

A man was singing 'Jimmy Crack Corn' on the wireless. 'That's not opera, is it, Grandad?'

'No-o, not as I remember it.' Grandad lifted the tea strainer and kept on pouring. 'It's Wild West music.'

' "Chapel in the Valley"'ll be on in a minute, Simon.'

'Oh, will it, Nan?' Nan was letting the fat drip off the bacon with a fish slice. 'I like this kind of music.'

'Well, it's nearly finished now, my duck. Do you want some fried bread.'

'M'm, yes please, Nan.'

'Aye, and some tom-atoes.' Grandad put my tea down by my place and we sat down together.

I balanced my spoon on the surface of my tea and guessed it would fill up and sink before Nan gave me my porridge and put the eggs and bacon in the oven to keep warm. She put two bowls down and gave Grandad the saucepan and closed the oven door and then my spoon sank and she sat down.

I twirled my porridge spoon in the syrup and let it down in a snake's head at the top and then made the body coil around the edge of the bowl until the tail petered out into a series of sticky drips and then I stirred it in.

'Porridge all right, lovey?'

'M'm lovely thanks, Nan.' It was always thinner and more creamy tasting made with almost all water and I hoped Nan wouldn't tell Mum I'd eaten it all.

'And how's the world with you, Simon?' Grandad took a last scrape at the pan and reached behind him and put it on the cooker.

'All right, thank you, Grandad.' I licked my spoon and looked at my reflection in it like I'd done when I lived here, before Dad had come back from the POW camp and Mum was still working at the Admiral's, and we'd had our

228

breakfast together and he'd taken me to work with him to Mrs Evans's in the wheelbarrow.

'And school all right, Simon?'

'M'm, s'pose so, Nan.' I gave her my bowl and ran my hands down the back of the chair where it was warm from the range. 'You still got that old wheelbarrow over at Evans's, Grandad?'

He rested his elbow on the table and scratched the corner of his mouth. 'Blimey no, Simon. That went west years ago.'

'Oh.' I took my bacon and egg from Nan. 'Did it?'

'I expect you'll be making pretty good progress now that you've settled in a bit, Simon.'

'Yes thank you, Nan.'

I'd been able to sit up straight against the back-board in the wheelbarrow and sometimes he'd given me his mackintosh to sit on to make me comfortable. The wheel had made a squelching sound as it went through mud and I could lean my head back and look up at him and say 'I'm glad I'm not having to stabble through that lot' and he never bumped me when he put it down to open a gate or close it after him.

'And plenty of sport and mates to play with, I'll be bound.'

'We can't play very much, Nan.'

'Why not, my duck?'

'Field gets all wet when it rains and the stones come through when it's dry.'

'Oh.' Grandad waited for Nan to give him his bacon and egg and sit down and then he poured more tea.

'Did you get all covered with fire when you were confirmed, Grandad?'

'Not as I recall, Simon. That was the disciples after Pentecost, if I'm not mistaken.'

'Was it?'

Nan cut the rind off her rasher and looked up. 'What brought that up, my love?'

I scraped a cross in the fat on my plate with my knife-point. 'Cos Mum said that's what happened to her.'

'Well then' – Grandad rinsed tea round his back teeth and swallowed – 'if she says that's what happened, then I s'pose it did, don't you?'

229

'Yes, Grandad.' I scratched the tail on my cross out longer and then edged out the outline of the body. 'Wouldn't it've burned her though?'

Grandad mopped up the rest of his egg with a crust of bread. 'Shouldn't't've thought so.' He popped the bread into his mouth. 'It'd've been holy fire, you see, more'n likely.'

'Poor little soul.' Nan collected the plates together. ' 'e shouldn't tease oo, should 'e?'

Grandad put soap flakes and soda and hot water in the galvanised bowl and washed up and I sat back in the chair by the window watching a blackbird searching for grubs amongst the leaves under the russet-apple tree. I'd never heard of this fire stuff settling on anybody in real life but it would be just my luck if it came down on me and the boys got to hear about it and spread it around at school that I was a bible-thumper or a sky-pilot or something.

There was the pattern of a rose on the oil cloth on the kitchen table. I sat picking at it and listening to Sandy MacPherson's 'Chapel in the Valley'. It was mainly prayers and hymns and then a parable but nothing about what Grandad had called the Holy Spirit and I was still thinking how I'd have made jolly sure I didn't waste seed slinging it in the hedge or chucking it about on stony ground if I was ever a sower, because Grandad had told me what seed cost nowadays, when Mum and Dad got back.

'Many there, son?' Grandad moved the kettle back on to the hot-plate and refilled it from the galvanised jug they'd used, Dad said, when they had to get water from the well at the bottom of the Simms's garden.

'M'yeah.' Dad was yawning and thinking at the same time. 'Us and Peters's four, and the Dainties an' son seven, and Miss Turner eight and Bill Lovesey – not Mrs – nine, an' a new couple from up the Redvins way, eleven.'

'Eleven, my goodness!' Nan took the tea cosy off and felt the pot and put the cosy back again. 'I should put a spoonful more tea in that pot if I were you, Art. It's still freshish.'

Grandad squeezed past her to get to the tea caddy. 'Eleven, eh. Cuppa tea?'

Mum and Dad took their coats off and said they'd sit down for a minute or two, although Mum said they'd have to be getting back to do a bit of squaring up before they came up again for dinner and that reminded Nan to look at the turkey, that she'd got up at half-past five to put in, so that it could cook slowly and be tender without falling apart, and she explained how she still couldn't get used to cooking with electricity and that she wished she'd never let herself be talked into parting with her old range and that in future she'd concentrate on making the jelly and trifle and getting a nice piece of ham from Greig's for supper and rely on somebody else to cope with cooking the turkey.

'And now I suppose I'll be expected to spend all bloomin' Christmas morning up there for now and ever more.' We were halfway down Nan's path and Mum was still doing up her headscarf. 'And would you please get a move on, Simon, because it's far later than I'd anticipated being home and I'll have to move like stink to catch up.'

Old Gran's friend, Mrs Ewicker, who she'd known ever since she'd kept the post office in Hanover, wasn't at all well and I heard Dad telling Mum he'd just pop up and see her for half an hour later on and then we'd go straight up to Nan's and meet her there. I didn't hear what Mum said but I didn't think she'd like it much because she hated walking up through the village on her own with everybody gawping at her.

Crouch Cross Lane on Christmas morning was like walking through a market. Derek Brown and Jerry Henry were standing on the bank in front of Derek's house showing each other their new shoes and their sisters were clopping around in their mums' sling-backs, with bits of curtain draped around them because Jerry's sister Shirley had been given a box of stage make-up for Christmas and they were practising at being grown-ups. One of the Vickers boys had got a pedal car for Christmas but he hadn't got the hang of pedalling it. He was sitting in it, with his goggles down over his nose, making brrum-brrum noises that sent an avalanche of bubbles down his chin, and zigger-zaggering backwards

231

and forwards about six inches and swinging the steering wheel all over the place with his brothers and sisters and the younger Gander children yelling at him that he was doing it all wrong.

'I'm glad you didn't keep on about having toys like that, Simon.'

I looked back. 'Never thought about 'em.'

'Cost a fortune and they're never satisfactory. Kids're mad on 'em for a day or two and then they go wrong and they get fed up with them and they finish up rusting out in the garden. Complete waste'a money.'

'Is it, Dad?'

Most of the houses had their lights on and some had hung their Christmas cards across their windows on bits of shiny string and one or two were lit up with Christmas trees with coloured lights so that the darker the house the brighter it looked. It was misty and muggy and didn't feel at all like Christmas although nearly everybody we met had a new pullover or a new coat and little girls went by carrying new handbags or wheeling new dolls' prams and it made me wonder whether Christmas presents weren't really just all the things people would have bought throughout the year if they hadn't had Christmas to stuff them all into, and I felt so miserable that I was glad to get through the village and up past the hall.

The mist on the elm trees by the Wobble gates drip-dripped as if it was raining and on, up to Hanover, there was a smell of rotting apples, that reminded me of cider, coming from around the base of some scrubby bushes.

'Why d'they call them crab-apple trees, Dad?'

'I dunno, Nip. Cos they're sour and've got a bite to 'em, I suppose.'

'Crabs aren't sour.'

'No, but they don' arf bite!'

We crossed the road by Brindle's coal yard. The heaps of coal had been covered with tarpaulins and the double doors to the blacksmith's shop were closed and it looked as if life had been closed down and was never going to open again.

The bricks in Cabby's yard were lifting in places and the weeds were growing up through them and there were still a few unpicked apples, on his espaliered apple trees, with the middles eaten out so that they looked like the insides of skulls. He still kept a pig or two and one was rubbing itself against the door of its pen and its weight made the padlock bulge. I'd never understood why they didn't just barge their way out and escape instead of staying cooped up all their lives.

Cabby's lorry was half in the garage and half out of it. It had A. McANDREW – GENERAL HAULIER written across the back and I wondered what the A stood for and if he was ever sorry that he couldn't call himself A. McAndrew and Son, or even Sons, and why he'd never had any children when he had a nice big garden for them to play in and he'd always been keen on football, Dad said.

'Smarten yourself up then, Nip.' Dad turned off the pavement into a low doorway and straightened his cap and pulled his shoulders back and knocked on the door. 'We'll just pay our respects and then get home for some lunch.'

Mrs Ewicker's daughter let us in and pointed us up the stairs. 'I shouldn't stay too long if I were you, because she gets ever so tired.' Miss Ewicker looked too old to be anyone's daughter. 'And if she gets over-tired she goes to sleep and then we can't get her off at night.' She said this from the living room and then disappeared into a dark little kitchen with a blazing fire, and a pair of man's boots sticking out in front of it from behind the kitchen door.

The stairs creaked as we climbed them and Dad's tap on the bedroom door seemed to reverberate through the house.

There was a long pause, and I was wondering if perhaps she'd died, when a thin voice called, 'Come in.'

Old Mrs Ewicker was nearly ninety but she looked even older. There were big spaces in her hair and it looked like bits of spider's web that had blown there and would blow away again if the wind caught it. She was yellow and wrinkled and bony and I couldn't see much point in getting that old.

'Just popped up to wish you a Happy Christmas from Old Gran, Mrs Ewicker.'

The old lady lay there with her eyes blank and Dad got closer to her and said it again.

'Thank you. Young George, isn't it?' Her eyes had a

233

cloudy skin over them and they didn't move. 'Give 'er my best wishes.' She coughed and drew her shawl more round her. 'Don't s'pose she gets about much nowadays.'

'Oh she's marvellous really.' Dad was right up against her ear and I could have heard him in Tangmere. 'But she couldn't've walked all up 'ere. The damp gets on 'er chest.'

' 'asn't got a vest?' Old Mrs Ewicker started forward off her pillows.

'The damp,' Dad yelled. 'It gets on 'er chest.'

Old Mrs Ewicker's head shook as if it was going to come off. 'Well I never. It's 'ard when you get old. Very little to give thanks for. But no vest. Poor old Fanny Grainger without a bodice to 'er name.'

'No, *no* . . .' Dad used his hands. 'Chest, CHEST.'

'I know all 'bout that, young George. You don't 'ave to tell me where this damp weather catches you.' She was pulling at the bedclothes. ' 'specially if you've nothing warm to wrap up in.'

'Saints preserve us!' Dad was so far over the bed it looked as if he was getting in with her. 'What are you doing, Mrs Ewicker?'

'Got to get to my drawer there.' The outline of a knee was drawing up under the bedclothes. 'Got one or two spare ones in my drawer.'

'Oh, for pity's sake.'

'Mr Wilson!' Miss Ewicker burst in. 'Mummy, whatever *are* you up to?'

Dad was still explaining as Miss Ewicker showed us out and 'Happy Christmas' got trapped in the door as she closed it behind us.

'That wasn't particularly successful, was it, Simon?'

'Not really, Dad.'

'Course she's getting on a bit you know, Simon.'

'Yes. Dad. Da-ad?'

'M'm?'

'Can I eat some of my fudge on the way home?'

'Don't see why not.'

I'd expected him to say 'no' but he didn't seem to notice what I was doing and the bag was empty by the time we got to Nan's gate.

*

They all said it was very thoughtless of me to fill up with fudge when I knew how much Nan looked forward to me eating a good dinner on Christmas Day, but I was starving by the time it was ready and then, just as they were going to serve it up, Old Gran said she wanted to go out the back. Nan had brought the sprouts to the boil twice and Grandad had carved the turkey and put it back in the oven before they started to get worried about her.

'Perhaps she's dropped off.' Grandad wiped the carving knife on the dish cloth.

'She never has done before, Art.'

'Well, there's got to be a first time for everything.'

'And it'd be dangerous to try to wake her. And where d'you think you're off to, Simon?'

'Nowhere, Mum. Shan't be a minute.'

I was starving and my stomach was aching and rumbling so I thought I'd hurry her up by slinging a few bits of earth at the flints around the toilet window until some hit the glass. Old Gran yelled back to know what the devil I was playing about at and soon after that she came out. By the time they'd made the gravy and sorted out who wanted stuffing and who didn't and remembered they'd been going to make bread sauce as well this year, I was feeling faint. Nobody really wanted bread sauce but they decided we'd all better have some as they'd made it and I couldn't wait any longer and popped a sprout into my mouth and sat there sucking it while Grandad gave thanks for what we were about to receive.

'Remains to be seen whether it's worth giving thanks for ...' Nan went on to tell us how turkey was one of the few meats that still agreed with her but that she was so fagged out with all the preparation that she would only be able to manage the tiniest piece of breast, to be sociable, and even that would be a bit of a struggle.

'It's as tender as tender can be.' Mum held a piece up on her fork to show how tender it was.

'Not overcooked, is it?' Nan cut a slice of stalk off a brussel-sprout and pushed it to the side of her plate. 'Only

I'm sure I'll never get the hang of this new oven and I do like always to give everybody a nice—'

'There's nothing wrong with it.' Old Gran never cut meat: she always sorted out which way the grain ran and pulled it apart with her knife and fork. 'But the veg could've done with a pinch more salt.'

'Well, I'll go to—' Nan glanced at Grandad as if she expected him to tell Old Gran off but he wasn't listening. 'I've been putting the same amount of salt in for the past forty years and you've never complained before.'

'I'm not complaining.' Old Gran manoeuvred a minute piece of potato onto her fork and cemented a bit of cabbage to it with a splash of gravy and held it still while she chibbled away with her front teeth at what she'd picked up before. 'I was just saying, it's probably the salt. Salt nowadays doesn't salt like it used to years ago.'

I'd eaten mine from the outside and gone round in a circle to make it last longer but I'd almost come to the end now and they were so engrossed in a conversation about whether the Russians were watering down the salt from Siberia to pay us back for getting more of Berlin than they'd got or if it didn't matter anyway because we probably got ours from one of the Commonwealth countries and the wireless said there was a plan called Zeto to get electricity out of the sea and Dad reckoned they'd probably try to turn it into drinking water at the same time and they might as well extract the salt while they were at it, that I had to keep scraping at the gravy stains until Nan noticed and said she thought there might be the odd sprout left. I stayed holding my plate out until she scraped some gravy up off the bottom of the meat dish and then found a potato or two that nobody else wanted and then Grandad said there was a stack of turkey left and that he'd be contending with it till Easter if he knew anything about it. He cut me off a wing and then cut a slice or two off the other side to even it up and I managed to dislodge another chunk that was joined by a bit of crispy so I finished up with nearly as much as I'd had at the start.

'You don't think that might be a little too much, do you, Simon?'

'Nope.' I squashed the soft centre of a roast potato in

gravy and sucked it through my teeth. 'Jus' right, thanks, Dad.'

Mum and Dad had got into the habit of not taking any notice when I was cheeky, so long as I wasn't too cheeky, but they sometimes looked at each other in a way that left me wondering what they really thought and their silence seemed to spread as the window clouded over with the steam from the Christmas pudding and the condensation inside the windows where the misty rain lay like pebbledash on the glass.

'Be lighting up time by the time the others get 'ere.' Nan had suggested they wash up before she made a pot of tea.

'Yes it will. Oh dear oh dear,' Mum said, so loudly that the others stopped and looked at her and she coloured up and pulled the sleeves of her frock up more above the line of the soap suds by sliding her arms against her ribs. 'Well, I do hate it when we have to shut the daylight out.'

'Cor, I don't.' I finished pencilling in the eyes on Joe Haverty on the back page of the *Daily Express*. 'I love it when we can draw the curtains and get a good old fire roaring away up the chimney.'

'Yes, well I do wish you'd stop talking about it roaring away up the chimney with such relish, Simon.' Mum scratched her top lip and left a blob of suds on it. 'The very thought of a chimney fire sets my nerves on edge.'

'Gonna light the fire in the front room, Grandad?'

'Aye.' He twisted and stretched as if he had damp wings drying.

'When, Grandad?'

'Better get on with it now.' He winked at me. 'Else it won't have time to burn up.'

We went through to the front room and I started laying the paper and kindling wood and then I followed him out into the old wash-house where he'd just lit up a Woodbine and was leaning against the stone copper.

'You remember when we used to boil the Christmas pudding in there, Grandad?'

He looked down at the charred grate and touched his toe against the blackened brickwork. 'Aye,' he said. 'You're

237

going back a bit now, Simon, but I remember.' He flicked an ash towards the grate and it lodged, grey against the damp black, on the twisted metal bars. 'But we'd best get a move on else the others'll be here before the fire's established.'

Grandad stood with his hand on the brown varnished top of the wireless on the cupboard where they kept the biscuits and Ovaltine and Nan's pills. His hand moved down to the On/Off knob and he twisted it. There was a click and the light on the dial faded and the voice died. The photograph of Uncle Steven, which Nan had etched with black silk again this year, looked down with the same stare that I remembered right back to when I was a baby. Grandad's hand slid back from the wireless and one finger left a trail in the dust on the rim round the dial where Nan had told Old Gran not to flick around with her duster in case she messed up the reception.

'They're here!' Grandad pinched a dead leaf out of Nan's Christmas cactus and crumpled it between his fingers. 'Better get the kettle on, I s'pose.'

Uncle Edward's car pulled up and the rear door half opened and stayed half open until a blue car stopped behind it and then they all got out.

'Uncle Roger got a car, Grandad?'

'Next door's. He sees to it for him.' Grandad shook his box of matches and then turned the hot plate on: they'd never had a gas cooker but he always said it felt as if the electric one should be lighted.

Michael and Jonathan waited on the pavement while Uncle Edward opened Aunty Sarah's door and stood back to let her out. Stephen and little Rachel were out of their car first. Stephen rushed towards the gate with his coat flying behind him like the tatters of a raggedy jackdaw and Rachel tried to follow him but he slipped inside the gate and closed it on her and she turned to Aunty Doreen, who was climbing out of the front seat with their new baby, and walked to the gate holding her mum's hand so that Stephen had to open it.

Rachel's coat and skirt pulled up and showed her pants

238

and bottom as she reached for Uncle Roger to carry her but he was holding a blanket around the baby and I imagined him, all tight-fisted and screwy-eyed, snuggled up in his blankets smelling of milk sick and talcum powder and I prayed that Mum wouldn't make me look at him and see what tiny little hands he'd got and ask me if I could credit I'd had hands as small as that at one time.

They all kissed each other and then Uncle Edward went to open the gate for Aunty Sarah but Stephen had stayed there and he held his hand out, as if he was asking for something for letting them through, and Uncle Edward strained against the gate until Uncle Roger came up and made out he was going to box Stephen's ears and Stephen danced away and put his hands up to his head and made a pair of Mickey Mouse ears and then he flew up the garden with his arms out and waving up and down and making a noise like a jet up the garden path and past the kitchen window with Rachel puffing along behind him like a bee in her yellow coat with the shiny black belt. Michael and Jonathan followed in their short grey trousers and school macs, like a couple of toy soldiers. Aunty Sarah and Aunty Doreen came next with the baby and Uncle Edward and Uncle Roger came last, sauntering along like a couple of bulls in a field who couldn't be bothered to escape out of the open gate.

I met Stephen at the back door. He zoomed round the corner, skidded to a halt and jabbed his fingers into my tummy.

'Hello, Steve.' I tried to grab him round the head but he squirmed away.

Rachel clitter-clattered round the corner and came straight at me with her arms wide and I bent and scooped her up. 'Hello, Rach?' I humped her a bit higher so that she was sitting on my forearm. 'Thought you'd've had a cold little bum?'

'No.' She giggled and rubbed her nose against mine. 'Nice and warm,' and then she kicked to be let down as Michael and Jonathan walked round past the laurel bushes.

'Hello, you two.'

239

'Hello, Simon.' Michael looked embarrassed but Jonathan rushed forward with his hand clenched up in his trouser pocket.

'C'mon, Simon. I've got something to show you.'

We went round by the rainwater butts and got Rachel in on the inside of us so that we could keep an eye on her. Jonathan was red in the face and dancing about from one foot to the other as if he was waiting for somebody to come out of the toilet.

'What'cha got then, Jon? Packet'a fags?'

'No.' He peeped his head out round the corner to make sure his mum and dad had gone in. 'Better than that,' and he pulled his hand out of his pocket slowly and opened his fingers.

'What is it?'

'A pipe.'

'I can see that. But what's so special about a bubble pipe?'

'It's not a bubble pipe. It's full'a baccy.'

I took it from him and smelt it. 'So it may be but it's still a bubble pipe jus' the same.'

Jon took it back and turned it over. 'Still light though, won't it?'

'Yeah, spec so. But it'll taste 'orrible if you've been blowing bubbles in it.'

'Well I haven't.' He put the stem in his mouth and gave it a good suck.

'You don't know it hasn't been used as a bubble pipe, Jonathan.'

'Why doesn't 'e?'

'He got it from school, Simon. Gave a boy sixpence for it.' Michael bent and straightened his sock. 'And he shouldn't put it in his mouth.'

'Be all right if he washes it first.'

'Yes, course it will.' Jonathan gave it a last sniff and put it back in his pocket. 'Shall we light it up after tea, Simon?'

'M'm, can do. S'sh.' I stood up straighter and looked casual as the back door opened.

'Yoo hoo! Anybody about?'

'That's Nan.'

'What we gonna do?'

'Nothing. It's all right.'

'Are you all out there, my loves? Don't you want to come in the warm?'

'Jus' comin', Nan.'

'Oh there you are.' Nan came padding round, in her blue fluffy slippers. 'Aren't you comin' in to say 'ello to us?' She reached out to Rachel. 'And you'll get all cold-a-coddle-a-whimey out 'ere.'

'Yeah, we're jus' comin' in, Nan. We were just thinkin' what we could play.'

'Well, come on in now.' Nan stood aside and we trooped in as if we were soldiers who'd been discovered and taken prisoner.

They were all giving their hats and coats to Mum and she was trying to balance them on one arm and open the door to the stairs with her other hand. Dad squeezed between Uncle Roger and Grandad and opened it for her. Old Gran was holding the new baby and the only place we had to stand in was alongside the kitchen table and against the sideboard.

'He's a pretty little fella.' Old Gran was looking for someone to give him to. 'But 'e's a bit of a handful. Makes my arm ache.'

' 'ere, let me 'ave 'im a minute.' We squashed back against the sideboard as Nan pressed past. 'Just while Doreen takes 'er 'eadscarf off.'

They were gradually getting settled. Aunty Doreen and Aunty Sarah were on the sofa and Uncle Edward was moving round in front of the fire and Uncle Roger had found the little stool and was perching on it with his back against the cooker so that there was a space left on the sofa for Mum.

'And how's things with you, Edward?'

'Oh, mustn't grumble, Dad.'

I leant back and trapped my finger between my back and the edge of the sideboard. They always said they mustn't grumble but they usually did and then they'd start talking about the price of things.

'Got a new estate going up just outside Lavant but

it's the devil's own job getting hold of the materials.'

'Shortages, shortages, shortages!' Dad had been reading about the threatened dock strike in yesterday's *Express*. 'Can't think what they think they're going to achieve by it all.'

'Higher wages, George' – I'd felt it coming – 'and then up'll go the prices.' I tried to look away but Dad saw me.

'What the devil's up with you, Simon?'

'Nothing, Dad.'

They gradually stopped looking at me and Grandad told them about what a rotten summer we'd had again this year and that he was blowed if he was going to get a new strawberry net until we started getting summers you could count on again and then Nan suggested they all went into the front room, now the fire had had a chance to burn up, while she and Mum got everybody a piece of cake and a cup of tea because she didn't suppose they'd be ready for their tea yet so soon after dinner so we wouldn't have any but have supper later.

'Course I blame the unions.'

Michael and Jonathan and Stephen and I were sitting in a tight circle on the floor picking the glacé cherries out of our cake and putting them on Rachel's plate because we didn't like them.

'. . . absolutely disgraceful how the country's being held to ransom by one lot of layabouts after another.'

'And I can't see the sense of it, Edward, because all it means is that prices'll go up so they'll be no better off in the long run.'

'Well, I can't think what's got into the miners lately.'

'Cor, I like that, Ina.' Dad was polishing the head of his lighter with the blunt end of a match. 'Where'd they've been without the unions?'

'Well, I'll say this, once and for all . . . if I get any more moaning and groaning about extra pay for working in wet weather, shorter hours, more overtime or any blessed thing else I'll shut up shop altogether and they can see what they make of that!'

242

I'd picked up the last of the crumbs with the wet end of my finger and was studying the crack pattern in the glazing.

'It's not their fault if they want to follow the boss's spending pattern.'

Grandad's foot stopped its heart-beat rhythm on the carpet and there was a pause in Nan's knitting and Uncle Edward went a deep shade of purple.

'Perhaps you'd like to sit down for a moment, dear?' Aunty Sarah patted the inch or two of space between her and Mum but she needn't have bothered because Uncle Edward was fixed as if he'd been pinned to the wall with a nail through the heart.

They seemed pretty well agreed that they didn't know where I got it from and that it was all wrong anyway and even if it wasn't there was a time and a place for everything but I couldn't understand what they were making such a fuss about because it had sounded all right when Taffy Davis had said it up at the Men's Club when I was waiting for a haircut one night, and everyone there had agreed with him.

I tried to sneak a smile from Mum, when they started talking again, but she wouldn't look at me so I whispered to Michael to ask the others if they'd like to go and play in the kitchen.

'But it's all nice'n snug in 'ere, my duck.' Nan sounded as if we'd decided to emigrate. 'What you wanna go off out there for?'

I put my hand over my mouth and hissed 'play cards' at Michael.

'Play cards, Nan.'

'Well, couldn't you play in 'ere, my duck?'

I nudged Michael again. 'No room.'

'Did you say something, Simon?'

'No, Dad. But it is a bit cramped down 'ere, an' there'd be nowhere to put the cards.'

Mum sat straighter and stared at the pair of stuffed sparrow-hawks in the glass case on the shelf above the cabinet where they kept the glasses.

Dad was watching her. 'Couldn't you do something else then, for a few minutes?'

'Oh but, Dad—'

'Oh, for goodness' sake.' Mum rounded on me in a flash. 'Go on out into the kitchen and play if you must. But pity help you, Simon, if you get into any mischief out there.'

'We won't, Mum.' I pushed Stephen out first. 'And we'll be ever so quiet.'

'And, Michael . . . ?'

'Yes, Daddy.'

'No misbehaving, mind.'

There were times when I wished I played football against Uncle Edward but all I could do was give him the kind of curled-lip look that Doug Ritson gave the masters at school, that they couldn't get you for, but that only made me feel worse because it would have been nice to have been friends with him so that I could have gone and played with Michael and Jonathan more, but he'd looked away and the others had gone on ahead so I followed them.

'Are we going to play cards, Simon?'

'Nah.' I ruffled Jonathan's hair.

'So that was a lie, Simon?'

'Wasn't a lie exactly.' I pushed my hair back and drew the curtains. 'Blimey, we were stuck in there like sardines and there was nothing to do except listen to their boring natter.'

'What we going to do?' Michael was beginning to look like his mother.

'You got any ideas, Simon?'

'Dunno, Jon.' I slung my arm over Jonathan's shoulder. 'What you wanna do? Play draughts or something?'

'Only two can play draughts.' Michael was beginning to sound like his mother.

'Okay then. What about hide'n seek?'

'Cor yes!' Jonathan was dancing up and down.

'I'll hide first.' Stephen tried to get behind the sofa.

'Hang on then. You can't hide until we've got our eyes hid. Dopey little mush.' I smiled at Michael and he smiled back. 'You wanna hide first, Michael?'

He looked around the kitchen. 'No, it's all right, Simon. You go first if you like.'

'Me. Me. I'll go first.' Stephen was jumping about from

one foot to the other and Rachel was looking up at him with her thumb in her mouth.

'Tell you what.' I bent towards her and she lifted her arms up to me. 'You let go out and stand on the stairs and close the door and I'll hide Rachel. I'll call you when she's ready and you can come and find 'er.'

'That'll be easy.' Jonathan was pressing the tobacco in his pipe down with his thumb. 'She'll never find a good place.'

'Won't she?' I chucked Rachel under the chin. 'We will, won't we, Rach? You'll see. Off you go.' I opened the door to the stairs for them and they filed out. 'And we'll only hide in the kitchen and in the passage. Nowhere else.'

I stood in the empty kitchen and looked at all the obvious places. 'Where you going to hide then, Rachel?'

She took her thumb out of her mouth and kicked to be put down.

'Under the table? No, they'd see you straight away. And not behind the sofa either. That's the first place they'd look.'

Her thumb went back into her mouth.

'Tell you what . . .' I touched my fingers to my lips and opened the kitchen door to the passage with my thumb against the latch to stop it making a noise, and took her by the hand.

It struck colder in the passage but she didn't seem to notice. I searched amongst the coats and macs hanging on the wall until I found Grandad's old gardening jacket and then I lifted Rachel up so that she was standing inside it on top of the umbrella stand that Grandad used for his walking sticks. Her arms fitted inside the sleeves and I buttoned it up and let the other coats fall back over it.

'All right, Rachel?'

'Yeth.'

'Good. You stand completely still and don't say a word and if they can't find you I'll give you a sweety, OK?'

'Yeth.'

'Right then.' I went back into the kitchen and stood the little shovel up in the coal scuttle, so that it scraped a bit. I waited a moment or two and then I went and

245

sat down by the wireless and stared at the light. 'Re-eady.'

The door flew back. It hit the wicker table and sent a shiver through Nan's Christmas cactus. In they flew.

'She's over here.' Michael made a bee-line for the back of the sofa by the scuttle. 'I heard them banging about over here.'

'Look under it.' Jonathan was down on his hands and knees but Stephen was in the way watching Michael, who'd overbalanced over the scuttle and got stuck between the back of the sofa and the wall so that he had to be helped out.

'She's not there,' he said as he brushed coal dust off his white ankle socks.

'Give us a clue, Simon.'

'Ah, go on. Surely you can find 'er. There aren't many places she could be.'

They set off again looking in all the places they'd looked before and pressing into the cushions and curtains.

'Oh do be sensible, Jonathan.' Michael had his hands on his hips. 'How could she be behind a picture?' His eyes moved on past the chimney and the cooker to the cuckoo clock and down to the dresser. 'P'raps she's in— Oh, lor'!'

A jar of jam rolled out. It hit the carpet sideways and the lid fell off. The sticky mixture oozed forward. Jonathan dived and scooped it up and held it in both hands.

'Blimey, that was close. Lucky it didn't go all over the carpet.' I took the jar while Stephen put the lid back on.

'Well, I give up.' Jonathan jammed his hands into his pockets so that his braces buttons showed on the tops of his trousers below his jumper. 'Don't you, Michael?'

Michael bit the inside of his lip. 'No, not yet.' He looked from me to the window. 'You didn't put her out there, did you?'

'No, course not. She'd've froze to death.'

'The larder!' Stephen was off like a rocket. 'He could've doubled back.' And the others followed him.

I went after them and stood by the coats while they clattered about amongst the old water jar of pickled eggs and the bottles of cider and port and sherry. The coats didn't move. A chill went through me. She might have suffocated.

'She's not there.'

The coat still didn't move. Maybe she'd slipped and hung herself.

'Let's get Daddy.' Jonathan looked suddenly brighter. 'He'll find her.'

'All right.' I tried to sound casual. 'Go and get him.'

They disappeared into the front room but I held back and whispered, 'You all right, Rachel?'

'Yeth' came back as if it was being breathed out through the walls.

'Good girl. Just stay quiet now.'

'But I wanna come out.'

'S'sh, just a bit longer.'

'Do tinkles.'

'Oh blimey, you don't, do you?' I looked towards the back door. I could get her out but I'd never be able to get her back in without them seeing. 'Just 'ang on a minute. Cross yer legs or somethin',' and then I went and stood by the front-room door.

The boys were fidgeting in a line in front of Uncle Edward.

'Came as no surprise to me when the police changed to Jags.' Uncle Edward flexed his shoulders as if his jacket was tight and, from an angle, I could see the back of his head reflected in the mirror above the fireplace. 'Not a bit of it. The bonnet's crammed full of engine. You'll have to have a look at it sometime, Roger.'

'Daddy.'

'There's not another engine to touch it.' Uncle Edward rocked backwards and forwards in front of the fire. 'Course, I needed a more powerful car to keep hopping about from one site to the other. One I could rely on.'

'Daddy!'

'I have to be everywhere at once. You can't afford to take your eyes off the men for a minute.'

'Da-addy?'

Red creases formed on Uncle Edward's neck as he leant forward. 'Yes, Jonathan.'

'Daddy. Simon's hidden Rachel and we've looked every-

247

where and we can't find her.' He'd taken hold of my uncle's hand and was towing him. 'So you come and help us.'

'Doesn't leave him much option, does he?' Mum laughed as she said it and I wondered what was so funny and why it was never funny when I tried to do something like that.

'Crikey,' Nan sat back and held her hand out to the fire, 'that makes a difference.'

'He's always appreciated an open fire.' Aunty Sarah was knitting something navy.

'Wonder he didn't catch fire.' Aunty Doreen seemed to laugh when she spoke.

'Probably fire-proof, Aunty.'

'Simon!'

'What, Mum?'

'I'm sorry, Sarah.'

'Don't worry, Ina.' Aunty Sarah smoothed her knitting out on her lap. 'Probably picks it up at school.'

'I don't know where he gets it from but we're getting pretty bloomin' browned off with it.'

The chair moved slightly as Grandad uncrossed his legs and bent towards me. 'She all right?'

I twisted up closer to him. 'Yes, Grandad. She's on the umbrella stand under your old gardening coat.'

He grunted and closed his eyes.

'Thought you were asleep, Art?' Nan was knitting socks and the light reflected off her glasses.

'Just resting my eyes.'

'Huh! You seem to be doing a lot of that lately.' Nan's needles slowed and Aunty's stopped. 'Stays out in that blessed shed until it's as black as yer 'at and then when 'e does come in and wash an' change 'e sits straight down with a book an' goes to sleep.'

'P'raps been at the 'omemade wine.' I winced as soon as I'd said it.

'Will you button your lip, Simon?'

'You what, my duck?'

'I was only joking, Nan.' They were all staring at me again.

'Do you know, Doreen . . .' Nan gradually looked away from me. 'When my old dad was alive an' made parsnip wine he used to be off out to work at seven in the morning until half-past six, seven and sometimes eight o'clock of an evening and then come 'ome an' get out in that shed with that blessed jug of 'is and come in for 'is supper as silly as an owl.'

Aunty Doreen was pressing holes in a piece of newspaper and unfolding it so that it looked like a flower. She held it up to me and smiled and then she refolded it and did some more.

'And how's work with you, Roger?' Old Gran had moved to the piano stool. 'You're looking tired.'

Uncle Roger rubbed the corner of his eye. He was thinner in the face now and looked more like the pictures of my dad before he went away to the war. 'Pretty busy, thanks, Gran. Plenty of overtime.'

'And plenty of tax.' Aunty Doreen let her pattern fall out and now it looked like a cake doily. 'The harder he works the more he gets taken off him. It's not fair.'

I felt Grandad move slightly and his hand went to his inside jacket pocket. An envelope crinkled and Mum and Dad exchanged glances.

'You should do what Roger's done, George.' Nan knitted a few more stitches. 'And you should 'ave done it years ago, Roger.'

'Yes, I know.'

'Could've 'ad a nice little bit put by now an' got a little car to take me out of myself occasionally and Ina'd love—'

'Edward's taking his time, isn't he?' I'd heard Mum telling Dad she didn't want a car at any price, when they thought I was asleep, and that she'd always said she'd be perfectly happy with another motor-bike, like they'd had before the war, so long as Dad didn't expect her to go up to Northumberland again on the back of it. 'Wonder if everything's all right?'

'Where d'you hide her, Simon?'

'Oh, she's hanging about somewhere, Nan.' I leant my head back and Grandad winked at me.

A log burned through and broke in a shower of sparks and Uncle Edward came back and stood in front of it. 'It's cooler out there,' he said and he looked straight through me.

'Couldn't you find her, then?'

'Oh, I followed them around for a while, you know, Roger. No point giving the game away.' He stepped forward a pace and folded his hands behind his back. 'She's quite well hidden.'

'Well, I think it's time she was found.' Mum looked as if she was going to do it herself.

'Come on, Grandad.' I leant back against him. 'You have a go.'

'Yes, yes. You find her.' Jonathan and the others had come in but now they dashed off out again.

'Hanging about somewhere?' Grandad bent forward as he stood up. 'Well, I don't know about that.' His leg brushed against my ear and his matches rattled in his pocket. 'Perhaps I'll have a look and then just turn the heating up a shade in the greenhouse before we get all boxed in for the evening.'

'Yeah,' I thought, 'and have a smoke while you're out there.'

Nan and Grandad and Old Gran had come down to lunch with us on Boxing Day but we'd come back to 64 with them for tea because they'd said Old Gran would have difficulty with the cracks in the pavement after dark and that if I wanted to preserve my eyesight I wouldn't keep on about going to the pictures from morning to night because that was jolly nearly as bad for your eyes as insisting on darning by lamp light when the Estate had just forked out a small fortune to have the place wired up for electricity.

'Don't be so silly.' Old Gran peered over her glasses at Nan as she snipped her darning wool off the sock she'd been mending. 'Load of old codswallop!'

'Yeah. Ol' Gran was darnin' by lamp light for bloomin' ages an' she'd got eyes like an' 'awk.'

'Do stop speaking in that slovenly way, Simon.' Mum was putting the cups away. 'If you please.'

'A nawk?' Dad was leaning back on the sofa with his hands behind his head. 'That's a sort of deer-thing, isn't it?'

250

'You're thinking of an elk, dear.' Mum was reaching for her dictionary. 'If I'm not very much mistaken.'

'You're right, Ina.' Nan took a liquorice allsort and passed the tin to Dad. 'And we may as well do the crossword now that you've got your dictionary out, Ina.'

Dad passed Mum our *News of the World* and Nan woke Grandad up because he was sitting on hers.

Old Gran finished drawing the seams together on her other glove and then she drew out a pair of Grandad's old gardening trousers from under her chair. 'Don't know where all this needlework keeps coming from.' She held them up to the light to show us the great hole in the pocket. 'If I've darned this 'ole once I've darned it a hundred times.'

'That's a bit of an exaggeration, Mum.' Nan was pencilling in 'aloes' into 11-down to see if the letters fitted while Mum made sure it meant what it ought to mean.

'Exaggeration or no, it wouldn't need doin' at all if he'd only learn to keep his penknife in the other pocket for a change.'

'Then they'd both wear out.' Grandad opened his eyes and winked at me.

'Thought you were asleep, Art.'

'I was, Madame. But I woke up.'

'And it's not so much with it being dim.' Old Gran reached forward to put her needlework basket on the table and her neck stuck out of her black blouse like an ankle from a boot.

'H'm?' Nan was looking over Mum's shoulder. 'Don't think "quaint" would quite fit there, Ina. Although we do need an "n" for four down.' She tested a couple of letters in the margin of Friday's *Express*. 'And 'oo's dim, Mum?'

'I didn't say anything of the . . .' Old Gran sometimes knew when people were teasing her and she sat for a moment running her tooth over a blood-blistery spot, that showed black under the violet colour of her lips, and settled deeper into her chair still mumbling as if she was chewing on something stringy from dinner. 'I was just saying, Fran, if anybody took a blind bit of notice of anything I say, that it's not the dimness that damages your eyes, but the brightness.'

251

'D'you mean the harshness, Gran?' Mum sounded as if she was trying to make a word fit better.

'Harshness, brightness! I can't for the life of me see the difference.'

Nan dabbed the corner of her mouth with her handkerchief. 'It's all the same but it's the screwing your eyes up in the half dark that messes your eyes up.'

'There's all the difference in the world, Fran. I can't abide these blessed electric lights. They're not natural.' Old Gran looked around the room. 'They don't even cast proper shadows. Give me a good old-fashioned oil lamp any day.'

'You wouldn't be so darned fond of them if you 'ad to clean them. Sweet, Ina?' Nan passed the tin to Mum.

Old Gran's head twitched like a bird hearing a movement in a hedge nearby. 'Cleaned a jolly sight more dirty mantles than you 'ave, my girl.'

'And sooty wisps blowin' about all over the place.' Nan looked up and ducked as if one was settling on her now. 'And flinging shadows in all directions enough to give you the creeps.'

Dad uncrossed his legs from the right and crossed them to the left.

'None of those horrible reflections off everything.'

'Poking about the place like a lot of moles.'

I'd drawn my legs up and was resting my chin on my knees. There was a black ridge of shadow under the sideboard at the point where the light stopped and the dark started. If I was a mole that's where I'd go. Moles were cheery, busy little things, especially Mole in *Wind in the Willows* when he got fed up with decorating and slung his paint brush down and said, 'bother it' . . . or was it 'botheration' . . . and went off to meet Toad and Ratty and had the sort of adventures I'd always hoped would happen to me when I couldn't find the boys and went off up the woods on my own. I leant further forward so that I was level with the table top. At the other end Old Gran was dozing over her needlework and her head was lolling forward as if she was pushing with her nose and I could imagine her burrowing about in the garden and popping her head up in the middle

252

of a pile of earth in somebody's lawn and asking if she'd had her dinner yet.

'Probably nothing to do with the brightness anyway.' I started when I realised she wasn't asleep and she sat up and shielded her eyes against the light. 'Probably more to do with what you eat.'

'Whatever—' Nan squared her shoulders and pulled her cardigan down. 'Whatever in the world's that got to do with it?'

'Over-weight, Fran. Fat people've always got bad eye-sight.'

'Well, I never did.' Nan sat up even straighter. 'Never heard such a lot of silly non—'

'Cream especially.' Old Gran smoothed her long black dress out over her legs and rubbed her bad knee at the same time. 'Cream's about the worst thing you could possibly eat.'

Mum was sitting with her pencil poised over her cross-word but she hadn't written anything for ages and Grandad opened his eyes and closed them quickly and Dad leant back with his hands behind his head again and blew a hum through his lips.

'Little dob of cream on a little trifle with a thin slice of bread and butter occasionally never did anybody any harm.' Nan was bolt upright now as if she was on the front of one of Grandad's Sexton Blake books having her fingerprints taken. 'And I do like a square of chocolate occasionally, but surely that's not too much to ask.'

Dad's head went further back.

'And the odd sweet now and again of an evening's not a crime.'

Grandad's fingers were drumming silently although it still looked as if he was asleep.

'And do you think I can find a decent dressmaker nowadays?'

'Time was when you made your own.'

Nan opened the palms of her hands so that they lay flat on the table. 'Time was, Mum, that a body could sit in of a Sunday evening and not be criticised all the time.'

Dad's hum got louder and I made out 'bonkey-doodle-ido'

coming through and then 'follow the sergeant-major'.

'That mean I can go then, Mum?'

'Go where, Simon?'

'Pictures. Cos I'm as skinny as a rake and it wouldn't hurt my eyes.'

'I'm not sure that's the point.' Mum looked round at Dad but he was yawning.

'And Sat-dee mornin' pictures is only once a week.'

'Oh, I know all about that.' Mum put her pencil down. 'But will it stop there or will you be wanting to go gallivanting there during the week as well?'

'Bloomin' bus fares on top'a what it costs you to get in, Simon. D'you think money grows on trees?'

'That mean I can go then, Dad? It's only sixpence to get in.'

'Blimey, *yes*, if it'll satisfy you.'

'It will. Thanks, Dad. And the boys usually take a tanner extra for an ice cream or some chips or something afterwards.'

'Oh do they? Bloomin' good start to the New Year this is.' Dad released his arms from behind his head and folded them and sat forward and Nan, who'd been sitting awkwardly so that she had her back to the sweet tin, said I shouldn't expect too much and Old Gran peered at me over the top of her glasses, as she was threading her needle, and Grandad opened one eye and then closed it and then they seemed to forget about me and I ran my finger around the rim of the brass ashtray that stood beside Nan's cactus on the wicker table under the window, and traced a swastika with my fingernail in the dust at the bottom.

ᑌᐢ *10* ᑭᐧ

*W*e'd all heard the camp kids talking about Saturday morning pictures and I'd suggested to the boys that we should go.

'That's a lot of sissy stuff,' Geoff Gibbs had said when we'd been sitting in the bus shelter one evening. 'We'd be far better off stayin' at 'ome and 'avin' a game'a football. An' anyone 'oo doesn't must be a traitor an' deserves to be beaten up.'

I'd been thinking of going on my own but I knew they'd find out if I did, but then they changed their minds.

'We're fed up with soddin' football.' Geoff Gibbs had a hole in his plimsoll and it bruised his toe when he kicked the ball. 'If we can get the ten pas' twelve 'ome from Chi, me an' Col'll be in time to get out for pheasant-beatin' by half-past one. So we can go to the flicks.'

'Thought you said it was sissy?'

'We thought it was when you suggested it, Nipper. But me an' Col looked into it, din' we, Col?'

'What, you went?'

'Yeah, las' week an' it's great.'

'Don't that make you traitors?'

'You wan' a thump, Nipper?'

'Not much.'

'Well shut up then.' He put his clenched fist against my chest and pushed. 'So all them 'oo don' wanna 'ang aroun' their mums an' dads 'a gotta come ta Satdee mornin' pitchers.'

Jerry Henry couldn't come to Saturday morning pictures because he had to do jobs for his mum. He got me and Jimmy Phillips to be witnesses for him while he had a row with her about it and she gave us a whack each with the copper-stick, as well as him, when we said we were all going; and Derek

255

Brown couldn't come because, Geoff said, 'his ol' man was too bleedin' stingy ta give ya the snot off 'is nose,' and he'd sent Derek home crying and holding his ear for saying he wasn't.

I leant back on the old school wall, by the bus stop, and felt the sun on my forehead melting my Brylcreem, and looked at the back of Geoffrey Gibbs. His Gran had made him have his hair cut short, so that it stuck out like a pile of nails, and he had his tweedy jacket on with pockets like fishes with their mouths open; the top button had ripped off his flies and he'd pulled them across with the buckle of his belt, but the flap-over was hanging out like a dog's tongue. He was getting tall too, and his trousers were short even though his turn-ups had been turned down, and he'd got a spud in his socks where his shoe rubbed where he trod over trying to walk bow-legged to look like a cowboy. Geoff hoiked and green flashed against the filtered sun from the Spanish oaks and dripped off the wall.

'Nearly gotch'a, Nipper.'

'M'm.' I leant away from it.

'Good one, that was. Think I'm getting a cold.'

'Oh yeah.'

Geoff sniffed and searched around in his throat and sucked through his teeth. 'W'a's up, me ol' Nipper.' He slung his arm around my shoulder and squeezed his fingers into my arm, and his breath smelt of onions. 'Got the gripes?'

'No I 'aven't.' I pulled away from him. 'An' get off.'

'Snooty sod.' He pushed me back against the wall and held his fist under my nose. 'You'll get this if you don't behave yourself,' and he went and told Colin I was scared to go to the pictures without my mum to hold my hand. Just then Kenny Lane and Jimmy Phillips came sauntering up the road. I started towards them but Geoff called them over and they stayed whispering with him until the bus came.

I looked for the RAF kids from Tangmere on the 66 but they must have caught the 57 earlier or perhaps they were going in later. Geoff and the others went in the two seats in front upstairs and I got in behind them. They talked to each other all the way and Geoff and Colin told them about the Superman serial that was on every week, and that there was always a big picture on with it and sometimes it was Hopalong Cassidy and sometimes it was something called the Bowery Boys and they started to talk in funny voices and call each other Chiefy and Satch and I started to laugh with them until Gibbser said he hoped they could get four seats together so then I stopped listening to them and looked out of the window.

We got off at St Pancras and walked down to the Gaumont. The doors weren't open yet and there was no queue so Geoff suggested looking in the windows at the January Sales and then we went up to Woolworth's.

We took in the smell of the coconut ice and the chocolate truffles and the colours of the wrappers on the bars and the jars of loose sweets and moved on to the shiny silver-capped pens and finely chiselled pencils, sharpened down so smoothly that you could see the wide grain, and the wooden rulers and the plastic see-through rulers and then we went on to the diaries and calendars and the warm-smelling leather wallets, with their secret pockets for putting stamps and pound notes and things in and then I saw an assistant watching us and followed the others along the counter to where they sold foreign stamps. Most of the other countries had better stamps than we had and some of the smallest had the biggest and most colourful; some were triangles or oblongs instead of squares and had pictures of birds and fish and mountains and rivers and even hockey players and footballers on them. The cellophane packets rustled when I shook them, to see what stamps were underneath, and some of them had smudgy postmarks, that they sold little magnifying glasses to see with, and there were packets of stamp hinges, so that you could move the stamps about, and then we came to the stamp albums that cost from two and sixpence up to a pound, some with spiral bindings and some with card covers with pictures on, and some with glossy covers and some with dark leather, like an old-fashioned book, that you'd have to be a bloomin' millionaire to afford and I could imagine sitting in front of the fire at home on a rainy winter's night sticking stamps in and explaining to Laurence from next door which countries they all came from.

'You going to buy anything, sonny?'

'Ain' got'ny money.' I dropped the front cover of an album.

'Well, don't get them all finger-marks then.'

'Yeah. Come on, Nipper.' Geoff Gibbs hustled me along the counter towards the door. 'Can't keep yer bleedin' 'ands off anything, can you? Bleedin' nuisance you are.'

We had a look around the covered market, where Dad got the fish on a Wednesday, and then stopped and looked in the shoe shop by the Cross and then went down East Street and stopped opposite the Granada where a queue was forming.

'Cor.' Kenny Lane pointed across the road. 'They got a Walt Disney film on there,' and he started across.

' 'old on, Laner.' Geoff hauled him back. 'Tha's jus' a cartoon. Tha's jus' kids' stuff. You don' wanna see that. Nipper might, but you wanna come with us, don' ya?'

Kenny shrugged. 'S'pose so.'

'Yeah, course you do.' Geoff had him by the arm. 'Go on, Nipper, if you're so keen on little girls' things.'

'I'm not.' There were pictures of Donald Duck and his nephews going ice-skating. 'What makes you think I am?'

'Well, you're always going on about Bambi an' Snow White an' the seven drips or something.' The others laughed and they went into Bartlemy's together.

Bartlemy's counter was like the bar in Aunty's pub in Petersfield, with tea chests in front tilted forward, full of grass seed and dog biscuits and chicken pellets and bonemeal and the two at the end were full of broken biscuits, digestive in one and shortcake in the other, and there were pairs of shears and cans of turps and spades and shovels and wellingtons all over the place and a paraffin stove by the door sent out waves of wet warmth like a hot fog.

'And what can I do for you young 'erberts?' A newspaper lowered behind the counter and a hand reached out and laid a burning cigarette on the furry grey nest of ash in the ashtray next to the till and a man stood up.

'Pound'a broken biscuits, please.'

The man looked from Geoff to Colin. 'An' you?'

'Pound'a broken biscuits, please.'

'M'm?' He nodded at Kenny Lane.

'Pound'a—'

'I know. Pound'a broken ...' He took a last pull at his cigarette and squashed it between his finger and thumb into the bed of ash and tossed the end behind the counter somewhere and the beheaded ash smoked and burned out. 'Every perishin' Saturday the same. Dozens an' dozens of 'em! Pound'a broken biscuits, pound'a broken biscuits ... as if their mothers can't be bothered to feed 'em.' He took a scoop, like a giant metal thumbnail, from the grass-seed box and wiped it on his overalls and jammed it into the chest of biscuits and came up slowly and turned and poured the bits into a high-sided metal bowl on the scales until the bowl on the scales went down and the weight went up. 'Can't get on with anything.' He reached round and brushed a ginger cat off a pile of rough brown paper bags. 'Soon as one lot've left we get more.'

Kenny Lane was a penny short for threepenny's worth so I'd agreed to buy a penny's worth from him as I didn't really want any anyway, and we spilled out onto the pavement and went up to the Gaumont.

'Yeah.' Geoff Gibbs stood back so that Jimmy and Kenny were on either side of him. 'An' we all know what that means, don' we, boys?'

'What?' Kenny Lane still had to look up at Geoff: it didn't seem as if he'd grown at all since we'd been at the Lincs.

' 'e'll wolf the bloomin' lot.'

'I won't.' I felt my face going red and I said it again, more softly, because some girls in the queue behind us had heard.

' 'e will. That proves it. 'e always goes red when 'e's lyin'.'

'You can only have a few, Simon.' Kenny Lane screwed the top of his brown paper bag tighter and held it in his other hand.

'I only wanted a few, Lane.' My fists went into walnuts. 'In fact I don't want any.'

'See, Mush.' Geoff's arm was over Kenny's shoulder. 'You'll be all right with us.'

' 'e can stuff 'is biscuits, Gibbs. Right up 'is—'

' 'scuse me.' A man in a long grey overall coat came out of the furniture warehouse, on the other side of the cinder track that ran down to the Gaumont car park, and spread his arms and moved us back against the wall. 'I got a delivery comin' in. An' you can watch that language too, my lad, with all these little girls about.'

Gander's eyebrows went up and Gibbser shook his head and muttered, 'Wan' my fault,' and then they both turned their backs on me and faced the front as the man flattened us back further and a lorry wheezed and banged its way up through the pot holes, with the driver running his eye along the warehouse wall and his mate leaning out of the cab window measuring the distance between the tyres and the children's toes, and I hoped that Colin Gander would sneeze or something and jog Geoffrey Gibbs so that he fell under the wheels but he didn't and by the time the lorry had passed my fist had unclenched and I just wanted to go home, but then the queue began to move.

The people at the head of it started to dissolve around the entrance like a drain unclogging and we craned forward to see over the people in front, but then it stopped and when I looked back I saw the queue stretched away behind us and right round the corner of the building to the car park at the back.

'Think we'll all get in?'

Geoff looked back past me. 'If we don't there's a lot of others 'oo won't.'

'M'm.' I shrugged myself off the wall and took my weight on my other foot. 'Borin', ain' it, jus' standin' aroun'?'

'M'yeah.' Geoff Gibbs was getting taller but I was taller than he was. 'S'pose so,' and he turned back to the front but he didn't whisper anything to Colin and I stood up straighter and folded my arms so that my elbows took up a lot of space and forced my eyes to stare straight into the sun that had peeked above the top of the pub roof on the corner where the Hornet merged with Market Street just to see if I could stand it, and refused to duck when blue and black dots came zooming in to attack the corners of my eyes like meteorites.

'Oh crumbs, watch out!'

'What?' I shook my head but my eyes were still blind and I was being pushed from behind again as the line moved forward. 'What is it?'

'S'sh. Don't say nothin' 'less 'e speaks to us.'

I clenched my eyes tight and wrung the sunlight out of them and stared ahead. It was like looking out of a rain-smeared window, but I could make out Doug Ritson standing at the head of the queue and looking down it. He had a long dark blue blazer on with silver buttons and a stardust shirt, with a very narrow collar, instead of a great floppy one like mine, and a woolly-looking sort of knitted blue tie, like a lot of holes joined together, and narrow grey trousers and white socks and crêpe-soled black suede shoes and his yellowy hair was sleeked back at the sides like the folded wings of a young dove. I looked for Pete Farmer and Gipsey Hill and Chunky Halstow and the rest of the Firm but they weren't there.

'Is 'e on 'is own?' Geoff Gibbs was trying to look through people's legs. 'P'raps we'll be all right.'

'What's up then?'

'They tried to get us, last week, down by St Martin's gents.'

'Oh yeah?' I stood back from him so that I could say it louder. 'What for?'

'Shuddup, Nipper.' The whites of his eyes showed as he glanced sideways and ducked down lower. 'Bleedin' great gob you've got.'

'Doug's all right.' I hung back as the line moved down. 'Mate'a mine in fact.'

'Yeah, well 'e ain't no mate've ours.' Geoff Gibbs's yellow teeth had straight-up streaks of green in them. 'Said 'e was gonna stick my 'ead down the bog an' pull the chain.'

'Yeah, but 'e didn't.' The way Colin Gander said things sometimes made me wonder whose side he was on.

'Bet he couldn't.' Kenny Lane was giggling behind his fist. 'Be too big to get it down there.'

Geoff's eyes gleamed like a rat down a hole. 'I'll do you, Lane.'

'Watch out.' Colin stood up straighter and smiled and said, ' 'ere 'e comes,' out of the corner of his mouth.

Doug Ritson was walking down the queue as if he was looking for a gap in a hedge. He was on his own, except for a little boy trotting along beside him who looked like the one in the cassock and surplice on the front of our

261

Christmas card this year from Dad's prisoner-of-war pal, Bill Pitney, from Birmingham.

'Doug.'

'Nipper. Gibbser, what'cha Gander.'

'Goin' pitchers, Doug?'

'Yeah, s'pose so.' He took his hand out of his trousers' pocket and looked at the two half-crowns in it and put them back. 'Gotta look after the little mush, 'ere. 'e's me cousin.'

'Oh yeah.' Gibbser looked grey and greasy beside Doug's cousin and I wanted to move in between them in case he breathed on him. 'W'a's 'is name then?'

Doug shook the little hand he was holding as if he was waking the boy up. 'Go on. Tell 'em your name.' He smiled. 'Loses 'is tongue sometimes.' He smiled again as if he'd forgotten who he was. 'He's only five.'

'You 'lowed in the pictures at five?' Kenny Lane gulped as Colin elbowed him in the ribs.

'If Doug wan's ta take 'im in 'e will, won't ya, Doug?'

The look Doug gave Gibbser made me think he must be measuring his head for the pan in St Martin's gents but he turned to me and said, 'They wouldn't stop 'im going in, would they?'

'Shouldn't think so, Doug.' I could still see Gibbser end up and head down, his hair straggling like seaweed, and I got rid of the grin by shaking my head. 'We'll all go in as a group with 'im in the middle.'

'They'll see 'im.' Gibbser was making a 'no' face at me from behind Colin.

'No they won't.' Doug threaded in amongst us and he only said 'mind out' when he trod the heel off Gibbser's shoe.

The queue was moving quickly now and we all stood over Paul as Doug got the tickets and we swept in past the usherette, who Doug called Linda and looked about seventeen, and started to go into the fourth row from the back. Jimmy and Kenny went in first and I was next and then Colin but Gibbser saw that Doug would be sitting next to him so he barged past and I could feel Doug getting restless because he was stretching over to see why they weren't sitting down so I stood aside and let Paul in and he went next and I sat at the end.

The rows of seats fell away to the stage and children were swarming over the seats and fighting and chasing each other and there was a steady stream of toffee papers and paper planes coming down in front of us from the balcony upstairs. Paul stood up, holding on to the top of the seat in front so that he could stretch up higher and his big solemn eyes ranged across the crowds in front of us and then he turned to Doug and pointed and Doug had to lean up to him to see what he was showing him.

The noise in front got louder and there were shouts and screams as the boys crept up behind the girls and grabbed them and the girls made out they hadn't seen them coming and turned round and spat out what they'd do if they ever did that again and I couldn't think why they didn't sit down in the first place if they didn't want the boys to get at them.

The noise got still louder until all the different shouts and screams merged into one and then I heard another noise, a long thin tinny rattling noise, that came one, two, three and then paused and sshlip, sshlip, sshlip again and I noticed people down towards the front stop, occasionally, and touch their necks or cheeks and look up again and then there was another whizz and something bounced off Doug's knee.

' 'scuse me.' He stood up slowly and edged past me.

I looked round as he went back three rows. 'Up,' he said and he made a lifting movement with his hand, like the thing they put under paving slabs to raise them when they needed to be re-positioned. Three or four boys stood up and he passed along the line to two boys from Lavant. They didn't move. Doug held his hand out. One of the boys looked at it and then away. Doug stuck his hand out a bit more and the boy shook his head. Doug's fist shot out and was back again as a thin dark line broke out above the boy's top lip. He reached down the side of his seat and put something like a pencil in the palm of Doug's hand. The other boy did the same. Doug bent them in two and twisted them and gave them back and then came back and sat down.

263

'Bleedin' peashooters.' He sat back and put his feet up.

All this time the noise had been getting louder and there were two or three fights going on in the aisles and one little boy got his ear clipped by the usherette for swinging on the curtains to the toilets. Then the noise changed to boos and stamping and a shower of crisp packets and apple cores and things were thrown at the front as a man in a black suit came on from the side of the stage holding a microphone. He held his hand up and yelled 'quiet' but it came out very softly and the booing turned to laughter and he shook the microphone and yelled 'quiet' again very loudly and a great cheer went up and then they started booing again.

'Your behaviour gets worse every week!' He held his hand higher against another wave of cheering. 'And if it doesn't improve we'll have no alternative but to close the club. You're more like animals than children, some of you.'

Those who were still standing up melted back into seats.

'And now I want us to give Aunty Joan a proper Saturday morning welcome.' He backed off the stage as the curtain closed and a fat lady in a tight shiny blue dress came out and took the microphone from him as the lights went down and she waved and called out 'Good morning, children.'

'Good morning, Aunty Joan.' It was the same grumbling sound of the infants' class repeating the words of the Old Lob stories reading book to Miss Anderson at the village school.

'And now, our club song.' She fixed the microphone into a bracket on the piano and sat down as a flimsy, transparent curtain peeled back and the lights went down and showed some smudgy blue writing on the screen. She gave an enormous bang on the piano and started to sing in a tinny voice and the rest of us followed after her:

> We come a-lon-g
> On Saturday morning,
> Greeting ev-ery-body with a smile.
>
> We come along
> On Saturday morning,
> Knowing it's well worthwhile.

It went on for a couple more verses about how we all looked forward to it all week and I wondered if Aunty Joan got paid for this or if she did it for love and then she did another long note and everybody stood up and she started off 'God Save the Queen' and we started singing and then we stood up as well.

We'd nearly finished the national anthem when I noticed the boys behind us were leaning forward and looking down and sniggering and Doug was standing awkwardly and leaning sideways and I looked behind him.

Paul had let his seat fold back and was kneeling down on the floor. He had his hands together and his head was bowed and his eyes were closed. He stayed like that until the national anthem was over and then he stood up and rubbed the grit and cigarette ash off his knees and pulled the seat down and scrambled up into it and folded his arms.

'Funny little mush, in'e, Doug?'

Doug Ritson turned and bared his teeth at me. 'Why? 'e didn't do nuffin', did 'e?'

'Didn't he?' I shook my head. 'No, Doug. I didn't see a thing.'

Doug didn't say a word throughout the Superman serial: his knees stayed propped up against the seat in front, even when Superman's car had gone over a cliff and he was hanging on by a tree root, and I found myself watching him more than the film to see if he was watching me. He didn't laugh, or even smile, when the big picture came on, of Old Mother Riley, and he just muttered 'prat' when I laughed when she caught her bootlace in a door as she was closing it and kept walking and tripped over and I wasn't sure if he was saying it about me or about the film. He pushed past me, later, when Paul wanted to go to the toilet, and I wasn't sorry when he ignored me and left as soon as the film finished, but Gibbser spotted it.

'And I suppose that now Lord Snooty's friend's disappeared 'e'll think 'e can get back in with us again.' He yelled this along the row as I was waiting for room to get out into the gangway. 'Well, 'e needn't think 'e is cos 'e isn't.'

I made sure I got separated from them in the crush on

265

the way out and caught the 57 from outside the Horndean Arms while they went up to the fish and chip shop by the Red Lion. I got home before them and Mum wanted to know what I'd been up to to get back so early when she saw Jimmy Phillips come home about twenty minutes after me.

I'd caught Mum looking at me at breakfast. I searched back through the last few weeks but I couldn't find anything I'd done wrong that she could have known about. I'd written Christmas 'thank you' letters to Nan's friend, Mrs Kaley, at Eastergate, and to Grandad and Grandma Peterson in Northumberland, and I'd been ever so polite to Mrs Keen, next door, when she'd asked us to go and play racing cars somewhere else because she had a headache; in fact I'd been so polite that Mum wondered if I was really being as polite as I made out. We had got told off by Mr Henty for putting a frozen turnip under each of the rear wheels of his bread van but we'd stopped laughing as soon as he'd finished skidding down the road and we hadn't cheeked him at all when he asked us what the devil we thought we were playing at.

I hung around when they were washing up and it was like having an itch that I couldn't find to scratch.

'. . . and I can't believe the number of snowdrops we've had this year, dear.' I caught Mum looking at me as she passed Dad a handful of knives and forks to wipe up.

'Just goes to show what a mild winter we're having, Ina.'

I went into the shed and made out I was messing about with my bike, then crept up to the back door to see if they were talking about me now they thought I couldn't hear.

'. . . didn't realise what a state things had got into out there.'

'It'd've been a darn sight better if young Farouk'd stuck to polo and spent a bit less time hanging around night clubs and film stars.'

I decided they must have heard me after all so I marched into the kitchen and through to the bathroom and made a noise locking it and then I unlocked it quickly and quietly and crept out again.

266

'. . . hope to goodness Dad makes it through the winter this year without another bout of bronchitis.'

'Well, he certainly won't if the silly old twirp insists on going out without a scarf and gloves on, George, and whatever is he on about saying he can't hold a fag-hook properly with nice woolly gloves on. It beats me what he wants to be hacking about at graves for with a fag-hook in the middle of January anyway.'

They must have known I could hear from the bathroom because I knew something was up that they weren't talking about and I waited until Dad went out and then I followed him. He went down Crouch Cross Lane and across the road into Church Lane to the vicarage and I hid behind the hedge when I saw Pop come out to meet him but I had to crawl right round the edge of the garden to come up on them from behind his garage before I could hear what they were saying.

'. . . and we'll probably finish at about half-past eight, George. Quarter to nine at the latest.'

I held my breath. They couldn't be planning for me to carry the cross at the half-past nine service.

'And that'll be six consecutive evenings?'

'Strewth!' I elbowed forward more on my tummy. It wouldn't be Monday because nothing ever happened on a Monday, or Tuesday, I hoped, because I went out to play on Tuesday; it would be just my luck if it was Wednesday because I'd have to miss 'Ray's a Laugh' and 'Take It From Here' and Thursday was club night and Friday was bath night and I didn't want to do it, whatever it was.

'Yes, I think so, George.' Pop's telephone rang. 'They may need a week or two longer but most of them are ready for it,' and he went on into the house and Dad followed him.

'Sod it.' A long forsythia runner went limp in my hand where I'd been bending it. 'Wonder what that's all about?' and I crept down the hedge to the church wall and sat picking a fir cone to bits until I was down to the stalk and then I went home.

None of the boys said anything about a church meeting or anything and by Wednesday evening I was beginning to wonder if I was the only one involved and then, when I was looking through some fag cards, I had a brainwave.

'Ain't arf lookin' forward to Friday, Mum.'

'Oh are you?' She pulled her darning wool slowly through Dad's sock and stitched a knot into it and cut it off. 'And why's that, pray?'

'Oh . . .' I leant back and tried to stretch. 'Jus' that I'm goin' out.'

'Oh yes? And just where d'you think you're going?'

'A party. Down the camp.'

'Oh are you?' She dug her needle into her pin cushion and closed the lid of her sewing basket. 'And don't you think it might've been polite to warn us what you were planning to do in advance?'

'I didn't plan it. I jus' got asked. What's up? I can go, can't I?'

'It's very thoughtless of you to spring things on us like this, Simon.'

'Why, Mum?'

She straightened Dad's socks out and folded them together and laid them on the top of her sewing basket. 'For all you know we might've been thinking of doing something else.'

'Yea-ah. We never do anything.'

'We do, Simon. That's just not true.'

'Like what?'

'Don't talk to me in that tone of voice.' Mum sniffed and looked away. 'We might have been going to do something important.'

'Like what, fer cryin' out loud?'

'Is that any way for a boy to speak to his mother?'

'What like then? You've fixed something up for me. I know you have. Just tell me.'

'Confirmation classes.'

'Wha-at?'

'You're going to be confirmed.'

'I'm bloody not.'

'I beg your pardon, Simon.'

'Oh blimey, Mum. I don' wanna be confirmed. And the boys'll all take the mickey out of me an' – an' – what night's it goin' to be? What night you goin' to ruin then? Friday, I s'pose.'

'No, Simon. Thursday—'

'Blimey, Mum. Thursday's the only decent night of the week and now it's been messed up and everyone'll blame me and—'

'Well, it's the only night Pop could have you so the club'll just have to take a back seat for a week or two, my lad. And several of the boys'll be going so—'

'I'll bet Gibbser's not.'

'*And* it'll please Grandad.'

'Bugger Grandad.'

'SIMON!'

I stood rock still. She was quivering with rage and the sting of her hand across my cheek hung on like an echo.

'Now get to bed.'

I turned with my face still stinging and went to the bathroom and cleaned my teeth until they bled.

Dad said everything depended on what frame of mind you were in. Randy Turpin was in the right frame of mind when he beat Sugar Ray Robinson but he wasn't when he lost the return; Denis Compton was usually in the right frame of mind and so was Len Hutton and Tommy Lawton, until he went over the hill a bit, and Mum said that if I was going to get the most out of my confirmation classes and enjoy them I'd better get myself into the right frame of mind or I might as well not go at all, but if I didn't Pop would be upset and didn't I know what a lot he thought of me and what a fuss he'd used to make of me when I was a baby and if I didn't go now goodness knows when I'd get another chance because the bishop had other things to do of an evening than go chasing around devoting special services to children who couldn't make up their minds, and so had Pop for that matter, so perhaps I'd better buck my ideas up and get changed without any more arguments or silly nonsense.

It was cold in the bathroom and my feet stuck to the floor. Mum had put the damper over for hot water and it squirted out in chunks and a fluffer of steam. By the time it was cold enough for my hands it was too cold for my

269

neck and armpits, and when I did what Mum called my unmentionables they shrivelled up and it took my breath away and made me stand on tiptoe and I was getting hairy which made it more difficult for me to get dry and I sat down on the toilet seat with both towels round me and wondered what Frank Parfit would do now on a Thursday evening and what there was left that was worth living for now that they'd ruined the only decent night of the week.

'You gone to sleep in there, Simon?'

'No I 'aven't.'

'Well, get a mivvy-on.' Mum was all light and airy now because she was trying to make me believe that going to confirmation classes was one of the first things you did when you started to grow up and that most things you had to do when you grew up were things that you didn't want to do and I did want to grow up, didn't I? 'Dad's going to walk up with you as far as Crouch Cross Corner if you're not too long thinking about it.'

' 'n what if I am?'

'Well then, he won't be able to, will he? And don't be cheeky, Simon, please.'

I curled my lip at my reflection in the tap handle on the washbasin opposite and twiddled the coarse hairs between my fingers until it made a twirled bit like Grandad used to have on his moustache and then I pulled the chain and slung the towels over the side of the bath and raced out of the bathroom and down the passage to my bedroom before the cold could get me.

Mum had laid my second-best clothes out and a clean handkerchief and clean pants and vest. She'd got me some new pants from Stevey Bacon on Wednesday, when she'd been in to Chichester with Nan to get the fish, and she'd left them in the bag for me as a sort of present. They had a stretchy band around the middle, that nearly cut me in two, and elasticated legs that clung to me as if they were wet, and they itched, but Mum said that would all get sorted out when they'd been through the wash a couple of times.

It was one of those nights, outside, like they had in my Wild West book, where Annie Oakley'd be sitting by the camp fire at the side of the trail with the Wells Fargo stagecoach parked behind her, and the fire light flickering on the frightened faces of the passengers, and she'd be pointing out towards the moon, that looked like half a Dutch cheese with a light behind it, and a wolf silhouetted against the line of the Rocky Mountains with his head flung back making a blood-curdling howl that the passengers thought was Indians and made the businessmen pull their hats down further over their ears and the card-sharper check the bullets in the derringer that he kept in a tiny holster up his sleeve, and she'd be saying that they needn't worry because Buffalo Bill would be along presently and that he knew these trails and plains and hills like the back of his hand, and I wished I could have had a tasselled scouting jacket made out of buffalo hide and a pair of pearl-handled six-guns and a Winchester repeater rifle, in a scabbard slung to the flank of my pinto pony, before I'd get too old for all that sort of thing.

'Nice night for a run, Nip.' Dad turned the collar of his mac up and rubbed his hands together.

'M'm.'

'P'raps start going out footer training again if the weather stays like this for much longer.'

'Yes, Dad.'

'You concentrate on what Pop's telling you tonight, won't you, Simon?'

'Yes, Dad.'

'You have to take this confirmation lark seriously and he'll be telling you about—'

'Yes, Dad.'

'What the devil's up now, Simon?'

'Nothin', Dad.'

'I hope you've been listening to what I've been telling you.'

'Yes, Dad.'

'M'm.' We'd got to the end of Crouch Cross Lane now. 'You be all right down Church Lane?'

'Yeah, course I will. We play hide an' seek chasin' down roun' 'ere.'

'Yes, well just remember what you're supposed to be up to tonight and don't go sloping off anywhere.'

'Yeah, bye, Dad.' I ran across the road and then scuffed

down Church Lane running my hand along the slatted fences of the cottages.

The light was on in Pop's study but the curtains were drawn and I couldn't see who was inside. I put my ear to the glass but the conversation was so muffled by the heavy curtains that I couldn't hear anyone distinctly. I rang the bell and Mrs Pope opened it and stepped back at the same time so that it looked as if it had opened on its own. She always did that when she was expecting somebody and the way she never spoke made it difficult to say anything and that made me feel embarrassed because it was rude to go into people's houses and not speak to them and I couldn't see why I should get told off for being rude when it was her fault anyway.

'A-ha, and here's Simon at last.' Pop had his Harris tweed jacket on and green corduroy trousers. 'And not looking as if he's particularly at one with the world.' He clasped his hands together so that his fingers interlocked and then he bent them back as if he was making a cat's cradle and leant forwards towards me. 'Close the door, Simon and come and sit down.' He'd put the chairs in a circle and I sat down in the one he patted. 'And now we're sitting comfortably, we will begin.' He smiled around the room as if reminding us of 'Children's Storytime' on the Light Programme was funny but he caught me raising my eyebrows at the ceiling. 'Something the matter, Simon?'

I could have told him that my pants were itching and that I wanted to go to the toilet and that I was wishing I'd gone in his rhododendrons before I came in and that it was perishing in here and why couldn't he put the other bar on on the electric fire but I just shook my head and said, 'No, sir.'

'Good, splendid.' He beamed again and sat back. 'And now, do we all know each other?'

The girls all whispered 'yes' and stared at the floor and we boys nodded and looked at the floor.

'Well, I think' – he looked around so that nobody was left out – 'that we'll all introduce ourselves one by one and say who we are and why we're here, just to break the air of formality. Would you like to start, Simon?'

272

I blushed to the roots of my hair and held my breath.

'Off you go, Simon.' Pop reached out to me as if he was helping me over a high step. 'Don't be shy.'

'I'm Simon.' I studied the outline of a gold circle in the carpet.

'And do we have another name? I'm sure we do.'

I gritted my teeth and imagined my hands round his throat. 'Simon George.' I was sitting opposite Kenny Lane who had his hand over his mouth clamping it closed.

'Simon George . . . ?'

I'd have gone to bed early for evermore and kissed Nan every time I saw her and let her friend, Mrs Kaley from Eastergate, hug me and never be unkind to those less fortunate than myself for ever and ever, amen, if I could have been released from this. 'Wilson. Simon George Wilson.'

'Good.' Pop's hand was still stretching out to me and he turned it over so that it was palm upwards and he raised it as if he wanted me to jump higher. 'And why is Simon here?'

'Get confirmed.'

'Get confirmed?' Pop spelled it out slowly as if he'd put a word in each of the trays of a pair of scales and was watching to see if they were evenly balanced. 'To prepare for confirmation, perhaps?'

I nodded.

'To prepare for confirmation, Simon?'

'Yessir.' My fingers were knotting so tightly together it felt as if they'd fused.

'Say it.'

' 'pare'fa'conf'mation.'

'Good. And the next?'

I could have strangled Derek Brown and Kenny Lane for getting away without their middle names and chirping up that they were preparing for confirmation and I cringed when Pat Smith and Jenny Wright, who didn't speak to each other since Jenny'd got to the High School and Pat hadn't, said it was so that they could take Holy Communion and Victoria Vickers, who'd never even been to church, blushed scarlet and said it was because her mum wanted her to and

Pop infuriated me by letting her off. Then he put his glasses on and took the little notebook he used for sermons out of his pocket so I sat back and started to tidy my fingernails by pushing the skin back around the half-moons.

He started off about how God made the world in six days and rested on the seventh and I found a piece of loose skin at the corner of my thumbnail and was pulling it back as he got into the bit about Jesus being conceived of a Virgin Mary and lived a pure and holy life and was tried and crucified to save us all and was buried and rosa-gain according to the scriptures and sittith on the right 'anda God the father and reigns with him for ever and ever.

Derek was peeping out Kenny's way and Kenny was watching a spider that was crawling across the carpet towards the new girl. It speeded up and then slowed down and stopped: then it jerked forward again and stopped as if it was deciding which way to go. It was getting closer to her and I was wondering what kind of squawk she'd make, if it went up her leg, when the sole of her shoe lifted. The spider did another little scuttle and the foot dropped. I ground my teeth together as Kenny Lane spluttered and Derek Brown's eyes watered and I had to look away.

Pop was going on about how we'd all been sinners from birth; even a baby who was one hour old. I couldn't believe a baby could have done anything wrong at that age because he wouldn't have been able to talk or think or muck about or anything so I started following the pattern of the vine on the wallpaper until Pop stopped talking and started handing out some books he said he wanted us to read during the next few weeks.

He gave the girls one each about Amy Carmichael in Japan and Kenny Lane got one about Livingstone and Stanley discovering Africa and Derek, the lucky blighter, got one about the Angel of Mons and I wanted that one because there was bound to be something about the English and the German soldiers playing football together on Christmas morning and what had made them stop and if they'd given each other time to get back into the trenches before they started shooting each other again, and then he was standing in front of me.

'And for you, Simon, C. T. Studd.'

' 'oo's 'e?'

'You like cricket, don't you?'

'Cor, yeah.' I held my hand out but drew it back when I saw the picture of a ragged Chinese boy, with a couple of buckets on a stick over his shoulder, on the front cover.

'C. T. Studd was one of our finest cricketers, and Captain of England, who gave up fame and fortune to become a missionary to Africa and China.'

'Did 'e?'

'One of the finest gestures of self-sacrifice ever known.'

'Oh.' I could imagine him walking up the gang-plank of an ocean liner with his bat in one hand and his bag in the other and the England team standing on the jetty waving him goodbye and pleading with him to reconsider and him trying to put a brave face on it. 'What the 'ell'd 'e wanna do that for?' I clenched my eyes shut and then opened them slowly.

'Well, I hardly think you need to put it quite like that.' Pop took his glasses off and rubbed them with his pocket handkerchief. 'Dear oh dear! I suppose he saw that as being the best way that he could spend his time.' – I could see myself opening the batting for England against the West Indies and stepping down the wicket and knocking Ramadhin and Valentine off their length and the wireless was talking about my second century of the series and all the wickets I'd taken and then I was standing in a bit of jungle with luminous eyes looking at me out of the darkness and a man with a bone through his nose and a darned great cooking pot and I just wanted to go home and I held the book by its edges in case it was catching. – 'And if you read it you'll see he was an even greater man than if he'd been captain of cricket and football and the Lord Privy Seal as well, for that matter, all rolled into one.'

The girls started laughing because they thought he was on their side and being nasty about football but they didn't know he'd been so proud of my Uncle Steven being good at sports he'd even used to go and watch him sometimes, so I mouthed 'Lord Privy what?' to Derek and Kenny and shrugged my shoulders and shook my head and screwed my finger between my eye and my ear to show I thought he was nuts and then we had milky cocoa and Tea-Time Assorted biscuits on a big plate with roses on it before we went home.

I read and re-read the first two pages of Pop's pamphlet about how C. T. Studd and his two brothers beat the Australian Test team when they were still only playing for Cambridge and I stared at a point of light where the sun caught Mum's china cabinet until everything went misty and I imagined how it would be if I had two brothers and we strode out onto the pitch at school and beat the High School and how we'd all be heroes and then I read it again and made out I was C. T. Studd smashing the Demon Bowler Spofforth to the boundary for successive fours on a sweltering day in July at Lords until Mum told me it was tea time and why couldn't I read my comic quietly like any other boy and not sit there waving my arms about like a wild thing and risking sending her ornaments smashing to smithereens off the mantelpiece and into the fender.

When I finally turned over from the preface it was all about him being a missionary in China and never doing anything much except stopping people smoking opium cigarettes that Mum said were made out of poppies and made you dream fantastic dreams but they didn't work properly because when I crushed some petals from a stray plant among Grandad's potatoes and rolled them up in some of Gibbser's uncle's cigarette papers, it wouldn't light and Gibbser said I'd rolled it too tight and he'd loosened it over a match as I'd dragged and I'd sucked the flame straight through and burnt my tongue and he'd said I could give him my Lash LeRue comic book or have a smack side the kisser as compensation for wasting his time, and then he'd gone on to America, where they didn't play cricket at all, or do anything much away from the frontier, and then on to Africa for ages. I flicked through the Africa bit expecting to find him playing for somebody or other because the West Indies were good cricketers and they looked a bit alike but he always seemed to have landed up in some jungly bit that was too uneven to play football, let alone cricket, amongst a lot of natives who spent all their time having tribal wars and getting sick and dying. The picture at the end was of an old man with wispy white hair and shining black eyes and a hooked nose and a scraggy neck, that made him look like a bald eagle, and a beard like candy-floss and two shirts on, that must have made him sweat like a pig out there in all that heat, and then I turned back to the inside-front cover, where he was at Cambridge and looked like the solicitor out of *The Old Curiosity Shop* before Uriah Heap got at him, and closed the pages and wondered if it wouldn't have been better for him if he'd stayed in Cambridge and played cricket for England: still, I liked the idea of belting the demon Spofforth all over the pitch until I started to call myself C. T. Stubbs when I was playing with the boys and they found out where I'd got it from and started calling me Alter-Walter so I took my bat and ball home and started playing with Laurence in the evenings.

Laurence had taken to waiting for me by the Close sign when I came home, and I went straight in and changed and came out to play with him. I wore my black leather balaclava and called myself the Masked Marvel and he was Bluebody, because he usually had a blue jumper on. Wrestling with Laurence, on a green canvas sheet Dad had in the shed, was like playing with a young puppy because he was light and soft and always landed on his legs so I could throw him around without hurting him. Sometimes I used to lie on my back and bend my knees up and sit him on my feet and then shoot him off, as if he was a doodlebug coming over to bomb London, and Billy Stroud used to stand and watch us, with his thumb in his mouth and his other hand down the front of his long khaki shorts. He stood watching us for days and never said a word until one day I asked him if he'd like to play as well and he took his thumb out and wiped it and grinned and trotted over and jumped on top of Laurence, who was already kneeling on my chest, and dug his knees into the pit of my stomach and started bouncing up and down and then stopped and asked me if he was doing it right. The game was for them to get on top of me and I had to try to stand up and they had to try to keep me down; and then I started standing up and we called that game Bear-baiting, because I'd seen a picture in our history books of a bear with two fighting dogs hanging from him, and they wouldn't let go even when I swung them round and round and round until that became a game called Chair-o-planes, and then they learned to use me as a fireman's pole and climb up onto my shoulders and slide down my back and fall on top of each other, like a couple of kittens, and then I'd spread my jacket out like a cape and change into a praying mantis and flop on them and eat them, through my mouth in my stomach, and have a nice lay down after my feed and they'd lie still until I'd gone to sleep and then they'd squirm about and give me awful indigestion so that I'd thrash about and then they'd escape and stand there laughing to see a praying mantis with tummy-ache until they stopped laughing and wanted to play something else.

When the Easter holidays came I said it was the cricket season and we ought to learn to play cricket but they kept swinging round and falling over when they tried to bat and when they bowled they either poddled it along the ground or slung it over each other's heads and I had to keep running after the ball so I said I'd teach them to play football. I went in goal between the drain covers in the road and they tackled each other. Laurence was taller and older and had a harder kick but Billy was what the *Daily Express* would have called 'a gritty little tackler' and kept on skittering about but he so seldom got the ball that when he did he didn't know what to do with it and stood there with his thumb in his mouth until Laurence took it off him again and then he took a deep breath and grinned and put his head down again and wood-peckered away into Laurence while I stood there in goal wondering if they'd ever run out of energy and if I'd ever get a shot to save. I did try to teach them to play passing and shooting but they kept kicking it into people's gardens and Dad got to hear about it and said we'd wear the stitches all to blazes out of the ball so we didn't play so much, except when Mum went up to Nan and Grandad's in the afternoon. She came home early one day and caught us playing and asked me if I'd heard what Dad had told me and then she asked me if I'd forgotten it was Thursday and the last of my confirmation classes and hadn't I better come in and get washed and changed and finish off my book about China so that I could make a good impression on Pop on my last night.

I had a bath and put on my second-best clothes and had my tea early so that I could sit down before I went out, and not get indigestion, and flicked over the pages of my book. If C. T. Studd had kept playing cricket instead of going off to China we'd have probably beaten every team under the sun and still have been winning all our Test matches even now and I left for Pop's feeling annoyed with all of China and Africa that we'd lost the last Test against the West Indies for no good reason.

Laurence and Billy were playing their own game of football down in the turning circle and they were calling out to each other about being Stanley Matthews and Tommy Lawton, like I'd done with them, and jogging on the spot to get supple like I'd shown them and they were too busy to more than look up when I called out to them as if they'd suddenly grown up together and were quite capable of amusing themselves without me. I kicked at a stone in the road but it went down the drain hole and I couldn't find another one so I walked quicker to Pop's and wondered what I could do with myself for the rest of the holiday, but I soon forgot that when Pop announced we'd all passed, except Victoria Vickers who wasn't ready for it and hadn't been since the first week, and that we were going to be confirmed at West Tarring Church on Wednesday 14th July at half-past six.

279

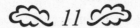

I looked out over the hills and wished I was up there instead of being jammed in the back of Mr Peters' car between Mum and Kenny Lane and Derek Brown. The hills and woods looked so inviting, with little pathways leading off to places you couldn't see, that I ached to be out there. I shifted my backside and hunched my shoulder over and down so that I could see out of the other window. Mum spotted me and gave me what looked like a sweet smile of encouragement, out of some book about the Queen Mother, and patted my knee. I moved it and she looked away. But then I looked at her again, when she wasn't looking at me, and saw how pretty her outline was against the passing hedges, and how much – with her face all relaxed and serene and her hands folded neatly on her lap with the skin all ruffed-up and chapped just sitting there quietly with only nice thoughts in her head and waiting to get back home and start washing and ironing and cooking and her dear gentle green eyes looking at things gone by – when I saw how much she loved me and remembered the smoothness of her, that I'd cuddled into when I was small but which seemed to clog the pores of my skin now and make me sweat inside, and how upset she got when I pulled away from her . . . when I saw all this I felt drawn to her to give her a last, long love before it was too late. But the boys were watching, and the way they could just sit there, fed up and without a care in the world, made me clench my fists and grind my teeth because they'd got parents who didn't insist on coming to watch them be confirmed and I had, and I looked straight ahead through the windscreen, over Mr Peters' shoulder, so that I didn't have to look at any of them and the sunshine paled and a wind shadow passed across a field of swaying corn.

West Tarring church was nothing like as nice as ours in

the village, Mum said, although it was bigger and had more fancy bits. I bet Kenny Lane it had never been a monastery like ours but he said it must have been if ours had because the carved stone heads of the little boys on the corners, where the ceiling met the walls, had round holes in their mouths that connected up to the roof to let the water out where it collected and ours hadn't, so that must prove something. I stood there, wondering why they'd built roofs that flooded in the first place and what happened to the water when it came out of the little boys' mouths and if they'd been daft enough to do that what other mistakes had they made, until Mr Peters tapped me on the shoulder and nodded towards the front pews and eased me forward.

The front pews had been reserved for the ones who were being confirmed. Most of the others looked real softies, all done up in their best clothes, with their hands together and their eyes closed and looking a million times more religious than we were, except for Pat Smith and Jenny Wright who were showing off by kneeling down and praying before the service had even started, which we never normally did, and I felt as if everyone was watching us and seeing how much we shouldn't be here. Even Kenny and Derek were beginning to look religious. That made me the only one who shouldn't be here. I looked up at Jesus on the cross on a stone pillar, leading to what was probably their vestry, and said sorry to him that I didn't believe any of what was going on and hoped he'd believe me and not be too unhappy about it and then I heard a swishing, scuffing sound coming up behind us. I looked round and back down the aisle and then I looked to the front again and went rigid. An enormous gold cape, with a great gold hat on top shaped like a horseshoe, drew level with us and went by with a little white-faced man inside with black-rimmed spectacles. There was an old man on each side of the cape in a black cassock and white surplice with another man, even older, swinging the incense. The procession flowed on after the bishop like a flock of black gulls after a fishing boat, and then they set up a chant that made the hair stand up on the back of my neck. Some sort of signal must have been given because the ones at the back had suddenly raised their bibles, as if they

281

were presenting arms, and broken into this stony cold chant that kept the goose pimples running up and down my back and seemed to get louder and more dismal as the heel-tap of their black shoes left the stone flags and cushioned out quiet on the Persian carpet. The procession moved on beyond the carpet and through the altar rails: the old man with the censer turned round and marked time and carried on swinging while the bishop went up two steps higher and then turned, with his hands together, and bowed his head. His crown tilted forward and it looked as if it was going to fall off and the rest of the procession separated around them.

The bishop looked up and waited until the last whisper had evaporated into the roof.

'Let us pray.'

There was an avalanche of bending knees and scuffing shoes and the grating of wooden-footed hassocks, and the rustling swish of dresses being arranged and trousers pulled up, to preserve the creases, and when the last movement had been snuffed out by the heavy granite silence he cleared his throat from deep inside his cape. 'Lighten our darkness . . .'

I cocked my ear.

'. . . we beseech thee, O Lord.'

That was one of Mum's.

'That by thy great mercy,' I joined in with him, 'we might see thy good . . .'

I knew the rest of it and said it with him in my mind as my eye ran along the line of drooping heads for Mum, but I couldn't see her. There was a girl, however, at the end of a row and I felt my breath stop, like a lorry-load of bricks at a zebra crossing, and I had to go on along the line a bit and come back to make sure she was real. Her face was pale and powdered pink and she had lipstick on, but not too much, and blood-red ear-rings to match: her brown hair hung, like two curved rams' horns on a viking helmet, over her ears and I nearly broke my neck trying to stand up with my head still turned round when the bishop finished praying and said we were going to sing 'Rock of Ages'. She was grown-up under her white blouse and I couldn't see how they managed to stand up straight when they were supposed to be full of milk but I had to turn round and squiggled my hand in my trousers' pocket to take the pressure off and I prayed it would go down before I had to go up the front. When I next looked I saw Mum watching me and nodding her head for me to face the front again, so I looked to see what number the hymn was from the boy next to me and came in halfway through the last verse.

We had to go up and kneel down at the front, two rows at a time, but they started on the other side so the rest of us had to sit and wait and watch them. They all came back looking pretty sheepish but I couldn't see that any of them had caught fire, so perhaps it wasn't working. I sat there trying to work out what would happen to me if there really was a God and tried to think about C. T. Studd in China to try to get in the right mood but then the girl with the lipstick went up and I went stiff again and it felt as if an enormous air bubble had got stuck in my chest and I closed my eyes and hoped to die rather than have the boys at school say I'd had the bonk when I went up to be confirmed.

The pew shelf, where they put the prayer and hymn books, was cold against my forehead and smelt of lavender furniture polish. It made me think of the little bags Grandad used to sew up for Nan and sewing reminded me of Old Gran and I wished that, if anyone had had to come, they could have sent her and I looked to see if, by any chance, she'd slipped in on her own somewhere, but she hadn't and I followed the zig-zag blue pattern up the edge of the Persian carpet and then hopscotched from red flagstone to black to red to black again until I was looking just behind where she was kneeling. She was leaning forward now and the hook of her bra strap made a little bump where her blouse was tight across her backbone, and I tried not to see it; her blue navy skirt clung close to her thighs and was tight around her waist where her blouse slipped under it, and I tried not to feel it; her legs disappeared up her skirt from about the point of her knees, and I tried not to think about them, but a scalding ripple went through me as she crossed her legs by laying one on top of the other and I looked up to see if I'd been struck by lightning and prayed that God would forgive me and I put my hands together and bowed my head and dried out the wet palm impressions on the pew with my elbow.

The bishop moved along the line with the bread and the wine. He stopped and said a few words to each of them, as he put his hands on their heads, and then he moved on and they waited a few seconds and then got up and bowed to the altar and came back to their seats. I counted off how much each one waited. It was seven in most cases so I decided to wait eight, just to be on the safe side. He got to the girl and I clenched my fists at him when he put his hands on her head and I rivetted my eyes on the back of her neck and counted. She hadn't got up at eight and I was beginning to wonder if something had happened when, by ten, she drew one leg up and rocked back on her heel and slid up and turned and she seemed to be looking straight at me. I ducked my eyes away but I knew she'd seen me and when I stole another peep at her she was looking over my head. I could feel her warm movement as she got closer, but then one of the old men in a cassock and surplice got in the way and tapped a boy at the end of the row in front of me on the shoulder and it was his row's turn and then mine.

I trailed my finger along the top of the pew to steady myself and stopped at the end to step down carefully in case I tripped. My mouth was like corrugated cardboard inside and there was a whistle in my chest as I breathed in. I walked up without looking at anyone.

My shoes sank into the carpet and the soles clung to the fibres as if they had suction pads underneath and I leant forward to keep going. The altar rail, with the line of white kneeling pads, spread out in front of me like the wings of an aeroplane and I fancied I was in a cockpit and swerving up and down, and then it was coming straight at me and I was among the laurel bushes in Nan's back garden looking up into the belly of the plane as it spattered bullets into the dull red brickwork of the house and I closed my eyes and when I opened them again it was to the light grey of white-washed stone walls and intertwining laurel leaves of gold and silver-green, woven into the altar cloth, and a vast expanse of green branches and ferns in a bowl on a pedestal, and I was rubbing a graze on my arm where I'd scraped it on the sharp edge of the communion rail and

284

I buried my face on my hands, like the boy next to me, and hoped to die.

There was a whispering movement at the other end of the rail and I splayed my fingers and looked to the right. A pair of highly polished black shoes were sticking out from under the folds of a black cassock. They moved towards me and were followed by what looked like a quarter of the end of a shaft of arc-light, covered in needleworked gold flowers and peacocks and shrubs on quilted silk with goldy gems stitched into it. I let my eyes run up the black cassock until they came to an arm laid across its tummy, as if it was resting on its brown leather belt, holding a thing like a flat silver ashtray that reminded me of what the dentist's nurse held the dentist's tools in. The bishop came next and he was bending from the middle and putting his hands forward and mumbling and moving on; and as they got closer I picked up the odd word and then I started to be able to put them together until 'Do this as oft as ye shall take this in remembrance of Me' came over as clearly as when Pop said it at the half-past nine service at home, when me and Gibbser had been carrying the candles, and I couldn't see what all the fuss had been about and why Pop couldn't have done us and save all this waste of time.

The arm in the white cassock reached across the boy next to me and held out what looked like a splash of congealed candle grease. He cupped his hand under it as the bishop started off again, 'This is the body of our Lord Jesus Christ that was broken . . .'

I knew I ought to have had my hands up above the altar rail by this time but it was high and that meant my elbows would stick out so I looked to see what the boy next to me was doing with them just as the bishop was saying 'Amen' again and he put them down.

The black-polished shoes slid across the carpet and the black cassock swirled and stilled and I bent my head as the bishop's robes stopped in front of me. It had thongs up the front, instead of buttons, so that it looked like a wigwam.

'This is the body . . .' Now it was my turn. The bishop was like a wireless that had been left on with nobody listening and I knew I should have had my eyes closed, but

285

I wanted to keep track of what was happening and I could see the man in the cassock was sorting out a bit of that wax bread for me.

I gripped the cup of my left hand into the cup of my right one, to keep it still, and looked to see if it was clean as the man put the wafer in and I held my breath as the bishop pressed down on my head. Was I supposed to pick it up with my tongue now, while he was still praying, or wait until he'd finished? And what would happen if I did it wrong? And would they let me have another go if doing it wrong meant I'd go to—

'Wha—' Something was forcing my head up. They'd finished and the bishop was lifting me under the chin.

I knelt there, like Mum had told me to, waiting for the wafer to dissolve, but it stuck my tongue to the roof of my mouth and it was still there when he came back with the wine. I could barely get my lips open for the cup and the boy on my right had gone and the bishop had nearly finished the boy on my left before the wine dissolved it enough to swallow. I stood up and nodded my head at the altar and turned away. I walked back with my eyes half-closed trying not to hurry or look at anyone in particular but then I saw the girl again. She smiled, or seemed to smile, and I looked round to see if she was smiling at anyone else and when I looked back she had her head bowed and I couldn't be sure if she'd smiled at all. I kept looking at her until I had to turn off and squeeze past the people who'd been done before me and then I had to keep leaning back to let the others in, and couldn't see her at all. The people behind started getting up then and going out as our row finished and by the time they'd all gone the first ones were coming back and when they'd all got settled it was time for the sermon and I had to look to the front.

I tried to listen to the bishop but he kept saying things like 'conferring with the Holy Spirit' and 'justification' that I couldn't understand even when I tried to think about them, and thinking about them made me miss what he said next and by then I'd lost the thread of what he was saying altogether. A man behind us kept saying 'Amen' when it wasn't even the end and an old lady, with a frock like curtain material with a flowered pattern, raised her glasses at me when I tried to turn and she sat squarer in the way of where I was trying to look.

The sermon ended and we all stood up. We sang 'Fight the Good Fight' and I wondered how I was going to get out through all these people and evade Mum and find the girl in the white blouse. And what could I say to her? 'Do you come to this church regularly?' She'd think I was a proper Nelly if she'd only come because she had to. But if I said it had all been a bloomin' waste of time and she was all for it, she'd think I was a hooligan. Perhaps she was one of those girls who don't want anything to do with boys.

The back of my left knee started to quiver as we got to the last verse and I was about to give up hope, when I spotted a little Jesus on a black cross hanging from a nail in the cement between two blocks of stone in a column supporting a small chapel down the left-hand side of the church. I crossed my hands in front of me and whispered, 'Please let me see her. I promise I won't try to kiss her or anything. Just let me talk to her, Amen,' as the hymn finished and I kept my eyes open when we all knelt down again and I shot out as soon as the first head came up.

I waited around the entrance, making out I was looking at postcards, as the people came out. I had to keep dodging about to see who was coming and I could imagine Dad getting annoyed, if it had been him, and asking Mum why it was that people insist on blocking up the doorway when other people wanted to be getting off home? There was one old man who couldn't get his overcoat on and his wife and grown-up daughter were helping him into it. He stood there, swaying from side to side, until I had to move somewhere else to see past him, and then they moved so they were in my way again. Then I saw Mum coming and I said 'sod it' under my breath and tried to look away.

'My goodness, Simon.' She was flushed and breathing heavily. 'You soon got out of there, didn't you? And whatever are you looking at me like that for?'

'Like what?' I froze my face so that it didn't look like anything.

'Really, if looks could kill. You've just been confirmed, for heaven's sake. But by the look on your face it looks as

287

if . . . well, I really don't like to think what it looks like. Whatever's the matter?'

'Nothin'.'

'This was supposed to have been a very special occasion.'

There was a flaky bit of concrete mixed in with the gravel and I squashed it with my heel.

'Something that only happens once in a lifetime.'

A movement of white towards the gate caught my eye but it turned out to be a lady blowing her nose.

'Are you listening to me, Simon?'

'Yes, Mum.' We were getting nearer the gate.

'Yes, well . . . you just hold on here while I find out where Mr Peters is.'

'Blimey, Mum. Can't we just meet 'im at the car?'

'Will you do as you're told. Anyway, he might be looking for us.'

I leant back against the gate post and kicked the backs of my heels into the wall and muttered 'waste'a soddin' time' under my breath as the people came out past me saying what a nice service it had been and. hadn't we been lucky with the weather but it couldn't last and hadn't dear Isobel Newton's daughter looked a picture and *yes* they'd simply love to come to tea on Saturday afternoon at about four.

There wasn't anywhere I could look without seeing them and I could feel my face burning as if their lardy-dar way of talking was scorching my skin and I could feel perspiration breaking out on my top lip and I wanted to blow my nose but I was too embarrassed to—

'Your name's Simon, isn't it?'

I looked around but it was just a sea of faces.

'You are Simon, aren't you?'

"Who . . . o-oh!' It was the girl in the white dress and she'd been hidden behind two big men.

'And your school came to Chidham to play netball and football once.'

'Did . . . er, yes, I think so.' She looked like a pinky-white lily with a deep red centre and I could feel my legs winding themselves round each other.

'Before we went to the Lincs.'

'Yes.' At least she didn't go to the High School so

288

she couldn't look down on me for that, and I tried to look behind the curving loops of hair and the sudden, sharp lines of her nose and chin to how she'd have looked when we were about eleven. 'Were you there, then?'

'Course I was.' Her eyebrows rose and she looked up at me with a slight colour around her cheekbones, but it was the smile that sent lightning flashing through the pit of my stomach. 'Don't you remember me?'

'Well I . . .'

'You were with your friend Paul.'

'Was I?' I was scrabbling back through what had happened that day. 'Afterwards there was a social.'

'And dancing.'

'Yeah, an' dancing.' They'd had country dancing and me and Paul Craven and David Harris had stood together looking at their girls and watching old Dorothy Newton trying to get off with a dirty fouler on their side who'd dented Jerry Henry's leg through his shin pad, and Paul had started dancing with a girl who'd played in their netball team. 'You're not . . . ?'

She lay her head over on one side and set her face like a mask. 'No. That was Janet.'

'Oh.' I screwed my memory up like a sponge. There'd been another girl. Janet's friend that nobody fancied because she had freckles and a hair-lip. 'And it wasn't . . . ?'

She shook her head and pouted. 'That was Jennifer Fenton.'

I could see the whole thing clearly now. There was me and Paul and Dave and this girl, Janet, who was quite good-looking, and her friend, who was horrible, and there'd been some . . . little kid . . . I swallowed hard and moistened my lips. 'Blimey!'

She laughed and tossed her head, so that her hair ballooned, and her eyes flashed green in the sunlight. 'That's right.' She arched her neck so that her shoulders went back and her blouse went tight, as if she had two lemons under it, and I wondered if they'd rub sore where they came to a point, and I had to put my hands in my pockets again and lean forward in case she saw and slapped my face.

'Were you the littl'n we sent out for lemonade?'

289

'That's right. Didn't you recognise me?'

I shook my head. 'No, not right off. You've, well . . . you've grown up.'

'Well, it was a couple of years ago.' She bent her knee forward and picked a speck of fluff off her navy skirt. 'And I suppose we've all grown since then.'

'Yes h'I—' I cleared my throat. 'Yes. I suppose we have.'

'Alice.'

'What?'

'Alice. That's my name.'

'Oh yes, I remember.' Alice! I let her name roll around in my mind. Alice. Al-lice . . . Al-leese. It had a sort of glass-slipper sound about it – a royal court in an arctic kingdom all of snow and ice and I'd never known anybody called Alice before . . . 'But you've grown up such a lot.'

She glanced up at me and her cheeks went a shade redder, and I wondered if I'd said something I shouldn't, but she was still smiling.

'Look, my folks'll be back in a minute.'

'So'll mine.' I moved closer to her.

'I go to the Spelotti School of Ballet every Thursday at half-past four.'

'Oh, do you?'

'Yes.' She was much closer to me now and looking from side to side, like a cat bedding her kittens down and looking out for danger. 'So if you were there about half-past five you might see me when we come out.'

'C'h'or, yes but—'

'But what?'

'It's all right. I was thinking we'd have conf— But that's all over now.' We were so close now we were almost touching and her lips were so puffed up it looked as if they were going to burst.

'Half-past five on Thursday.'

'Yes.' Her eyes were half-closed.

'Bye then.' I leant to my left as I passed across her and my fingertips brushed the iced-shell surface of her nails and I turned back to her as she turned back to me, but then the space between us filled up with people.

I'd taken the same little case of Old Gran's to school with me ever since I'd started the Lincs. Mum had thought at first it would be nice for me to have a satchel to go with my cap, like Just William, and I'd said that would be fun because I could have my tie all over the place and one sock up and one down and my shoe laces undone and use my garters as a catapult, but then she said, on second thoughts, perhaps it wasn't such a good idea after all and that the next best thing would be for me to put my PE stuff and towel and things for school in the little brown case of Old Gran's that was still under the bed from when I'd had it to go up to Aunty's at Petersfield.

The next Wednesday I got home early from school and put my case under my bed and then went through my drawers and wardrobe to see what I could wear. My school shirts all looked like school shirts, even when I folded the pointed collars up under to make them straight, and I had no option with my blazer because it was too bulky to go into my case after school. I experimented by using my grey windcheater, with the claret collar and cuffs, as a shirt because my stardust one was in the wash and I wanted to wear a tie. I tried the yellow silk tie, out of Dad's tie box that he never used, with it because the boys said girls like boys with yellow socks and I hadn't got any yellow socks, and stood in front of Mum's mirror for ages pulling and loosening it and trying to get my windcheater collar to stay down and make the tie hang straight, so that it covered the zip at the front, but it kept swinging back and the knot kept getting too small and I lost my temper and pulled the knot so tight it wouldn't come undone so I gave it up and got my old green shirt with the dark green collar and short sleeves and my greeny-brown Tootal tie, that I hated but tied a good knot, and then I remembered that the very first time I'd worn it had been at the Chidham social where I'd first met Alice. Perhaps it would bring me luck this time too.

'I've taken some money out of my money box for my bus fare, Mum, because I won't be on the school bus tonight.'

'Oh, and why's that, Simon?' She'd been making me some sandwiches for the morning playtime.

'Because I'm joining the Chess Club on a Thursday after school and I'll get my bus fare back from the office tomorrow.'

'Oh, good boy. I'm glad you're taking an interest in something sensible at last, Simon.' She gave me a great big hug that made me feel guilty for telling her lies. 'I'm really proud of you,' and she made me some extra cheese and chutney sandwiches in case I was late home for tea.

'But don't, for goodness' sake, be a minute later home than six o'clock.'

'Why not, Mum? Confirmation classes've finished now.'

'Yes, I know that. But what always used to happen on a Thursday night?' Mum looked up from wrapping my sandwiches in greaseproof paper.

'Dunno, Mum,' but a sinking feeling settled over me as I saw her smile. 'You mean the club?'

'Of course the club.' She gave me another hug and I stood and let her, looking at my little brown case dangling from my arm down her back. 'Dad kept it a secret so that it'd come as a surprise and he's putting a notice up in the post office on his way to work so that the others'll know too.'

'Is he?' To get home by six I'd have to catch the twenty-past five 57 from the bus station.

'Aren't you pleased, Simon?' Mum pulled away from me.

'Yeah . . . smashin'.'

'What's up then?'

'Jus' that I was gonna see someone at half-past five.'

'Who?' She had her hands on her hips now.

'Jus' one'a the boys from the children's 'ome.'

'Oh yes?'

'About some fag cards.'

'Well, see him earlier.'

'What?' The sun suddenly broke through the cloud and sparkled through the glass onto the window sash she'd been polishing. 'S'pose I could. Might catch 'er . . . 'im going in instead'a . . .'

'You aren't up to something are you, Simon?'

'Course not, Mum.'

'Only I thought you'd've been over the moon about

having the club again. You made enough fuss about it when you thought it was closing.'

'I am, Mum.' I half shut one eye and looked into the sun. 'Yeah, smashin'. But I gotta go now, Mum, or I'll be late.'

I carried my case around with me all day so that I didn't lose it or have it pinched out of my locker and I opened it lots of times and refolded my shirt, hoping somebody would ask me why I'd got it.

'I'm not coming home on the school bus tonight, ya know, Col.'

'So what?' Colin was relacing his plimsolls where the lace had broken.

'I got a date with this smashin' girl.'

'She must be barmy to go out with you, Nipper, or blind. An' give us a sandwich.'

'Sod off, Gibbs. Get yer own if ya want any.' I wiped a smear of chutney off the corner of my mouth with the back of my hand and went and put my sandwich bag in the waste-paper bin and kept on going, on into the toilets, to wet my hair and try to comb it so that it stayed back.

Our last lesson that afternoon was Hoggy for Technical Drawing and he was in a worse mood than usual. He always made us line up in the corridor outside his classroom and walk in an orderly line when he arrived to open the door. He was always late but today he was later than ever and we stood waiting and listening as an almighty racket developed down the corridor in Sparrow Higgs's class. Pete Farmer and Doug Ritson and the rest of the Firm made us draw lots to see who'd go down and see what was going on and they chose a boy called Geach from East Dean, who wore the full school uniform and never said anything to anyone. He'd looked as if he was going to argue when Doug had first told him what he had to do but Doug had grabbed him by his tie and shirt front and squeezed him until his face looked as if it was going to explode, and then kneed him in the groin, and he'd limped off quietly enough to find out what was happening. The noise had stopped suddenly as he turned the corner and a few minutes went by and then Hoggy came out with his cane in one hand and Geach in the other. He walked past us without a word, opened the door and stood Geach over a chair and squashed him down into it and then stood back against the door.

'M'come in,' he said, in that tone of voice that made me feel as if I'd been doused in cold water and left out on an iceberg to dry.

We sat down and he strode to the front, tapping his cane against his leg the way a cat swishes its tail before it pounces.

'M'h'I will not tolerate bullying.' His eye was a searchlight. 'M'h'I will not tolerate sneaking and spying.' The searchlight played back again. 'Nor cheating and prying.' The tapping came slower and harder and I could feel fat Penniworth next to me breathing heavily. 'I won't have it!' The shriek of his voice merged with the swish and the wet crack of the cane across the desk pinned us against the backs of our chairs as if we'd been rivetted.

'M'who sent Geach out to spy?'

We stared at the front.

'M'who sent you, Geach?' The cane rose and slowly fell.

'Geach won't tell on his friends.' Up it went again and then down. 'Or is he terrified?'

'M'very well!' The cane rose and fell and rose and fell. 'How would the whole form like detention until quarter-past four tonight?'

'We gotta catch . . .' The colour in Penniworth's face drained as Hoggy swung round on him and his head dropped as he muttered 'school bus'.

'Did you dare to speak, Penniworth?'

'No, sir.'

'Half-past four . . . if somebody doesn't own up?'

My fingers curled.

'Quarter to five?'

I could imagine Alice looking up and down the empty street.

'I've got as much time as any of you.' The stick was going up and down so fast now that it turned into a steady rat-tat-tat. 'Five o'clock?'

294

I glanced at Ritson.

'M'Ritson?' It was like an exploding shell. 'Any ideas?'

'No, sir.'

'M'Wilson?' He was over me like a hawk on a rabbit. White strips of congealed saliva were clinging to his lips like tapeworm. 'Well?'

'No, sir.'

'No, sir! What d'ya mean, No, sir?' A great foaming sud flew out and landed on the back of my hand and then the cane lashed down between my fists.

I closed my eyes and prayed he'd keep a straight aim.

'Look at me, and tell me why you looked at Ritson?'

'Didn't, sir.'

'Filthy, wretched little liar!' The cane whipped and slashed again. 'I saw you.'

My teeth rattled. He shook me by the shoulders until my right arm pumped forwards. My fist fell short of his stomach and short again and then it hit him.

'Did you strike me, boy?'

'No, sir.'

'If I thought that you'd . . .' He'd let go but my arms still burned where he'd gripped them. 'Get out before I lose my temper with you completely.' I was suddenly up in the air as he lifted me over the back of my chair and almost threw me out of the door.

He'd said 'get out' but he hadn't said anything about staying and I was just turning to go across to the toilets to comb my hair before I went to meet Alice, when the door clicked closed against its return spring and I glanced back.

'Bugger!' My coat, with my bus fare in the pocket, was draped across the back of my chair. I stood and stared at it through the small square window. 'Bugger, bugger, bugger!' It was like seeing a new football being carried out to sea on the tide. I could have tried asking the Secretary for my fare but she would probably want to know why and if I went without my jacket the school would probably be locked up by the time I got back and I'd never hear the end of it at home. I leant my head back on the wall and banged it against the gloss-painted brickwork.

The light from the classroom filtered through into the locker-room. One locker door hung open. There were a pair of old plimsolls inside, with dust in the canvas. I laid them straight and closed the door. Hoggy had started the lesson now and he carried on after the bell. The corridors filled and emptied and a deep silence fell over the school. I went and sat in the cloakroom and watched the clock in the chemistry lab, across the corridor, tick round to half-past four and then to quarter to five. At ten to five Hoggy cleaned the blackboard while the boys put their compasses and protractors back and then the door opened and they came out. I didn't hurry and nobody spoke to me except Ritson.

'Did you 'it 'im, Nipper?'

I shook my head. 'Nah. Wish I 'ad'a done.'

'Bastard in'e?'

'Yeah,' and I went in for my jacket and case.

Hoggy was packing his briefcase. I waited for him to say something to me but he didn't look up. I tiptoed in and slid my case out through the legs of my desk. It wasn't my desk. We hadn't got our own desks. We hadn't even got our own classrooms or our own teacher. We had Hoggy for Technical Drawing and Music and Mr Jones for Science and Mr Hossack for Maths and Mr Titmarsh for English but nobody really knew us or took any notice of us, outside of their own lesson, and I wondered if they'd have missed any of us if it hadn't been for the squares against our names they had to tick in their registers to show we'd been there.

I could have caught the 66 from the bus station, but I went up by the Granada and stood on the pavement listening to the bumping up and down music coming from behind the sooty first-floor windows across the street. Alice was in there. Perhaps she was thinking I'd forgotten her, or maybe she thought I'd stood her up. I could have gone up the side stairs and looked in the window and pretended it was the wrong place if anybody'd caught me. But if she saw me she'd wonder why I hadn't waited for her. I looked around for a piece of chalk to write her a note on the pavement, but I couldn't find any. I looked all

296

around the borders of the houses down as far as the South Pallant but everything that looked like chalk turned out to be flints, until it was nearly twenty-five past five and then I had to run for the bus.

I caught the 57 from outside the Horndean Arms. I could have gone upstairs with some of the Tangmere boys, but I didn't. I sat down on the long seat by the door trapping my case with my heels against the bottom of the seat, and watched the road fly past. I could have got off at the school and walked home through the village, but the conductor was upstairs when we went past and I couldn't be bothered to get up and ring the bell so I stayed on and got off after the camp kids at Tangmere Corner. I waited in the hedge until they'd gone and then I went down to the main road and along by the policeman's house and home up the back field.

My feet brushed up clouds of dust and pollen through the long grass and disturbed the bees and insects and set them buzzing. There were millions of flittering skittering things in the grass. They seemed to go on crawling up things or over and in and out without any thought for each other as if each one of them was the only one there. A fat purply-silver bluebottle scuttled across a blackberry leaf and stopped with its bulging eyes looking all ways at once, and twiddled its front legs. Another one came up from the underside of the leaf and it stopped too and appeared to drop its head. Then they both twiddled their front legs and joined together for a couple of seconds and flew off in different directions.

I felt as if I'd walked a thousand miles as I bent to climb through the back fence and my case felt heavier as I changed hands to open the back door. Mum had just switched the kettle off and was waiting for it to finish steaming.

'Good boy, Simon. You're right on time.' She turned as she went to pour the water in the tea pot. 'Whatever's the matter? Dear oh dear! You look as if you've lost a shilling and found sixpence.'

'Nothin' much.'

She put the cosy on the tea pot and smoothed it round as she lifted it onto its mat. 'How d'you get on?'

297

'Lost.'

'Never mind.' Mum was putting milk and sugar into the cups. 'It's not the end of the world. You can p'raps have another crack at it next Thursday.'

'M'm.' I went through into the living room and put my case down by the brown armchair. 'I think I will, but don't expect me home so early next week.'